A SINISTER REVENGE

A
SINISTER
REVENGE

A VERONICA SPEEDWELL
MYSTERY

Deanna Raybourn

BERKLEY
NEW YORK

BERKLEY
An imprint of Penguin Random House LLC
penguinrandomhouse.com

Library of Congress Cataloging-in-Publication Data

Names: Raybourn, Deanna, author.
Title: A sinister revenge / Deanna Raybourn.
Description: First Edition. | New York: Berkley, 2023. | Series: A Veronica Speedwell mystery
Identifiers: LCCN 2022031842 (print) | LCCN 2022031843 (ebook) |
ISBN 9780593545928 (hardcover) | ISBN 9780593545942 (ebook) |
Subjects: LCGFT: Novels.
Classification: LCC PS3618.A983 S565 2023 (print) |
LCC PS3618.A983 (ebook) | DDC 813/.6—dc23/eng/20220708
LC record available at https://lccn.loc.gov/2022031842
LC ebook record available at https://lccn.loc.gov/2022031843

Printed in the United States of America
1st Printing

Book design by Kristin del Rosario

For Michelle Vega, with heartfelt thanks for joining me on this adventure. Excelsior!

A SINISTER REVENGE

CHAPTER

1

Bavaria, September 1889

Y ou must not go into the forest at night," the innkeeper warned, his voice trembling with fear. "Something dangerous walks there in the darkness."

He carried on in this vein for some time as I applied myself to a stein of Weissbier and a plate of crisp, excellent sausages. My friend and travelling companion, the Viscount Templeton-Vane, listened politely as the fellow grew more vehement.

"The creature that walks by night, it is part wolf, part man. It has but one eye, the other a gaping hole of deepest black. It keeps to the shadows, and if you dare to come near, it snarls like a bear," he went on, his eyes round in his chubby, shiny face. He was a character straight from a storybook, plump and bearded, an imp of a fellow, with lines of good humour etched upon his face. But there was no mirth to be found upon his visage as he told his tale, only fear, brightening his eyes and causing his mouth to tremble ever so slightly.

Behind him, a lurking barmaid whose ample charms were scarcely contained by the lacing of her dirndl threw her apron over her head and fled through the door to the kitchens.

The viscount—Tiberius to his friends—quirked up one expressive brow. "My good man, calm yourself. Surely this is some piece of local lore meant to frighten the feeble. We English are made of sterner stuff."

"But it is true," the fellow insisted, colour pinkening the cheeks above the white fringe of his beard. He glanced around and lowered his voice. "I have seen it, a hulking shadow, moving in the silence of the firs. And when I stepped in its direction, it reared back and it *growled* with the fiendish fury of a hound of Hell."

Tiberius, usually a man of cool logic, looked startled. "Growled, you say?"

"Like a wolf," the man confirmed.

I sighed. It was time to put an end to this. "My good man," I said politely to the innkeeper, "whilst I must concede that your use of alliteration is impressive, I think we can dismiss the notion of a hybrid monster roaming these mountains."

He gave me a look of profound injury and slunk away, muttering.

Tiberius met my gaze. "Can we? I realise the local folk are a superstitious lot, but how exactly would you explain the existence of such a creature?"

I ticked off the qualities as I said them. "A tall, unsociable creature that keeps to the shadows, shuns the society of respectable people, and growls its displeasure? Tell me, who does that seem to describe?"

Tiberius' mouth went slack, then curved into a smile. "You mean—"

"Yes, Tiberius. I think we have, at long last, found your brother."

The Honourable Revelstoke Templeton-Vane—Stoker, familiarly—had not been lost so much as slightly misplaced. For some months Stoker and I had enjoyed an intimate relationship that had proven thoroughly fulfilling, indeed *enrapturing*, in all the particulars. We were work colleagues, engaged in the endlessly fascinating task of preparing museum exhibits for our employer, Lord Rosemorran. We were also neighbours, each of us inhabiting a small folly on his lordship's Marylebone estate.

And we were occasional partners in detection, as falling over corpses had become something of a habit. In short, our lives were so fully entwined it was difficult to say where one left off and the other began. We enjoyed it all—from the scientific work to the investigation of crime, to the exuberant physicality of our more private endeavours. (Stoker is singularly suited to the amatory arts through a combination of bodily charms, robust stamina, and an enchanting thoroughness that might have startled a less experienced or enthusiastic partner than I.)

But following a painful interlude, Stoker had taken himself off to nurse his wounded feelings. When last he and I had been together, there had been a complication regarding my marital status. Not a complication so much as a husband—one I had believed dead and whose resurrection was most unwelcome. The fact that we had nearly died as a result of Harry's dramatic appearance into our lives had not endeared him to Stoker, and he had taken his leave of England whilst still believing me bound forever to a man with criminous tendencies.* As his parting words had been a directive to grant him time and privacy to smooth his ruffled feathers, I had naturally concurred. By the next morning he was gone, leaving only a hastily scribbled line to explain he was off to Germany in pursuit of a trophy—as a natural historian, his employment entailed procuring and improving a vast array of specimens—but no invitation to join him ensued.

At almost precisely the same moment, a letter had arrived from Tiberius urging me to come to Italy, where he had persuaded his host-

---

* *An Impossible Impostor*

ess, an aging papal marquise, to part with a prized collection of rare birdwing butterflies. I am, first and foremost, a lepidopterist. I did not hesitate to pack my carpetbag and board the first train out of London. Through the end of the spring and the whole of that summer I accompanied Tiberius as he made his way through Italy, sending boxes of butterflies back to Lord Rosemorran's burgeoning museum.

From Stoker, I had not a single line, although Lord Rosemorran frequently alluded to Stoker's peregrinations through the Black Forest in his own letters. I thus had a vague idea of where Stoker was, and I was not at all distressed by our lack of communication. I knew two things: the depth of our feelings for one another and the fact that absence makes the heart as well as the libido grow stronger. I had little doubt that Stoker missed me—*all* of me.

No, the fact that he had taken his leave so abruptly and with no effort at a proper good-bye did not distress me in the slightest. And while another woman might have grown increasingly irritated that the post forwarded from England brought not the merest *scrap* of a postcard, to say nothing of a proper letter, I naturally devoted myself entirely to the study of lepidoptery. I passed my days in hunting specimens that flittered and fluttered from the Dolomites to the Sicilian hills and back again. I grew leaner and more firmly muscled from scrambling over peaks and pastures. I set out at daybreak each morning from our lodgings, when the night's dew still bespangled the grasses at my feet. I did not return until the languid golden sun dropped beyond the horizon, leaving a few last gentle rays to show me the way back. I never used my net; its presence was merely a habit from my previous expeditions. Instead I followed the butterflies, making careful study of their mazy meanderings, their behaviours and habitats.

And when I returned to the solitude of my room, I spent long hours writing up my findings both for my private notes and for publication in the Aurelian journals. Invariably, I dropped into bed exhausted by my exertions, only to rise at dawn and repeat the process. Not for me the languid evening passed in mournful contemplation of the distance—both literal and figurative—between myself and the person I considered to be my twinned soul. I would not permit myself to waste away in pining and regret. I had the celibate consolations of science, and I made full advantage of them.

If I am to be strictly honest within these pages—and I have sworn to be so—then I will admit to the occasional wakeful night or interminable afternoon when I found my thoughts inhabited by his familiar form and face. When these moods came upon me, so strong was my longing for him, it required all of my discipline to refrain from flinging my things into a bag and dashing to him. The only remedy was another strenuous day spent in pursuit of my studies, driving myself physically harder than ever before even as I enumerated his flaws. I catalogued them as I strode the Italian hills, whipping up my annoyance.

"What sort of man just *leaves*? And without so much as a proper kiss good-bye," I muttered to the nearest rock in a fit of particular frustration on the isle of Capri. "What kind of fellow thinks it is acceptable simply to disappear for months on end and send no assurances of his well-being? Not a telegram, not a semaphore flag, not so much as a hint of a postcard with his current address? An *ass*," I told the rock.

But even as I said the words, I knew Stoker was not entirely to blame. He had left still believing I was the wife of another man. Only a handful of hours had passed between Stoker's departure and my learning the truth of my marital status—that I was not, and never had been, legally married.

Why then did I leap at Tiberius' invitation instead of rushing after Stoker to stop him before he left England?

It was some months before I could face the answer: I was a coward. When I learnt of Stoker's resolve to leave, to take time for himself to consider our attachment, my initial reaction, the longing of my heart, had been to go to him. And therein lay my terror. I, who had laboured and loved independent of real connection for so long, was entirely and besottedly enraptured with this man. When I most had need of a confidant, I had not turned to him out of fear of dependency, and when he left, the desire to run to him had kindled that fear once more.

So I drove it out with hard physical exercise, with time and distance, hoping I could blunt the sharp edge of my resistance to committing myself fully to Stoker. My demeanour, ordinarily so tranquil as to be remarkable, was frequently waspish as I came back, always, to the fact that even if I wanted to go to him, he had insisted upon the gift of time. If time was what he wanted, he should have all the time in the world, I decided. In fact, I would grow weary and withered and ancient before I would stir a single *step* towards him. If I suffered from the loss of his company, then he should suffer as well, I decided. I had my dignity, after all.

I do not know how long I might have maintained my lofty determination to wait for him to make the first move. I might still be wandering the Lombard hills, butterfly net in hand, had Tiberius not appeared one morning at breakfast, bags packed and travel arranged. Our hotel, a converted castello, was very fine and comfortable but with few of the comforts so beloved of the English traveller. The beds were hard, the pillows nonexistent, and the mosquitoes particularly aggressive. Worst of all possible woes, the tea was unspeakable and I had almost resigned myself to drinking coffee. I was peering into the murky depths of the teapot when Tiberius took the chair across from me.

"I wish to find Stoker," he said flatly. "Do you know where one might run him to ground?"

I put aside the crime that passed for tea in those parts and gave him a level look. "Somewhere in Bavaria, if Lord Rosemorran's letters are accurate. But his lordship can be vague about such things, and this is, after all, Stoker of whom we are speaking, a man inclined to follow his most wayward impulses. He might be in Batavia. Or Bolivia. Or Bechuana." He did not respond to my little witticism and I gave him a close look. Tiberius was, like all the Templeton-Vane men, a singularly handsome fellow. But there were plummy shadows under his eyes, and a line, slim but severe, etched its way across his brow. "Tiberius, why do you want to find Stoker?"

He hesitated, itself cause for alarm, and then said three words which chilled me to my marrow.

"I need him."

The fact that Tiberius Templeton-Vane, ninth viscount of the same, expressed any emotion as lowering as *need* of another person was mildly terrifying. He was the most self-possessed man I had ever met, his character having long since been shaped by the ineffable knowledge that he was the firstborn son of an aristocrat, heir to a fortune, a title, and an estate. His privilege was as much a part of him as his elegant hands or his superb sense of dress. Tiberius, so long as I had known him, needed no one and nothing—least of all his scapegrace brother. Stoker had, almost since the cradle, been considered the cuckoo in the nest. (The fact that their mother's dalliance with an Irish painter was actually responsible for Stoker's paternity only augmented this division.) Stoker had rebelled against the family's strictures, taking himself off for the first time when he was twelve years of age. His putative father, the eighth viscount, had him apprehended and returned to Cherboys, the family estate in Devon, but Stoker simply ran away again. And again. Every time he was hauled back to Cherboys, he bided his time and then left. In due course, the viscount stopped retrieving him and Stoker fell in with a travelling circus before studying medicine in Edinburgh and later becoming a surgeon's mate in Her Majesty's Navy.

Through his perambulations, he had lost the thread of connection with his family, and by the time I had met him, some three years previous to these events, there was almost no communication between Stoker and his three brothers, their father having died the year before I came into his life. He had been independent for so long that it had almost become a matter of pride for him that he did not rely upon the Templeton-Vane name or its influence to open doors for him. He lived by his own talents, and this was met by his brothers sometimes with good-natured bafflement and sometimes with resentful envy. Their own lives had been laid out for them by the late Lord Templeton-Vane, and none of the three had the courage or will to deviate from the appointed path. Tiberius, as the eldest, had succeeded to the title. The second, Sir Rupert, had been granted a baronetcy for his services to the Crown as a barrister who dabbled in secret diplomacy. The youngest, Merryweather—shoved into the Church, possibly against his will— had been granted the living of the parish of Dearsley, the village nearest to Cherboys. The brothers were settled, with varying degrees of satisfaction, in their roles.

And yet. Now and then, so fleeting I could almost believe it my own fancy, each of them had looked at Stoker with something akin to jealousy. I was not surprised. It was the same expression frequently aimed in my direction, usually by women with too many children and too much time spent embroidering tea cloths. To make one's own money, to direct one's own destiny, these were heady gifts indeed.

Such was the nature of my thoughts as Tiberius and I steamed our way north. Summer had lingered in Italy, but as we climbed into the forested mountains of southern Germany, the leaves shifted from glimmering green to the russet-edged hint of the coming autumn. Spirals of woodsmoke curled from cottages tucked in the woods, and lazy fogs drifted across the valleys. It was a fairy-tale landscape, a place to believe in witches and wolves, and the feeling of unreality grew the further into Bavaria we travelled. Lord Rosemorran's letters had not been explicit on the subject of Stoker's whereabouts, but I had a fair idea of where to begin our search, and it was in the third village we made enquiries where the innkeeper regaled us with the story of the beast that stalked the forest by night.

"You really believe it is Stoker?" Tiberius asked as I wiped the delicate foam of the Weissbier from my lips.

"Certainly," I said. "And tonight, I have no doubt, this particularly elusive game will be afoot."

The details of our search for Stoker do not bear relating. Suffice it to say the first few hours of our endeavour were spent scrambling over rocky precipices guided only by lantern light and my unerring instinct for Stoker's presence. We traversed hillsides, climbing over boulders and through the fir-forested thickets, an exhilarating adventure under certain circumstances. These were not those circumstances. Tiberius, to whom any form of physical exercise is anathema, kept up a steady stream of complaints, first loudly and then—as his breathing became laboured and his stamina began to flag—whispered in a sinking voice one associates with genteel invalids with wasting diseases.

"Really, Tiberius," I chided. "This is hardly more than a *ramble*."

"Ram-ramble?" he panted. "I am dying. My life has passed before my eyes," he added as he stumbled to a halt, grasping a low-hanging branch for support. "And if there were a clergyman to hand, I would confess my sins and lay myself down to my eternal rest."

I rolled my eyes. "You have all the subtlety of a melodrama heroine," I informed him. "And the endurance of a particularly tiny sea slug. Where is your spirit, sir? Where is your *grit*?"

"In my other trousers," he said, his jaws clenched.

I opened my mouth to remonstrate further when I heard it, the soft rustle of branches, disturbed not by the wind but by the movement of some stealthy creature.

"What," Tiberius demanded, "in the name of god's teeth is that?"

"A large deer, perhaps," I suggested. "Or possibly a bear? Maybe a wolf. Do they still have wolves in the Bavarian Alps?"

We turned as one as the sound grew louder, the gentle susurration of the tree limbs giving way to thunderous crashes and the sound of some mammoth beast moving through the darkness to where we stood in the deceptive security of our little pool of warm light.

I had been teasing Tiberius, but the fact of the matter was that bears did still inhabit those mountains, and even if the wolves had long since vanished, there might still be large, predatory cats with a taste for aristocratic, city-softened flesh.

I stepped in front of Tiberius to shield him from certain death as the branches parted to reveal an enormous furry form, its shaggy coat thick with brambles. It emerged on all fours, low to the ground and lumbering forwards, a great heaving growl issuing forth in a sort of mournful ululation.

I held my lantern high and stood my ground as the creature lifted its head—no doubt to bay at the rising moon, I decided.

But as the lantern light fell upon its hairy face, I smiled.

"Hello, Stoker."

CHAPTER

2

To say Stoker was not entirely pleased to see us is a slight understatement. In point of fact, he sulked all the way back to the inn where Tiberius and I had taken rooms. The innkeeper was not enthused about his presence in his establishment, and the maid—who once more flung her apron over her head and fled with a shriek—would only be coerced to serve us supper on the condition that she leave the tray at the door of the little parlour that had been put aside for our use.

Stoker had repaired to Tiberius' room to wash the worst of the grime from his person, but when he joined us, I could not detect much of a difference. The beautiful, masculine line of his jaw was completely obscured by a set of thick black whiskers that stretched from Adam's apple to cheekbone, concealing the slender silver scar which usually lent such character to his face. The eye patch he wore when his left eye was overtired was in evidence, grimy and tattered, and his clothing was unspeakable. Even his hands, normally stained with ink and glue and various chemicals, were unusually filthy. His hair, always brushing the bottom of his collar, had been left untrimmed and had taken on a personality of its own, the waves giving way to a tumble of witch-black elflocks that snarled over his shoulders.

I thought him the most glorious being I had ever seen, but Tiberius, refreshed after our long excursion by the better part of a bottle of excellent claret, regarded him with the offended fastidiousness of a very superior cat.

"My god, what are you wearing?" he asked, pointing in horror at the matted atrocity which passed for Stoker's outer garment. It was a collection of hides and pelts, stitched together in a monstrous patchwork that might have done credit to Mary Shelley's most fiendish imaginings. The various hairs and furs were tangled with burrs and leaves, and small twigs dropped every time he moved.

"It is a garment of my own design," he explained. "It is a variation on a traditional ghillie suit. It affords me perfect camouflage in the forest."

"I think I saw something moving within it," Tiberius told him.

"It does have a tendency to attract fleas," Stoker admitted. Tiberius shied like a startled pony, drawing his immaculately tailored legs as far away from his brother as he could. Stoker shrugged off the offending garment, leaving it in a heap in the corner. I could not be entirely certain, but I thought I saw a mouse scurry out from its folds as it fell.

I folded my hands in my lap and adopted an air of perfect composure. I had anticipated this moment for the past six months, but now that the time was upon us, I found myself a trifle unquiet, first adjusting my sleeves, then smoothing my hair.

"Good god, Veronica," Tiberius said as he came to sit. "You are as twitchy as a Roman street cat. Have some beer and settle your nerves."

"I cannot imagine what you mean," I told him with a repressive look.

Stoker took his seat at the table and I smiled calmly at him. "I hope you have been enjoying yourself," I said as I passed a plate of savoury sausages and buttered black bread. He fell upon the food and consumed several large bites before favouring me with a reply.

"I have," he said.

"And I presume there is a good reason for your roaming about the forests, frightening the locals?" I asked pleasantly. I was determined to be polite, no matter what the cost. I have already explained that I was in no way at all vexed with the complete and total lack of communication from him for the past half a year. Not in the *slightest.*

But I was perhaps a bit put out at the almost indifferent greeting he had offered when we found him. His first words were, "What in the name of the oozing wounds of Christ are the two of you doing here?" It was not precisely the romantic reunion of one's heated imaginings, I reflected as I stalked back to the inn. During the interminable train ride north, I had distracted myself by pondering exactly what form our meeting should take. My imagination provided a number of scenes of infinite variety, none of which included Stoker looking and smelling like something twelve days past death and with all the aloofness of one of the lesser pharaohs.

If he was not thoroughly pleased to see us, then I would kill him with kindness, I decided, as I considered his less-than-enthusiastic welcome. Murdering him seemed a very good plan indeed.

Stoker did not return my smile. He sat back and folded his arms over the breadth of his chest. "I am on the hunt for a wolpertinger."

In an instant, my good intentions were cast aside. I suppressed a snort of laughter, but Tiberius regarded him with polite curiosity. "What is a wolpertinger?"

"A mythological invention of German fantasy," I replied.

"We don't yet know that," Stoker riposted, clearly annoyed.

"We most certainly do. It is a singularly ludicrous creature," I explained to Tiberius, "with the body of a hare, the wings of a hawk, and a tiny set of antlers. Like a miniature deer."

"You forgot the fangs," Stoker said coldly.

"I do apologise." I turned to Tiberius and held my forefingers up to my canine teeth in demonstration. "It has fangs. Like a wolf."

"Where the devil do they come from?" Tiberius asked.

"Allegedly from the union of a deer and a hare," Stoker explained. "Unlikely, I grant you—"

"Unlikely! Impossible," I began.

Just then, something hard struck my ankle under the table and I realised Tiberius had kicked me. I stared at him in astonishment, but his face wore its usual impassive expression. He was, as ever, seemingly unruffled. But as I looked at the indolent features, I detected the wariness in the eyes, a new tightness about the lips. If I did not know better, I would say that Tiberius was *nervous*.

Then I remembered his heartfelt admission the morning he asked me to help him find Stoker. *I need him.* However much I had tried, I had not been able to pry further information from Tiberius on our journey to Germany. He would say only that he required Stoker's assistance and would explain everything when we saw him. Now the moment was to hand, he hesitated. Whatever he wanted from Stoker, he feared being refused.

I drew in a breath and blew it out slowly as I counted silently to ten in Farsi.

"Stoker," I said at last when I had reached dah, "Tiberius and I were travelling in Italy when he said he had to see you. Urgently. We have come a great distance and gone to inordinate lengths to find you. I know that he may rely upon your stalwartness in his hour of need."

I thought it a pretty little speech, but Stoker merely snorted. "Hour of need? What is the trouble with him?" He turned to his brother. "Is your newest waistcoat not tailored to your specifications? Your box at the opera given away? One of the servants brew your tea for five minutes instead of four?"

There was often mockery between the brothers. It was one of the ways they demonstrated affection. In fact, anything short of actual fisticuffs was to be encouraged. The last time they had had a significant difference of opinion, the matter had ended with Tiberius lightly stabbing Stoker. (Considering the fact that Stoker had just dislocated Tiberius' shoulder, a stabbing was not an entirely inappropriate reaction.)

But now there was an edge to Stoker's facetious enquiry, an impatience that seemed to mask a flash of real temper. It did occur to me that Stoker's anger flared just when I mentioned that Tiberius and I had been travelling together, and I suppressed a surge of resentment. I was a woman grown, and no matter what bonds of devotion tied me to Stoker, I would not be made to feel I had done wrong in spending time with a man I considered to be a friend. A very great friend, in fact. Tiberius was a restful companion in his own way. He had, upon several occasions and with complete thoroughness, indicated that he was entirely aware of my personal charms and under other circumstances might have been inclined to act upon them. Yet with his innate sense of honour, he would never trespass upon the boundary I had established between us. For Stoker to entertain, for even a moment, the notion that there was anything untoward in my travelling with Tiberius was not to be borne. But I would deal with that insinuation later, I decided. Tiberius' necessity was of the moment.

"Stoker," I said, returning the subject to the matter at hand, "I am certain Tiberius' request, whatever it may be, is nothing so frivolous."

"Not frivolous, but perhaps imaginary," Tiberius said with a frown.

"Imaginary? Like a wolpertinger?" I asked sweetly.

"Now, see here," Stoker began. I smiled. Goading him was ever one of my favourite occupations, and how I had missed it!

The smile stopped him in his tracks. He broke off with a growl and turned to his brother. "What is the trouble?"

Tiberius smoothed the crease in his trousers, as if playing for time. "Nothing terribly serious, except that—" He paused and gave us an apologetic little grin. "Except that I am rather concerned I am about to be murdered."

CHAPTER
3

Stoker and I stared at Tiberius, waiting for some acknowledgment that he was japing us, but none was forthcoming.

"Did you have anyone in particular in mind for committing the dastardly deed? Or is this a more general concern?" Stoker enquired politely.

Tiberius' smile thinned. "It is entirely particular," he assured his brother. He reached into his coat for his notecase and extracted a pair of newspaper cuttings. He passed them to me and I skimmed them quickly before handing them on to Stoker.

The cuttings were death notices, one written in rather florid German and taken from a newspaper published in Baden-Baden. The other was French, snipped from a Parisian periodical. The German cutting concerned the death of a gentleman called Kaspar von Hochstaden, a fossilist from Munich who had come to Baden to take the waters for his gout. His death was sudden but not entirely unexpected given his precarious health. The second cutting concerned the death of Alexandre du Plessis, a bon vivant whose end had come after suffering induced, it was supposed, by a bad oyster.

There was nothing particularly remarkable about the cuttings except for the notations which had been added by hand. In the margin of the German newspaper, dated the previous June, was a large numeral one. The French cutting was from August and carried a bold, slashing numeral two. And in the margin of this, penned in a crabbed, anonymous hand, were the words *You will be next. Prepare your soul.* **VENGEANCE FOR LORENZO.**

I regarded Tiberius as Stoker studied the cuttings. "I would suggest that anyone eating oysters in August has only himself to blame for his misfortunes, but these notes indicate something more nefarious. Do you know these men?"

He nodded. "Yes. Although it has been many years since I have seen or even heard from either of them." He paused, his gaze resting upon Stoker, whose furrowed brow grew more creased the longer he read. Stoker looked up.

"The Seven Sinners?" he asked softly.

"Just so," Tiberius said.

"Perhaps one of you would be good enough to inform me what we are talking about," I suggested.

Tiberius gestured towards the empty steins of beer upon the table. "I think we will require something stronger than that." Rather than ringing for the innkeeper to wait upon us, Tiberius rose and went to the sideboard, returning with a bottle of some dark liqueur and a trio of glasses. He poured out a measure for each of us and we drank. The stuff was dark and thick as treacle, sweet and tasting strongly of plums. Tiberius sipped at his slowly, pausing to stare into the depths of his glass as if scrying for answers. The silence stretched out, taut as a bowstring, and I realised the heightened atmosphere was coming from the viscount himself. He was reluctant to speak, it seemed, as if giving voice to his fears might make them real.

"Tiberius?" I prodded.

He sighed. "Very well. The Seven Sinners is the pompous name a group of us adopted at Cambridge. It was silly, boyish nonsense, of course. We weren't really all that vice-ridden." He paused to smile. "It was some years before I became truly accomplished at debauchery. But we were twenty-one and wild to see something of the world. I cannot remember who, but someone suggested a Continental trip of some duration."

"A sort of Grand Tour?" I suggested.

Tiberius shrugged. "An outmoded custom, even in 'sixty-five. But we were a cosmopolitan group. Kaspar was our resident German. Alexandre was from Lyon. There was another Englishman besides me, and a Scot. And two Italians. We were none of us eager to take up the mantle of responsibility, so we persuaded our parents that a bit of polish might be just the thing to finish us as gentlemen."

"'Mantle of responsibility'?" Stoker choked a little on his plum brandy. "What responsibility did you ever have besides sitting around and waiting for Father to die and pass on the title?"

"I did, as you well know, accompany him on numerous trips to the Continent to engage in missions of discreet diplomacy," Tiberius replied coldly.

"Missions of overt profit, more like," Stoker countered. "Father never visited a country without plundering it."

Tiberius inclined his head. "Be that as it may, Father saw the value in travel, as did the parents of the others. It was arranged that we would organise the tour around visits to one another's homes. Kaspar's family hosted us at their castle on the Isar. Alexandre's people had a château in the Loire Valley, and so forth. Naturally we slipped away whenever possible to take in the glittering sights of the nearest cities, but it was, on the whole, a sedate and thoroughly relaxing way to spend a year."

He fell silent a moment, a faraway expression in his eyes. "We used the time to explore our interests. Pietro Salviati and I were music enthusiasts, so we took the others to the opera in Milan. We visited private collectors to see the paintings that Alexandre admired. It was churches for Benedict Tyrell. Kaspar and Lorenzo d'Ambrogio were keen amateur natural historians and wanted to see our coastline at Cherboys."

He did not elaborate, but I knew enough about the surroundings of the Templeton-Vane family seat to understand it was perched on the Devon portion of the Jurassic Coast, a series of cliffs thick with prehistoric fossils. "And James MacIver did not care. He simply wanted to hunt. So we travelled, from the shores of the Italian lakes to a shooting box in Scotland when it was time to take the grouse. We ended at Cherboys, some fifteen months after we left Cambridge. Older, no wiser, and considerably more experienced. The Paris opera dancers were particularly accommodating, if memory serves. As were the gondoliers in Venice . . ." His voice trailed off as he lapsed into reminiscence, a fond one if the gentle smile upon his lips was any indication.

I turned to Stoker. "Do you recall the visit of these young men to Cherboys?"

Stoker shrugged. "I was nine years old or thereabouts. I spent most of my time with my tutor."

"Evading him," Tiberius corrected. "You were positively feral as a child. It was only a few short years later that you ran away to join the circus."

"It was a travelling show and I learnt some thoroughly useful skills—" Stoker began.

I held up a hand. "Another time, if we may. Tiberius, you were setting the scene, as it were. The Seven Sinners had concluded their tour with a stay at Cherboys."

"Strictly speaking, we were no longer seven at that point. James MacIver had acquired a fiancée, who came for a visit with her mother."

"And the Greshams came," Stoker put in.

"The Greshams?" I turned to Tiberius for elucidation. "Who are they?"

"Ah yes. The Greshams. One hardly knows how to describe them," he began, the corner of his mouth quirking up in amusement. "Timothy Gresham is a doctor of the very earnest and superior sort. He is always doing Good Works," he added, adopting an expression of mock piety.

"One cannot imagine any friend of yours engaging in such activities," I remarked dryly.

"Friend! What a terrifying thought. No, my dear Veronica, the Greshams are neighbours, the most gently born folk for ten miles and therefore often invited to Cherboys to make up numbers when required. Timothy is of a similar age and, before he became so desperately serious, could be amusing, so he was invited. His younger sister, Elspeth, was included for other reasons entirely."

"No doubt to make a pretty addition to your party," I concluded.

"Pretty! Veronica, I can assure you that neither man nor god has ever called Elspeth Gresham pretty. She is a spinster of unfortunate appearance and dogged intellect. Twenty years ago, she was being thrust onto the marriage market by her rather desperate mamma who was determined to see Elspeth properly wedded. Father threw a ball whilst the Sinners were staying at Cherboys, and old Mrs. Gresham prevailed upon him to include Elspeth."

I felt a rush of pity for the unfortunate Miss Gresham. "I suppose you were beastly to her on account of her overbearing mother and lack of physical attractions."

Tiberius assumed a hurt expression. "I am wounded you would think so. In point of fact, I danced with her in spite of the fact that she managed to break two of my toes. And I helped her make her escape from the party when it all became too much for her."

"Presumably so she could weep in privacy," I said, feeling waspish.

"You are determined to think the worst of me!" he protested. "I guided her to the library and showed her where Father kept the books on Devonian natural history. Believe me when I tell you she was over-joyed with the turn of events."

My gaze fell to the cuttings on the table. "Tiberius, from the information you have presented, it does indeed appear that two of your Sinner friends have met an untimely end in recent months and that your name is next on the murderer's list. Have you any idea why someone would be killing Sinners?"

He rolled the glass between his palms, studying the flickers of light in the depths of the brandy. "I have, I think. You see," he said, raising his gaze to mine, "Lorenzo d'Ambrogio died whilst we were at Cherboys. And I rather think it was our fault."

I poured another measure of brandy as a stiffener. "Go on."

Stoker had said nothing at this revelation. He merely waited in silence for his brother to continue.

When Tiberius spoke, he seemed to choose his words carefully. "Lorenzo, as I have mentioned, was a fossilist."

"He and—" I craned my neck to read the name on the cutting Stoker had tossed onto the table. "Kaspar von Hochstaden."

"Yes. They were mad for anything that came out of the ground. Ammonites, belemnites, brachiopods. God, the hours we spent listening to them natter on about *bones*." He rolled his eyes. "They were especially keen to come to Cherboys because of its location. That bit of coastline from Devon to Dorset is particularly rich in fossils. You may have heard of Miss Mary Anning?" he asked me with lifted brows.

I smiled. Her painting hung in a place of honour at the Hippolyta Club in London, an establishment devoted to women of accomplishment. She had never been a member—the club having been established some years after her death—but her achievements made her an honourary light.

"'She sells seashells by the seashore,'" I recited. The bit of doggerel known to all schoolchildren had been written in her honour. After the death of her father, she had earned her way by courageously excavating fossils from the crumbling cliffs of Dorset and selling the specimens to collectors. While still a girl she had unearthed the complete skeleton of an ichthyosaur, the first ever found, and it was this discovery that had set her on the path to greatness.

"When Lorenzo and Kaspar found out that Cherboys was so near to Miss Anning's favourite hunting grounds, they could hardly contain themselves," he went on. "They wanted nothing more than to comb the cliffs for their own dinosaur. And to everyone's astonishment, they found one."

I blinked at him. "A dinosaur? A complete one?"

"Yes, one forgets the name of the beast, but it was a 'somethingosaur,'" Tiberius confirmed. Stoker pulled a face. "Philistine," he muttered. He would have no doubt launched himself into a thorough explanation of the find, but I had little interest in a paleontological lecture when there was the drama of a potential murder at hand. I opened my mouth to discourage this diversion, but Tiberius waved an airy hand. "It hardly matters," he said repressively. "The thing was found and it was enormous, far larger than Miss Anning's ichthyosaur and of a kind never seen before. Lorenzo and Kaspar were beside themselves. They thought it would bring them renown, and we were all wildly excited."

"That would have been only six years or so after Mr. Darwin published *On the Origin of Species*," I mused. "A new fossil would certainly have added fuel to the particular fires his book ignited." "Conflagration" might have been a better choice of word. Mr. Darwin's book had challenged the understood order of things, setting forth ideas that had been circulating for some time amongst natural historians but which were met with alarm if not outright violence by the general public.

Charges of indecency and blasphemy were leveled against scientists as a result.

"What happened to the fossil?" I enquired.

Tiberius spread his hands. "Lost."

Stoker spoke up. "The cliffs were like sugar, crumbling to bits. That is how the beast came to light in the first place. There were storms that summer, sudden and violent. One uncovered it, and another washed it away."

"*Away?*" My voice rose in dismay.

"The cliffside where it sat was badly eroded," Stoker told me. "A particularly nasty storm saw it fall into the sea, taking the bones with it. There were a few rough sketches made, but no evidence of it remained."

"It was lost in the storm—as was Lorenzo," Tiberius added softly.

"Surely he would have known it was a dangerous undertaking," I ventured.

"A child would have known," Tiberius said dryly. "The cliff was unstable at the best of times. It grew far more precarious over the years, and periodically Father would order the thing roped off until a fresh rockfall rendered it stable again by sloughing off the rotten bits. He was most reluctant to let Lorenzo and Kaspar go pottering about, but they were so enthusiastic, he finally gave way. After the first storm exposed the dinosaur, Kaspar had a nasty little accident—a slip that might have hurled him into the sea. He managed to catch himself but he strained his shoulder badly—dislocated it, if memory serves. He went about looking pale and tragic with his arm in a sling. But it was enough to alarm Father, and he ordered ropes put up. He didn't want any of the village children from Dearsley falling into the sea."

"Not because he had any concern for them," Stoker put in. "He simply didn't want to pay off their parents if one of them was dashed on the rocks below."

"That was his primary motivation," Tiberius admitted. "Of course, it drove Lorenzo wild with frustration. All he wanted was to get his dinosaur safely dug out of the cliffside. But it was terribly wet at the end of that summer, thunderstorms almost every day, and bit by bit, the exposed cliff face was falling to pieces. Lorenzo feared if he didn't excavate it at once, it would be lost forever. So, one night when a tempest was upon us, he apparently left the house after everyone else had retired."

"Apparently?" I asked quickly.

"No one saw him go. There is a garden entrance at the back of the house. It gives directly onto a rose alley which ends at a path leading to the cliffs. The main doors are bolted shut every night, but the butler discovered the garden door was unlocked and told Father at once. The house was searched to see if someone had burgled us, but we realised almost instantly that Lorenzo's bed had not been slept in. We were organising a search party when one of the village fishermen arrived. He had come in early with his catch and seen Lorenzo." He stopped abruptly and Stoker filled in the rest.

"The sea has been lapping at those cliffs for centuries, and from time to time, a bit of the land falls away, leaving a treacherous collection of boulders, some rising just above the level of the water. Lorenzo had landed there. I was forbidden from going to look, but—" He paused with a shrug. I understood only too well the pull of the macabre to an imaginative child. "He lay on the rocks, just as he had landed. It was not a pretty death," Stoker concluded. "He looked . . ."

He turned to his brother, and Tiberius finished the sentence with a shudder. "He looked as if he had been flung there by the hand of God."

CHAPTER

4

There was nothing to be done," Tiberius went on wearily. "His body was retrieved, and Father, in his capacity as magistrate, ensured an immediate verdict of accidental death was returned at the inquest. It was all quite straightforward."

I spread my hands. "It seems it *was* an accident, Tiberius. A tragic one, but an accident nonetheless. If anyone is to hold responsibility for it, surely it must be Lorenzo d'Ambrogio himself."

He hesitated before shaking his head slowly. "I don't know. It was a simple matter at the time to believe it an accident, but I was uneasy."

"About?" Stoker asked.

"I cannot say. It was only ever a vague sense of disquiet. I did not examine it closely then. We were young and all of us bereft at his loss. His things were packed up and sent to his parents and the rest of us dispersed. We went our separate ways and that was the end of it. I wrote a letter of condolence to the d'Ambrogios. They had been enormously kind during our stay in their castello. Lorenzo was their only son, and I knew they would take the news very badly. He had been their pride and joy, you see. You know what Italians are. The d'Ambrogios wanted a dozen children, but in the end, they had only Lorenzo and a much younger sister, Stella."

His mouth curved into a smile. "A monster, spoilt beyond belief, but Lorenzo adored her. The rest of us thought she was diabolical, always putting salt into our wine or toads in our beds. Very unlike Kaspar's sisters—the most delectable Rhine maidens with golden braids and the ruthless stamina of Valkyries. I dallied with both of them and it was highly instructive," he said, his voice trailing off as he reminisced.

I snapped my fingers in front of his face. "The d'Ambrogios," I reminded him. "You wrote them a letter of condolence?"

He shrugged. "I hardly knew what to say to them. In the end, I wrote some nonsense about those whom the gods love dying young. I cannot think it was any consolation to them. I heard nothing in return, and I was not much surprised. No doubt they wanted to put all memory of us behind them."

I nodded to the cutting with its melodramatic notation. **VENGEANCE FOR LORENZO**. "If someone is targeting the former Sinners, then someone who loved Lorenzo is the likeliest candidate. Who better than his family to avenge him?"

Tiberius shook his head. "A tidy solution but impossible. The parents and sister died within a year or two of Lorenzo—an outbreak of fever, I heard, but I think it must have been something else."

"A heart can be broken so badly that the body can no longer recover," Stoker put in. I dared not look at him, but Tiberius held his gaze.

"Just so."

He paused a moment, in silent homage to the fallen house of d'Ambrogio, I fancied. When he went on, he seemed to collect himself a little. "The house party broke up as soon as Lorenzo was buried, the rest of us scattering to the four winds. James was newly engaged and he went off to marry his Augusta. Alexandre and Kaspar returned to the Continent, as did Pietro. Benedict decided to embark upon a series of missionary trips, and I applied myself, rather too successfully, to a period of studied debauchery in Paris and Vienna. I confess, I did wonder a time or two about the oddness of Lorenzo's death, but the longer I stayed away and the more I drank and dallied, the less often I thought of it."

"But why would someone hold you—or any of the other Sinners—responsible for Lorenzo's death?" I asked. "It was an accident."

"Because of Father?" Stoker suggested. "It was his land, after all."

"And he blocked the way to the cliffs, posted notices forbidding anyone from going there," I replied.

Stoker's smile was cynical. "Think of the twenty-year-old men you have known, Veronica. Forbidding them from doing something is utterly pointless. One might as well issue a formal invitation."

I turned to Tiberius. "Was Lorenzo like that? Bullheaded and impetuous, like most young men?"

Stoker protested. "I never said—"

"Hush, my dear. Tiberius is thinking."

Stoker subsided into glowering silence as Tiberius considered my question. "No," he said finally. "He wouldn't have gone out to see the fossil simply because it was forbidden. But he could be quite stubborn if he believed he was in the right."

"Again, his own fault," I pressed. "Not yours or anyone else's."

"And yet I cannot escape the conviction that somehow his death is on my conscience," Tiberius said simply. "I have, for the better part of twenty years, pushed it aside. But no more."

I did not blame Tiberius for failing to examine his own misgivings about Lorenzo's death. I knew myself how easy it was to put unpleasant things firmly to the back of one's mind, locking them away and living only in the moment.

Stoker's thoughts must have been much the same, for he gave me a quick, sharp look as we waited for Tiberius to continue.

"As I say, the rest of us, the remaining six, have never been in the same room together since. It was as though losing Lorenzo meant the magic of our friendship was lost as well."

"Lorenzo d'Ambrogio, Kaspar von Hochstaden, and Alexandre du Plessis are dead," I said, nodding towards the cuttings on the table. "You are here. That leaves three unaccounted for."

"Two," Tiberius corrected. "Benedict Tyrell died a decade back on one of his interminable missionary expeditions. He was attempting to convert the local folk of some island or other, and they took exception to it. Decided to make an example of him."

"One can rather see their point," Stoker put in.

"Quite," I agreed. I objected to missionary work on general principles. My philosophy was that any god who required the help of priggish sermonisers to spread his message was rather less than omnificent.

"Yes, well, having sat through more than one of Benedict's interminable lectures, I can only say that I would have happily sharpened the arrows," Tiberius added.

"And there is no question that his death was due to his missionary activities?" I enquired.

"None whatsoever," Tiberius assured me. "He travelled with a number of unimpeachable witnesses, also missionaries. Benedict was the only one murdered, no doubt to send a message that a hospitable welcome would not be in the offing. The others fled and gave the same account—an attack by the local peoples in order to drive the Englishmen away."

"Effective," Stoker mused. "Kill one and leave the others alive to spread the word that such efforts would not be met with any cordiality."

"Indeed," Tiberius replied.

"And there is no chance at all he was secretly spirited away? Perhaps, if he felt haunted by the matter of Lorenzo's death, he might have arranged an escape whilst a coffin was buried under his name?"

I dared not look at Stoker as I posed this question. Given our most recent adventure, it cut far too near the bone.*

---

* *An Impossible Impostor*

Tiberius shook his head. "I see I have been too courteous. Let me be explicit. He engaged in extremely offensive behaviour amongst people whose penalty for such infractions is death. And afterwards, he was consumed. As I say, in front of witnesses. With special utensils."

"Come to think of it," Stoker said, "I believe we have a particularly nice example of a cannibal fork somewhere in the Belvedere."

"A tale for another time," I said firmly. The matter of Benedict Tyrell's death being settled, I guided the brothers back to the subject of the Sinners. "So, subtracting Benedict Tyrell from the remaining Sinners, there are, as you say, two besides yourself, Tiberius. And their whereabouts are a mystery?"

"Not at all," Tiberius said smoothly. "I know where they are and how to contact them. In fact, I have already done so."

"You did what?" Stoker demanded.

"I have made overtures to the other survivors," Tiberius said with a mocking smile. "Pietro Salviati, now a count, having succeeded to his father's title, resides in New York with his American contessa, Beatrice. James MacIver—Sir James now, fourteenth baronet of that line—is a prominent MP and divides his time between London and his family seat in Glen Lyon in Scotland. His wife, the redoubtable Augusta, is a prominent society hostess, always raising large sums of money to be given away to the deserving poor and holding dinner parties for fascinating people."

"That is extremely specific information," Stoker observed. "You have done more than simply make overtures."

"I may have made a few discreet enquiries when I received the cuttings," Tiberius admitted.

"And what form have these overtures taken?" I asked.

"I have issued an invitation to both James and Pietro and their wives. I am holding a reunion of sorts at the end of this month at Cherboys. It is twenty years since Lorenzo's death, and I wish to mark the occasion."

Stoker's interjection was frankly phrased and not suited to polite company, so I will not relate it verbatim. Suffice it to say that he expressed a healthy skepticism of Tiberius' motivations.

I added my voice to Stoker's in remonstrance. "Surely it cannot have escaped your attention that with the d'Ambrogio family gone, one of the other Sinners is the likeliest villain in this endeavour."

"It did not," he said silkily.

"You want to set yourself as bait," Stoker accused.

Tiberius narrowed his gaze at his brother, but the eyes gleamed with something resembling respect. "And if I do?"

"Of all the pigheaded, utterly cotton-witted schemes," Stoker began. Tiberius held up a hand.

"Please. It is late and we have travelled far. Abuse me tomorrow after I have had a good night's sleep and a proper shave," he said, rubbing a hand over his still immaculate chin.

"Stoker is correct, Tiberius," I said mildly. "But so are you. If you believe these recent deaths are connected to Lorenzo's, then gathering together those principally involved is a most efficient method of investigating."

Stoker interjected again, launching into an eloquent tirade. Tiberius and I listened politely for several minutes until his lordship turned to me. "Do you mean to let him go on like this for much longer?"

"I have no very mechanical mind," I explained, "but I do have a grasp of the basic principles of the steam engine. Once the heated vapour builds to dangerous levels, one must allow it to vent or the entire apparatus may explode."

He nodded sagely. "Very wise."

We carried on, sipping our brandy until Stoker lapsed into furious silence. I gave him a bright smile. "You are entirely in the right. Tiberius is willfully ignoring the danger inherent in this situation and I am fostering this reckless behaviour. It may, as you say, very well end in tears. But surely you will admit that it is safer for Tiberius to bring the battle to his own ground? He will have the advantage at Cherboys." I paused and let Stoker absorb this before pushing the point gently home. "And you must also concede that if the others have not yet received a warning, it is the responsible—nay, the obligatory and honourable—course of action to alert them?"

Stoker opened his mouth and snapped it shut again. "He could send them a postcard," he muttered through gritted teeth.

"Indeed, but I hardly think such matters should be consigned to the vagaries of Her Majesty's post. No, this requires a face-to-face meeting, a reunion of the parties involved. And with us there to protect him, what could possibly go wrong?"

Stoker groaned and dropped his face into his hands. "No," he said, the voice muffled. "I refuse." He lifted his head. "Veronica—"

"Stop," I ordered. "This is the point at which you remind me that you have, in the course of our investigations, encountered mortal peril. You will complain of being stabbed, garrotted, shot—" I ticked the dangers off on my fingers. "Have I missed any?"

"Stripped naked, drugged, and stuffed into a trunk in preparation for being hurled into the sea and drowned," he said coldly.

"But you were, in point of fact, *not* drowned," I returned with equal hauteur. "We escaped, as we have escaped every murderous plot against us."

"I have also been chained—more than once," he added.

"And here you are! None the worse for your adventures and with stories to tell the young folk when you are in your dotage," I added briskly.

Tiberius waved me off. "Do not attempt to reason with him, Veronica. I know this mood of old. It requires bribery."

Stoker snorted. "What could you possibly offer me that I want? Your silk underwear? The contents of your wine cellar?"

Tiberius, with the instinctive timing of a consummate hunter, paused before saying two words. "The Megalosaurus."

Covetousness, we are told in the Bible, is a sin, but that did nothing to deter Stoker. His eyes kindled with an unholy greed. "The Megalosaurus?" he asked in a voice hoarse with lust.

Tiberius permitted himself a thin smile. "You may have it. It is not in perfect condition, but I will pay for the materials and you will return it to glory."

"What Megalosaurus?" I asked.

For a long moment, neither brother seemed to hear me. Stoker was lost in a slack-jawed reverie whilst Tiberius was doubtless congratulating himself on a perfectly executed gambit. I cleared my throat and he turned my way.

"It is a model, sculpted in the studio of Benjamin Waterhouse Hawkins in his heyday."

"Benjamin Waterhouse Hawkins—*the* Benjamin Waterhouse Hawkins?" I asked.

"The one and only," Tiberius confirmed.

Stoker began to recite, the facts tumbling over themselves in his excitement. "In 'fifty-two, the Crystal Palace was moved from the Great Exhibition site in Hyde Park to Sydenham. In the ornamental gardens there, Hawkins set up a studio to build life-size models of extinct animals. He was advised by Sir Richard Owen on their anatomy, and what they created was unprecedented."

I broke in gently. "I have been to the Dinosaur Gardens," I reminded him. "I have seen the creatures for myself."

"Then you will know they are hopelessly out of date with modern findings and have been badly damaged by vandals, the vicissitudes of weather, and time."

"They were not at their best when I visited," I said. "But I imagine when they were first installed, they must have been dazzling."

"*Dazzling*," Stoker confirmed.

"But they are not the only ones Hawkins sculpted," Tiberius explained. "One of his installations, an iguanodon, was the setting for a dinner party in 1853, quite a famous one. The story, complete with illustrations, was in all the newspapers of the time. It was so sensational, in fact, that when our dinosaur was lost, Father thought of the iguanodon model and decided to commemorate the vanished Megalosaurus. He commissioned Hawkins and Owen to come to Cherboys. It was larger, more impressive than the iguanodon, and Father's dinner party in it was legendary. But that sort of thing soon went out of fashion. It was Stoker's favourite hideaway until Father eventually had the thing carted away to punish him for one of his many transgressions. We never saw it again."

"How did you find it?" Stoker asked.

Tiberius shrugged. "How do I do anything, brother? Money. I made enquiries and ran it to ground in the Argentine. I had it shipped back in the spring. It has been sitting in the grounds of Cherboys since."

"And you did not tell me?" Stoker demanded.

"I meant it to be a surprise," Tiberius replied. "I knew that one day I would want something from you that you would not be inclined to give me. You do not gamble or collect horses or women or snuffboxes, so I have precious little to offer by way of a bribe. Except this," he finished, spreading his hands.

"Name your terms," Stoker said.

"As I said, restore it to glory. A few days' work at most."

Stoker's brow quirked upwards. "And?"

"And I require your presence for the duration of the house party," Tiberius told him.

"But why?"

"Because, although it pains me to admit it, you seem to have a flair for this sort of thing," Tiberius said, waving a hand towards the cuttings. "I want to know why someone is targeting us. And if Kaspar and Alexandre were murdered, I want to know who is responsible."

"And possibly save your life in the process," Stoker replied.

"Cynicism does not become you, brother. And there are other things I value more highly than my own life."

"You realise it will mean asking difficult questions," I warned Tiberius. "You will be entertaining people who may as easily be potential villains as victims."

The ghost of a familiar smile flitted about his lips. "I daresay not for the first time." He blew out a sigh. "What say you? Will you come?" This last was directed not at me, but at Stoker. Tiberius knew me well enough to understand that it required no bribery to lure me into an investigation. The prospect of a puzzle coupled with the zest of danger was precisely the sort of situation best calculated to pique my interest. Although, I reflected darkly, he might have at least attempted to offer me an inducement. A nice case of rare birdwings would have not gone amiss, I mused. Or perhaps a lively group of Morphos for my vivarium where they could flap about under my watchful eye.

Whilst I pondered butterflies, Stoker held Tiberius' gaze. "Very well. For the Megalosaurus." They shook hands upon it, as sober as judges, and Stoker rose to leave.

"What about your wolpertinger?" I asked pertly. "Can you bear to leave the quest unfulfilled?"

Stoker paused, his hand upon the doorknob. "Lack of fulfillment is nothing new to me."

It was not often that Stoker had the last word, but on this occasion, I formed no response, not even when the door closed softly behind him.

"Goodness," Tiberius said lightly. "Trouble amongst the lovebirds?"

"I am very fond of you, Tiberius." I rose and shook out my skirts. "Do not make me stab you with a cheese fork."

CHAPTER

5

I did not go to my own accommodations. I had a good idea of what lurked behind Stoker's cool reception of me, and I knew precisely how to overcome it. I went directly to the room Tiberius had arranged for Stoker and scratched upon the door. There was a pause before he opened it, just a little, his body blocking my access to the room.

"Yes?"

"Let me in," I said, putting my hands to his chest and pushing a little. It was akin to trying to move a tree trunk. He did not so much as waver under the pressure of my palms. "I want to speak with you," I told him. "It is a matter of some urgency."

How many times had I envisioned this exact meeting, torn between an urge to rap his knuckles soundly for his impetuous departure and a rampageous desire to bear him away to the nearest bed and inflict such sweet punishments!

And now the moment was at hand, I felt a fizzing in my blood, an ancient drumbeat of timeless anticipation, a heady commingling of souls and selves—

"We can speak here just as easily as inside," Stoker told me, breaking into my reverie with a tone so cool he might have been speaking to the chambermaid.

"Very well," I said, folding my hands together. "I received a letter from Harry after your departure from London. It seems we were labouring under a misapprehension. I am unmarried," I said slowly, infusing each word with meaning. "The wedding licence was never signed. He sent me proof of the thing. He is not my husband."

For a moment, Stoker said nothing, *did* nothing. Not by the flicker of an eyelash or the sharp inhalation of his breath did he betray his feelings.

I prodded him gently with a finger. "Stoker?"

He roused himself to speak, seemingly with a great effort. I had expected an eruption of temper, a lavish display of his delicious ferocity, but instead he sounded entirely bereft of animation.

"It did not occur to you to write to me this news?" His voice was dangerously soft.

"I thought it best to tell you myself." I took half a step forward. "Whatever distance Harry has put between us, there is no need for it."

"I did not leave because of Harry," he reminded me. "I left because you could not confide in me. When you had the greatest need of support, of understanding, you chose to hold your secrets close instead of coming to me. You are as elusive as one of your bloody butterflies, Veronica. And when at last we are brought together again, it is under such circumstances as these," he said, spreading his hands in sudden frustration.

I blinked in surprise. "Really, Stoker, I cannot believe your intransigence. I may have travelled in Tiberius' company, but there was nothing except perfect friendship between us. You have no cause for jealousy, I assure you."

The expressive brows drew together. "Jealousy? You think me jealous? Of Tiberius?" To my astonishment, he burst out laughing. Stoker's laugh is, upon most occasions, warm and rich and beguiling. In this context, it was merely annoying.

"Well, yes. I do think you are jealous. I have spent the summer travelling in his company, in conditions of some intimacy, and it is apparent to the most casual observer that our connection is a close one. Anyone might have leapt to the wrong conclusions, although I must tell you this particular conclusion requires a jump over an especially broad chasm."

His smile was one of cool mockery.

"My dear Veronica, credit me with enough perspicacity to know that Tiberius, while blessed with the morals of a not very particular tomcat, would think it beneath his dignity as a gentleman to seduce a woman attached to his own brother. And although you live by your own Byzantine code of ethics, you would likewise consider it a crime against decency to climb into Tiberius' bed. The notion that the two of you might have been disporting yourselves around Italy is not my grievance."

"Then what is?" I demanded.

Anger flared in his eyes. "Six months," he told me. "Six months without a word from you. Not a letter. Not a telegram. Not a carrier pigeon. Not even a bloody postcard. Instead, you let me go haring off to Germany without protest, without objection."

"You asked me for time," I reminded him hotly. "And I gave it you! I was respecting your wish for some distance so you could gain perspective on our relationship. What would you have had me do? Run after you? Throw myself at your feet? Drag you back to England?"

"Yes," he said succinctly. "To all."

"You cannot seriously expect me to believe that you wanted me to engage in such histrionics. One might as well be Italian."

I smiled at the joke, but no answering grin touched his lips. His expression was serious as he leant forward, his gaze fixed upon mine, his voice unaccountably soft. "Veronica, I have loved you always. I love you still. And I will love you so long as time endures. I have proven the depth of my affection by every conceivable means, including risking certain death to save your life."

He leant closer still, a breath all that divided us. My lips parted in anticipation. Just before his mouth would have touched mine, he stopped. "But I am finished with running after you and dancing to your tune. It. Is. Your. Turn."

"What the devil does that mean?" I demanded.

"Veronica, you are the cleverest woman I have ever known. Apply your deductive powers and work it out for yourself."

With that, he stepped smartly back into his room and closed the door. As I stood there, reeling from his words, I heard the bolt slide home with quiet decisiveness.

Applying a forceful kick to the door seemed, in retrospect, not the most dignified of responses. Nor was it particularly wise, given the thinness of my slippers. I hobbled back to my room nursing what I was certain would prove to be a broken toe and a bruised sense of amour propre.

Such histrionics! I thought sulkily as I flung myself into bed and lay staring at the shifting shadows upon the ceiling. He was simply in a state of vexation at not finding his wolpertinger, I decided. Once we had spent some days in one another's company, once we were happily engaged in an investigation, testing our mettle and our wits together, facing down danger hand in hand, arm in arm, then he would come round. One way or another.

I dared not imagine what might happen if I were wrong.

CHAPTER

6

The twin advantages of Tiberius' deep pockets and formidable will ensured that within a very few days we arrived back in England. We paused briefly in Paris for him to consult his tailor and for Stoker to pay a visit to his favourite taxidermic suppliers to secure the necessary materials for his revival of the Megalosaurus. These chores completed, we travelled on to London where we parted company with our travelling companion. Tiberius enjoyed his solitude at his town house whilst Stoker and I returned home at last to our lodgings at Bishop's Folly, the Marylebone home of our patron, the Earl of Rosemorran. It was our base when in London, providing us with accommodation in the form of pretty follies on the extensive grounds—I claimed a tiny Gothic chapel for my use whilst Stoker's preferred residence was a little temple set at the edge of a duck pond. Our work was housed in a freestanding structure called the Belvedere. Built as a ballroom for a previous earl, it was stuffed to the rafters with the collections assembled by various family members over the centuries. Statues and antique arms sat cheek by jowl with paintings and rare coins, and other, less expected offerings. I had unearthed a sarcophagus full of prosthetic anatomical devices, a camel saddle, Napoléon's camp bed, and enough papyri to fill a pyramid. Jewels, stamps, assorted oddments—all could be found within the walls of the Belvedere.

But its greatest and most comprehensive collection comprised the natural history specimens. Over the centuries the practices of taxidermy had greatly improved, leaving many sad, lumpen animals oozing sawdust from broken stitches. Stoker's task was to remount the most valuable trophies according to the latest methods. He was both craftsman and artist, fashioning something majestic out of the ruins of each, resurrecting the creatures so that one could feel they were almost alive, restoring dignity to the animals in death akin to the vitality they had enjoyed in life.

The bewinged specimens of the lepidoptery collection were my own pride and joy. Many were the happy hours I toiled over birdwing and swallowtail, cleaning, labelling, and arranging the jewel-like insects. It was also within my scope of responsibilities to attend to the vivarium, a small glasshouse that had been fitted with steam heat and an assortment of lush plants to facilitate the breeding of butterflies and observation of their habits. Along with these duties, Stoker and I were tasked with sorting and cataloguing the entire Rosemorran collection in preparation for its eventual opening as a museum. At least, that was Lord Rosemorran's intention. Between our frequent absences from the estate and his lordship's penchant for adding to his treasures, Stoker and I estimated it would require a further few decades' work to bring the collections into some semblance of order.

Amongst the treasures housed in the Belvedere was an extensive library acquired for a pittance by his lordship from the estate of a destitute duke. Hundreds, perhaps thousands of volumes were stacked precariously in the upper gallery of the Belvedere. I made my way there the morning after our return, followed closely by the dogs. Huxley the bulldog was Stoker's companion of some years, but the others were more recent acquisitions. Betony, his lordship's enormous Caucasian sheepdog, trotted adoringly after the diminutive Huxley, never minding the disparity in their stature.

The rest—Nut the Egyptian hound, Vespertine the deerhound, and Al-'Ijliyyah the Italian greyhound—were all souvenirs of our various investigations. Each had come to us after their owners were murdered or arrested or went away to gain some education. It was only the mercy of a Divine Providence that none of our cases had involved monkeys, I reflected as I climbed the winding stair to the stockpile of books. I picked my way carefully through the teetering piles, grateful that we had at least had the presence of mind to sort them by subject matter. As was often the custom with libraries of the nobility, the books had been bound according to the owner's specifications. Once shelved, the assorted volumes would form a harmonious whole, although I deplored the duke's choice of dull yellow kid for the binding. The front covers were heavily embossed with the ducal coat of arms featuring a pair of hedgehogs rampant, and I suspected few of the books had never been opened, being commissioned to impress rather than to inform.

It took the better part of an hour to discover the exact title I required, but I found it at last. *A Tour of the Great Country Houses of the Southwest: Dorset, Devon, and Cornwall* by the Reverend Ellswater Pondlebury.

"A most unlikely name," I murmured as I opened it. The binding cracked like a gunshot.

"Just for show," I advised the dogs who were listening attentively. "Most dukes of my acquaintance are barely literate." I skimmed the table of contents. "Ah, here we are. Cherboys and the village of Dearsley, seat of the Viscounts Templeton-Vane, page seventy-eight and following." I turned to the page indicated to find a handsome drawing of Cherboys and gave an exclamation of surprise. I knew the Templeton-Vanes were aristocrats; I knew further that they were wealthy. I did not, however, anticipate a house as substantial as the one depicted. It was a miniature palace, sprawling across the page in a mass of chimneys, bay windows, turrets, and square towers.

Vespertine cocked his head and I read aloud. "'Built in 1516, the original edifice was a Tudor manor house extensively remodeled in 1698 and 1743, when additions were made in the Queen Anne and Georgian Neo-classical styles, respectively. Finding the result to be both inconvenient and unattractive, the seventh Viscount Templeton-Vane pulled down the structure and had it rebuilt in 1837 in the "Jaco-bethan" manner. Constructed of red brick and boasting some 133 rooms, it is faced with dressings of Mansfield stone. The interior features a top-light Picture Gallery and a bedchamber reserved for royalty after the 1856 visit of Queen Victoria.'"

Huxley made a flatulent noise and I raised a brow. "I quite agree, Huxley. Reserving a bedchamber for thirty-three years simply because a dumpy little woman once slept there is ludicrous." The fact that the dumpy little woman in question was the Empress Queen of the British Empire and my natural grandmother was beside the point. I thumbed through the following pages which featured a floor plan of the interior, tracing my way along the various corridors and up the tiny staircases. The last page featured a brief description of the setting of the house.

"'Perched atop the Devonian cliffs, Cherboys boasts impeccable views of the sea on one side of the house and gently rolling upland on the other. Extensive gardens established by John Tradescant the Younger in 1638 were improved upon by Lancelot "Capability" Brown in 1753 with the addition of an artificial lake featuring an island. Brown is also responsible for constructing the hill at the edge of the garden which is crowned with the famous Pineapple Pavilion folly.'"

I peered at the map provided, noting the vast bulk of the house from which half a dozen paths and drives wended, leading to a cliff-top overlook, the various gardens and bowers, the lake with its man-made island, and the aforementioned and frankly enormous pineapple. A pair of paths, one quite direct and another lazily meandering through tiny copses and over little footbridges, led to a tidy cluster of houses that marked the village of Dearsley.

Bordering one side of the estate was a narrow blue line, the River Dear, which flowed from the high ground down towards the distant port of Lyme Regis and the broad expanse of the sea. Beside the village green in Dearsley was a duck pond, a church, a school, and an assortment of neat houses, each with a bit of garden. A railway station, so tiny as to be almost invisible on the map, stood just a little apart from the rest of the village, and beyond this lay woods and fields dotted with farmhouses, cottages, and barns, all connected by a series of footpaths, demonstrating with a few narrow strokes of the pen how neatly the lives of the Dearsley folk were intertwined.

"Very handsome," I said, closing the book with an audible snap. I have always found it is best to survey the topography of an expedition before one embarks upon one's travels. Whether one is bound for the spice-scented tropics or the cosy familiarity of the English countryside, forewarned is forearmed.

Whilst we prepared for our sojourn in Devon, Stoker maintained a coolly polite distance. I was tempted upon more than one occasion to try to persuade him to join me in a health-giving session of physical congress, but in the end my pride would not permit it. He was polite, demonstrating towards me the sort of distant courtesy one reserved for one's spinster aunts. Our usual raillery and repartee had been abandoned in favour of cordiality. He offered no spectacular flashes of temper or biting oaths; he kept his Vesuvian temperament on a tight rein. The Stoker I knew of old was mercurial, easily roused to passionate displays of annoyance or affection, and both were scintillating. I was accustomed to grumping and glowering when he was displeased, but now he withdrew into excessive civility, using words like "please" and "thank you," as he might to any lady. I had been his equal, fighting back to back and standing hand in hand during our various adventures. Now I was firmly and politely placed upon that most hideous of perches—the pedestal. He enquired about draughts and whether I had eaten. He insisted upon wiping the dogs' muddy paws while I sat in front of the fire on a stormy day. Worst of all, when I attempted to reposition a heavy Wardian case full of Nymphalidae, he plucked the thing out of my hands and carried it for me. I thanked him in a hollow voice as I realised he had ceased thinking of me as a partner and begun to view me as a woman, enfeebled and helpless. His excessive good manners were a means of punishing me, and I returned the favour, thanking him elaborately for every act of kindness.

It was galling, a state of affairs that could not be allowed to continue. But confronting him directly was out of the question. He was clearly still furious and there was no point in forcing him to discuss the matter before he was ready. I knew Stoker, better than anyone, and I understood he possessed an innate stubbornness that any donkey would admire. No, there was only one course of action—to smother my own mounting irritation for the time being. When the moment presented itself to act, I would know, and I already had a strategy in mind. With the single-mindedness of a battlefield commander, I had mapped my plan and secured my matériel for the clash to come, one that I was certain should see me victorious.

So it was with a renewed sense of optimism that I boarded the train to Devon. Stoker and I had lingered in London to finish securing the supplies he would require, whilst Tiberius had gone ahead to prepare the house for guests. Tiberius seldom visited Cherboys, preferring his London residence and travel upon the Continent to its bucolic charms, Stoker informed me.

"Is it not comfortable?" I enquired. The sketches of the house had been staggering in scale, but it was entirely possible nothing had been updated since its rebuilding in 1837. We had only the previous spring stayed at a house on the north Devon moors that still featured prominently in my nightmares, more for its lack of modern plumbing than its legendary ghost.

Stoker gave me a look of understanding. "If you are thinking of Hathaway Hall, I can assure you that Cherboys is much more amenable to the creature comforts. There is a difference between the rural residence of a baronet and the country seat of a viscount, you know. Father was the most terrible snob," he went on. "He put in the latest plumbing—at least it was the latest thing when he installed it. There was a fire in the family wing and several of the bedrooms were damaged. It provided him the opportunity to install the very newest hygienic arrangements. I don't think an hour went by in my childhood that there was not the sound of hammering or falling stone."

Stoker had mentioned a fire previously—something to do with igniting Tiberius' bed whilst he was sleeping as retaliation for a bit of brotherly bullying, but I thought it best not to turn over that particular stone at present. Stoker and Tiberius' relationship was tenuous at the best of times, and reminding him that he had once resorted to an act of arson was not calculated to bring out the best in him, I mused. I decided instead to prod him in another direction.

"Your father had an interest in architecture?" I enquired. Stoker seldom spoke of his father, and when he did it was rarely with affection. The late Lord Templeton-Vane had been Stoker's sire in the legal sense of the word only, and the fact that Stoker had been the result of Lady Templeton-Vane's indiscretion with an Irish portrait painter had done little to endear him to the viscount. His attitude towards Stoker had apparently swung between active dislike and bored disinterest with occasional forays into mistreatment.

"He had a passion for making things exactly the way he wanted them," Stoker corrected. "Tiberius had to be the perfect heir. Rupert was primed for diplomacy and the law. Merryweather was groomed for the Church. Everything had to be just so. God, how I disappointed him!"

Bitterness limned his words. "I think he ought to have been proud of the man you have become."

He gave a sharp laugh. "Proud? With these hands?" He held them up. They were clean, washed free of his usual embellishments of ink and glue, the nails neatly trimmed. But they were marked with scars and calluses, the hallmarks of his profession, the hands of a man who worked.

And yet capable of such delicacy of touch! Such gentleness and such ardor. A thousand memories tumbled in my mind, each more delicious than the one before. How many times had those hands lingered upon my corset laces and stocking tops? And how many times had they consoled, protected, petted, loved? How many times had they been raised in defence of my person against pernicious peril?

Awash with such tender memories, I very nearly faltered in my resolve to bring him to heel. It would have been so easy then to reach out to him, to offer him conciliation.

I opened my mouth. "Stoker—" I began.

Before I could finish my thought, the train lurched to a stop. "Dearsley! The stop for Dearsley!" cried the conductor.

We had arrived.

CHAPTER
7

As is my custom, I travelled lightly, with a carpetbag and a small valise comprising the whole of my impedimenta. Stoker, on the other hand, required the support of several local fellows to extract his heap of trunks from the baggage compartment and pile them into a wagon. This was something to which I was accustomed from some months of travelling in Tiberius' company. His lordship never set foot outside his own home without packing half his wardrobe, a saddle custom-made from the finest Circassian leather, a toilet case befitting one of the more pernickety archdukes, a Sèvres tea set, and a substantial quantity of his favourite foods and liquors. He even, to one region notable for its remoteness and the rudimentary nature of its plumbing, conveyed a canvas bathtub with assorted salts and scented waters.

Stoker was nothing like half so fussy. His trunks held the various oddments of his trade—several types of clay for modeling, tools, sawdust, scraps of fur, needles, thread, and eyeballs. Boxes and boxes of eyeballs.

"Must you bring so many eyeballs?" I had enquired politely as I watched him wedge yet another tray into his trunks.

"They are very particular eyeballs, Veronica. I cannot trust my mounts to just any pedestrian eyeballs," he chided. He was, of course, correct. One of the qualities unique to his specimens was the bright, lively gaze he managed to achieve, due entirely to the fact that he had worked diligently to achieve mastery of the lampworker's art. Many a peaceful evening had passed with us tucked in the Belvedere bent contentedly over our work, Stoker with rods of glass and a fiery torch and me with a case of lepidoptera in need of attention. (As Stoker tended to work stripped to the waist, I was often distracted from my own scientific efforts, but we shall draw a veil over these diversions for the moment.)

We were the only travellers to alight at Dearsley, but an absolute pack of porters descended upon us, maneuvering the baggage swiftly into its own wagon as we were guided through the miniature station. "I know where I am going," Stoker muttered. His mood had grown increasingly gloomy through the duration of our journey, and I turned to him, suddenly intuiting what lay behind his fit of the morbs.

"How long has it been since you were last here? At Cherboys, I mean?"

"Not long enough," he said as one figure, more unkempt than the porters and wearing a black cassock and the tabbed white collar of a vicar, detached himself from the crowd.

"Stoker!" The clergyman hurtled towards us with the rumbustious enthusiasm of youth. I had only met him once before, but I recognised him instantly from a meeting at Bishop's Folly where he had deeply embarrassed himself by offering an insult to my reputation. The fact that Stoker had threatened immediate bodily injury did not in any way diminish the handsomeness of his forthcoming apology in my eyes.

I smiled broadly to show I bore him no ill will. "Hello, Merryweather." It was a less than conventional way to address a vicar, but the lad bore far more resemblance to a shaggy, shambling dog than a man of the cloth.

Merryweather came to a stop just short of us and gave me a shy smile, flushing to the roots of his curling hair, the tresses dark as a polished chestnut. His eyes, like those of every Templeton-Vane save Stoker, were bright brown—lively and watchful.

"Miss Speedwell, good afternoon to you. I am so pleased you have come to Dearsley," he said, putting his hand out in a show of friendliness. "I have long since wished to repeat my apolo—"

I thrust my carpetbag into his outstretched hand. "Take my bag and we shall say no more about it, Merryweather. Your contrition is noted and appreciated. Now, lead on. I am longing for a cup of tea."

He took my bag but did not move, his gaze fixed upon his elder brother. "It is good to have you here again at last," Merry said. There was a wariness in his expression, and I realised he was in a state of some nervous anticipation. Hardly surprising, considering the fact that the last time they had been in the same room, Stoker had called him a carbuncle and lifted him clear off his feet by his clerical collar.

"Hello, Merry. I see you're still in harness," Stoker said, dropping his gaze to his brother's distinctive garments.

Merry shrugged with a rueful twist of the lips. "Yes, well." He said no more, but there was a resignation to his tone that I did not like. It was customary for the youngest Templeton-Vane son to enter the Church, and Merry had dutifully taken holy orders in spite of lacking both temperament and vocation. But he had not dared to cross his father and, later, Tiberius. I felt a pang of pity for the boy, locked as he was into a fate quite different to that of his desiring. I knew only too well the sort of determination it required to chart a course of one's own choosing. Perhaps Merryweather might manage it for himself, if only he had the proper encouragement.

But that was a matter for another time, I decided, and I prodded Merryweather with the point of my parasol. "Tea, Merryweather."

"Of course, Miss Speedwell," he said, instantly contrite as he led us away.

Waiting for us was a luxurious conveyance marked with the arms of the Templeton-Vanes. Merry handed me in and proceeded to give me a thorough tour of the village as we bowled along. A fair number of people were milling about and I wondered if it were market day although I saw no telltale stalls or bunting.

"No, they've come out to see Stoker," Merry said, grinning, when I ventured the question.

Stoker had lapsed into silence and sat glowering in the corner of the carriage. Merryweather went on, pointing out the tiny street of shops and the various other landmarks and amenities. I recognised them from the map in the book I had unearthed in the Belvedere, but it was pleasant to have a guide, and I let Merryweather continue without interruption. "There is the village green with the duck pond, and the doctor's house is Wren Cottage, that pretty little Georgian house with the dispensary attached. Most convenient for the villagers. Just there is the school, oh, the children are at the windows, waving." He paused and raised a hand to them, smiling, as Stoker slunk further down in his seat.

Merry pointed. "And there on the other side of the pond is the church—*my* church, St. Frideswide the Lesser's," he added, should I be in any doubt on the matter. We rode swiftly along the main road as it swept in an arc around the walled churchyard and into a narrow, leafy lane that led away from the clustered cottages. The whole village could not have encompassed more than fifty houses, but it was snug and prosperous, neat as a pin with late roses rambling over the warm honeyed stone.

"You'll notice there are no thatched roofs here," Merryweather pointed out. "Father thought them unhygienic, so he had every last one stripped and replaced with slate." The effect made the village only slightly less picturesque than it ought to have been.

"They are also a fire hazard," I remarked. To my astonishment,

Merry began to cough, a sort of choking wheeze that ended only when I slapped him forcefully upon the shoulder.

"Are you quite well?" I asked when he had recovered his breath.

"Perfectly," he rasped.

I was content to let the matter rest, but Stoker's expression was stern. "What have you done now?" he demanded of his brother.

"Stoker! What makes you think poor Merryweather has done something?"

"Experience," he replied dryly. "Well, Merry?"

"I may," his brother said in a small voice, "have burnt down the vicarage."

"Good god," Stoker said.

"Was anyone injured?" I enquired.

"Oh no, thank heaven," Merry said fervently. "We were entirely blessed in that regard. My housekeeper, you see, had gone out. She went to have words with the fishmonger about the quality of his whitings. Putting him in his *plaice*, as it were."

He paused for us to appreciate his joke, and since Stoker continued to glower, it seemed only kind to smile. Merry threw me a grateful look and carried on.

"Anyway, I was terribly hungry—I had been gardening, you see, and digging in the herbaceous border always builds up an appetite, I find. And Mrs. Nettlethorpe left only a single cutlet, a very *small* cutlet, and some vegetables for my luncheon. I remembered a pork pie in the larder and decided it would be just the thing if I warmed it through. So, I banked up the oven—"

"Merry, you didn't," Stoker said. "You know better."

Merry hung his head.

"Why are you not permitted the use of the oven, Merryweather?" I enquired.

He raised mournful eyes to mine. "I am afraid I have had one or two accidents in the past," he said.

"One or two!" Stoker interjected. "You very nearly burnt down the house when you were seven."

"I thought *you* were the one who burnt down part of Cherboys," I said to Stoker.

"Oh no. That was just Tiberius' bed I set alight. Merry managed to bring down an entire wing."

"I was playing castle siege with my tin soldiers and I needed a flaming ball of pitch for my trebuchet," Merry protested.

Stoker turned to me. "He took a live coal from the fire in Father's study up to his bedroom and launched it with his toy siege machine. It landed in the curtains and kindled a fire that took forty men the better part of six hours to extinguish. And," he added with a repressive look to his brother, "it cost me my eyebrows."

"You were warned not to go in," Merry said, lapsing into a sulky tone.

"I wasn't going to let Pomona burn!" Stoker returned fiercely.

"Pomona?" I asked.

"His dog," Merry said. "He insisted on going back for her and playing the hero."

"Well, I quite understand not wanting one's dog to be immolated," I said reasonably.

"It was *stuffed*," Merry retorted.

"Mounted, damn your eyes," Stoker roared. "And I never did get the stink of smoke out of her fur."

"You mounted your pet?" I asked, only faintly disturbed.

"It was my first attempt at taxidermy," Stoker muttered. "Father had an extensive natural history collection. I saw his specimens and I thought if I could—" He glanced at Merry and broke off. "Never mind. The point is, Merry is a walking calamity. And his misadventures are not limited to fires. As soon as Father had plumbing installed in the house, Merry flooded the entire nursery wing."

"I had built a model of the *Argo*," Merry explained with solemnity. "I wanted to see if it would float in Mamma's bathtub."

Stoker continued, numbering the mishaps upon his fingers. "He knocked over a particularly valuable vase—Chinese, Fourth Dynasty—and shattered it. He fell into the River Dear, which flows from the village, past Cherboys, and down to the sea. He was only saved from drowning because his trousers snagged upon a branch. Then there was Father's horse, Tinchebray—"

"Enough," I said, holding up a hand. "Youthful peccadilloes. If a child is energetic and inquisitive, accidents will happen." I looked warmly at Merry. "I accidentally asphyxiated a kitten in a blancmange once. I managed to revive it, but only with great difficulty."

"Then you understand," he said in some relief.

"Quite. Now, since Stoker appears disinclined to play cicerone for me, why don't you tell me about our surroundings?"

This Merry did with alacrity, pointing out that we were descending almost imperceptibly from the village proper towards the sea, passing wide swathes of fields, some dotted with wagons full of hay, others freshly furrowed and planted with winter wheat or barley. Lambs born in spring had been fattened and weaned and were grazing in pastures that gave way to orchards heavy with fruit. The scene was one of sleek prosperity, well managed and abundant. In the fields, farmers and hands paused in their work to watch the carriage pass, most tugging their forelocks as Stoker shrank further back into his seat.

"They seem happy to see you," I remarked.

"Then they can wave," he replied darkly. "The hold this family have on the area is positively feudal."

Merry went on, pointing out the narrow rush of the River Dear as we crossed it via a small but handsome stone bridge. "From here, the river borders the estate," he explained. The road we travelled sometimes paralleled the river and sometimes curved away, leaving small, pretty patches of dappled woods between. From the uplands of the rolling hills, down we moved towards the cliffs standing sentinel over the water beyond, and as we emerged from one particularly lovely little copse, the vista before us opened to reveal a broad sky, deep blue and tufted with cotton-wool clouds stretching to the horizon above a dark grey sea.

"Spectacular," I breathed.

Merry smiled. "Grandfather had that last bit of wood planted in order to make the view more striking. The trees are so dark and then suddenly one is in the open, dazzled by the light."

He nodded ahead to where a house sat perched near the top of the headland, its face set to the sea. "And that is Cherboys."

He might have said, "And that is Heaven," for the note of reverence in his voice would have been the same.

As we travelled ever nearer, the house loomed larger and more impressive. The sketches I had seen had failed to do it justice, for how could mere lines upon a page encompass the grandeur of Cherboys? From battlements to towers, from galleried pillars to lavish parapets, it embraced every possible embellishment. Not a single enhancement had been overlooked. Every bit of stone that could be sculpted or carved had fallen under the workman's chisel. Every ornament, every turret, had been chosen with exacting specificity so that all fitted together in harmony. Remove one fluted stone facing, eliminate a single balustrade, and its perfection would be compromised. But it was a cold perfection, austere in its majesty, and I suppressed a shiver as we passed beneath its shadow.

The carriage rolled over the gravelled sweep of the drive, coming to a halt in front of the grand front doors. They were open, and down the wide flight of steps stood a battery of servants, each spotlessly attired and standing stiffly at attention. A pair of footmen, bewigged and be-stockinged, wore the livery of the Templeton-Vanes, dark blue edged in silver. The maids wore dresses of the same shade of blue with crisp white aprons and enormous mobcaps to cover their hair.

"Christ," Stoker muttered. "Was this really necessary?"

"Tiberius' orders," Merry said by way of apology. "He knew you wouldn't like it, but they are all very excited you've come home."

"No doubt Tiberius is hiding behind the door, watching it all and laughing up his sleeve," Stoker said darkly.

"Hardly," Merry replied. "He is squirrelled away in his office. Something about estate business." He paused and looked at his elder brother anxiously. "Of course you may stay in the carriage as long as you like, but it is nearly teatime. Perhaps we ought to think about getting out?"

Stoker said nothing, but I sensed the tautness of his nerves. A homecoming after a long absence is often a difficult thing, and Stoker's travails had been dramatic and painful. Infamous gossip had been published in the London newspapers—*untrue* gossip, I might add, and all at the behest of his former wife, whose depravity is exceeded only by her malice. Stoker had never said, but I suspected one reason for his avoidance of his boyhood home was the fear that the rumours had spread even so far as the wilds of the Devonian coast. He had often enough found judgment in the eyes of those he had counted friends. He had no wish to receive it from those he had once held dear. He had been seduced by Tiberius' offer of the Megalosaurus, but I knew him well enough to understand that returning to Cherboys, the site of so much of his boyhood unhappiness, would feel like a reckoning.

Merry handed me out of the carriage and I stepped aside to wait for Stoker. For one long moment I thought he would not appear, but at last he emerged, ducking his head as he descended. He drew a deep breath as his foot touched the gravel and straightened, raising his chin in defiance.

Suddenly, a diminutive figure in grey and white detached itself from the others. She was plump and wore long, full skirts of an old-fashioned design. A cap of snow-white lace perched atop hair of the same colour. She stood at the top of the steps, arms crossed over her chest as she regarded Stoker, scrutinising him slowly from scuffed booted toe to tumbled hair. Without saying a word, she pursed her lips and turned on her heel, tapping smartly as she walked into the house.

"Oh no," Stoker murmured, his face going pale.

"I ought to have warned you. She is rather angry," Merry whispered, looking quite sorry for his brother.

"Who is that?" I asked. Stoker did not reply. He merely mounted the steps, slowly, with the tragic and dignified air of a French aristocrat mounting the tumbril on his way to the guillotine.

"Courage, man," Merry called to his back. Stoker squared his shoulders and followed the tiny woman into the house. The other members of staff stood looking after him with expressions of mingled fear and amusement.

I turned to Merry. "Why does Stoker look as though he were preparing to face a firing squad?"

Merry's expression was sober. "It is far worse than a firing squad, Miss Speedwell. Far worse indeed." He paused and gave a grim nod towards the house. "That is Nanny."

CHAPTER

8

Merry guided me up the steps past the bobbing and curtseying staff and into a grand entrance hall that seemed to go on for miles. The floor was black-and-white marble, austere in its glossy perfection. The walls were dotted here and there with alcoves, each fitted with a plinth to hold a statue from antiquity. Various gods and goddesses watched eyelessly as we passed, footsteps ringing upon the marble. It was formal and impressively large, designed for one purpose: to display enough wealth and power to strike terror into the heart of the casual visitor.

But the décor was not the only thing to terrify. Stoker stood in the center of the hall, head bowed as his nanny heaped scorn upon him in a thick Scottish accent.

"—this many years without so much as a visit and hardly even a scrap of a postcard to say if you be alive or dead. When I think of the hours I spent cuddling you to my bosom and you fair screaming the house down with the colic. I can hardly hear now for the damage you did me, but would I consider it a loss? Nay, I would not, if only I had a *word* from you now and again—"

She was warming to her theme and heaven only knows how long she might have carried on had Stoker not interrupted her. I was tempted to suggest to Merry that we ring for tea—watching Stoker squirm is a thoroughly entertaining proposition and refreshments seemed in order—but Stoker clasped his nanny's wagging finger in his large hand and brought it to his cheek.

"Dear Nanny," he said gently, "there are no words sufficient to convey my regret that I have caused you a moment's trouble. Can you find it in your heart to forgive me?"

The little harridan slipped her hand from his and slapped his cheek—but lightly. "That is for giving me more grey hairs than the rest of the lot combined." Then a smile warmed her withered apple face. "And this is for coming home at last, my wee Stokie." She reached up on tiptoe and kissed him soundly on both cheeks before tucking his arm through hers. "Now, you must come to my cottage and have tea with me."

He cast a glance backwards at me as she moved to drag him off. "Nanny, I must introduce you—"

She paused and gave him a quelling stare. "Do you mean to agitate me again, Stokie?" She pressed her free hand to her bombazine bosom. "Do you know that I have palpitations now? From all the *worry*," she said meaningfully.

"Of course, Nanny," he soothed, patting her hand. "We will have tea."

He sent us a helpless look, but she grasped his hand and tugged him along relentlessly. She turned back just once to dart a look of triumph in my direction, and Merry regarded me anxiously. "I hope you are not offended, Miss Speedwell. Nanny can be a trifle possessive where her boys are concerned, particularly Stoker. She always had a soft spot for him."

"Don't you mean 'wee Stokie'?" I asked with a grin. I put my own arm through his. "Never mind, Merryweather. I will have tea with you and we can get to know one another better."

Merry played the tour guide, naming the various rooms we passed through—picture gallery, garden entry, library, morning room— until we came at last to the drawing room, a long, handsome chamber furnished in gold silk.

"I brought you the long way round," he informed me, sketching a broad circle with his hands. "We have made a loop, clockwise, through the main public rooms, and if we passed through that door," he said, pointing behind me, "we would find ourselves in the entrance hall once more. At least it makes a start to learning the house. Best to take it in stages," he finished kindly.

Having seen the floor plan in the Pondlebury book, I knew he spoke wisdom. "It is a considerable property," I said as he rang for tea.

"Oh, quite! You have seen less than a third of this floor and there are two more above with the attics atop that. Stoker always used to say that it needed Ariadne's clew to find one's way around." A fleeting smile touched his lips, and I realised then what genuine affection he held for Stoker.

Before I could broach the subject, the tea appeared, hot and fragrant and served with such a vast assortment of cakes, sandwiches, and tarts that I began to fear for the state of my corset strings. When we had dusted the last of the crumbs from our fingers, Merry suggested a tour of the grounds after I had been shown to my room.

"Splendid idea!" I told him as I rose and smoothed the skirts of my travelling costume. "Trains are diabolically stuffy inventions and a bit of fresh air is just the thing to blow the cobwebs away."

We returned to the entrance hall, where a trio of servants waited. I spotted a familiar figure and gave an exclamation of real pleasure.

"Collins!" I said as I extended my hand. I had visited Vane House—Tiberius' establishment in London—often enough to have become quite well acquainted with his butler. "How nice to see you again. How is your lumbago?"

Collins seemed startled at the proffer of my hand, but he shook it gravely. "Tormenting me day and night, but it is kind of you to ask, miss."

"I have only recently read of a new treatment—a kind of baking apparatus to warm the limbs. I shall speak to Stoker and have him sort one out for you," I promised.

"That is not necessary—" he began, looking thoroughly alarmed at the notion.

I smiled. "It most certainly is. I know how much Lord Templeton-Vane relies upon you, and how can you work or enjoy your leisure if you are suffering?"

He gave me a feeble smile. "How indeed, miss? May I present Mrs. Brackendale, the housekeeper?" He gestured towards the woman behind him, tall and composed and with an enormous ring of keys at her belt that rattled as she moved.

"How do you do, Mrs. Brackendale?"

"Miss Speedwell," she said, inclining her head. "This is Lily, one of the upstairs maids. She will be responsible for taking care of you during your stay."

Lily was a plump and cheerful-looking country girl with rosy apple cheeks and a twinkle in her eye that spoke of barely suppressed amusement. Her dark blue dress was uncreased, her white apron spotless.

"Hello, Lily," I said.

She bobbed a curtsey, the edge of her mobcap fluttering a little. "How do, miss?"

"I am sorry that his lordship is unavailable to receive you at present, Miss Speedwell," Collins said. "But he was confident you would take no offence."

"Certainly not. His lordship and I are long past standing upon ceremony," I assured him.

"Still wrestling with the accounts, is he?" Merry enquired.

"No, Mr. Merryweather. I believe now it is the rents. It is nearly quarter day," Collins replied, pursing his lips.

"Oh dear," Merry murmured. He looked at me. "Tiberius is not the most attentive of landlords, and quarter days are when the rents are due from every cottager, farmer, and tenant on Templeton-Vane land. And every one pays in person, coin in hand. He will be inundated with visitors from morning to night. Tell me, Collins, has he begun drinking yet?"

"Only a little whisky in his morning coffee," Collins admitted. "And then a very nice full-bodied Burgundy with luncheon."

"An entire bottle?" Merry's brows rose skyward.

Collins discreetly held up two fingers before turning to me. "No doubt you will meet other members of staff during your stay, Miss Speedwell, but you may rely upon myself, Mrs. Brackendale, or Lily to attend to any of your wants. His lordship has issued strict instructions that you are to be afforded every possible comfort whilst at Cherboys. Now, Lily will show you to your room."

Merry and I arranged to meet after I had freshened myself, so I trotted obediently after Lily, listening to her cheerful prattle as she pointed out still more features of the house as we mounted the broad principal staircase. "Now, the family portraits is all in the picture gallery, and I wager you've never seen the like of that room, miss. It has a window in the ceiling it does, three stories above. It makes me giddy to look up at it, it does. The billiard room is where the Russian paintings is, all grim-looking saints and a Jesus as wants a good meal, I reckon. Here in this staircase hall is the Italian collection," she said, waving a hand to indicate the paintings hung in heavy gilded frames. At a glance I noted a Leonardo, a pair of Titians, a gloomy Caravaggio, and a particularly fine Tintoretto triptych.

Looking up, I saw that the ceiling of the staircase hall was covered in frescos. "Heaven." She pointed upwards. "The walls below used to be painted with . . . *the other place*," she said in a low whisper. "The late Lady Templeton-Vane didn't think it decent, so it were all painted over and these pictures hung instead, although why anyone would want a painting of some dirty boats is beyond me." I smiled as we passed a Canaletto series of gondolas.

We left the stairs at the first landing and I saw that we had emerged into a wide rectangular gallery open to the floor below. "Stand just here, miss, and you can see how it is arranged. Below us is the pictures what I did tell you about, the family portraits and such." I peered over the railing and saw beneath us the long expanse of the picture gallery. On the floor above us, another corridor circled the opening to the gallery, whilst far above, a top light permitted illumination. It was a clever architectural conceit, permitting light and a sense of spaciousness.

Lily, no doubt trained well by the redoubtable Mrs. Brackendale, did not point but gestured by nodding her head. "Across that way is the children's wing, the nurseries and governess quarters and schoolrooms, although none of those are in use now, of course. Overlooking the drive and away to the sea is his lordship's suite." She turned. "Along the back of the house is one of the large guest suites, meant for guests that haven't yet arrived. Italians, I'm told."

"That would be Count Salviati and his countess," I said.

"Aye, that sounds right. In the back corner, overlooking the garden, that is where your room is, miss. It has a wee balcony for sitting should you take a mind to admire the view. Them Italians in their suite come next to your room, then the back stairs, the linen room, and the sitting room for visiting ladies' maids."

"I'm afraid I haven't one of those," I told her, knowing well I would lower myself in her estimation by the admission. Travelling without a lady's maid was as scandalous as losing one's maidenhead in certain circles. Of course, I did not have one of those either, but the loss hardly troubled me. "I am sorry it will make extra work for you, but I assure you I am entirely capable of looking after myself."

"As you please, miss, but if you need a hem whipped or a bit of lace mended, you come to me," she told me firmly. "Mrs. Brackendale will have my guts for garters if she thinks I've not taken care of you properly."

She clapped a hand over her mouth. "I am not meant to speak like that in front of guests."

"Well, I am not your customary guest, Lily," I advised her.

"God's own truth, that is," she agreed. She relaxed enough to point upwards. "The other large guest suite is meant for the Scots and it is on the floor above us with the bachelors' rooms. Mr. Revelstoke is in the corner, just above your room, miss, and the vicar is next door, over his lordship's suite, as it were. And the floor above that is the attics, maids' rooms and lumber rooms and so forth." Along the walls were alcoves housing assorted seminude statues of nymphs and warriors in Classical poses. "These are called nimps," she informed me. "They're ladies what had special powers—talking to trees and whatnot. And some of the statues are men with their bits out, so mind you don't get startled."

I suppressed a smile.

"Thank you, Lily. You have been a most informative guide."

"Thank you indeed, miss." She pinked with pleasure. "Come this way and I will show you to your room. Mind you look out the windows as we move to the back of the house. The views are of the gardens, not the sea, but for my money, Devon is as pretty a country as you'll find."

S he led me to a bright and airy room of generous proportions. It was furnished and carpeted in delicate shades of green and violet. "The Pomona Suite," she said, throwing out her arms.

"Pomona? After the Roman goddess of spring?" I enquired.

"No, miss. After that," she said, nodding to a dog basket in the corner. Lying in state was a sleeping dog—at least it seemed to be sleeping.

"Stoker's pet," I observed, recognising the creature from the story Merry had told.

"That it is, miss. After it did die, Mr. Revelstoke stuffed it and Lady Templeton-Vane said it was a masterpiece, but old Lord Templeton-Vane wouldn't have it in the public rooms and ordered it destroyed. Her ladyship had it moved here instead. I can take it out if it troubles you," she said, moving towards it.

"No, thank you," I told her. "It doesn't bother me in the least." There was something oddly touching about having a bit of Stoker's childhood in my rooms, and although I might have chosen a more decorous item, I could not choose a more meaningful one.

CHAPTER

9

I washed and changed into a walking dress and stout boots, longing for fresh air and a bit of late summer sunshine. I retraced the route I had taken with Lily, making my way to the entrance hall, where Merry was waiting. We left the house through the garden entrance, a small lobby hung with an elaborate green glass lantern. The little room gave on to the terrace, which ran the distance of the back of the house. From there, shallow steps descended to a series of small out-door rooms, each with its own distinct style and purpose.

"The knot garden and the rose alley were laid by my mother," Merry told me with some pride as we made our way down a long, straight corridor of roses, great flowering shrubs heavy with perfumed blossoms. In the middle a sort of bower had been made, with benches and an archway of roses meeting overhead and sprinkling petals like so much silken, scented confetti. Merry gestured towards a gap in the shrubbery. "This path here leads through the little copse we saw as we drove in. It will take us out onto the cliffs."

He pointed out various landmarks along the way, some of which I recognised from my researches—the pavilion shaped like an enormous pineapple, a fountain featuring a goddess with exuberant breasts and a basket full of grapes, a picturesque hermitage long since abandoned but still attractive. It had been built to resemble a mushroom, the roof carpeted thickly with moss. "My grandfather hired a man to live there and pretend to be the hermit. Apparently it was all the rage a century ago. Ah, and here we are," he said as we broke from the trees and out onto the wide expanse of headland giving on to the sea.

The beauties of the Devon cliffs are best described by poets. A natural historian will speak of limestone and strata and mineral deposits, but a poet will sketch with words the grandeur, the limitless, stark beauty of white chalk cliffs bearing down to the ink blue sea. This part of the world brooks no beaches; no pleasant stretch of shingle softens the base of these cliffs. They rupture abruptly at water's edge, broken off as if in midsentence. If one is careful and has a good head for heights, one might perch precariously at cliff's edge and peer over the side, spotting the dark shadows that hint at caves forgot since the start of mankind. But tarry too long and it seems the earth shifts under the feet, crumbling away like so much demerara sugar. It is easy to lose one's head and succumb to giddiness, and as we approached the edge, Merryweather looked a trifle unwell.

"Are you quite all right?" I enquired.

"Entirely," he said.

"For a clergyman, you are frightfully mendacious," I told him. "You are positively green, Merryweather. Have you a poor head for heights?"

He looked abashed. "I am afraid so."

I drew a flask from under my skirts. I offered it to him and he pulled in a long sip, swallowing, then gasping, choking, and heaving all at once. I thumped him hard upon the back until he regained his breath. His complexion had turned from green to a violent shade of pink.

"Not water," he managed in a broken voice.

"Certainly not. Aguardiente," I explained. "It is a refined spirit from the sugarcane plant. Potent but effective for restoring the nerve. Already you look much improved. Would you care for more?"

He reared back like a frightened pony and waved me off. "Thank you, no." His voice was still hoarse but he managed to stand. "I am quite recovered. I think I saw stars for a moment," he added, blinking furiously.

"Yes, it can have that effect." I tucked the flask back into place and found him regarding me with a lively interest.

"You are an extraordinary lady, Miss Speedwell," he said.

I held up a hand. "I am on a first-name basis with the rest of your family and see no reason for formality amongst friends, Merryweather."

"Veronica," he said, with one of his charming blushes. "It is difficult to make new friends here. I am glad to think of you as one."

"You do not much care for being a vicar, do you?" I enquired as we began to stroll. I made certain to keep myself between Merry and the edge of the cliff path. Where we walked, the path was bordered by a grassy verge some feet from the brink of the precipice, and the footing was sound enough.

Merry shrugged. "One has no choice in such things."

"No choice! You speak like a Russian serf. You are not tied to the land, you know. You have two strong arms and a strong back. You have a reasonable intellect, one presumes, as well as the advantage of youth. The world is yours for the taking."

"But take it *where*? I have been educated for this," he said, tugging at his dog collar. "I am fit for nothing else."

"Feathers," I said firmly. Merryweather, like so many born into the noble class, had little imagination and less initiative. But liberating him from his torpor could wait. We had come to a section of the cliffs which looked as though a giant had bitten a piece away, leaving a long curve edging inland. A landslide had happened here, I realised, carrying away part of the path itself. Some distance from the edge, a pair of wooden posts had been knocked in, flanking the path. Between them stretched a heavy chain, thick with rust, and a painted notice, the edges peeling away from the salt-laden winds. **DANGER**.

"That is where the cliff collapsed," Merryweather told me. "When I was a child. It happened when Tiberius was having friends to stay—you must know, the people he has invited for this house party. It is a reunion of those who were here then."

The sea was louder here, as if the sheared-away cliff cupped it, amplifying the sound and sending it up to where we stood.

"There was a fossil, was there not?" I asked, stretching on tiptoe. I could see nothing. The notice was some six feet from the edge, and even as I stood there, I observed a tiny ripple of pebbles as the ground shifted. They shivered and then disappeared as a minute portion of the cliff fell away.

Merry grabbed my arm and pulled me several feet further back. "I am sorry, but it is not safe. When Father had the notice put up, it was some twenty feet from the edge. Every year more of it slides down into the sea." He shifted and raised his gaze to the sky. "The autumn storms will come, bringing heavy wind and rain, soaking the earth and causing the ground to crumble away. And that is when the situation is most unstable."

He looked distinctly uncomfortable, so I allowed him to lead me up to safer ground. A boulder had shrugged itself free of the earth, making a sort of rustic seat, and we scrambled up to perch atop it.

"St. Frideswide the Lesser's chair," he said.

"And who is St. Frideswide the Lesser?" I asked. "Besides patroness of your church."

"A Saxon lady of gentle, some say even royal birth," he told me, his hair ruffled by the sea breezes. "Not to be confused with the original St. Frideswide, of course."

"Of course. What makes this your St. Frideswide's chair?"

"Legend says St. Frideswide had become a Christian, unlike the rest of her family, who remained firmly pagan. Her father arranged a marriage for her with another Saxon lord, who refused to permit Frideswide to practice her faith. Frideswide came here and sat upon this rock and said she would not be moved until her intended husband promised to allow her to do as she pleased. Naturally, her father and brothers and prospective husband thought it would be a simple matter to carry her off the rock and to the church to be wed."

"Naturally."

"But when they came, they found that none of them could shift her. It was as though God himself had bound her to the seat. For six days and nights she sat, taking no food, no water, and resisting all attempts to remove her. One by one, the menfolk gave up, all except the would-be bridegroom, who insisted he would be master in his own house and that Frideswide would bend the knee to him."

He paused for dramatic effect. "But on the seventh day, his strength broken, the bridegroom gave in. He promised Frideswide she should do as she wished, and instantly he made his vow, the rock released her and she went happily into his arms. To this day, folk around here believe that if a woman sits upon St. Frideswide's seat before her intended, she will be master in her own house."

"And if a woman does not wish to marry?" I asked archly.

He grinned. "Then I believe she does not need St. Frideswide's help in the first place." I smiled back before turning to the panorama before us.

"What a marvellous view!" I exclaimed. Sea and sky met at a single dark line on the horizon and the world seemed to fall away as we sat there under the scudding clouds. The wind whipped and gulls cried, diving for fish as the whitecaps rose.

"Before we spoke of St. Frideswide, you asked about a fossil," Merry said. "It was a Megalosaurus. The largest ever found on this coast—or in the world, I am told."

"But it was later lost, was it not?"

He nodded. "Along with one of the guests at Tiberius' house party. An Italian fellow—I don't remember much of that time. I was very young, you understand. But I remember Lorenzo."

"Do you indeed? Why?"

He paused as if groping for words. "He was kind to me. He had a sort of toy he used to carry in his pocket—a bit of card tied between two pieces of string. One side of the card had an illustration of a bird, the other a cage. When he spun it between his fingers, it looked as if the bird were actually inside the cage. I thought it magic," he said with a nostalgic smile.

"A thaumatrope!" I exclaimed. "I had one as a child. Only mine had a butterfly on one side and a net on the other. Quite appropriate, as it turned out, given my chosen occupation. What happened to yours?"

"Oh, it was not mine. He bought it to take home to his little sister. But he was kind enough to oblige anytime I asked him to show it to me. He was generous like that. Always doing things for other people. At least that is what I remember. I don't even recall what his voice sounded like or the features of his face. But I do recall how he made me feel."

"And that was?" I prodded gently.

"Important. Fourth sons are rarely noticed," he added with a rueful smile.

"Neither are orphan girls," I replied.

"I am sorry," he said instantly. "I did not know."

"No need to be sorry," I assured him. "Children know nothing beyond the upbringing they have. It is only adults who regret what they lacked." I nodded towards the edge of the cliffs. "You said the fossil and this Lorenzo were lost?" I knew the answer, but I was interested in Merry's impressions. Children, unburdened by the prejudices of adults, were often keen observers, in my experience.

"Yes, and more's the pity. Lorenzo was a fossilist. It was he who discovered the Megalosaurus. He would have become quite famous from it, but the poor beast was carried away in the same landslide that took his life."

"But it was on your father's land," I pointed out. "Would he not have received the credit for the discovery?"

Merry shrugged. "Father was not a generous man, but he was shrewd. Lorenzo's family were wealthy and influential, and Father wanted to make use of their influence. He had ties to diplomacy and business. Making friends with the d'Ambrogios was a stratagem, nothing more. Allowing Lorenzo the credit for discovering the Megalosaurus would cost him nothing. Lorenzo was a gentleman and a scholar. He'd never have sold the fossil. He would have donated it for study and published a paper on it. In the meantime, Father would have ever-so-gently made certain the d'Ambrogios never forgot who was responsible for their son's happiness." He paused, no doubt intuiting my thoughts. "No, I did not understand that at the time. I was four years old. It was only much later I realised what sort of man Father was. He did nothing that would not bring him a benefit, and every word, every gesture, every kindness had a cost." Merry broke off suddenly. "I am sorry. One ought not to speak ill of the dead, particularly if the dead is one's father."

"On the contrary, my dear Merry," I said, rising and dusting off my skirts. "The dead are the very best people about whom one may speak the truth. They are far less likely to bring suit for slander."

He grinned and offered me a hand as we clambered down from St. Frideswide's seat. I paused at the edge of the cliff path. "How did Lorenzo d'Ambrogio happen to find the beast in the first place?" I enquired.

Merry explained how the creature had been situated within the face of the cliff, a thin layer of black marl, rock, and soil that concealed the skeleton until a sudden storm had caused it to be revealed, as perfect as the day it had lain down to die. He went on for some time in vivid detail, laying out how the earth comprised layers, each formed uniquely in its own epoch and containing a perfect microcosm of its history and its fauna, one atop the other since the beginning of time. It was all information I knew perfectly well—one had only to look a single time at William Smith's geological map of England to understand the principle—but there is no better way to win a man's regard than to let him believe he is teaching one something new. Besides, there was something adorably schoolboyish about his enthusiasm, so I let him carry on about the fossil until at last he wound down.

"Imagine," he finished, "it was simply *there*, this magnificent specimen of Creation, resting within the stone for millions of years."

"You know rather a lot about fossils," I observed. "And you do not seem to have the usual clerical aversion to believing the Earth is considerably older than four thousand years."

"If the Lord God can make a universe in six days, then he is capable of anything," Merry said.

"I admire your faith, Merry," I told him sincerely. "It is good to have something in which to believe."

"What do you believe in?"

"Science," I said with promptitude. "But for those who wish to find it, the hand of God may be detected there. One may see the glory of a creator in the artistry of a butterfly's wing or the perfection of a shark's design. I have no quarrel with your occupation," I assured him. "Only with its tendency to inflict itself on the unwilling."

"I am no proselytiser," he assured me. "I can scarcely minister to the flock I already have. I could never find it within me to go and collect others."

"Is the work of a country parson so arduous?" I teased.

"You would not imagine it, but yes," he replied with fervour. "I am called upon for births and deaths and baptisms, which I anticipated. But there is so much more! Every quarrel, I am asked to adjudicate. Every wayward youth, I am expected to find honest work. Gainful employment for a man who has lost his position. A bit of firewood for a cold hearth, a home for a fisherman's orphan. Every problem, no matter how large or small, is laid at my doorstep. I must be all to them—father, landlord, master, shepherd, teacher. It is . . . it is a great responsibility," he said finally. His colour had risen during his outburst, and he had spoken quickly, with great passion. But as he wound down, he seemed to collect himself. "I am sorry. I ought not to complain."

"It is as you say—a great responsibility to be so much to so many. Is there no one to help?"

He shrugged. "It is because I am one of the family—a Templeton-Vane. If Tiberius were here, it would fall to him, but . . ." His voice trailed off as he shrugged.

"Is there no curate? No estate manager?"

"Tiberius does not believe there is work enough for me to require a curate, and the estate manager has held the job forty years and more. He grows tired and is often ailing. And he is not from Dearsley. He is a Bristol man, and even though he has lived amongst them for four decades, the villagers consider him an incomer still. He does a fine job of keeping Cherboys in order, but if there is a misunderstanding between the villagers who work on the estate, they bring their troubles to me. It is just the way of folk here. They have been under the dominion of the Templeton-Vanes for so long, they cannot imagine an existence where they are not cared for by the family."

"And Tiberius has neglected his duties," I supplied.

Merry turned to me with shocked eyes. "I would never say that. It is not neglect. It is apathy. He simply chooses to spend his time in London and abroad, and we are forever the afterthought."

"And it does not ameliorate the situation to have no lady of the manor, I imagine. A viscountess in residence would look after the poor of the parish," I ventured.

His expression was rueful. "Yes. If Tiberius married it would ease the burden a little. As it is, the Greshams do much to help."

"The Greshams?" I recollected Tiberius mentioning the brother and sister who had joined the fateful house party when Lorenzo d'Ambrogio fell to his death.

"The doctor. I pointed out his cottage as we passed through the village," he reminded me. "He and his sister are most beneficent. They do what they can, but it is not the same as if Tiberius were here."

"It seems unkind that they have all left you here to shoulder the burden alone," I said at last.

"I would not mind so much if I thought any of it truly mattered. Tiberius is a viscount, after all, and sits in the House of Lords. Rupert is always doing something important with diplomacy—and most likely running the government behind the scenes, if I know him, as well as standing as the member for his district. And Stoker, well. Stoker used to be the wayward son, the prodigal who would never make anything of himself, to hear Father tell it. But one only has to look at him to find a man who is utterly content within himself. His work, his friends, you—" he added, dropping his eyes bashfully. "He has found purpose, real purpose. And what he does makes a difference to those around him. Sometimes I fear I am sinking into shifting sands here, just drifting in the current instead of *acting*. I ought to be doing something, I feel, but I do not know what, and so I am left to wonder what is the point of me?" Before I could respond, his smile turned wistful. "But you are wrong. I am not alone now. At least for the duration of this house party. I am glad you have come. And I know Tiberius would want me to tell you to consider Cherboys your home."

"I will," I promised, "as I shall consider you my friend."

"I am honoured. Veronica," he said, carefully, as if testing my name. "Are you ready to return to the house?"

"Not just yet. I would like to enjoy the view a while longer."

"Then I will leave you if you think you can find your way back?"

"My dear Merry, I have navigated the jungles of Costa Rica with nothing more than a broken compass and my own wits. I promise you, I will be perfectly fine."

After he had gone, I stood staring out to sea as the sun lay long golden rays upon the rippling waves. I never tired of the ocean, the promise of it, the enduring way it beckoned to me, suggesting adventures just beyond the horizon. But the sea was not the reason I stayed behind.

When I was certain I was alone and Merry did not mean to return, I climbed carefully up St. Frideswide's seat, settling comfortably onto the sun-warmed stone. The notion that a long-dead saint could imbue a woman with the power to determine her own fate and keep true to herself even in love was so much superstitious flummery, I knew.

But one can never be too careful.

CHAPTER
10

With Tiberius wrestling with the demands of his estate, Stoker using his Megalosaurus to elude me, and Merry locked in the study, struggling with his next sermon, I was the sole focus of the staff's efforts. No sooner had I awakened than they sprang to action each day, plying me with food and drink, running baths, suggesting walks, and lighting fires in the various rooms they thought I might frequent. Library, music room, portrait gallery, morning room, billiards room—all were kept in perfect readiness for me. And when I ventured out of doors, it was to find fresh flowers and pitchers of elderflower cordial waiting in the Pineapple Pavilion or a basket and secateurs sitting expectantly in the cutting garden.

In the end, I took to hiding, filling my pockets with apples and biscuits to escape the endless courses of a formal luncheon served in the solitary splendour of the dining room. I darted behind doors whenever I heard Mrs. Brackendale's familiar jingle, and I rose and washed before Lily could appear with my morning tray. The library soon became my favourite hideaway. It was a vast chamber, shelved from floor to ceiling, with a gallery circling the perimeter. The cases were stuffed with novels and tomes on every conceivable subject. Folios of maps were stored in wide wooden drawers and plinths held busts of famous thinkers.

Glass terraria and Wardian cases housed specimens from around the world, ferns and flocks of bright songbirds mounted in flight. It smelt of beeswax and book leather, and I passed a good many hours tucked in the window seat of the library, reading and munching apples behind the draperies, which hid me from view. Only Nanny avoided me, for which I was entirely grateful.

But I missed Stoker acutely, an eventuality with which I was not entirely comfortable. Dependency upon anyone was an abomination to my independent spirit, but one cannot resist the lure of the twinned soul. One afternoon, the day Tiberius' guests were due to arrive at last, I dropped my apple core into a handy aspidistra and went in search of him.

The Megalosaurus had been hauled into position on the island in the middle of the man-made lake. This had been dug some distance from the house and could be reached via the rose alley. Willows trailed their green sleeves into the dappled water, and a pair of particularly nasty swans paddled serenely past. On the near side of the lake, there was no bridge to spoil the view, only a tiny rowboat. But having once nearly met my doom after an excursion in a rowboat,* I elected to circle the lake and cross the narrow footbridge on the far side. More willows had been planted here, and it was with a sense of entering an enchanted glade that I pushed my way past the languorous fronds into the clearing at the center of the island.

The Megalosaurus crouched there on all fours, a long, low lizard of mammoth proportions with a small head and stout, lumbering legs. Its back was humped, the barbed spine running to a long, thick tail, and its head was ungainly, the heavy brow lowering over a pointed snout full of unpleasantly sharp teeth. It had been painted a violent shade of green, and the eye sockets had been fitted with glass orbs that glowed with malevolence. It was a dreadful creature, and I was not at all surprised that Stoker loved the thing. He had always been drawn to the outré.

---

* *A Dangerous Collaboration*

I circled the beast, finding no means of ingress and no sign of Stoker. But I could hear him, his lush baritone raised in a cheerful, perfectly filthy song he had no doubt learnt whilst in Her Majesty's Navy. I rapped smartly upon the side of the Megalosaurus. There was a pause in the song, and after a long moment, the beast began to shudder. A sort of panel, running from the base of its head to the start of its tail, rose slowly to reveal a wide opening. Stoker stood inside, begrimed and thoroughly happy. He was stripped to the waist, streaked with paint and glue, hair tied back with a leather thong, muscles rippling in the golden light of late summer's afternoon. Tiny tufted catkins danced in the air, lending the whole tableau a fantastical air, and if I had not been a woman of science, I might well have imagined myself in the presence of some primitive god of myth, a divine being with dominion over great monsters and perhaps even the weather itself, a powerful lord of creation who would lift me as easily as thistledown and with one mighty thrust—

"Veronica?"

I blinked to find Stoker staring at me quizzically. "I beg your pardon?"

"You were woolgathering," he told me. "I called your name twice. What on earth were you thinking about?"

"Never mind," I said hoarsely. I fixed a cordial smile to my lips. "Won't you introduce me to your friend?"

He nodded. "It is stable enough for you to come inside." He put out his hand and I took it as I stepped into the shadowy belly of the beast.

"Careful of the paint there," he advised. "It is still wet."

The creature smelt of fresh glue and wet plaster. The sculpted rib cage formed a curving back wall, each bone fitted with a sconce to provide illumination.

"I have been working by candlelight to make certain of the effect during the dinner. It is rather successful," he said, looking thoroughly pleased with himself.

"My god," I breathed as the flames flickered suddenly. It was a vision straight from the depths of Hell, the small fires dancing over the bones. I was reminded then of the first time I had seen Stoker, in a similar state of dishabille, working to remount a massive elephant amidst a litter of bones and specimen jars.* He turned to me then, his eyes bright with excitement.

"Here, come out and see what I have done with the head," he urged. We climbed out of the beast and moved to the front. He pointed to where he had installed a lamp in the head of the creature. "I have made the eyes translucent so they will glow."

I circled slowly, taking it all in. It was monstrous and unnerving and I could only imagine how unsettling it would be to dine in such surroundings. "I love it," I told him truthfully.

"It is as faithful a representation as I can manage without ever seeing the fossil in situ," he explained. "I changed the angle of the neck. You can see here from the way the vertebrae are seated—" There was more, *much* more, but I confess I did not hear it. Stoker was never so happy as when he was engaged in his work, and although this creature was merely a facsimile of a Megalosaurus, the chance to apply recent findings to its appearance was an activity calculated to delight him. Somehow, for all their quarrels and grievances, Tiberius had struck upon a task that beguiled him more than any other I could imagine. And this pleasure seemed to dim his annoyance with me—at least so long as he enthused about his model, he was prepared to lower his guard just a little. It was an imperfect rapprochement; none of the troubles between us had been settled, but at least the rough waters had calmed a little. I listened, happy for the moment for us to be, even if fleetingly, as we once were.

He broke off several minutes later. "Why are you smiling? You do not care for dinosaurs."

"No, I do not." I said nothing more, wondering if he would intuit my thoughts.

---

* *A Curious Beginning*

He cocked his head, his eyes gleaming. "You have the most peculiar expression, Veronica. Are you going to try to seduce me now?"

Before I could respond, I felt a sharp rap upon my arm.

I turned to see a pair of shrewd eyes regarding me from below a ruffled cap.

"Nanny MacQueen, I believe," I said faintly. "I am Veronica Speedwell."

"I know who you are," she told me. "And it is past time we had a chat. Come with me."

I turned to Stoker, but he spread his hands helplessly even as he grinned at my discomfiture.

"And you put on a shirt, Stokie. I'll not have you taking a chill and me left to nurse you back to health," she told him severely.

"Yes, Nanny," he said, obediently reaching for a shirt.

She poked me firmly in the ribs. "Come along, then. I haven't got many years left and I'll not waste them waiting for the likes of you."

Nanny pivoted on her dainty heel and stalked over the footbridge, never glancing around, so certain was she of being obeyed. And obey I did, trotting meekly behind as I followed her to a small, sedate Georgian house that had been tucked neatly into a copse between the coast path and the rose alley.

If Nanny MacQueen were an old family retainer from a storybook, she would have had a quaint little cottage covered in rambler roses with polished copper pans hanging over a merry hearth and a pretty calico cat sleeping in a basket. But Nanny MacQueen was not that sort of retainer. She led me into an elegantly proportioned room furnished with excellent Regency pieces of fruitwood inlaid with mother-of-pearl, and the only pet in evidence was a fat grey parrot that stood upon its perch and regarded me with as much obvious distaste as its mistress.

She pointed to a low chair upholstered in pearl-pink silk. "Sit," she ordered. When I had done so, she rang a little bell and a cowed maid-servant trotted in with a tray. Upon it stood a bottle and two small crystal glasses. Nanny dismissed the maid with a wave and poured out equal measures of a cloudy yellow liquid, handing me a glass.

"Parsnip wine," she told me. "Of my own making."

Why people insist upon fermenting vegetables for wine when grapes are handily abundant is a thing I shall never understand, but I could hardly make such an observation to her. She was watching me closely, and I realised the parsnip wine was a test of sorts.

Very well, I decided. I should prove myself. I took a deep draught of the wine and instantly understood that I had made a terrible mistake. When one is drowning, the whole of one's life is said to flash before one's eyes in a sort of magic lantern show with oneself in the starring role. Death by parsnip wine is not half so pleasurable. At least when one drowns there is the possibility of choking in a bit of air. With parsnip wine, there is only fire, an explosion of flame behind one's nasal cavities searing a path straight to the belly.

Tears filled my eyes and I choked out a word. "Delicious."

She gave me a grudging nod as she took a deep swallow from her own glass. "You have courage at least." She continued to scrutinise me as I drank, matching her sip for sip.

I waited for her to speak, but she was content to let silence stretch between us, punctuated only occasionally by my coughs and the odd piece of invective from the parrot.

It completed an especially racy limerick just as Nanny came to the end of her drink. "Another!" she said, pouring out a full glass for herself. She seemed not the least affected by the spirit, although my head was beginning to spin. I knew to refuse would be to lose whatever sliver of ground I had gained in sitting down to drink with her, so I accepted a second glass. She opened a box on the table beside her and drew out a small, very dark cigarette. A second box, where she must have kept her store of vestas, proved empty, and she clucked in irritation.

"Permit me," I said, reaching into one of my capacious pockets. I produced a vesta and struck it, leaning forward to light her cigarette. She drew in a deep lungful of smoke, puffing it out until a little wreath circled her head.

When she had made herself comfortable with cigarette and parsnip wine, she settled back in her chair and began to speak.

"I do not like you," she said plainly.

"I did not expect you to do so," I replied with equal candour.

"My Stokie is special."

"On that we are entirely in agreement," I said.

"He is a sensitive soul. Like his father." She watched me closely as she spoke, no doubt wondering if I knew the truth of his parentage. From all I had learnt of the late Lord Templeton-Vane, an African rhinoceros boasted greater sensitivity. She was clearly speaking of Stoker's actual sire, the Irish portraitist who had come to paint Lady Templeton-Vane and done a good deal more.

"Artists are often thus," I said, parrying the thrust.

"So you know the late lord was not the one who had the getting of him?" she asked with narrowed eyes.

"I do. It changes nothing. Children should not bear the weight of the sins of the parents."

She gave a grudging nod. "That much we agree upon." She sat back in her chair, her expression one of fond nostalgia. "I came here as a girl, you know. I'd been nurserymaid to the late Lady Templeton-Vane when she were wee, and she wanted no one else to nanny her boys. 'Nanny,' she said, 'Nanny, I trust no one so much as you. I know with you, my boys will grow to be fine men.'"

"That they have done so is a credit to your good care of them," I said.

"Aye. Fine men, all four of them. Too good for the likes of you," she said, narrowing her eyes and pointing her cigarette at me.

"I beg your pardon?"

"'Tisn't your fault," she said mildly. "I say nothing against you." She paused and I sensed that she would have enjoyed saying a good number of things against me. "But there's not a woman born good enough for my lads."

"Lord Templeton-Vane has been married," I pointed out.

She snorted. "A duke's daughter with two centuries of inbreeding in her bloodline? She didn't last out the year. She hadn't the *bottom* to handle a man of spirit like my wee Tibbie. And the less said on that monstrous Caroline, the better."

Tibbie! The mind reeled. "I never met the poor lady, so I cannot say. But having made the acquaintance of Stoker's former wife, I quite agree that Caroline is a thoroughly nasty woman and it's rather a pity she has not met with a hungry crocodile. However, I must protest as to the character of Sir Rupert's wife. I had the pleasure of meeting Lavinia last year, and I found her thoroughly charming and quite spirited."

She snorted, a noise the parrot immediately imitated, one of the most distasteful sounds I have ever encountered. "Jumped-up, that one is. Her great-grandfather was *in trade,* you know."

"Her *great-grandfather*? But her father is an earl," I pointed out.

"New aristocracy," she said, pulling a face. "Hardly better than those German upstarts on the throne."

Nanny's opinion was not entirely surprising. Many of the old aristocracy of England had lost their regard for the royal family when Queen Anne died and the Hanoverians ascended the throne. The fact that George I had not spoken English had done nothing to endear him to the powerful Whig families who considered themselves the true backbone of the nation, and his unattractive mistresses had impressed them still less. The news that the current German branch of royals happened to be my extended family was not one I cared to share with Nanny.

She went on. "I invited you here to make certain we understand one another, my girl. I am taking your measure, and thus far I have found you wanting."

I set my glass carefully aside and fixed a polite smile upon my lips.

"Thank you for the wine, Nanny MacQueen. You have certainly given me much to think about."

I rose, but Nanny remained seated. With the parrot perched near her shoulder, she resembled an elderly lady pirate.

She fixed me with a warning look. "If you think to make trouble for my boy—"

I held up a quick hand. "I would never make trouble for Stoker. Of any sort. You are wrong, you know. He is not a good man. He is the best of men."

I had expected my loyalty to Stoker to demonstrate that Nanny MacQueen had nothing to fear from me. We might presently be at odds—although how much Nanny knew of that I could not say—but I felt, in my marrow, that we would somehow come right in the end. I could not contemplate a destiny that unfolded otherwise.

I waited, anticipating an accord with Nanny.

Instead, she surveyed my figure slowly from top to toe. Finally, she took a long draw on her cigarette and spoke. "I'll grant you've a good set of milkers if you mean to nurse any bairns you might have, but your hips is far too narrow to make easy birthing. I'll give you even odds of making it out of childbirth alive."

She sat back, primming her lips with the air of a duelist who has just put a bullet into the heart of her opponent.

"Thank you for the warning, but I can assure you, motherhood is one adventure I shall never undertake."

I left her with as much dignity as I could muster, but as I shut the door behind me, I could distinctly hear the sound of wheezing laughter—whether from Nanny MacQueen or the parrot, I could not say.

After leaving Nanny MacQueen, I was feeling both slightly tipsy and entirely out of sorts. Being both reluctant to ring for a maid and sorely in need of sustenance to counteract the effects of the parsnip wine, I went directly to the kitchens, muttering about poisonous old women as I wound my way through baize-lined doors and around passages until I heard a voice that pulled me up short. The tone was rich and melodious, and the accent lilting and familiar.

"Julien!" I exclaimed as I entered the main kitchen. Julien d'Orlande, one of Stoker's dearest friends and a particularly beloved acquaintance of mine, was standing in the middle of the room surrounded by a heap of crates newly arrived on the early train from London. He never wore a proper toque, preferring instead slouching caps of luscious velvet. This one was raspberry pink, a delectable foil to his dark skin and starched white coat and a wonderful contrast to the plain black dresses of the kitchen maids. He was standing in a lordly pose, arms folded over the breadth of his chest as he issued orders in a calm, stern voice. Various maids and boys hopped to attention, carrying out his commands as Tiberius' usual chef was nowhere in evidence.

"Veronica!" Julien came and kissed my cheeks in the Continental fashion. He had been born in the Caribbean and educated in France, accounting for both his exquisite French and his even lovelier manners. He was a sensualist, loving food and women in equal parts, and the fact that he invariably fed me rather than attempted to seduce me was in large measure why I adored him so.

"What on earth are you doing here?" I demanded.

"I am cooking," he said, giving a Gallic shrug. He looked over my shoulder to where a maid in a vast cap that hid half her face was hefting a crate that rattled ominously. "That champagne cost more than your entire family earns in a year," he told her severely. "Let one of the boys carry it. That is why we brought them. Take the grouse to the larder."

She muttered something unintelligible and put the crate down, exchanging it for a basket that dripped a little blood as she hurried from the room.

"But Lord Templeton-Vane *has* a chef," I said, turning back to Julien.

"Is he as good as me?" Julien demanded.

"No one is," I promised him.

He smiled, showing one deep dimple in his left cheek. "You see, this is why Lord Templeton-Vane needs me. He wants dinners to dazzle his guests, dinners fit for royalty. I am his man." He puffed out his chest a little.

"Where is his usual chef?" I asked, poking into a basket of cheeses.

Julien smacked lightly at my hand. "Leave those. They are for tonight and they must breathe."

"I thought only wine breathed," I protested.

What followed was a string of fluently insulting French, so beautifully delivered I did not even mind when he called me an unsophisticated philistine.

"But I require sustenance," I protested.

He sighed and dove into one of his assorted baskets, emerging with a small pie of the most delicate proportions and delectable aromas. He tied it into a bit of linen and presented it to me with a flourish.

"Julien will never let you starve," he promised. "But you must not spoil your appetite for tonight. I will give you such a dinner!" He kissed his fingers and released them heavenwards. "And now you must leave. I have much to do."

He fairly pushed me from the kitchen, and I went with good grace. It was curious to find him at Cherboys—I knew they had met but did not realise Julien was well acquainted with Tiberius, much less ever employed by him. Julien's usual place of work was the Sudbury, one of London's finest hotels, an expensive and exclusive enclave that charged hideous prices, in no small part to pay his extortionate salary as their head pastry chef. But he would not be the first to accept independent commissions to create fanciful meals for special occasions. The queen's own chef at Buckingham Palace often did the same. And there was nothing suspicious in bringing some of his own staff to help him prepare the meal. After all, who would be more likely to know his ways and cater to his whims than his regular chefs, maids, and porters?

No, there was not an untoward thing about Julien or his people. Except one.

I found her in the larder, removing the feathery corpses of grouse from the basket and grimacing at the blood dripping onto the stone floor.

"If you are going to pass yourself off as a kitchen maid, you really oughtn't be squeamish over a bit of blood," I said as I stood in the doorway.

The maid gave a start and swore as a streak of blood soiled her apron. "Hellfire and damnation! That is my last clean pinny, Veronica." She shoved the enormous cap away from her brow and gave me a resentful look.

I sighed. "J. J. Butterworth, lady reporter and frequent scourge of my existence. What are you doing at Cherboys?"

She dropped the last grouse into place. "I call that rude. I thought we were friends."

"We are. Occasionally. When you are aboveboard about chasing a story."

J. J. was a freelance journalist and the most ambitious woman I had ever met. Her age was very near my own and our paths had crossed with such regularity that she was one of two women in London I considered a friend—at least when she was not gently blackmailing me to get her way about something.

"The last time we saw each other, you extorted a trip to Windsor Castle out of me under extremely difficult circumstances," I reminded her.

"And I have kept many more secrets than I have revealed," she said, setting her chin at a mulish angle. J. J. knew the truth about my parentage but had thus far been willing to keep my secret. Whether she did so out of true loyalty or because it meant I was perpetually in her debt, I was not entirely certain.

"Pax," I replied, putting out my hand.

She shook it gamely enough—J. J. is not the sort to bear a grudge, particularly against someone who has inadvertently provided her with front-page features on more than one occasion. Her entrée into Windsor Castle had resulted in a spectacular story in the *Daily Harbinger* that had taken down a junior Cabinet minister.*

"Now, why are you here?" I demanded. She often worked as a chambermaid at the Sudbury, the same hotel that employed Julien, in order to dig up tawdry stories on the great and good who stayed there, but posing as a scullery maid seemed a comedown. "I should have thought your success as an investigative journalist would have seen

---

* *An Unexpected Peril*

you doing far more interesting and elevated things than plucking grouse."

She pulled a face, and not just at the entrails of the bird she was cleaning. "You would think. One of the staff writers at the *Harbinger* convinced the editor that he was responsible for exposing the corruption in the minister's office. Claimed I had used 'underhanded and unethical means' of getting the story."

"You did."

"Yes, but he wasn't to know that! I had proof, notes in the minister's own hand. Little matter how I got them. In any event, I found myself in disgrace. Again. And I was in need of a little extra money. Naturally, when I discovered Julien was paying double rates to anyone who came with him on this excursion, I leapt at the chance. Double rates—with good reason," she added darkly, pulling something wet and slimy from inside the bird.

"At least it is an honest day's work," I said with a bright smile, relieved that for once J. J. seemed bent upon something other than ferreting out a story. Although, I reflected, if she had any idea of Tiberius' true purpose in hosting this house party, she would be back to her old tricks in a flash.

She held up one bloody bird. "These are from the moor of one of the guests due to arrive today—Sir Ruddy McMoustaches."

"Do you mean Sir James MacIver?" I asked repressively.

"That's the one. Imagine having nothing better to do with your time than blast away at these poor things all day." She looked up suddenly with a sharp gaze. "He is an MP, you know. And I hear there is a count from the Continent abovestairs. Any potential stories with them? A bit of juicy scandal that might get me back in good graces in Fleet Street?"

"Heavens no," I said airily. "Dull as ditchwater, the lot of them. Mind you do a good job on those grouse. I shouldn't like to find feathers floating in my tea."

She muttered something unprintable and I made her a vague promise to meet up with her later in the day. I trusted her as far as I could hurl Stoker's favourite woolly mammoth.

Still pondering J. J.'s presence and how it might complicate our undertaking, I went to my room to prepare for the evening. Lily appeared, harried and gently perspiring, nearly an hour after I had rung for her. She bustled in and thrust me into the chair before my looking glass.

"I am that sorry, miss," she said as she hurried to jam pins into my hair. "The guests have arrived, and as it happens, neither lady has brought a maid, so it has fallen to me to take care of Lady MacIver." Her mouth tightened. "Polly, who has been here seven weeks less than I have, has been given the countess."

I was well enough acquainted with belowstairs politics to know this was a serious breach of staff etiquette. The Contessa Salviati, as the highest-ranking lady in residence, had claim on the services of the senior chambermaid. Upon such slights were feuds of generations built.

Lily went on, pinning as she talked. "And Lady MacIver hasn't hair as nice as yours, and that's a fact. Took me half an age to pin her false curls in place, it did. Although I will say her skin is good as a woman ten years younger. Like milk it is or what is that white rock?"

"Alabaster?" I guessed.

"That's the one." She paused and stepped back, scrutinising the effect of her efforts. "Pretty as a picture, if I say it myself. Now, for a bit of powder."

Before I could stop her, she pummeled my décolletage with a swansdown puff, sending great drifts of the stuff up to cloud the room. It smelt strongly of roses, but it shimmered prettily against my skin and as I wore no jewels, it would have to suffice.

I thanked her for her efforts and made my way downstairs. The gong was just sounding as I entered the drawing room. The gaslights had been lit and the gold silk on the walls gleamed in their glow. Stoker, washed and attired in clean and formal if not fashionable clothing, joined me where I stood in front of the fireplace. I had dressed in a new evening gown of luscious violet taffeta, cut in a severe style and edged with black velvet, and Stoker eyed me with silent appraisal.

Tiberius appeared for dinner dressed impeccably as usual. But as he entered I saw new lines upon his face, no doubt etched by the strain of the situation. As I returned his greeting, I exhaled, realising suddenly that I had been rather worried about him. Whilst we had been alone at Cherboys, he had been safe enough, in my estimation; now that the house party had assembled, a possible murderer walked among us. But no harm would come to him on my watch, I vowed.

"Whatever are you thinking, Veronica? You look quite fierce."

"Only that it will be a significant task to keep you safe now that your guests have arrived." I counted them off on my fingers. "The Count Salviati and his contessa, Sir James and Lady MacIver—"

"The Greshams," Tiberius put in.

"You invited them?" Stoker asked. "They are not members of the Seven Sinners."

"But they were here at the time. It is too much to hope they might have seen or noted anything of interest, but one never knows."

"Six potential murderers, then," I said. "You must be well guarded at all times, Tiberius."

"Six?" Stoker raised his brows in an imperious gesture of enquiry. He looked like one of the younger and more alluring Roman emperors, attractive and possibly lethal.

"Six," I said firmly. "Surely you of all people understand that the female of the species may prove deadlier than the male."

This oblique reference to our past ordeals made no impression

upon him, and Tiberius hurried to agree. "Augusta was newly affi-
anced to James that summer, and Beatrice only married Pietro somewhat recently. No, I think we may safely acquit the ladies of any
suspicion."

"But—" The tiniest twitch of amusement tugged at Stoker's mouth.
I broke off what I had meant to say. "Clearly you are in agreement," I
said.

He shrugged. "It does seem thoroughly unlikely in the present circumstances. And you might as well add Elspeth Gresham to the list of
unlikely murderers."

"On what grounds?" I demanded.

"I simply think her incapable of the act of murder. No, it will be
either Sir James or the count," he assured me.

"Or Timothy," Tiberius put in.

Stoker shook his head. "As unlikely as his sister. Your visits to
Cherboys are rare and remarkable, but they *do* happen. Either of them
might have happily poisoned or garrotted or stabbed you these past
twenty years."

"True," Tiberius agreed. "And neither of them has stirred a foot
outside of Dearsley these past two decades. Highly improbable that
Elspeth or Timothy managed to murder Kaspar or Alexandre on the
Continent."

"Just so," Stoker said. They were nodding in unison, the family resemblance suddenly so striking and maddening I wanted to do nothing so much as knock their heads together.

"Do not agree with one another," I said in considerable alarm. "It is
terrifying."

"It will not last," Stoker assured me. "But I am right. One of those
two men will be our villain."

Tiberius regarded him with a look of approbation. "I quite agree."

Both Templeton-Vanes in agreement with one another against me was a novel and wholly unsettling experience. I felt my equilibrium shift, knocking me into a reckless reaction I hoped I would not later regret. "Would you care to wager on that?" I asked.

Tiberius blinked. "I beg your pardon?"

Stoker grinned. "It is one of Veronica's favourite pastimes during our forays into investigation. Invariably, she becomes too attached to a pet theory and cannot turn loose of it for pride's sake. We have wagered in the past, and I believe I have come out the winner more times than not, haven't I?" he asked, tipping his head and widening his eyes like an innocent.

"I do not recall," I replied with icy hauteur. "But I will wager *both* of you that Kaspar and Alexandre's murderer, the fiend who sent those threats in the post, is a woman."

"How much?" Tiberius enquired.

"A pound would be the usual wager," Stoker informed him.

"I shouldn't think of engaging in any wager less than five," Tiberius said, shaking his head. "How about it, Veronica? Five pounds?"

"Guineas," I countered firmly.

The three of us shook hands on it. I had just ranged myself against the combined intellectual and physical and financial resources of the Templeton-Vane brothers. It was a chilling thought, but I have never been one to shrink from a challenge.

"Of course," Stoker said mildly, "we are still assuming the murders are connected to Lorenzo d'Ambrogio's death."

Tiberius waved a hand. "Let us not complicate matters unnecessarily, brother. We may assume that only one person is seeking to murder me."

"For now," Stoker said pleasantly. "I could probably think of others." It was the sort of banter they had always shared, but there was a new mellowness to it now. The sharp edge that had characterised their relationship had dulled, and I wondered why.

Tiberius took no offence at the jibe. "No doubt, no doubt," he agreed. "Have you finished the Megalosaurus?"

"Almost. Just a few little spots I want to touch up early tomorrow. It will be ready," Stoker promised.

"Good. The flowers and entertainers I have ordered from London will be down on the first train."

"Entertainers? Where will you put them?" I asked. "The Megalosaurus is hardly large enough to accompany a quartet."

"They will disport themselves outside the beast, and we will be able to see them and hear the musicians. Food, music, flowers." He ticked them off on his fingers. "And plenty of expensive wine. That should set the mood nicely."

"I tremble to ask," Stoker put in, "but set the mood for what, precisely? Surely you cannot intend to accuse your own guests of a spot of homicide during dinner."

"I might," Tiberius said, his expression suddenly inscrutable.

"How?" Stoker demanded. "A casual mention between the starter and the fish course? 'Oh, do try the turbot, and by the way, did any of you happen to poison Kaspar von Hochstaden?'"

Tiberius gave him a repressive look, very much assuming once more the mantle of elder brother. "Do not, I beg you, lapse into vulgarity. I would never serve turbot."

I held up a hand. "Boys. The guests will be down any moment."

Tiberius grinned. "You know how arousing it is when you speak to us as though you were our nanny," he said in a seductive growl.

"Having now met your nanny, I do not find that comparison remotely flattering," I told him. "Now, I am not at all comfortable with the notion that one of your guests might be an experienced murderer intending to wreak some sort of vengeance upon you. I think one of us should stay with you tomorrow. At all times."

Stoker thrust his hand into the air. "Not It."

"I was going to suggest myself," I told him, "but there will be times I cannot accompany Tiberius and you should make yourself available."

"To act as his keeper?" Stoker asked, frankly incredulous.

"No," I said sweetly. "His protector."

At that, both brothers swore furiously. "I have a Megalosaurus to finish tomorrow," Stoker said. "I shall spend the better part of the day inside my dinosaur. Tiberius, do try not to get yourself murdered."

Before Tiberius could reply, Collins appeared, escorting the guests into the drawing room. Tiberius made the introductions as Merry slipped in, adjusting his collar and running a hand over freshly brushed hair. I scrutinised the guests carefully with an eye to who might most easily play the villain.

First, Pietro, the Conte di Salviati, and his American wife, Beatrice, entered. They were an extremely handsome couple, and the countess, a vivacious personality, was several years her husband's junior. She was a brunette, beautifully dressed in a gown so fashionable, it could only have come from Paris and only within the last few months. It was cleverly cut in a shade of shimmering pearl grey that suited her complexion of pale olive and showed off her elaborate parure of garnet intaglios to perfection. Her only other jewel was a rosary worn at her belt, the beads polished onyx and the cross glittering with tiny diamonds. She had wide, dark eyes which went often to her lord and husband.

It was obviously a love match, I observed, for the count's hand caressed his wife's waist and his eyes rested adoringly upon her. His profile was his chief attraction, marked by a hawklike nose and high forehead punctuated by a sharp widow's peak. It was an attractive, even a noble face, although his expression was watchful as his gaze lingered upon his wife. There was some anxiety in his manner, an unease about bringing her here, amongst these strangers. It was never easy to befriend the companions of one's husband's youth, and I noted a certain nervousness in her fluttering hands and quick glances. The count kept a steadying arm about her, and I found I liked him for his gentle attentions to her.

This pair were followed closely by another, Sir James and Lady MacIver, the very picture of Scottish aristocracy. He looked the sort of gentleman more at home in country tweeds than evening finery, and his formal black coat strained slightly at the shoulders, as if his presence were simply too large to be contained by seams. He had thick moustaches, very like those of *Odobenus rosmarus*, save that his turned upwards at the ends, giving his expression the appearance of a perpetual smile. Some gingery hair remained on his head, brushed neatly over a gleaming pate, and his brows were lavishly tufted. In old age, they would wave about like the antennae of one of the livelier beetles, I had no doubt.

Lady MacIver was tall, her height nearly matching that of her husband, and she was only a few years his junior, I judged. Fine lines webbed her lovely blue eyes, and her figure was only slightly thicker than it must have been in girlhood. The result of childbearing, I supposed, thinking ruefully of Nanny MacQueen's pronouncements on my own deficiencies. Lady MacIver moved with considerable elegance, a cool counterpart to the more animated American countess, and she was dressed in the silvery blue of newly bloomed periwinkles. I did not care for her gown—far too much lace for my taste, and one can bear only so much ruching—but it was obviously expensive, as were the enormous pearls hung at her throat and ears.

The introductions were made, and the greetings exchanged were of the convivial sort.

"Stoker," the count said in lightly accented English. "I remember you, although you were just a boy in short pants. And Merryweather! Look at you, a man of the Church. You were still in skirts the last time I was here, scarcely out of your cradle."

Merry flushed to the roots of his hair, but Stoker merely grinned and shook the count's hand. "Come," said the count, "you must meet my Contessa Beatrice," he urged, giving her name the Italian pronunciation.

The lady smiled, revealing very even, white teeth. "How do you do?" She held a gloved hand to Stoker first, then Merry, as the count turned to me.

"Ah, the estimable and beautiful Miss Speedwell! How well Tiberius speaks of you, and yet he has done you no justice, for you are enchanting," he said, sweeping a courtly gesture in my direction.

"Lord Templeton-Vane is too kind by half," I replied.

"Nonsense, my dear," said Lady MacIver, coming forward and extending her gloved hand. "Tiberius says the most remarkable things about you, and it is already apparent he has not exaggerated in the slightest. James, come and shake hands with Miss Speedwell," she instructed her spouse. He shambled over and took my hand in his enormous, beefy one.

"How do, Miss Speedwell?" he said gruffly.

These then were Tiberius' guests, and we made polite noises at one another as he completed the introductions. Just as he finished, Collins came to the door.

"Dr. Gresham and Miss Gresham," he intoned solemnly. He stepped aside to permit the last pair to enter. Unlike the two couples who had travelled down from London, the doctor and his sister were clearly countryfolk by their dress, and I remembered the pretty cottage Merry had pointed out in the village. They were of similar years to Tiberius, well past the first flush of youth. The doctor wore his evening suit a little stiffly, the collar clearly chafing him, and he blinked at the assembled company as if nearsighted. He bore a passing resemblance to a common hare, with a twitching nose, slightly pink at the tip, and tall, slightly pointed ears. But he smiled jovially and greeted the others with warmth.

His sister, I judged, was a trifle more acidulous in personality. Her hair was threaded with silver and her cheekbones stood proud, as if time itself had whittled away all excess flesh. On Lady MacIver, such signs of maturity only served to heighten her sophistication, marking her a woman of the world. On Miss Gresham, they gave an air of dustiness, like a bit of mantelpiece china rarely polished and seldom appreciated. Her gown was half a dozen years out of date and smelt strongly of mothballs, which she had attempted to cover by a lavish application of violet toilet water. I saw Tiberius' nose vellicate in protest as he bent over her hand, but his greeting was every bit as gracious as one he would have shown to the highest lady in the land.

"Timothy. Elspeth. I am so glad you could join us. You know my brothers, of course, but it is some time since you last met these three," he told them, drawing their attention to the MacIvers and Count Salviati. Polite murmurs were exchanged on the part of the men, but it was Augusta MacIver who came forward with real warmth. "Of course. Dr. Gresham, I believe you were newly arrived in Dearsley when last we met. And Miss Gresham, you had only just come out," she added, perhaps a trifle tactlessly. Elspeth Gresham must have nurtured matrimonial hopes if she had been brought out into society, and they had clearly been thwarted.

Miss Gresham gave her a stiff little smile in return. "You look very well, my lady. I see the years have been kind to you."

Lady MacIver laughed. "It is you who are kind. I find more wrinkles every day."

Tiberius stepped in once more to introduce Countess Beatrice, who inclined her head graciously. "How do you do?"

"Oh, an American!" Dr. Gresham said with enthusiasm. "You must tell me all about automobiles. I understand one of your countrymen has purchased the very first and I long to know more."

The countess blinked a little at his exuberance. "I am afraid you have the advantage of me, Doctor. I am unversed on the subject of automobiles."

He tried manfully to cover his dismay, but it was obvious the countess had disappointed him deeply. "Never mind, never mind," he murmured.

Tiberius completed the introductions. "Here is Revelstoke's colleague, Miss Speedwell."

We exchanged polite greetings, but I detected a distinct coolness in the physician's. His ears seemed to twitch at the word "colleague." "Indeed! A lady of science, are you, Miss Speedwell? What a singular thing. Can you imagine, Elspeth? How very extraordinary. A lady scientist!"

Elspeth Gresham's thin lips stretched into a semblance of a smile. "Extraordinary."

Her tone was sour, and I did not know whether she bore an antipathy towards other women or was simply bashful of strangers, but I was grateful when Collins stepped in once more.

He raised his chin and in his most refined tones pronounced the words for which we had been waiting.

"Dinner is served, my lord."

CHAPTER 12

A s an unattached lady—and Tiberius' unofficial hostess—I was led in by the viscount himself, with the Salviatis and the Mac-Ivers following, Stoker partnering Miss Gresham, and the remaining bachelors bringing up the rear. It was a flagrant breach of etiquette, but I suspected Tiberius had his reasons.

"Oughtn't you be escorting the countess?" I whispered to Tiberius as he escorted me through to the dining hall. "It would have been proper."

"You know that nothing delights me as much as the improper," he chided. "Would you care to be improper with me later tonight?"

He was merely japing—Tiberius had long since given up any serious attempts at seduction. But if his guests overheard, it might prove awkward.

I poked a stiff finger into his ribs and he gave a short cough. He grabbed my hand and dropped a kiss to my gloved palm. "The first rule of rough play is never to leave bruises, my dove."

I suppressed a sigh as I took my seat at the foot of the table. Tiberius sat with the two married ladies flanking him, which left me tucked neatly between the count and Sir James, the two highest-ranking male guests. Stoker, Merry, and the Greshams were fitted in between. The table was a large one, spacious enough to accommodate our party of ten but small enough to make general conversation possible if we chose. It was heavily laid with starched linen embroidered with the Templeton-Vane crest. Several enormous candelabra wrought of Renaissance Italian silver and wreathed in creamy hothouse roses dotted the table. More milky roses were grouped in low silver bowls and still more filled a lavish display on a pedestal at the end of the room.

The countess gasped at the sight of the décor, for the walls were painted a striking shade of green and embellished with life-size figures of smooth white plaster. More plaster had been worked into vines and pilasters, and the effect was like walking into a living piece of Wedgwood.

"How magnificent!" she said, hand fluttering to the garnets at her throat.

Tiberius favoured her with a smile as everyone took their seats. "Thank you, Beatrice. My father designed it as an homage to a small dining room in the palace of Catherine the Great. He was a tremendous Russophile."

"I know exactly the one you mean," she assured him, and they launched into a discussion of their respective travels as the first course was carried in. Julien's delectable food was complemented by vintage wines and pleasant conversation, yet as the meal stretched on, I detected undercurrents, small notes that seemed faintly out of tune, like a badly plucked string on a violin.

The countess continued to chat with Tiberius, and while I attempted to make conversation with her husband, the count's manner often seemed distracted as his gaze lingered upon his wife. She dazzled, with an arch manner and a winsome smile that would have won a far less susceptible man than Tiberius. When she turned her charms upon Merry, he blushed to the roots of his hair and ducked his head whilst she teased him gently.

Not all of her repartee was reserved for the gentlemen. She made an effort to include Lady MacIver in their discussions, although that lady seemed far less talkative than her American counterpart. She conducted conversation according to strict custom, speaking with Tiberius during one course, Timothy Gresham the next, alternating for the duration of the meal. I caught only scraps of their discussion, Lady MacIver's tones being elegantly modulated.

"I know you would be most interested in our work at the Milverton House for Mentally Unbalanced Ladies," Gresham said in some earnestness as he took up a forkful of peas. "I am merely the consulting physician, but I can assure you, we take the greatest care of our ladies. We are committed to treating them *humanely.*"

Sir James took note of their conversation. "A great philanthropist is my wife," he said to me, sotto voce. "If Timothy is clever, he will get something out of her for his little hospital." He finished this with a wink.

Across the table, Miss Gresham kept a hand pressed to her stomach and refused two of the courses and all of the wines after giving them a fastidious sniff. Sir James was not half so pernickety; he ate with the relish of a devoted trencherman, clearing his plates swiftly and with resounding and appreciative smacks of the lips as he lay down his utensils. The count tore his gaze from his lady and regarded Sir James with obvious amusement.

"James has always been thus," the count told me, loudly enough for Sir James to hear. "Greedy for his food."

Sir James patted the gentle curve of his belly with a rueful expression. "Much good it has done me. I am growing stouter by the year."

"You are a fine figure of a man," the count declared. "In your prime, my friend," he added, raising his wineglass in a toast.

Sir James gave him a grin, clearly pleased. "Well, I do still play a bit of rugby—usually when the boys are home from school. Does them a world of good to see their old papa can still move like an athlete if needs must."

"You have children, Sir James?" I enquired. I am seldom interested in other people's domestic arrangements, and never in their offspring, but it is a useful topic to introduce. Parents who are proud of their children will invariably say something dismissive and change the subject to something more engaging, whilst those who are not terribly keen on them will spend half an hour enumerating their virtues, more to convince themselves than anyone else. If they are the former, they will think me polite for asking and we will discuss something diverting instead; if the latter, I can offer a blank smile and think about Papilionidae whilst they carry on.

Sir James beamed. "Four boys." He rattled off their names in a string of Caledonian syllables I promptly forgot. All of them seemed to be named for Scottish kings, most of whom ended badly. "The eldest is sixteen, the youngest just seven. They're at school, of course. Left for the autumn term just this morning. The eldest will have the managing of the estate in time. Our seat is in the Trossachs. Do you know the area?"

I gave him a rueful smile. "I am a lepidopterist, Sir James, and my occupation dictates my travels."

"And Scotland has not much in the way of butterflies to entice you," he said with an understanding nod. "Well, if you ever decide to specialise in sheep, you will know where to come."

"Sheep and grouse," the count put in. "James boasts the finest hunting in all of Scotland, is that not the truth, my friend?"

"'Tis so, 'tis so," Sir James said with obvious pride. "The birds you're eating came from our land," he added with a nod towards our plates. Fresh grouse are a delicacy on their own merit, but Julien had roasted them to crisp perfection and sauced them with a concoction one could only describe as poetry.

"How many acres is it? Thirty thousand?" the count enquired.

"Forty thousand, actually," Sir James corrected. "And the largest grouse hunt in the country."

"Ah, yes! The Glorious Twelfth!" The twelfth of August marked the start of the annual grouse season, and the day when the peaceful air of the Scottish moors would be shattered by the volleys from shotguns. "And what distinguished guests have you had this year?" asked the count.

Sir James pinkened with obvious pleasure. "I do not like to boast, but His Royal Highness himself numbered amongst our guns."

There were a few dozen royal highnesses he might have meant, but only one required no further title. He meant the Prince of Wales, and I felt the usual thrust of emotion when his name was mentioned. He was my nearest living relation, but he would not—nay, *could* not acknowledge me. The fact that he had a daughter who predated his marriage to Princess Alexandra would have been scandal enough. The fact that he had entered into a form of marriage with my mother, making me semilegitimate, would have rocked the very foundations of the monarchy itself, I had been warned. So I pretended not to have a father, and he pretended not to have a daughter, and we did not meet. It was a thoroughly unsatisfying situation on all counts.

Sir James told some anecdote of my father's skill in the hunting field—the Prince of Wales was, according to the newspapers, very fond of killing things—before leaning towards me with a smile. "If you are ever in mind to shoot birds instead of netting butterflies, you must come to us. We would be only too glad to have you, and Augusta is the best hostess in all of the north."

"You shall be my first port of call," I promised.

"You will find much better hunting for your butterflies in Italy," the count put in.

"Indeed I have," I told him. "I spent the summer collecting in the Dolomites."

We fell to discussing the merits of the Italian mountains—Sir James, a keen walker, had much to add on the subject of hiking in the alpine heights of that region—and the meal passed quite companionably. As soon as the sweet course was cleared, Tiberius gave me a significant look and I realised what was expected of me. I sighed. It chafed my principles to participate in so regressive a custom, but it was his house, after all.

I bared my teeth at him in what a naïve person might have mistaken for a smile and rose from my chair. "Countess, Lady MacIver, Miss Gresham." I gestured and the other three rose. The gentlemen leapt to their feet and I noticed Stoker's lips twitching. He knew well enough my feelings on the ladies being made to withdraw, as did Tiberius. But I understood the futility of resistance, so I took my leave with as much dignity as I could muster.

And as I saw Tiberius' mouth curve into an inscrutable smile, I would have given the rarest and most perfect imago of a Kaiser-i-Hind to know what he was thinking.

CHAPTER

13

Collins, the butler, waited in the corridor to conduct us to the drawing room. The gold silk draperies had been drawn against the cool evening fog and a fire had been kindled, crackling merrily and smelling faintly of applewood.

"I will bring tea and coffee, Miss Speedwell," Collins said quietly to me as we seated ourselves.

"Thank you, Collins. And port," I added.

His steely grey brows lifted almost imperceptibly. "Port, Miss Speedwell?" His training was too good to permit any display of the shock he must have been feeling.

The countess smiled and even Lady MacIver, more serious and reserved than her American counterpart, seemed to unbend a little. Miss Gresham looked as if she were wrestling with her conscience and I wondered if her abstinence at dinner meant she was teetotal.

"Port," I repeated firmly. "Perhaps the same vintage his lordship is serving in the dining room?"

Collins pursed his lips. "If I may, Miss Speedwell, his lordship prefers ruby, but there is a particularly fine vintage of tawny I have only just decanted?" He let his voice trail off hopefully, and I grinned.

"Excellent suggestion, Collins. We will have the tawny."

"Very good, miss." He bowed his way out of the room, returning a very short while later with the promised decanter and a tray of glasses. A young footman trotted behind with a tray. "I have taken the liberty of bringing a Stilton as well as some dried fruits and a dish of almonds, roasted to bring out the flavour of the port," Collins advised, nodding towards the accompaniments with an air of satisfaction.

I thanked him and he withdrew as I poured out for the other ladies. The countess raised her glass. "Do forgive me for preempting you, Miss Speedwell, but I should like to propose a toast. To friends, old and new."

We lifted our glasses in response and sipped. The vintage port was smooth as caramel velvet, and the countess gave a little sigh. "How delicious," she murmured as she put the glass aside. "And now some peppermint tea, I think," she said apologetically. She did seem a trifle delicate, and I wondered if she were possibly expecting. That might account for her husband's attentiveness as well as her slight fragility.

As if intuiting my thoughts, she blushed a pretty rose pink. "I am not with child. But I am often indisposed. My heart is not strong, for which I take a tonic, and frequently my digestion troubles me," she explained as I rang. "At home I eat very simply, a vegetarian diet with a little fish and no wine. Dinner tonight was a trifle rich."

"Then peppermint tea is just the thing," Miss Gresham told her firmly. "Or a nice ginger tisane." They fell to discussing remedies until Collins appeared bearing a small pot steaming fragrantly with the crisp, green scent of peppermint. The countess took a small bottle of smoke-coloured glass from her pocket. It was a pretty thing, shaped like a pilgrim's cockleshell and small enough to fit into the palm of her hand. She twisted off the silver cap and poured a measure of liquid into her cup. "My tonic," she said with a smile. She sweetened the concoction with a drop of honey and settled back against the cushions with a sigh as she sipped. "That is better."

Lady MacIver, having finished her first glass of port with startling rapidity, held it out for a second measure. I obliged her and poured another for Miss Gresham, who had gone very red about the cheeks. The flush suited her, but as I handed her the glass, I saw that her eyes were gently crossed.

"Thank you, Miss Speedwell." Lady MacIver regarded us thoughtfully over the rim of her glass. "I think, as we are so small a party, we might be familiar, do you not agree? I am Augusta."

"Veronica," I told her.

"Beatrice," the countess added, using the English pronunciation of her name. She smiled. "Or Bey-ah-tri-chey if you want to sound like my husband."

Miss Gresham hesitated, then blurted out, "Elspeth." She gave a dainty little hiccup.

"A good Scots name," Augusta told her kindly. "And after all, we did meet long ago, did we not?"

"That we did," Elspeth agreed.

Augusta turned back to Beatrice, cocking her head. "Have you been married long, my dear? Only the count seems terribly smitten. Like a newly wedded bridegroom."

Beatrice gave a low, throaty laugh. "More than a year, yet the happiness does not pall. And yes, he is entirely smitten." Her smile was one of feline contentment. "Pietro is a tremendous romantic. All Italians are, I daresay. And so dramatic! He is forever picking little quarrels just so we can have a few slammed doors and then make it all up with a pretty bauble he has bought for me. It is thoroughly exhausting." But she said this with another smile, and it was clear the count and countess were devoted to one another.

Augusta held her glass between her palms. "Then he is not changed from when I knew him," she said.

Beatrice sat up a little straighter. "Yes, you said you were here the last time he visited. That means you knew him as a young man. Both of you did," she added with a conspiratorial glance at Elspeth. "You must tell me all of his secrets."

Augusta laughed at Beatrice's question. "There is not much to tell. I met him only once. Here," she said, glancing about. "It is quite strange to come back to Cherboys after so much time has passed. Twenty years gone now—it was the summer before James and I were married."

"The famous Grand Tour of the Seven Sinners!" Beatrice crowed. Her garnet earrings fairly danced as she laughed. "Pietro has told me all about that trip. What laughs they had together. That is why we are all here now, is it not?"

She looked from Augusta to me and back again. "Yes, a reunion of sorts, Tiberius tells me," I replied. I was aware of Elspeth quietly draining her glass of port as the rest of us talked. "I believe Tiberius has planned a special dinner to honour the memory of those who have since been lost," I said.

Beatrice gave me a tight smile. "How very kind." I raised a brow and she sighed. "Forgive me. That was churlish. Of course Pietro should be here to mourn with the others. It is just that I had hoped to see England properly, you understand. It is my first time here. I wanted to take in all the famous sights of London, the Tower, Buckingham Palace, the Houses of Parliament. I was thinking only of myself. A common American failing," she added with a flicker of mischief in her expression.

I smiled back to show I bore her no ill will and Augusta hastened to reassure her as well. "You must come to us in London. I will host a dinner for you and introduce you to anyone you care to meet."

Beatrice fairly glowed with excitement. "Royalty! Do you know any royalty?"

Augusta demurred, but I spoke up on her behalf. "Sir James tells me you recently hosted the Prince of Wales on your grouse moor."

Beatrice nearly upset her teacup in her enthusiasm. "The Prince of Wales! Did you really?"

"Well, yes," Augusta admitted.

"You know the Prince of Wales," Beatrice breathed. "I should so dearly love to meet royalty."

"He would be quite taken with you," Augusta promised. "He is very fond of the young American ladies who have married into European society, you know. He likes their high spirits and informal manners."

At that, Beatrice gave a peal of laughter. "You mean our uncouth ways! You are the soul of tact, Augusta." Beatrice returned to the subject of her husband once more. "But you must tell me, what was Pietro like as a very young man? Leave nothing out," she ordered.

Augusta tipped her head, thinking. "I found him charming in the way so many Italians are. Very much obsessed by music. He was forever asking me to sing duets."

Beatrice gave a merry trill of laughter. "He has not changed at all, my darling Pietro. He still loves music above everything. If we are not careful, we will find ourselves being made to sing Verdi until all hours of the night."

"I can think of worse pastimes," Augusta said kindly. "The last time we were all gathered here, it rained so much we were often forced to rely upon music and games to amuse ourselves."

"I remember that," Elspeth said suddenly. "You were a fair hand with silhouettes."

Augusta waved a hand. "You are too kind, Elspeth. I merely pottered about with black paper and scissors, but it did pass the time."

"I still have the one you cut of me," Elspeth told her gruffly. "I look rather better in it than any photograph I have ever had made, at least that is what Timothy says."

I felt a flicker of annoyance that Timothy Gresham should be so unkind to his sister, but Augusta looked pleased. "The fact that you kept it all these years is gratifying indeed. You know, I do not think I have cut one in years! Is it not silly how the hobbies of one's youth simply fade away as one grows older? I ought to cut silhouettes of the boys before they are fully grown. They go away to school and come back complete strangers, you know." She paused and turned to Collins. "Do you think his lordship could spare a bit of black paper?"

"Certainly, my lady. And sharp scissors?" he enquired.

"As sharp as you can find, but not very long, please," Augusta instructed. "The blades must be short enough to maneuver easily."

Collins sped off to do her bidding and she turned expectantly to the group. "Elspeth, I have already done yours, and I hope, Veronica, you will excuse me if I begin with Beatrice? If it comes out well, perhaps Pietro would like a paper portrait of his bride."

Beatrice clapped her hands together and I arranged the room according to Augusta's direction. I moved a pair of lamps onto a small table to provide strong light and with Elspeth's help and some handy vellum unearthed by an obliging Collins, we fashioned a sort of screen onto which Beatrice's image could be projected in shadow.

When everything had been assembled to Augusta's satisfaction, she settled Beatrice in a chair and began. It was instructive to watch her. In spite of her protests of being an amateur well out of practice, she bent seriously to her task, furrowing her brow as she surveyed Beatrice's outline on the screen.

"What a lovely profile," I observed. "Classical in proportion. Praxiteles himself could do no better."

"Not quite fair," Elspeth said under her breath. Augusta was absorbed in her cutting and Beatrice was on the other side of the screen. Only I heard her, and I turned in some surprise. She flushed, an unattractive mottled shade, and set her mouth stubbornly. "Some people have everything is all," she said.

I made a note to ask her to elaborate when circumstances were more conducive to private conversation. In the meantime, I read aloud from the newspaper. Florence Maybrick, accused of murdering her husband with arsenic and strychnine, had been convicted the previous month. The death sentence had shortly afterwards been commuted to life imprisonment, and we debated the lady's fate until, with a flourish of her scissors, Augusta finished the silhouette.

"There you are, my dear. Mind, it is nothing a professional artist would manage, but I think it has come out well enough to please Pietro." Augusta quickly pasted the bit of black card onto a piece of stiff white paper. Beatrice gave an exclamation of delight.

"Oh, but it is wonderful! You are indeed an artist. Look how you've captured the way my nose tilts up just so at the end. How clever you are—Pietro will adore it."

Just then, the door opened and the gentlemen joined us, expressing delight (Tiberius) and mild shock (Dr. Gresham) at the sight of the port decanter.

"I carried that tawny home from Oporto myself, cradled in my arms like an infant," Tiberius said. "I am glad it is being properly appreciated."

He glanced at the other gentlemen, but they were slow to respond. I realised then that a certain frisson had accompanied them. Sir James' colour was higher than ever whilst Timothy Gresham twitched, his eyes darting here and there. Merry, whose innate shyness had rendered him almost inaudible during dinner, was now entirely mute, clearly distressed about something, and Stoker looked frankly annoyed. Only Tiberius seemed himself, a silent satisfaction simmering below the surface. His gaze settled on Sir James with pointed intensity.

The baronet roused himself to reply to Tiberius' remark. "And you palmed us off with an indifferent ruby!" He finished with a laugh that trailed off weakly.

If the others were subdued, the count seemed almost aggressively talkative. He threw back his head and laughed loudly. "As if anything at Tiberius' table could be called indifferent! Hey, now. What is this?" he asked, plucking the silhouette from his wife's fingers. He burst into impassioned Italian, praising the effort as he studied the image.

"Augusta cut it for me," Beatrice explained. "Isn't it lovely?"

"It almost does justice to my bella sposa," he said. He uttered a few phrases in florid Italian before turning to Augusta. "You are a true artist, my friend, but then you had such a muse!" He blew a kiss to his wife and tucked the silhouette carefully into his breast pocket. "Now I can have your beauty with me, always," he said. The sentiment was romantic, loving even. But something in his tone struck me as possessive, and I found myself wondering about the count and his youthful bride.

Pietro turned to the rest of us with a smile. "Now, what were you ladies discussing? Something entirely scandalous, I hope." He settled himself on the arm of his wife's chair, stroking her neck absently. She twined her fingers through his before replying.

"I was saying that we would all be very lucky indeed if you did not force us to sing Verdi."

"Verdi!" The count's eyes lit with pleasure and he darted to the pianoforte in the corner.

His fingers, long and limber, were perfectly suited to the keyboard, and he played beautifully, with great feeling. The notes trilled under his fingers as he began the prelude to a lively folk tune, which Tiberius sang with competence if not virtuosity, until the count moved into his beloved Verdi. It proved too low for the doctor, so Stoker stepped up to the piano and began to sing, his baritone round and supple. It was not as elegant as Tiberius', but it had more feeling, and more than one eye gleamed brighter as the last notes died away.

Then the count began to play "Già nella notte densa" and Beatrice joined him in the duet.

The performance was bravura. Beatrice's voice was a high, pure soprano, but with a lushness that blended at the end with her husband's rendition of Otello into something quite magical. It was almost enough to make one forget Desdemona's end, I reflected dryly.

When they finished, the count immediately swung into a peppy tune, gesturing for us all to join in. "It is 'Funiculì, funiculà'; surely you know it, my friends!" He pounded out the sprightly rhythm and we sang with gusto, Timothy Gresham proving the greatest surprise as he thundered out a deep and thoroughly unlikely basso profundo.

As the last note died away, Beatrice suddenly seemed to falter. She paled and the count sprang to her side, murmuring into her ear as he put an arm out to support her. She looked up and smiled wanly. "I am sorry, friends. I hope you will not think me unmannerly, Tiberius, if I retire? I am fatigued, the travel . . ."

She let her voice trail off and Tiberius rose, beckoning to Timothy Gresham. "Beatrice, you will let Timothy attend you, I insist." She made to wave him off, but the count murmured once more in her ear and she assented with a wan smile. Together, the two men helped her up the stairs. Tiberius poured another measure of port for himself, but no one else partook. The pleasure of the evening, dimmed with the appearance of the men in a curious mood, had been entirely eclipsed by Beatrice's sudden turn. A chess game was begun between Stoker and Merry whilst the rest of us passed the time in desultory conversation. Elspeth Gresham was blinking furiously, as if fighting off sleep, and the clock struck midnight before Timothy reappeared.

Augusta looked up. "Is Beatrice better?"

The doctor rubbed at his rabbity nose, his expression one of concern. "For now. Heart troubles, she told me," he said soberly.

"Is it serious?" his sister asked.

He gave her a reproving look. "Elspeth, you know I cannot say." But his expression was eloquent in its gravity. The little contessa was clearly quite unwell, and her prognosis could not have been a good one.

Augusta made an exclamation of gentle dismay. "How dreadful! Poor Pietro. They seem so happy together."

Sir James patted her hand. "Then they must make the best of the time they have," he told her. A minute expression of exasperation flickered across her face before she mastered it. I understood it well enough. It was unthinkable that this vital and contented young woman should be so unwell—unthinkable and deeply unfair, I mused.

The news dampened what little amusement had been left in the atmosphere. Tiberius looked about and addressed his guests. "I think a good night's sleep is what we all need. It promises to be a fine day tomorrow and we ought to make an early start to see the estate at its best."

Everyone nodded agreement and rose to move into the hall, where Collins waited with footmen holding the Greshams' wraps and lighted candles for the rest of us. Elspeth was weaving slightly, and her breath was heavy with the smell of port as she bade me good night.

"Mind you drink a good glass of barley water before you retire," I advised. "Or you might find your head a little sore in the morning."

She smiled and her eyes went from side to side, as though she were seeing two of me and trying to decide which to address. Just then her brother came to her holding out a heavy cloak of serviceable green wool.

"Come now, Elspeth, let us get you home," he said with a chuckle.

He tied her cloak under her chin for her with gentle fingers and patted her arm. "I am rather sleepy," she admitted.

He pulled a rueful face over her head as he led her away. Collins was handing candles to the others as Tiberius turned to Merry with an oblique look. "Merry, would you be good enough to show Sir James and Lady MacIver back to their suite on your way up?" He smiled at the MacIvers. "I know you've already settled in, but Cherboys is a veritable maze and we haven't given you bread crumbs to leave a trail."

Merry yawned broadly as he took his candle, shuffling up the stairs like a small bear. Only Stoker, Tiberius, and I remained, affording us the opportunity to compare notes from the evening's events. But before I could suggest a council of war, Stoker took his candle and bowed from the neck. "Good night to you both." He followed Merry up the stairs, taking them two at a time and leaving me staring after him in considerable irritation.

"Are you quite certain there is nothing amiss, Veronica?" Tiberius asked lightly.

"Certainly not."

"I notice, and you will forgive my frankness on such matters, my dear, that my brother goes alone up to his virtuous and solitary bed."

I opened my mouth to utter a witty riposte but somehow could not, in that moment, manage anything other than the truth. "We are not entirely as we were," I admitted.

"Then you are fools, the pair of you," Tiberius replied. He gave me a long look. "Veronica, I hope that you have, in the course of our acquaintance, come to know that you may confide in me," he said simply. The usual theatricality of his gestures was absent; his tone was gentle and his expression warm with regard.

I swallowed hard. "I am not much in the habit of confidences," I admitted. "I have, perhaps, been too long upon my own."

"You confide in Stoker," he pointed out.

"Not as much as I should," I said with some bitterness. "Besides, that is entirely different."

"Yes, I believe it is." He paused, uncomfortable as always, it seemed, with genuine emotion. "I am sorry to see the two of you having troubles. I rather thought you were the one woman upon the face of this good earth who might understand him."

A sudden pricking behind my eyes was the only indication I required that the conversation had gone too far. "Do not be absurd. This difficulty is of the moment. Not even worth speaking of, I assure you. Now I am off to bed. I must be well rested if I am to act as your protector tomorrow."

He did not laugh, but his smile deepened. "Tell me, shall you be armed?"

"I always am."

CHAPTER

14

By the time I reached my room, I had come to a decision. If even Tiberius had noticed the strain between Stoker and myself, the moment to act was at hand. Our division had gone on quite long enough, and it was time to seize the nettle, as it were. With a rising sense of anticipation, I made my preparations. First, I bathed, taking full advantage of the late Lord Templeton-Vane's passion for the latest in plumbing advancements. After refreshing my person I changed into a particularly flattering ensemble du nuit. I had purchased it in Paris with Stoker in mind. I had discovered an establishment specialising in confections of artfully wrought satin and lace during a stop the previous spring when we were returning from a visit to the Alpenwald. I had commissioned several garments from the place, and so successful had they been that even the mention of the name of the atelier was enough to bring a blush to Stoker's cheek. He had not seen this particular costume. It was fashioned of exquisite black lace and dotted strategically with silken butterflies the exact violet of my eyes. The whole affair was laced together with narrow satin ribbons in the same shade, finishing artfully in tiny bows that simply begged to be untied. I smoothed the stockings into place, slipped my feet into a charming pair of velvet mules, and covered the whole with a long, concealing dressing gown of dark Turkey red paisley. I did not anticipate encountering any visitors as I crept through the darkened corridors of Cherboys—the other ladies were attached and accompanied by their husbands, after all—but I thought it best to err on the side of decorum. I tucked a particular book of verse into one of the capacious pockets and sprayed myself strategically with Stoker's favourite perfume.

I tiptoed from my room on slippered feet, moving down the corridor and behind the discreet door to the back stairs. The servants would make use of this staircase to gain access to their rooms, but they would have retired some time ago, the whole of Cherboys settling into a midnight silence. Remembering what Lily had told me about the arrangement of rooms during our tour, I knew that Stoker's chamber was directly above mine. In order to reach it, I had to pass first the principal guest suite—assigned to the Salviatis—and then the linen room.

As I passed the door of the Salviatis' suite, I heard movement and low voices. They were probably far too engrossed in one another to notice the odd noise in the corridor, but I took no chances. I held my breath and tiptoed noiselessly past.

The door of the linen room was slightly ajar, and I hoped Lily was not the poor maid responsible for such slackness. I had heard Mrs. Brackendale when her ire was roused, and I did not envy the girl if she found herself on the receiving end of it.

On silent feet, I crept up the back stairs, emerging on the floor above. A gentle snore rumbled from behind the door of the suite assigned to the MacIvers, and I took even greater care as I eased beyond it to Stoker's room. A narrow band of light shone beneath his door, and I surmised he was still awake. He had with certainty availed himself of his brother's extensive library and was most likely propped up in bed with a glass of whisky and the latest French romantic novel. I had often seen him thus, the bedclothes resting carelessly on his bare hip-bones, iliac furrows sharply delineated with such grace and finely developed musculature . . .

I shook myself firmly and scratched at the door, a soft noise, scarcely audible, but I had no wish to rouse the rest of the wing. After a moment, I heard the squeak of mattress springs and then the door opened a crack. As expected, Stoker was stripped to the waist, the candlelight playing over the planes of his muscles. "Yes?" he asked politely.

"You do not seem surprised to see me," I observed.

"Your methods are as predictable as your libido," he said dryly. His gaze stayed fixed upon my face, but his nostrils flared slightly and his breathing seemed to come a little faster. He was holding himself in check, but not without difficulty.

I opened the dressing gown and let it slide from my shoulders without a word.

It was a long moment before he spoke. "My god," he rasped. Stoker was no stranger to blasphemy, but this was uttered in the worshipful tones of prayer and I smiled.

"May I come in?" I stepped forward, but he blocked the way with his body. I plucked at one of the tiny bows and it burst open, spilling pale, curving flesh.

"I think not," he said, dragging his eyes upwards again.

I blinked. "But—" I took a slow, deep breath and his gaze fell. His jaw went slack, and something entirely feral kindled in his eyes. He clapped his hands over them.

I tugged his hands from his face. "Look at me, Stoker. Why can we not put our brangling behind us? We are entirely and utterly free," I reminded him. "And we have both been exceedingly stubborn."

"Veronica, that is not the point."

I pressed myself against him, putting my hand to a particularly vulnerable and receptive part of his anatomy. "I believe *this* is the point," I remarked, pitching my voice to seductive tones. "You are not entirely unhappy to see me and heaven knows I am very happy to see you." I edged closer and touched my lips to his neck. I felt his knees tremble a little, but suddenly, with a smothered roar, he drew back, setting me gently away from him.

"No," he said with a sternness I found both maddening and adorable. "I will not be manhandled. Or *womanhandled*, as the case may be. I was giving you an opportunity to make a grand gesture," he said, folding his arms over the breadth of his chest. I moved closer still, my perfume wafting as it rose from my heated flesh. He put out his hands as if to ward me off. "Get thee away, succubus."

I paused. "Are you entirely and completely serious? Do you really mean to refuse me? I am trying to *woo* you." I lifted the small book of poetry from my pocket. "I even brought Mr. Keats to assist me. Let me quote something." I flicked through the little volume to a particularly apt passage. "'Now, a soft kiss—aye, by that kiss I vow an endless bliss.'" I stretched forwards on tiptoe, puckering my lips into a rosebud of invitation.

He kept his hands firmly in front of his body, shielding himself from me. "Do not make me hang garlic at the window or summon Merryweather to perform an exorcism to get rid of you. He frightens easily."

"You are being thoroughly ridiculous," I began.

He peeped through his fingers, and I saw the merest gleam of mischief in his eyes. He was still angry, but he was also amusing himself, I realised suddenly. He was *enjoying* this. He meant to make me dance to whichever tune he meant to play, to establish himself as the one with the whip hand in our relationship, and I would have none of it.

"Very well," I said, wrapping the dressing gown tightly about my body and tying it neatly into a bow.

He dropped his hands in surprise. "You surrender?"

"Not now," I replied tartly. "If you wish to play games, you may play them *alone*, Revelstoke."

I turned on the tiny heel, preparing to stomp down the corridor. I do not know if it was my reply or Stoker's burst of laughter that roused Merry, but suddenly his door was flung open. The young vicar stood in his nightshirt, feet bare and nightcap askew. He gaped, speechless.

I strode to him and thrust the volume of Keats into his hands. "Here. May it do you more good than it has me."

Stoker was still laughing when he shut the door.

CHAPTER
15

As soon as Stoker shut his door with a decisive click, Merry turned on his heel and fled into his room, no doubt barricading it against dangersome females, I thought darkly.

I tugged my dressing gown about myself even more tightly as I hurried down the back stairs. This time, as I passed the Salviatis' door, I heard voices again. Where before they had been low and almost inaudible, now they were raised, quick and impassioned. They were quarreling, I realised, and I stepped a few inches nearer. I paused, darting behind a handy statue to effect concealment.

Suddenly, a hand clapped over my mouth and a voice whispered in my ear.

"It's only me." The hand lifted away and I hissed one of Stoker's favourite oaths.

"J. J. What in the name of a dozen devils are you doing skulking about the family wings?"

"Looking for a story, unlike you," she said, giving a salacious wink. "Am I to understand the delectable and Honourable Mr. Templeton-Vane will not oblige you with his attentions?"

"That is none of your affair," I told her.

"Come now, you can confide in me. What's the trouble? Have you quarrelled? Do you snore? Are you indelicate in your attentions?"

"I am prepared to be indelicate with my fists if you accost me again," I muttered.

"Temper! You are in a foul mood. I shall have to tell Stoker it is in all our best interests for him to attend to your needs. Unless you think prayer might help. That young parson is quite personable."

"Leave Merryweather alone or else," I began.

She raised her chin. "Or else what?"

"Or else I shall tell Mrs. Brackendale that I discovered you sniffing around the family rooms, no doubt looking for silver to steal."

"How dare you! I've never stolen anything in my life," she whispered angrily. "But I need a story, Veronica. Help me."

"Not likely," I told her, clipping the words.

"Tiberius does not come to Cherboys, ever," she said. "That is a deviation from his normal habits. Deviations are where the stories are, and I can smell this one. Do not think I won't find out what he is about, Veronica. And when I do, I will write about it."

"Sharpen that quill and you just may prick yourself," I warned her.

She snorted. "I am content to take my chances." She glanced at the statue in front of us, scrutinising the impressive backside. "What is this meant to be anyway? It is just a big fellow being strangled by snakes."

"It is Laocöon. A Trojan priest who tried to warn his people not to accept the horse left by the Greeks. Poseidon sent sea serpents to kill his sons and Laocöon was killed in the attempt to protect them."

"He has an exceedingly nice bottom," she observed. "Almost as nice as Stoker's."

The gleam in her eye told me she was being deliberately provocative in hopes of a reaction. I summoned my dignity, refusing to give her what she wanted.

"Mind your manners, J. J. And stay away from the Templeton-Vane men. They are troublesome in ways you cannot imagine."

"Aren't they all?" she asked with a rueful twist of the lips. "Aren't they all?"

"J. J.," I began, but she held a finger to her lips. She pointed to the door of the Salviatis' suite.

"At it hammer and tongs," she whispered. "I've been listening in the linen room. It's been going the better part of an hour now."

That bit of news trumped my annoyance with J. J. "Good heavens. They were quiet enough a moment ago."

"That's when the fighting stops and they kiss a bit. Then one of them says something and they're off again." Just then Beatrice's voice rose on a sob and J. J. leapt into action. She held up a glass and positioned it between her ear and the door.

"What are they saying?" I demanded in a whisper.

She listened a moment longer, then shrugged. "Devil if I know. I don't speak Italian. Here, you listen."

She pushed me towards the door and thrust the glass into my hands. I took up the post and listened attentively for some moments. The voices had fallen again and I made out only snatches of the conversation. And a single, chilling word: 'morto.' *Dead.* It might have been significant, but without the proper context, I could draw no conclusions. And I had no intention of sharing this scant information with J. J. For all I knew, they were discussing bedbugs.

At length, I heard a few stifled sobs and then a long, low sigh. They lapsed into silence and I shook my head at J. J.

"Gone to bed," I mouthed at her. She pulled a face and I motioned for her to follow me. I led the way back to my room and closed the door softly behind us.

"That wall is shared with his lordship's suite," I told her. "You will have to whisper." She nodded and we settled onto the bed to talk. "Why were you eavesdropping on the Salviatis?" I demanded.

She waggled her brows at me and I peered closely. "Are you having some sort of nervous storm? A fit?"

"I am attempting to arch a brow at you. I am being *scornful*," she said in a lofty tone. "Was that not conveyed?"

"Not in the least. If anything, you looked demented. And why should that question elicit such a response?" I demanded.

"Because you are being deliberately obtuse, Veronica. I am obviously in pursuit of a story."

"About the Salviatis?" I leant closer. "Are they worthy of a story?"

She shrugged. "Not yet, but I have high hopes. You see, working belowstairs is extremely informative. If you keep your ears open, you can learn quite a lot, and I have been learning about the Salviatis. It's a terribly romantic tale, apparently. She is an American heiress, you know. Very good family and her uncle is some titan of industry. Railways or some such. He has settled a handsome amount of money on her, and with her looks, she was absolutely besieged by suitors when she made her debut. She has apparently left them all dangling for years. Scores of handsome American fellows with deep pockets and very white teeth all paying court and asking for her hand. But it was not to be."

She paused—no doubt for dramatic effect, and I suppressed a sigh of impatience. J. J., like all storytellers, could never be rushed.

But she did expect an appreciative audience, and a little rapt attention would not go amiss, I decided.

"Go on," I encouraged with wide eyes to show I was listening closely.

"She met the Count Salviati, older but very handsome and with lovely, Continental manners. Apparently she has a weakness for all things Italian," J. J. said, waggling her eyebrows again, but this time to better effect. I understood at once that she meant to imply Beatrice found European gentlemen to be extremely alluring. "The other suitors dangled diamonds in her direction, but all it took was a few whispered sonnets from Salviati, and she was so much putty in his nimble hands. They were married a shockingly short time later."

"There must have been a bit of talk; after all, he is much older than she. Although he does bring the title and the wealth, I suppose. Beauty has been traded thusly since time began," I mused.

J. J. shook her head. "The contessa is the one with the money. The Salviati family were tremendously important during the time of the Borgias and have been gently declining ever since. There's no grand castello left to restore or anything like that, but I did hear of a tiny Roman palace, scarcely larger than a town house in Belgravia. Perhaps they'll use her money to do it up. In the meantime, they like a bit of travel. They're having a belated honeymoon and slowly making their way to Egypt so they can spend the winter amidst the pyramids." She stopped, her expression dreamy. "Can you imagine anything more romantic than sleeping under the desert stars, observed only by the unseeing eyes of the statues of pharaohs?"

"And the guides, and the tourists, and the local folk, and rather too many smelly camels," I told her with some asperity.

"You just want a place that has butterflies," she said pointedly.

"I do not deny that is an attraction. Now, what else have you discovered about the count and his bride?" I cursed myself silently as soon as the words had flown from my lips. Either my persistence on the subject of the Salviatis or my tone alerted her. She lifted her nose in the air as a predator will when it smells blood.

"Why do you want to know? You aren't here just for a bloody house party," she accused. "You are engaged in an investigation!"

The last word rose loudly, and I clapped a hand over her mouth. "Hush! Do you want everyone in the house to know?" I removed my hand to reveal a Cheshire Cat grin.

"But they will know if you do not tell me exactly what this is about," she assured me.

"That," I told her in an icy voice, "is extortion."

"It is," she agreed happily. "But it's quite like old times. Now, tell me."

"Impossible!"

"Veronica," she said pleasantly, "our friendship is of recently short duration, but I think you know me well enough to understand the depth of my persistence in pursuit of the truth. Now, we can spar and spat until the proverbial cows come home, but in the end, you will tell me because you simply cannot risk what I might do if left to my own devices. Why waste the time and effort when we both know you will tell me in the end?"

It sounded so reasonable when she phrased it thusly. "Harpia harpyja," I muttered.

"I beg your pardon?"

"The Latin name for the harpy eagle. A thoroughly nasty bird that will tear a small deer into pieces so it can devour the poor creature. I cannot imagine why that particularly predatory beast came to mind just now."

She waved an airy hand. "I am impervious to insult, Veronica, and you are stalling. Tell me."

So, recognising the inevitability of my defeat, I gave a bone-deep sigh and capitulated. She listened attentively, asking intelligent questions and homing in on pertinent details. It was, I found, not so much a chore to share the story with her as an unexpected pleasure. I had not realised how much I feared for Tiberius' safety until I halved the burden, as it were. That I would have had a true partner in this endeavour if Stoker had not proven intransigent was a bitter thought and one not worth dwelling upon.

"And those two arrogant foozlers have actually wagered against you on the outcome of this case?"

"They have. I suspect they have done so as much to keep Tiberius from meditating too much upon the possibility of his imminent demise as from any true sporting spirit."

"Oh, you think so?" she demanded. "Then why did they find it necessary to cheat?"

"Cheat! They would never. They are gentlemen of honour."

J. J. grimaced. "I *might* concede that point where Stoker is concerned, but Lord High-and-Mighty? Never. He wants to win this wager and he is prepared to soil his pretty hands to do so. In fact, he has already begun."

"How?"

"After the ladies withdrew from the table, the gentlemen remained behind for port and cigars and a spot of gossip."

"Gossip! Of what sort?"

"Lord T-V shared the newspaper cuttings."

"He did what!" It was my turn to shout, and J. J. shushed me to silence.

"His lordship's suite," she reminded me. "And we don't need him alert to the fact that we are working together." I ignored her certainty that we would be partners and gestured for her to go on. "He gave them the broad strokes of what you told me, then said he had been threatened and handed round the cuttings."

"And what were the reactions?"

"Stoker looked like thunder. Of course, he often does, but this was *properly* stormy. It was very clear he didn't approve of Tiberius sharing the story with his friends. Young Merryweather looked bewildered, like a lost puppy."

"And the others?"

She tipped her head, thinking. "Timothy Gresham, the medical fellow that looks like a rabbit? Well, by the time his lordship finished, Gresham looked like a perplexed rabbit. As if you had asked him how to do advanced mathematics in his head. He said precious little. Sir James blustered that it must be a joke but that it was in damned poor taste. And Count Salviati simply murmured some phrases in Italian. I think he was saying it was a pity or a tragedy. They hadn't much time to talk about it because they did not want to keep you lot of ladies waiting, so they resolved to discuss it another time."

"That is why there was an air of tension when they came to the drawing room," I said slowly. "They had just been informed a murderer is likely walking amongst us."

"Indeed. And it is up to us to find him," she finished happily.

"J. J.," I began.

She held up a hand as she slid from the bed. "Do not bother, Veronica. I am going to help you whether you like it or not."

"And no doubt find yourself a meaty story," I said acidly.

She shrugged by way of response and said nothing, waiting for me to reply.

"I suppose I cannot stop you," I said finally. "But you will confine your efforts to the servants' quarters. If you are caught someplace you oughtn't be, you can always plead losing your way. If you're discovered in any of the family or guest rooms, I shall not lift a finger to protect you."

"Agreed," she said, putting out her hand. I shook it, feeling that if I were not quite making a deal with the devil himself, I was certainly throwing my lot in with one of his lesser demons.

J. J. made to leave.

"Wait," I called, and she stopped at the door, her hand resting on the knob. "How do you know what they said in the dining room after dinner? Female staff are never permitted in the room when port is being served."

"Poor old Collins was rushing so much between the dining room and the drawing room, he left the door ajar. There's a particularly large potted aspidistra just outside. Very handy for hiding behind."

"J. J. Butterworth, you are a deceitful trollop. You knew about the entire story before you came in here this evening and yet you blackmailed me into telling you anyway?"

She grinned. "Best get your beauty sleep now, Veronica. It is late and we have a case. See you tomorrow, partner."

CHAPTER
16

The next morning I woke in a dangerous mood. I was thoroughly annoyed at being manipulated into taking J. J. on as a partner, and I was more than a little vexed with Stoker. In spite of my protests to J. J., I was not in the least surprised that Tiberius had decided to skirt the rules of fair play. But Stoker's gamesmanship had taken a new turn I did not like. Hitherto, we had been partners in our investigative endeavours, even when we pursued separate lines of enquiry. Now, he seemed content to carry on without me, and it would not do. I had to plot precisely how to bring him to heel. It never profits a lady to permit a man to gain the advantage in matters of the heart, I reflected. *I* must have the whip hand, I told myself as I dressed. It was an unfortunate choice of words. That particular phrase led me to woolgathering in an especially saucy vein, and it was some minutes before I recalled myself to the task at hand: protecting Tiberius from a possible murderer.

Of course, we had no absolute proof that the murderer was even amongst us, I reminded myself as I pinned my hair neatly into place. We had gathered a collection of potential victims, and it might take considerable unravelling to make progress. The situation called for keen observation and patience, skills innate to a lepidopterist and honed to a razor's edge in the field.

In a burst of exuberance, I put aside the simple country walking dress I had selected and dressed instead in my hunting costume. It was a collection of garments whose design had been refined over the course of many years' experience. I owned several in various fabrics, and this was a particularly suitable pale violet twill, light enough for the warmth of the day. The ensemble began with trousers, cut tight to the leg but with good freedom of movement for scrambling over rocks and hillsides. A fitted white shirtwaist came next with an immaculate white collar pinned at the throat by a small brooch bearing a cameo of Medusa's head. A waistcoat and jacket followed, and atop the trousers went a slender skirt fitted with various pockets and an ingenious system of buttons so that it might be secured out of the way when necessary.

Into the starched white cuffs went a set of minuten, the small headless pins used by butterfly collectors to secure specimens. They were used more in the laboratory than the field, but I found them particularly convenient for warding off predators of the two-legged variety. More than once an importunate suitor had made to grab my hand only to draw back, bleeding and thoroughly cowed. I filled my pockets with various tools and the odd knife or two—I had, after all, promised Tiberius I would be his stalwart protector. The last to go on were my boots, flat and flexible of sole and laced tightly to the knee. The effect was eccentric but not unbecoming, and I pinned on a hat with a broad brim to shield my face from the late summer sunshine. I preferred a wide brim for the shade, and the necessary hatpins were another handy weapon. I kept mine sharpened to a needle point, and once suitably kitted, I felt equipped to meet any threat that might befall Tiberius.

I found him on the terrace outside the morning room, dressed with his usual fastidious neatness and explaining the lay of the land to his guests.

"I am sure you all remember, but Beatrice is new to Cherboys and the rest of you may care to refresh your memories. To the south," he said, sweeping his arm, "is the sea, just down the rose alley and beyond that copse of trees. Do be careful if you go that direction. The cliff paths can be hazardous."

Someone, I could not determine who, made a strangled sort of sound and the count gave a dry little cough. Tiberius' smile was grave.

"I am certain you recall the dangers," he said. He fell silent a moment, and I had no doubt he was thinking of Lorenzo. Then he gave a little shake and lifted his chin. "That direction is the village."

The countess furrowed her pretty brow. "But surely we came the other way yesterday?"

"The road is the long way round," Tiberius explained. "If you wish to go to the village, there is a path directly through the trees on that side of the estate. Two, in fact. One more direct and the other a meandering walk but more picturesque. It comes out at the wall of the churchyard, which is well worth a visit. The church is quite pretty."

"Norman," Merryweather put in proudly. "With a rather fine window of St. Frideswide the Lesser."

"Popery," Sir James muttered under his breath with the true vigour of a Scottish Presbyterian. Merryweather drew back as if stung and I decided instantly that Sir James was my favourite candidate for pushing Lorenzo d'Ambrogio to his death. Anyone who could offend so amiable a spirit as Merryweather was entirely capable of murder.

Tiberius went on. "If you wish to ramble further, then to the north you will find chalk downs and a few hills worth climbing for the views down to the sea. I have interviews with my tenants this morning and cannot accompany you, I regret, but you cannot lose yourselves. The paths are well maintained and it is quite easy to find your way," he promised. "Just make your way back by one o'clock so that Collins may serve you luncheon in the dining room."

The guests moved into the topiary garden, debating the merits of the various walks, as I stayed behind, fixing Tiberius with a gimlet eye.

"I thought you meant to spend the day with them," I said, nodding towards the assorted group in the garden.

"And I thought perhaps it might be better to let you do what you do best."

"Ah, you mean employ the keen observational skills of a trained lepidopterist?" I asked, feeling a tiny thrust of satisfaction.

"I meant follow people about and ask impertinent questions," he replied. "It is damnably rude, but it does get tremendous results."

"Speaking of rude," I murmured.

He laid a hand upon my sleeve. "Said with the greatest admiration, Veronica. You know the depth of my regard for you."

The bantering tone was almost right, but an undercurrent of something melancholic flowed beneath. "Tiberius," I began.

He waved me off. "Don't let us get distracted, my dear. I am fine, I promise."

"I am fond of you too, Tiberius. Mind you do not get yourself murdered. I should be very cross indeed."

"Because of your regard for me?" he asked lightly.

"No, because I shall never collect my five guineas. By the way, it seems the gentlemen were quite unsettled when they joined us ladies last night after your port and cigars. I cannot imagine what you might have been discussing to raise such a reaction. Is there anything you would care to share with me?"

I watched him closely for any sign of duplicity, but Tiberius was an accomplished liar. "We were talking about the Prince of Monaco. He died last week, and we were contemplating whether his successor will keep the casino open. It would be a grave disappointment if it were shuttered."

I resisted the urge to snort. Count Salviati looked like the sort of man who might enjoy a flutter or two, but less likely gamblers than Stoker, Merry, Timothy Gresham, and Sir James were hard to imagine.

"How very concerning," I replied.

He fixed me with a piercing look. "Yes, it is. So concerning, in fact, that I was wakeful long after I retired. I thought I heard voices coming from your room, Veronica. Is there anything you would like to share with *me*?"

I widened my eyes. "Why, no, Tiberius. Nothing at all."

With the thrill of the hunt rising in my blood, I hurried to begin my surveillance of the houseguests. A brisk walk of a few minutes' duration brought me to the top of the hill crowned with the folly shaped like a pineapple. Inside, a narrow staircase spiraled up into the crown, providing a perfect crow's nest at the top. From that vantage point, I could—with the aid of a spyglass taken from my lepidoptery kit—ascertain the whereabouts of Tiberius' guests. They had divided up, I soon discovered. Sir James and the count were ambling gently towards the coast path, seemingly relaxed in their attitudes. The count was swinging a walking stick, using it to rustle the tall grasses on either side of the path, while Sir James told a story, sketching broad gestures with his hands. Whatever their reactions had been to Tiberius' revelations about the threats against him, they were clearly unconcerned.

From this amiable duo, I swivelled the spyglass, finding a lone figure dressed in elegant white making its way to the bower of the rose alley. It was Beatrice, her face shielded by a wide hat tied with a soft blue ribbon. She settled herself comfortably in the shade of the bower before drawing a book from her pocket. If she was distressed about the quarrel with her lord and master the previous night, she showed no sign of it. The brilliant sunshine, the glittering sea, the rosebushes heavy with blossom and fragrance—all seemed to conspire to bring out the holiday spirits of the houseguests.

Still, the web of intrigue had given me plenty of threads to pluck, and I meant to question them all. I decided to begin with the countess.

I tucked the spyglass away and descended, taking up my butterfly net from where I had left it at the bottom of the stairs. There is no more useful tool than a butterfly net for lending purpose to one's presence out of doors. No matter the country, no matter the season, the pretence of lepidoptery is a perfect ruse. I slowed my steps to a casual amble as I approached Beatrice, hoping to give the impression I had come upon her by happenstance.

At the sound of my footsteps, she looked up, letting the book in her hand fall closed. It was a slender volume, bound in blue kid and stamped with a tiny gilded bee that shone dully. The edges of the pages were heavily foxed and the cover was spotted with mould. Poetry, no doubt, or a popular novel, and a much-loved one judging from the condition. Beatrice was an engaging person, but she did not strike me as the sort of woman who would wrestle with Aristotelian philosophy on a glorious summer's morn.

"Veronica!" she said, greeting me with real warmth. "How have you been spending this lovely day?"

I held up my net. "A-hunting I shall go."

"In this weather! You are a lady of unusual vigour, Veronica. I envy your stamina," she said, her smile only lightly tinged with something more. Envy? Wistfulness? It seemed wrong that so young and lovely a creature could suffer from serious ailment, but I recalled how quickly she had faltered the previous evening, and how sober Timothy Gresham's expression had been after he had examined her.

I decided to approach the matter obliquely. "I am happy to see you looking so much better than last evening. I hope you are feeling recovered?"

"Recovered is not possible," she said simply. She paused, as if making up her mind, then forged on, stating the facts quite plainly and without undue emotion. "I am afraid my heart is not sound, Veronica. I was given the news shortly after I came out into society. All those balls and dances! I used to faint so often, my poor aunt used to carry feathers to burn under my nose to every party. When it finally occurred to her that I wasn't trying to be genteel, she took me to the best doctors in New York. Cardiac troubles, they said. And they prescribed rest, lots and lots of rest. So I spent the next year in a place called Vermont, reading and admiring the views."

"It sounds lovely," I offered.

"It was dull beyond belief," she confided. "But it did seem to help. The doctors finally said I could return to the city and take up some sort of social life again." She paused. "You know, during that time away, I had the chance to think, quite deeply. And I decided it wouldn't be fair to marry—to my husband, I mean. I made up my mind that I would remain a spinster."

"What happened?" I enquired.

Her smile was wry. "Pietro. How can a girl from Manhattan possibly resist a European gentleman with that profile who can make love in three languages? I discouraged every suitor who tried, and yet I was powerless against Pietro. I tried to talk him out of it—the first time he proposed, I mean. I explained about my heart. That I wouldn't make old bones and shouldn't have children. But he said he would rather have a year with me alone than a lifetime with anyone else and her houseful of children. Isn't that the most romantic thing you've ever heard?"

Stoker's declarations were so eloquent as to be unmatchable, but I would not argue the point. "Terribly romantic," I murmured encouragingly.

"Anyway, I found I couldn't resist him in the end. I married him, against everyone's good advice, and we have been blissfully happy," she finished with a contented sigh.

Some flicker of doubt must have kindled in my expression, for she laughed suddenly. "You heard our quarrel last night, didn't you? I told Pietro we should have been more discreet."

"I heard only raised voices," I said, pausing for effect. "And then a word. 'Morto.'"

She laughed again. "My poor Pietro! He worries constantly that I will overtax myself. He began by lecturing me very sternly on allowing myself to be too excitable. He said I had had too much stimulation with the travel and meeting new people, and I should be more restful or I should find myself dead." She rolled her eyes. "The Italianate temperament is so emotional! I wonder how they ever managed to conquer the world under the Caesars."

Her tone was light but she was watching me closely, as if trying to decide if I believed her explanation for the raised voices. I smiled blandly.

"I am so glad to know that is all it was."

Before she could form a suitable reply, Augusta appeared. Like Beatrice, she had protected her pale skin from the sun, but she had chosen a pretty Chinese parasol instead of a wide-brimmed hat. She wore a light gown of biscuit silk and gave a sigh as she fanned herself with a hand. Tiny pearls of perspiration beaded her hairline.

"A spectacular day but a trifle hot after Scotland," she proclaimed as she joined us. Her eyes fell on Beatrice's book and she paused. "My dear, do not tell me you are wasting this glorious weather on reading! Or are you still suffering a malaise from last evening's turn?"

Beatrice gave her a gentle smile. "I am quite recovered, thank you. Today is one of my better days, although I promised Pietro I wouldn't exert myself."

"What are you reading?" Augusta enquired, peering at the book.

"Have you found something scandalous in Tiberius' library? I confess, I looked for a novel and was mightily disappointed in how little light reading was to be found. Has ever there been so much Suetonius in one collection!"

Beatrice shrugged. "A book of poetry I acquired some time ago."

"Poetry," Augusta said, making a slight moue of distaste. "I can never bring myself to like poetry. Far too much about *feelings*, I always think."

Before Beatrice could reply, we heard a shout—a sort of muted roar that echoed through the gardens.

"That sounded like Pietro!" Beatrice exclaimed. She rose to her feet, but before we could move towards the sound, Pietro appeared, waving his hand in the air and declaiming loudly in Italian.

"A bee has stung you? Caro mio, I am so sorry," Beatrice said, hurrying to his side. He brandished his hand for all of us to see. There was a large red weal, puffing angrily around what looked like a thorn.

"The stinger is still in his hand," I pointed out.

"It hurts," he said, puffing his breath and groaning.

"Because so long as the stinger is there, it will continue to envenomate you," I explained. "Do hold still and I will try to help."

With the encouragement of his wife, who held his other hand and murmured gentle words of solace, he let me minister to him. I retrieved the tweezers from my lepidoptery kit and made short work of extracting the stinger. He moaned gently as it came away from the swollen flesh.

"You will want to clean that immediately," I advised. "And a bit of honey might help the pain."

Beatrice put her arm around her husband's waist. "Come, my darling. Let us go up to the house and take care of this."

He moaned again as she coaxed him away, and I turned to Augusta. "Such a fuss over a tiny bee sting!" I exclaimed.

She smiled. "I do not know Pietro well, but I can tell you he has always been a man with a propensity for dramatics." She suddenly gave a start. "Oil of lavender! I have some in my room. One of our boys is forever being stung. He simply will not keep out of the heather and it is fairly awash with bees in the summer. I should go and search it out for Pietro. Do excuse me, Veronica."

As she turned to go, she paused. "And Beatrice has forgot her book in all the excitement."

"Take it to her," I suggested. "She may not be back for some time, judging by Pietro's histrionics. And it might be spoilt if rain comes later." I pointed to the clouds gathering on the horizon.

Her lips thinned a little in obvious distaste at handling the book. "I rather think a good dousing would do it little harm. It is filthy." She lifted it with her fingertips, wrinkling her nose. "Enjoy your hunt," she added with a nod towards my butterfly net.

"Thank you, Augusta. I intend to."

CHAPTER 17

I decided my next target should be Sir James, and I deduced that the count must have left him somewhere on the grounds before seeking out the tender ministrations of his wife for his bee sting. I made my way to the cliff path, striking out with a long stride, filling my lungs with the fresh salt air. Out on the cliffs, the glory of the day was even more apparent, the late summer sun glittering and glimmering on the sea with just enough wind to whip the waves to a froth. Without Merryweather's caution to hamper me, I ventured near the edge a time or two, testing the ground carefully. It was possible to find sound footing even quite close to the precipice, and I stood right at the earth's end, perched precariously but exultantly on the brink of disaster. It is a heady thing to test oneself thus, to push one's mettle to the sharp point of endurance, but it is essential to know one's limitations. I am never giddy at heights, but even a steady constitution can take a turn when faced with such a prospect.

I suspected that is precisely what happened to my quarry. When I came upon him, Sir James was perched on St. Frideswide's seat, looking a trifle peaked, his expression distracted.

"Good morning!" I called brightly. He gave me a nod, raising a hand in greeting as I joined him. "Sir James, if you will forgive the observation, you seem unwell."

I had designed my hunting costume with the utmost practicality in mind, but Stoker had made improvements. Wherever possible, he had carefully picked open the seams and inserted capacious pockets. I carried about my person not only the impedimenta of my occupation but various oddments, such as a book—a pocket edition of Ovid's *Ars Amatoria* does wonders for passing the time when one is forced to wait out a sudden storm in the shelter of a friendly grotto or hollowed-out tree—a compass, needle and thread, a sandwich of thick-cut bread laid tenderly with slices of rosy ham and good Cheddar, and a basic kit for attending to various minor medical emergencies. (I had also about my person assorted weapons, a waterproof tin of vestas, and the flask of aguardiente I had shared with Merryweather. It had been my habit to carry also a cheese wire until Stoker confiscated it. I do not admit to carrying it for the purposes of garrotting should circumstances necessitate, but I will concede that it was this possibility that caused Stoker to remove it from my person.)

"Are you giddy? I have strong liquor if the height has affected you."

He roused himself to respond. "What's that? No, no. Nothing like that," he murmured. He looked about the windswept bluff and shook his head. "I have not been on this path in twenty years."

"The late Lord Templeton-Vane forbade it, I hear," I offered.

He nodded. "Yes. It was far too dangerous at the time."

"A pity it isn't shored up. With the proper engineering, it might be usable again, a shortcut from the village down to Lyme. That might be a convenient thing for the local folk when the road floods."

"They would not want to walk here," Sir James put in suddenly. "Not after what happened to Lorenzo."

"Lorenzo?" I enquired, pretending innocence.

"Lorenzo d'Ambrogio. Our very dear friend. He died upon this cliff. Twenty years ago."

"I have heard something of the matter. He was your school friend and travelling companion, Tiberius tells me. His death must have been very tragic," I observed. "To die so young . . ." I let my voice trail off invitingly, and as I expected, Sir James carried on. He was the very embodiment of the bluff British gentleman, feelings bound and buckled so tightly I doubted he would have spoken of them if any of the other gentlemen had been present. But it is remarkable what confidences a little womanly sympathy can coax from the most reluctant breast.

"A boy," Sir James said. "Just a lad from Umbria. Or was it Florence? I can't even remember." He made a gesture of dismissal. "Foreign parts, anyway. But he was a good fellow, even if he was a Continental. Loyal to a fault, always thinking of honour."

"You believe this is an English virtue? In my experience, Italians are keenly devoted to the matter of honour."

"I do not count their duels and vendettas and whatnot," Sir James said with a touch of pomposity. "I mean real honour, the sort that pays its debts and lives up to its promises."

"And that is the sort of man Lorenzo d'Ambrogio was?"

Sir James grunted. "Aye. He was occasionally ridiculous, even if he was my dearest friend. He could make an utter mountain out of the tiniest of molehills if he thought something touched his honour. One time," he said, settling himself a little more comfortably, "we were staying near Chambord with our friend Alexandre. Quite a nice château it was, but a very tiny village. The sort of place that sees one train per day and one train only." He raised his index finger for emphasis. "There we were, packed up and ready to leave, standing on the platform, and suddenly Lorenzo starts bemoaning the fact that he's just realised he hasn't settled his bill with the cobbler in the village for mending a boot. Fairly upset he was, insisting he had to settle the debt before he left because he'd given his word as a d'Ambrogio. Now, we pleaded with him, explained we'd miss our train to Paris and it would spoil our plans. And mind you, he could just as easily have sent the money on from Paris, and the cobbler wouldn't have been the poorer for more than a day. But does Lorenzo listen to us? Does he heed our warnings? He does not."

"What did he do?" I asked.

Sir James, like most men with an encouraging woman to talk to, opened like a flower as he finished the story.

"I will tell you what he did! He ran off down the road, and sure as the seasons, he missed the train. And so we all of us missed the train. Back we had to go to the château and stay another night. And fairly furious we were with him, I don't mind telling you."

"Did it really matter so much, the delay of a day?" I enquired.

He gave me a knowing look. "You've not come between Pietro and the opening night of the opera in Paris or you'd not ask that." He thought a moment before he went on. "He was a kind fellow, though, Lorenzo. Old Lord Templeton-Vane held a country dance here in our honour. Lorenzo was the only one of us besides Tiberius to ask Elspeth Gresham to stand up with him."

He looked around as if to make certain we were not overheard. "I don't like to say it, but that woman scares the life out of me, and there's no two ways about it."

I could well imagine Elspeth as a debutante, dressed in stark, un-flattering white and trembling with nerves. She was unprepossessing enough with the confidence of age; being paraded like livestock at the county fair in the full flower of her youthful awkwardness would not have brought out her best. I felt a thrust of pity for her, unwanted and unadmired, and I could not resist a waspish little jab.

"It would have been kind for all of you to have asked her and not just Lorenzo."

Sir James blustered in response. "I was newly betrothed. It would not have been appropriate to dance with another lady."

"It was a country dance," I said serenely. "What harm could it have done?"

Sir James rose immediately to the bait. "I had to have a thought to how it would look if Augusta should see me dancing with another lady," he protested. It was far too easy to pluck at Sir James' puppet strings. He was an uncomplicated fellow, and I realised that, in common with many British gentlemen, he was far more concerned with appearing to possess virtue than actually having it.

But it made him an extremely apt subject for my little manipulations, and I carried on, changing tack with ruthless speed.

"I must confess, I did know something of your little group's misadventures," I informed him. "Tiberius showed me the cuttings."

The unexpected swiftness of the charge disarmed him. He turned to me with frank astonishment, then abruptly looked back out to sea. "Oughtn't to have shown them to a lady. I would never trouble Augusta with such a thing. If I had had one," he amended hastily.

He had spoken in the conditional tense, but I knew a diversionary tactic when I saw it. "Haven't you?" I challenged.

He turned back to me, surprise writ upon his features. "How can you . . . that is to say, what makes you believe such a thing has happened?"

I decided that a strategy of artfully constructed truthfulness would be the most effective. I leant towards him, assuming a confiding air.

"Sir James, I presume that I may trust you? That you are a man of your word?"

"Naturally," he said stiffly.

"Then I may tell you that I am very well acquainted with Sir Hugo Montgomerie of Scotland Yard." I gave him a knowing nod.

"The head of Special Branch?" His bushy brows rose in amazement. "What business have you with Sir Hugo?"

"That is just the point, Sir James. I have *business* with him. He has, over the course of many months, entrusted me with various and sundry undertakings. I am by way of being a consultant of sorts to him. On matters of extreme delicacy."

I paused to let him consider this. He sat staring at me for a long moment, his mouth slack. "A young lady? *Working* for Scotland Yard?"

"Not for Scotland Yard," I corrected hastily. "But for Sir Hugo from time to time. When he is confronted with a matter of such delicacy that he cannot involve himself personally."

"But a young lady," he repeated, stupefied.

"Who better? After all, if you were a villainous wretch bent upon some criminal mischief, would you suspect a lady with some refinement of being an agent of justice?"

He shook his head slowly. "I cannot say I would."

"Exactly." My tone was triumphant. "So, you see, Sir James, I am an experienced confidante. I have heard secrets which could topple the government, nay, the very Empire itself," I said in a whisper charged with emotion. "You may trust me with whatever troubles you."

I thought I had persuaded him. I had used both intellect and emotion, appealing to reason and feeling, and he was a susceptible fellow. He opened his mouth as if to speak, then clamped it shut.

I put a hand to his sleeve, startling him into looking directly at me.

"If you have received a set of cuttings, you might be in danger, Sir James. Won't you let me help you?"

"Danger? My dear young woman, what sort of danger do you imagine I might be in?"

"If Lorenzo d'Ambrogio's death was not an accident, someone may be exacting vengeance for him."

He shied, drawing his arm swiftly away from my touch. "Rubbish," he said almost angrily. "It is absolute rubbish. Lorenzo's death was an accident, and there is nothing else to say upon the matter." He rose abruptly from the boulder. "I think I have had enough of the view. I shall leave you to enjoy it."

He hurried on, but I did not bother to follow him. I had learnt something from my discussion that I doubted Stoker or Tiberius knew.

Sir James MacIver had received a set of cuttings of his own.

And Sir James MacIver was frightened.

CHAPTER

18

I found myself in much better spirits after my conversation with Sir James. Tiberius might jape at my burrowing about and asking questions as so much meddlesome interference, but even he had seen the effectiveness of my methods, and I had just been vindicated yet again. It had been my experience that gentlemen, particularly those of the upper classes, were heavily inclined to permit ladies more familiarity than they would indulge in another man. And if the lady were young and comely, she might ask him almost anything. If Sir James had had his wits about him, he would have curtailed our discussion, firmly returning us to a more appropriate topic. Instead, he permitted a frankly outrageous interrogation. He had lied, of course—gentlemen often do when the truth will make them look bad—but what is concealed is often more illuminating than what is revealed.

I was convinced, for example, that he had indeed received a set of cuttings identical to those sent to Tiberius. I was further persuaded Sir James had not shown them to his wife. Most gentlemen are apt to think of women as delicate, shrinking creatures whose sensibilities must be protected. I had little doubt Sir James was one of these. (The fact that Augusta clearly ran his household, reared his children, entertained on a lavish scale, and engaged in vigourous philanthropy would not penetrate the brain of such a fellow. He would still think her fragile whilst I observed Augusta possessed all the skills necessary for commanding a middling-sized battleship under enemy fire.)

I was still contemplating Augusta's brisk virtues when I reached the village of Dearsley. After my cliff-top walk, I realised I was enjoying the brilliant sunshine far too much to partake in the formal luncheon indoors. Instead, I ate my sandwich in the cool shade of the Pineapple Pavilion and, dusting the crumbs from my fingers, decided to pay a call upon Elspeth Gresham. She was a curious woman, fussy and a little prickly, but I suspected her sharp eyes missed little, and as a young woman during the fateful house party some twenty years past, she might well have formed impressions of those in attendance. I was interested in her thoughts on the young men who had neglected her at that long-ago ball in favour of more attractive ladies such as Augusta, who must have been even handsomer in her youth.

As I reached the front gate of Wren Cottage, where the Greshams lived, I noticed several details I had missed upon first passing when we left the train station. A rambler rose, thick with late, saucer-sized pink flowers, grew over the arched gate, shrouding the entrance in blossom. It required only a few steps to carry one from the gate to the door, but in that space grew a profusion of country flowers. Buddleia and fuchsia clustered beside the sturdy stems of hydrangeas, and rosy geraniums nestled cheek to cheek with the fragrant petals of lavender. It was all tidy and free of weeds, carefully tended by an exacting hand. A handsome little Painted Lady drifted about the blossoms, but *Vanessa cardui* is perhaps the most ubiquitous butterfly in existence. I watched its lazy progress for a moment before noticing a noise coming from the front door of the adjoining dispensary. It was housed in a long, low addition having little of the charm of the main cottage apart from a deep, latticed arbour fitted around the door, blooming thickly with purple clematis. A shadow moved within, rapping smartly upon the door.

"Timothy, I say, Dr. Gresham, are you there?"

I recognised Augusta's voice and called a greeting to her. She peered around the edge of the arbour, smiling when she caught sight of me. "Oh, hello, Veronica! If I had known you meant to come to the village, we might have walked together." She came to where I stood upon the front step of Wren Cottage.

"I didn't know myself until a few minutes ago," I told her.

She nodded a trifle impatiently towards the dispensary. "I am supposed to meet Timothy to discuss his work at Milverton House. Do you know it?"

"No, but I heard a little of your conversation last night. An asylum for unbalanced ladies, I believe?"

"That's the one. Ah well, I suppose Timothy must have been called away. The lot of a country doctor! Did you mean to call upon Elspeth? I may as well come with you."

If I meant to question Elspeth discreetly, there was no hope for it now. I could not refuse Augusta's company with anything approaching courtesy, so I merely smiled and gestured for her to precede me as I glanced over Wren Cottage.

The house itself bore the same attention to detail that made the garden so charming; the doorstep had been neatly scrubbed and the brass knocker polished to a high sheen. The knocker was a charming little dormouse, and my hand went instinctively to the tiny velvet mouse in my pocket. Chester had been my most constant companion, much loved and carried around the world and back. The fact that he had been mended once or twice with Stoker's painstaking stitching only made him the more valuable. I stroked his back with a fingertip while Augusta rapped at the cottage door.

The windows of Wren Cottage were hung with starched curtains of very white linen, and upon one sill perched a cat of lordly propor-tions. It looked down its nose at me as we waited upon the step. I had expected a maid to answer, but when the door swung open, Elspeth Gresham stood there. She was dressed in a well-washed gown of faded grey cotton, serviceable, but not flattering. A crocheted lace collar was her only offering at the altar of Vanity.

"Lady MacIver, Miss Speedwell," she said in some surprise.

"Hallo, Elspeth. We did decide not to stand upon ceremony," Augusta said.

Elspeth looked at me uncertainly. "Veronica," I reminded her. "I hope the hour is not inconvenient for callers."

"Not at all," she said, stepping back. "I was just putting up some jam. Brambleberry. It is Timothy's favourite, although I cannot abide the pips."

She gestured towards the doorway immediately to her left and we entered a small, neatly kept parlour. Everything was polished and shin-ing, neither crumb nor hair marring the gleaming perfection. A tiny sofa and two armchairs stood in the middle of a freshly brushed carpet, and a bowl of roses took pride of place in the center of a table that had been set for tea. There was no cloth, no embroidered linen or fine embellish-ments, but the tea things were good—old Wedgwood, mended skillfully.

"What a pretty room!" I exclaimed.

It was only a slight exaggeration on my part. The room was not pre-cisely handsome; the flower-patterned plates hung upon the walls were a trifle too fussy, the bits of souvenir glass and china a bit too garish. But there was a homeliness that had clearly been accomplished with a great deal of care, and I assumed Elspeth took pride in her little nest.

She smiled tightly. "It fills the time." She glanced to the little plate of thinly cut bread and butter on the tea table. "I shall go and put the kettle on. I won't be a minute."

She hurried away and Augusta and I settled ourselves onto a hard, narrow sofa. Behind us, the cat in the window stared balefully. "She must have been expecting someone," I ventured. "The table is already laid for tea."

Augusta shook her head. "Not necessarily. I suspect Elspeth spends much of her time dispensing tea and sympathy to the villagers. I've known many a lady like her—so busy with Good Works they've no time for their own pursuits. Look around, my dear. Everything neat as a pin and polished to within an inch of its life. That will be at Timothy's insistence."

"You think?"

"Depend upon it. There is no one so pernickety as an aging, unmarried man."

"Indeed." I studied the room, curious about our hostess. A statue of a shepherdess carrying a lamb stood upon a bookshelf. It was lettered in gilt with the motto *A SOUVENIR OF LYME REGIS*. I had not realised they were so fond of their sheep in Lyme, and the shepherdess's expression was entirely vapid.

"That belongs to Timothy," Elspeth said as she came into the room bearing the steaming teapot. She lifted a cloth off a plate of freshly cut bread and butter and another of thinly sliced seedcake. "He is forever filling the room with bits and bobs and I am forever clearing them away."

I looked at the assorted bric-a-brac jostling with the shepherdess for pride of place. A model of Wellington's head, the articulated skeleton of a small bird, a spray of shells artfully arranged on a bit of driftwood, a broken ammonite. His interests seemed as varied as his taste was questionable, I decided.

"He has never even been to Lyme," she said as she settled in over the teapot. "He bought that at a sale of bric-a-brac at St. Frideswide's."

Augusta smiled. "James is entirely the same. The castle in Scotland is of course furnished completely in stag's heads and miles of tartan carpet, but he wants to do the same in the London house and it is all I can do to keep him from serving haggis to the guests."

They fell to gently abusing their menfolk while I sipped and munched contentedly at the bread and butter. There are few pastimes as uninteresting to me as listening to women complain, but it is often highly instructive. In this case, I learnt that in spite of Elspeth's frequent scolding, Timothy often forgot to change his muddy boots for slippers, spoiling three carpets this year alone. And I learnt that James could not be trusted to handle the ordering of the wines, no matter how often Augusta attempted to leave the matter in his hands.

"If it is not good Scots whisky, he has no interest whatsoever," she said in affectionate exasperation. "I could pour him out a measure of cough syrup and tell him it was the most exquisite vintage from Bordeaux and he would believe me. He simply has no palate."

I do not know what reply Elspeth made, for the cat had leapt to the mantelpiece and I went to scratch its chin. I am not usually fond of cats, but I had unwisely helped myself to a piece of rather foul seedcake and I thought a little sleight of hand might permit me to fling it into the fire undetected. I stood with my back to the others and dropped the cake into the fire as I raised my hand to pet the cat. It was a surefooted creature, for it had stepped around another collection of Timothy Gresham's miscellanea—a marble model of a child's hand, a bird's nest complete with ossified eggs. And then I saw it, tucked behind the nest, barely visible: a handful of small bones so distinctive I knew them at once.

They were the bones of a dinosaur.

CHAPTER

19

I pondered the implications of those bones as the conversation flowed gently past. They burbled on about village affairs and the demands on their time whilst I considered Timothy Gresham and his little bones. That they were ancient, I had no doubt, and I knew them to be the remnants of a prehistoric beast. Of what kind, I could not say. Dinosaurs had never held much fascination for me except as an abstraction. I preferred living creatures, particularly my beautiful butterflies that fluttered and flapped, animated and quixotic.

But these bones were of interest thanks to Lorenzo d'Ambrogio. Had they come from his specimen, excavated from the very cliff that had been the scene of his death?

I could not put the question to Elspeth without betraying my interest, and before I could devise a stratagem, Augusta rose, dusting her fingertips of crumbs.

"This has been so pleasant, Elspeth, but I know you must be longing to return to your handwork," she said with a nod towards a basket sitting on the sofa. It was filled with balls of thin yarn and four pointed needles which held the beginnings of a sock.

"Never enough hours in the day," Elspeth said a trifle wearily.

"I knocked at the dispensary, but Timothy was not in," Augusta told her.

Elspeth nodded. "A confinement case. Had him up before cock-crow and he still hasn't returned."

"Ah, well," Augusta said kindly. "Another time."

Elspeth guided us to the door. She had seemed animated enough when we arrived, but as she showed us out, her steps seemed to drag, and as soon as we were out of the gate, Augusta turned, shaking her head.

"I must admit to being rather too happy to take my leave of Wren Cottage," she said ruefully. "Does that make me dreadful?"

"The room was a trifle stuffy," I agreed.

"Not simply the room!" She dipped her head towards mine confidingly. "Elspeth is unhappy. And nothing poisons the atmosphere like an unhappy woman."

"Is she really as dissatisfied as all that?"

"My dear Veronica! Were you not listening? A lifetime of service to the villagers. Assisting Timothy, knitting and sewing and carrying beef tea to the infirm. Reading to the elderly."

"It is a very common life for a spinster in a country village," I said mildly.

"Indeed. And I wonder at what cost," she said. She put her arm through mine and we walked along the village road. "I wonder how different our lives would be if we were free to do as we pleased."

"But I do," I said.

She turned to me with an expression of real interest. "Tell me."

So I related to her the life I led, the voyages of exploration to secure specimens for my exacting clients, the work I did for Lord Rosemorran in his burgeoning museum, the private collections I assessed and repaired.

"And not without companionship," she ventured slyly.

I slanted her a look and she burst out laughing. "Forgive me. But I noticed a frisson between you and Stoker. And you make a devastatingly attractive couple. Is marriage in the cards?" she teased.

"It is not," I assured her. "I mean to keep my independence—as does he."

"There is so little security for us ladies. Do you not fear for your future?" Her voice was no longer gently mocking. She was concerned, sincerely so, and I appreciated her worry.

"I do not fear what I cannot control," I said stoutly. "I have taken care of myself since I was eighteen years of age. And I will do so as long as I am able. Beyond that, I cannot say."

"You are either very wise or very foolish," she said at length. "I wish I knew which."

"I wish I knew myself," I told her truthfully. "But I cannot be other than I am."

"It is astonishing to me that men think us such delicate and irrational creatures. You say you have known your own mind since you were a slip of a girl. As did I. We have never wavered from our convictions. We are not shifting sands or changeable weathercocks. We are women of principles," she said, warming to her theme. I had, in fact, wavered once and permitted myself the luxury of dependence upon a man who did not deserve it. The lesson had been a bitter one but perfectly learnt. I would not deviate again, for any man's sake.

"But they sit in judgment upon us like the lords of creation," she went on in the same tone of mild exasperation I had heard her use in conversation with Elspeth. "I confess, I do wonder sometimes what it must be like to be them, to go through life with such unerring confidence, such unquestioned supremacy. To make all decisions and never feel obliged to defend or discuss."

I smiled at her. "I think it is apparent how much Sir James defers to you," I said. "The London house is still furnished according to your taste, is it not? And the cellar full of drinkable wine?"

She laughed. "Very well. I do manage to get my way rather often, I will admit. James is easily talked round. But it is the *effort* I mind. How much simpler to devote oneself to one's pet interests instead of always having to justify what one does with one's time."

"And what are your pet interests?" I enquired.

"The needs of women," she said promptly. "Particularly those who have fallen from virtue. I have a house in Finsbury where girls who wish to leave the sinful trades are welcome and taught their letters and useful skills as well as Bible lessons. And I do other charity work, raising funds for an orphanage in Leeds and an asylum in Surrey—the one I wished to discuss with Timothy. I am keenly interested in the treatment of incurable insanity. It must be, above all, humane," she said firmly. "I would give all of them up in order to support suffragists if James would hear of it. But that is one cause to which I am not permitted to lend my name. He is utterly apoplectic at the very idea." Her smile turned suddenly conspiratorial. "I did manage to donate twenty pounds by telling him it was for an anti-vivisection society, but you mustn't tell him."

I twisted my fingers against my lips as if turning a lock. "Your secret is safe with me."

She tipped her head like a bright bird, assessing me with those lovely eyes. "You are a breath of fresh air to me, Veronica. An absolute tonic. I am very glad to have made a new friend."

I considered the paucity of such friendships in my life and discovered I was glad to have met her as well.

"Come," she urged. "Let us hurry back to Cherboys. I am in need of a proper cup of tea."

"Thank you, but no. I mean to explore the village a little more. Oh, I quite forgot—how is the count after his bee sting?"

She made a little gesture of dismissal. "Still moaning, the last I saw. But I gave Beatrice the oil of lavender and I have no doubt it will help him. I only hope he is recovered by dinner. Tiberius has promised us a spectacle!"

She left me then, waving her hand in farewell as she turned to the shortcut through the Cherboys woods and I started around the duck pond. I ended at the churchyard attached to St. Frideswide's. This was a burying ground of some obvious antiquity, the engraving of the stones smoothed by the hand of age. Soft grass carpeted the ground, and thick layers of moss crept up the draperies of the various statues. Most of the stones were carved into simple designs of crosses or left as granite slabs, but a few were more elaborate confections of marble lace, inscribed with the names of the prominent families of the area.

But one family's preeminence stood out from the rest. In the center of the graveyard was a stone edifice, a mausoleum executed in the Neo-Gothic style. The ironwork that formed the fence around it was picked out in fresh black paint, and the brass embellishments were carefully polished. I knew what the name over the door would be before I even stepped near enough to read it. *TEMPLETON-VANE*. I touched the door, but it was locked, and I was not certain if that came as a relief or a disappointment.

Above the door was chiselled the family motto: *NULLAE EXCUSATIONES. NULLAE PAENITENTIAE.* No excuses. No repentance. A list of the tenants of the mausoleum had been inscribed on a bronze plaque and fixed to the door. A few assorted viscounts and their wives had been interred within at the start of the century, but two names were much brighter than the rest, the letters sharply incised. Stoker's mother, Annabelle, was the first. Below hers was that of her husband, dead only these three years past. I read the name and blinked, then read it again. I had seen Stoker's name written formally on a handful of occasions. The Honourable Revelstoke V. Templeton-Vane. I had never asked what the "V" stood for, but as I read his putative father's given name for the first time, I found myself smiling. I tucked the information away for future use and turned to go.

As I moved down the pair of marble steps, I knocked against a small vase of late summer roses, upending it onto the ground. I hastened to put it right, noticing the small note tucked into the petals of one lush bloom. *For Mamma*. The handwriting was similar to Stoker's but rounder, younger, and I cast an indulgent look towards the church itself. Merry might be a man fully grown, but he had been a child at his mother's death, and it was apparent he still felt the loss most keenly.

Well, it would not do to disarrange his lovely token of remembrance, and I scrambled about, retrieving the flowers. One had fallen a little further than the others, caught in a bit of long grass. I reached for it and grazed my hand upon a stone half-hid by the greenery. Unlike most stones, it was plain to the point of austerity. No graven angels here, only the name, writ in stark capitals. ***LORENZO D'AMBROGIO***. And the date of his death. The Templeton-Vanes had given him a resting place, I realised. But he had died violently, and I wondered how restful he had found his afterlife. Stoker regularly chided me for entertaining such thoughts, but as I had pointed out to him with considerable patience, germ theory had been a far-fetched notion until it was proven. The most outlandish ideas might have merit, even if science occasionally proved laggard in confirming them.

As if to echo my fanciful turn of mind, a soft susurration of wind ruffled the grass, rustling it uneasily. A prickle rose along the back of my neck, and the afternoon, which had been decidedly hot, turned suddenly cool.

A cloud passing over the sun, I told myself firmly. But there was no accounting for the feeling of being watched. I crouched there, bent over Lorenzo's stone, as voices suddenly reached my ears. I glanced in the direction of the church, perfectly concealed from view but able to see the door open. From the dim interior two figures emerged into the porch, quite close together. One was Merry, his head bent low to the other, slighter form at his side. A gloved hand came up to touch his cheek, and even at that distance I sensed him blushing. The woman with him never turned, never sensed my presence. She did not tarry but lowered her veil and left him. He stood, staring after her as she went, before lifting his shoulders in a sigh and turning to go back inside.

I stayed crouched there for some minutes, until I was quite certain Merryweather was gone. And then I got to my feet and made to follow Beatrice.

CHAPTER 20

I trailed the countess, soft-footed as a lynx—walking quietly is a skill one must hone early as a lepidopterist; a startled butterfly is a lost opportunity. But even if I had crashed through the shrubberies with the unsubtle energy of *Diceros bicornis*, I doubt she would have heard me. She seemed lost in thought, her footsteps slowing and then speeding up again. Her perambulations were not, I surmised, undertaken with any sort of purpose or design. She was simply making her way back to Cherboys in a leisurely fashion.

It was no great effort to follow her. In fact, she moved so glacially that at one point I stopped behind an accommodating oak to eat another of Julien's delectable sandwiches. When I resumed my surveillance, she was hardly further along than when I began, pausing now and again as if puzzling something out. I might have thought her distracted by the beauties of the surroundings—the trees were beleafed in green newly tinged with gold, and the late summer flowers were still offering themselves in lush-throated abandon. Even the clouds were engaging, soft and pillowy white, the sort of clouds to coax a romantic soul into lying out on the grassy Downs, imagining shapes hidden amongst them.

But the countess showed no interest in these. She kept her gaze fixed firmly ahead as she passed quite near to my place of concealment in a handy bit of bramble. A notably pretty Silver-Washed Fritillary—*Argynnis paphia*—swooped by in a slow arch of orange wings, but I refused to be diverted. Beatrice was not so single-minded. Her expression was one of complete distraction. She was not diverted by the bounty of the natural world because she simply did not perceive it. She was woolgathering, building castles in Spain, and it was this activity which caused her to pause now and again as she turned over some troubling thought.

I am not, as the casual reader may wonder, gifted with clairvoyance. I could not read her mental wanderings or hear the inner workings of her mind. But I am, by virtue of my occupation, a keen observer, and I noticed that every time Beatrice stopped, she raised her hand to her mouth, nibbling the corner of one thumbnail. A tiny furrow etched itself above her nose as she did so, marring the smoothness of her brow. After each reverie, she would gather herself with a little shake and move on. She was, it was apparent, working something out within herself, and I did not much care for the obvious inference: to wit, that she was debating the merits of engaging in a dalliance with young Merryweather.

The most obvious construction to put upon what I had seen was that Beatrice, as a lady suffering from a devastating illness, had sought spiritual counsel with the nearest source. But I dismissed this possibility at once on the grounds of her rosary. I could not imagine a Roman Catholic turning to an Anglican vicar for clerical consolation.

As any scientist knows, hypotheses are made to be discarded. They are *working* suppositions, the beginnings of frameworks that may lead much more easily, and far more often, to failure. They are slender and insubstantial things, light as will-o'-the-wisps and designed to collapse at the first incongruous fact. Anything that does not fit within the hypothesis must be discarded. But to begin with, the facts must be assembled to see if a pattern may be detected.

So I settled onto a comfortable patch of moss and assembled my facts. First, Beatrice was a lovely woman, and men are vulnerable to the allure of physical attractions. Some, particularly clerics, are not, but I knew Merryweather well enough to know that he was a normal red-blooded fellow in all essential regards and therefore susceptible to the temptations of the flesh.

Was the little American countess likewise attracted? Possibly. Like all the Templeton-Vane men, Merry possessed the physical attributes one might find in the recovered statues of Greek antiquity. He might be untidy and shamblesome, but he had strong shoulders and sturdy thighs as well as a certain regularity of feature and vitality that is extremely attractive to the right sort of woman.

Ah, but Beatrice was a devoted wife, I hear the faithful reader object! Yet even the most accomplished adulteress may conceal her sins beneath a veneer of affection for her spouse, I reflected. In fact, a cunning woman would make a point of behaving with tenderness to her legitimate spouse in order to throw off any suspicions that she harboured feelings elsewhere. Was Beatrice capable of such machinations? I could not say. Our acquaintance was of a brief duration, but she was American and, in my experience, Americans are capable of anything.

No, I could not say with any certainty what her designs upon Merry were, but she would bear watching, I decided firmly.

I rose from my musings with a brisk air and continued on my way.

As I made my way up the staircase at Cherboys, a heavy silence pressed upon me from all sides. It was the curious hour after teatime and before the dressing bell when households are invariably scattered to the winds. I had little doubt the others were out on the estate, enjoying the lazy, golden afternoon. The maids would have long since finished in the guest rooms and it was not yet time for them to reappear to assist with collars and clasps as we prepared for dinner. It was, in short, a perfect time for a little sleuthing.

I was convinced that Sir James had received a set of cuttings, and I longed to know what they said. It rankled that Stoker and Tiberius had introduced the subject of the cuttings when the ladies were absent from the dining room. It more than rankled, I decided. It was manifestly unjust to use our gender against us when they were the ones who enforced the archaic custom of withdrawing. They deserved to be pipped at the post, and by whatever means necessary. I might have deputised J. J. to investigate Sir James' room—in her guise as a maid, she could devise a far more plausible reason to be in his suite than I—but I defended my decision to go on my own on the grounds that J. J. would be needed in the kitchens as Julien worked feverishly upon his dinner party menu.

In truth, I did not want to miss one atom of the possible delights of an investigation. I placed my butterfly hunting kit in my room and stepped out of my boots and into a pair of soft slippers. On silent feet, I slipped from my room and up the stairs to the suite assigned to the MacIvers, closing the door softly behind me. The rooms were, unsurprisingly, neat as a pin. Mrs. Brackendale ran the tightest of ships, and I pitied any member of staff who left behind an errant crumb or bit of dust. There was a bathroom with all the appropriate furniture, the porcelain polished to a high sheen, and a fresh bath mat laid upon the floor. Sir James' shaving things were laid tidily on a stand next to the sink, and a new cake of soap had been left beside the bath. There was nothing to be learnt from this room, so I moved on to the dressing room where the dressing table held an assortment of Augusta's toilet waters and powders and a tin of rose lip salve. I smiled at this small evidence of vanity. Augusta was so self-possessed it was amusing to find she had any foibles at all. The drawers of the dressing table were empty, clear of even traces of powder, so thorough were the maids.

Wardrobes had been assigned to each of them. Augusta's held a few handsome evening frocks and assorted sensible country clothes for day, everything neatly in its place. Sir James' wardrobe was just as orderly, each shoe arranged with its mate, each suit brushed to gleaming perfection. One of the drawers held a small leather folio of the sort gentlemen use to carry papers, but a swift glance through it yielded nothing of interest. Letters from his man of business regarding land issues, tenant rents, and a frankly appalling amount of information about sheep.

But no cuttings. If Sir James had received them, he had either destroyed them or carried them about on his person. Or, I realised in some annoyance, he might have left them in Scotland for safekeeping. He would hardly want Augusta to come upon them unexpectedly.

I closed the wardrobe with a decisive snap. There remained only the bedside tables to be searched, and I found no clue in these. Augusta's reading tastes tended towards modern novels of the moralising sort and a few fashion papers whilst the table on Sir James' side of the bed held only periodicals devoted to animal husbandry.

It had been a pointless endeavour to search their room, I realised in annoyance. Possessions can be an eloquent testimony to a person's character, but in the case of the MacIvers, they told me nothing I did not already know. Augusta was tidy and philanthropic; Sir James had no real interests apart from his estate.

Unless Sir James MacIver was playing a careful and canny game. I paused to consider the implications. He never confirmed he had received cuttings; only his evasive manner had convinced me that he had. *But what if he had sent the cuttings to Tiberius himself?* If he were our villain, he might well have sent Tiberius the threatening cuttings, assuming Tiberius would be too alarmed to raise the subject in front of the rest of the house party. The fact that Tiberius had done so would have come as a surprise. Quick thinking would have suggested that he ought to bluff it out, insisting gruffly that it must be a tasteless joke, all the while subtly insinuating that he himself was also a recipient. It was a clever solution, fiendishly so. It would require an ingenious brain as well as a sophisticated knowledge of human nature to execute.

And one had to ask, did Sir James possess any of those qualities? He presented himself as a hearty Scotsman, more concerned with the welfare of his sheep than anything of real import, but perhaps that was a useful bit of chicanery. After all, his estate was apparently profitable even in our challenging times when many of the old aristocratic families were experiencing difficulties. Once the source of limitless wealth, the land was no longer a dependable means of earning money. Real profits were made through technology and commerce while forestry, fields, and mines limped along, bringing in far less than they had once done. Sir James clearly possessed a good head for management if his sheep were earning well. Did those skills translate to murder? And if so, what had been his motive? Why seek vengeance on behalf of Lorenzo d'Ambrogio? Was there some connection between them as yet unexplored? They had spent time together as young men, but according to Tiberius, Lorenzo's great passion had been his fossils, a passion shared by Kaspar von Hochstaden, not James MacIver. Had their passion been of another variety? Lorenzo had been, by all accounts, an extremely handsome young man, and he had travelled in James' company for many months. James might have developed an unrequited affection for Lorenzo. Or perhaps an actual tendresse had sprung up, a love affair that James could not pursue, hampered as he was by his engagement to Augusta—an engagement arranged by their parents, I remembered. If he loved Lorenzo and had reason to believe his paramour had been murdered, seeking out the killer to exact vengeance was entirely reasonable.

I glanced around the suite. Elegant, like all the rooms at Cherboys, and giving absolutely nothing away. If there had been some attachment between James and Lorenzo, there was no proof of it. It was one of a few dozen reasonable hypotheses I could have offered as to who our villain might be and why. There were simply too many variables at present, and my little investigation had done nothing to eliminate any of them.

I made my way back to my room in a state of mild irritation. The scientific mind is never cast down by a lack of success. Failure is very often as instructive as victory, but in this case it meant a waste of time when I might have been comparing notes with J. J. I had high hopes she had learnt something of use belowstairs, but a quick glance at the clock revealed I would have no chance to ask her before the dinner bell. My musings had caused me to tarry longer than I had intended in the MacIvers' suite, and it was the purest luck I had not been discovered.

Happily, no one was about as I hastened down the back stairs—explaining why I had been on the floor above my room would take considerable ingenuity. I reached my bedchamber undetected and was just congratulating myself when I heard the door of the suite next to mine shut. The Salviatis, I realised. If Beatrice or Pietro had just returned, they might well have seen me darting about, looking furtive.

I eased my door open and peered out through the crack. I could see only a sliver of the corridor, but I caught a flash of black skirt and white apron. I eased the door open a little wider and saw an enormous white mobcap with streaming ribbons trailing behind. It was a maid, heading in the opposite direction to mine, taking the back stairs.

"J. J.," I muttered as I closed the door. That much was apparent by the colour of her dress, kitchen black instead of the smart blue of the chambermaids. She had clearly been sleuthing abovestairs in direct contravention of our agreement. No doubt she intended to steal a march on me by discovering some bit of tittle-tattle she could flog in her despicable newspaper.

Very well, I decided. If that was the game she meant to play, we would no longer be partners. With Stoker ranged with Tiberius and J. J. acting in her own interests, I was clearly on my own. I felt a thrust of emotion I had not felt in a long while. *Loneliness.* I had grown accustomed to having friends, partners, compatriots. It was a testimony to how important they had become to my happiness that I felt so wretchedly adrift without them.

I stiffened my spine and my resolve. If they did not wish to stand with me, I would stand alone.

And I would beat them all.

CHAPTER

21

I made a swift but careful toilette for the evening, surveying my simple hairstyle and violet taffeta gown with satisfaction. I had little doubt the countess and Augusta would present themselves in the first order of fashion and dripping in jewels, but I did not mind. Let other women compete for compliments. I was content with a single gown of excellent material and superb cut, ornamented only with a small spray of hothouse violets pinned into my hair.

We assembled in the drawing room, where the Greshams joined the house party and Collins was pouring champagne with a decidedly reluctant air. I took the proffered coupe from him and edged towards Tiberius.

"Why does Collins look as if he has been sucking lemons?" I murmured.

"He does not approve of serving champagne before dinner," Tiberius returned in a low voice. "He thinks it debauched."

"How in the name of all that is holy has he endured in your service without a taste for debauchery?" I enquired.

"He has hopes of reforming me," Tiberius replied with a smile. But it was nothing like his usual expression of amusement. There was a watchfulness about his eyes, a wariness that told me he was more concerned than he cared to admit. Whatever he intended for this night, it weighed upon him, I realised. I pressed his hand swiftly and he raised a brow into a perfect Gothic arch.

"I am not so unnerved as to require bolstering, although the effort is appreciated," he said solemnly. I eyed his glass and he smiled again, this time in genuine amusement. "I watched Collins open it myself and my glass has not been unattended, I assure you. Do you mean to sample my food at dinner as well?"

"Mock me if you please, but you will think yourself well served if I do indeed save your life," I informed him loftily.

He raised his glass in a silent toast as he moved away.

The others had assembled by then and he waited in silence until all were served. "My dear guests, I wish this evening to be a memorable one," he said slowly, resting his gaze in turn upon each of them. "Come. I have prepared for you an experience you will not soon forget."

Tiberius led the way out the garden door. I surveyed the party, but Stoker was not to be found. I suspected he was awaiting us in the garden, as nervous as an expectant father as he prepared to unveil his masterpiece. Along the rose alley, long silken banners had been hung to waft in the breeze. The hard heat of the day had softened as the evening settled over the estate. The air was heavy with the fragrance of the roses, the petals trodden under our feet as we walked, chattering excitedly. At the end of the alley and through the gate, we came to the edge of the lake. The setting sun turned the water to golden fire, and floating on its shining surface were a miniature flotilla. To the rowboat had been added a Venetian gondola, a tiny Chinese junk hung with lanterns, and a Greek trireme scarcely larger than a rowboat.

Tiberius divided us into groups—I travelled with Sir James and the count in the trireme—and we were rowed across to the island by masked youths. It made for a lovely picture, the little fleet moving slowly over the glassy lake, each carrying one lady and a male companion or two. Beatrice wore a gown of flame silk, cleverly cut to suggest the movement of a fire. Enormous opals nestled in her hair and at her ears, and she was a stunning contrast to Augusta's ensemble, an elegant affair of heavy oyster duchesse satin embroidered with clever little motifs of stylised thistles. She wore her pearls again, but this time they were augmented with several extra ropes and a small coronet. Even Elspeth had made an effort, wearing black satin and a cluster of her pretty pink roses tucked in her décolletage. Music filled the air, something sprightly—Vivaldi, perhaps—and for a moment I forgot entirely the danger at hand, revelling instead in the brief magic Tiberius had conjured for us. Only one thing was missing, and I found myself sitting forward eagerly as the trireme touched the opposite shore. Stoker would be here.

We pushed through the banks of willows just as the last rays of the sun died, emerging into the clearing in the center of the island. The garden had been set with cressets, the flames flaring up in a breeze scented by the sea. Amidst the torches, entertainers strolled, jugglers and fire-eaters lending a carnival atmosphere. And in the circle of the torches sat the Megalosaurus, the back open, the eyes gleaming with fire. Stoker had created a masterpiece. The beast, once a great lumpen thing of papier-mâché, now crouched in the shadows, expectant, predatory, the great mouth gaping open to reveal a crimson maw, hungry and shining damply in the fitful light from Stoker's deft applications of various varnishes. It was hideous and magnificent, and I heard the assembled gasps and exclamations as we beheld what Stoker had wrought. He waited at the foot of the small set of stairs leading up to the heart of the creature, extending a hand to assist as each of the guests climbed inside. He had trimmed his hair for the occasion and he was freshly shaven, smelling deliciously of verbena soap and his own ineffable scent. The extensive work on the Megalosaurus must have taxed the strength of his eye, for he wore his patch, but the effect was not unattractive. In fact, the patch, coupled with the glint of the golden earrings in his lobes, put me in mind of a swaggering Elizabethan privateer.

"Well done," I murmured to him as I passed into the belly of the beast. He gave me a grave nod. He might have been proud of his work, but he was not looking forward to the evening with any enthusiasm. Knowing Tiberius as I did, I could well imagine how he intended to confront his house party, and knowing Stoker as I did, I could anticipate his reaction.

But Stoker said nothing as we took our seats. Tiberius himself had arranged the table placement, fixing the elegantly penned place cards with his own hand. The table was narrow of necessity, for the Megalosaurus was not wide, but we squeezed into place with good-natured jostling and a bit of care. To Tiberius' right was Pietro. Next to the count sat Stoker, and then came Augusta. Beatrice was at my right, next to Merry, with Elspeth on his other side, squeezed in beside James. Timothy rounded out the party, sitting to my left. It was an odd arrangement, owing much to imagination and nothing to etiquette. But I saw at once what Tiberius had done. He had placed the other Sinners in nearest proximity to himself for greater ease of observation when he launched whatever stratagems he meant to employ. Merry, Timothy, and Elspeth were innocent bystanders in the affair, but Stoker and I were well-placed for our own observations. Our eyes met across the table and I felt a shiver, a goose walking over my grave, as the countryfolk say. But something ominous hung in the air, a sense of foreboding, and I did not like it.

As soon as we had settled ourselves, Tiberius rang a tiny crystal bell that had been placed at his elbow. Instantly, staff appeared bearing delicate cups of consommé. Usually, only footmen served at table, but I looked up, shocked to see J. J. placing my consommé before me.

"Miss," she murmured almost inaudibly, her cap pulled low for concealment.

"What are you doing here, Judas?" I hissed.

"Too small in here for the footmen, so maids were asked," she replied in the same low voice. "And what are you on about, calling me Judas?"

"Later," I said flatly.

She waggled her brows at me—I should have to speak firmly to her about using another means of communication—and I surmised from this that she intended to use the opportunity to study the guests. I darted a quick glance at Stoker, but he had not noticed J. J. and I intended to ensure he remained ignorant of her presence. If Stoker knew she were at Cherboys, he would shout the place down, perhaps even insisting she be sent back to London. For all that he liked J. J., he was occasionally very much a Templeton-Vane, and I suspected he would place Tiberius' privacy above J. J.'s. need for gainful employment. Besides, as irritated as I was with J. J., I still had hopes of extracting information from her. With an animal's instinct for self-preservation, she eluded Stoker's gaze and ducked away to serve Pietro.

I turned my attention to the consommé. It was lightly flavoured with mushroom, and a quick glance at the evening's menu showed the theme was one of autumnal bounty.

We spooned up the light broth and Augusta exclaimed, "How delicious! One expects mushrooms in this season, but these are so refined."

"Local to Cherboys," Tiberius explained. "I have a chef down from London for the dinner, and he has used much of our own produce apart from a few treats—such as your own grouse, Augusta," he added with a nod of acknowledgment.

Sir James guffawed. "Her grouse indeed! Augusta hasn't bagged a grouse in fifteen years."

"I do not care for the killing of things," she said with a shrug.

"But your grouse shoots are famous," the count put in.

Augusta smiled. "One must make allowances for the interests of one's guests. Give any Englishman a patch of open land and he must have a shotgun to blast away at something."

"Englishman, Scotsman, German, Italian, Frenchman, we are all the same," Pietro replied with a disarming grin. "We must be masters of all we survey."

"Hear, hear," Sir James agreed.

"'And thou shalt have dominion over the beasts of the land,'" murmured Timothy.

"Come again?" Sir James coaxed, looking slightly confused.

Augusta addressed her husband. "Timothy was quoting Genesis, James. Beasts of the land."

"Ah yes," her husband agreed. "Dominion over every living thing— they that walketh, they that crawleth, they that swimmeth. Is that right, Padre?" he asked with a glance to Merry.

"Near enough," Merryweather replied pleasantly.

"The covenant of the Almighty with mankind," Timothy put in. "To us is given authority over all living things."

Merry kept his lips pressed tightly together, no doubt biting back a pithy remark, but Stoker had no such scruples. "You mean to say you interpret the Bible literally?" he asked in a tone anyone might have mistaken for friendliness. But I saw the amusement in his eyes and realised he was merely laying a trap.

Timothy Gresham's expression was one of complete earnestness. "Indeed I do, Revelstoke." In spite of Tiberius' encouragement to be casual with one another, the doctor maintained a formality quite at odds with the bonhomie of Sir James or the courtly amiability of the count. He was not, I reminded myself, one of the Seven Sinners. Perhaps he felt the chasm which must extend between a simple country doctor and the group of accomplished and travelled gentlemen who had befriended him. And if he did, did he resent it? I watched him with greater attention as he listened to Stoker's questions.

"Then you believe there is a specific time and date at which the world began?" Stoker continued in a dangerously polite voice.

"Eight p.m., October the twenty-third, 4004 BC," Gresham replied with perfect assurance.

"You cannot be serious," Stoker said flatly.

Two spots of bright colour flared high in Timothy's cheeks. "Indeed I am, sir," he said, obviously offended. "The Scriptures are entirely clear upon the point."

"They bloody well are not," Stoker began.

Tiberius rang his bell again, cutting Stoker off before he could build a head of steam. The bowls of consommé were cleared with deft precision, and under the soft clicking sounds of porcelain and silver, Beatrice turned to me. "Men," she murmured.

I smothered a laugh and she grinned in return. I half expected Tiberius to introduce a less controversial topic over the following course, but the subject of the origins of the Earth suited him quite well, I realised as he merely turned with an air of expectancy towards Timothy Gresham as we lifted our forks and applied ourselves to plates of fried soles with parsley sauce.

"You were saying, Timothy?" Beatrice said, widening her eyes innocently. She was a minx, I realised, as proven by her eagerness for gossip during our earlier conversation. And now it amused her to provoke the doctor—or Stoker.

Timothy placed his fork carefully upon the edge of his plate. "I was merely observing that in spite of what the scientists would have us believe," he said, laying emphasis upon the word "scientists" as if it were something scandalous, "that the Bible is perfectly clear upon the length of time that has transpired since creation."

"But *you* are a scientist," Pietro pointed out.

"I am a physician," Gresham said stiffly. "I do not meddle with the divine truths."

"And you believe Adam and Eve were real people?" Stoker asked, once more adopting a tone of easy affability. "And that we are all descended from both of them?"

"Certainly," Timothy said.

"And their sons?" Stoker went on.

"Of course."

"So we are all products of ince—"

"Stoker," Tiberius put in lazily. "Pas devant les femmes."

"But this femme finds it most interesting," Beatrice assured him with a mischievous smile. "It is indeed as Stoker says. If we are all descended from Adam and Eve, then we must therefore be descended from the union of their son with their daughter. What other explanation can there be?"

She looked around the table, colour high and eyes shining as she waited for an answer. I had heard more than once of the propensity of American ladies towards outrageous and provoking dinner conversation, and Beatrice seemed determined not to let the reputation of her countrywomen down. This gift for sparking intriguing debate was a quality that endeared the Americans to the Prince of Wales, according to Augusta. If His Royal Highness were ever invited to sit at one's table, a lady could do no better than provide him with a partner from across the pond. He loved nothing so much as being mildly scandalised, and judging from the canary-fed cat expression on Tiberius' face, he was much the same.

The count smiled indulgently at his wife's conversational gambit while Augusta tactfully applied herself to her fish and Elspeth studied her plate. Timothy looked faintly apoplectic, and Stoker and Merry were regarding Beatrice with respectful looks.

Sir James laughed aloud. "Very good, my dear. Very good indeed," he said, raising his glass in her direction. He swivelled to fix an eye upon Timothy Gresham. "You have seen the fossils, man. You know perfectly well that Earth is *millions* of years old."

"Blasphemy," Timothy said with obvious distaste.

"Blasphemy! Look around you, Timothy. We are sitting inside a bloody great dinosaur. How do you think that happened?"

"It isn't *real*, you know," Gresham reminded him coldly.

"No, but it is based upon something real," Tiberius said suddenly. He spread his hand expansively. "This is what Lorenzo's fossil would have looked like if it had been saved."

Sir James gaped at him. "You mean, if we could have recovered it, we might have assembled it properly and it would have looked like *this*?"

His gesture sent one of the candles from the candelabra in the center of the table free, sparks flying upwards. Augusta gasped and Beatrice gave a little shriek.

Stoker said something far more blasphemous than anything else we had heard as he dove to extinguish the sparks. He spent a hectic few seconds stamping and smothering before resuming his seat. "This whole bloody thing is covered in flammable varnish," he warned us. "Another escapade like that and it will go up with all of us inside it."

Sir James muttered an apology, looking a little abashed, but Tiberius seemed entirely pleased with how events were transpiring. He rang for the next course and we sampled another of Julien's creations, a ballotine of poussin. He was gifted as any other artist, and the fact that his medium was food, to be consumed and never entirely replicated, was bittersweet. The impermanence of his masterpieces was a considerable part of their majesty. I gave myself up to the sumptuous plateful and noticed Beatrice was suppressing little moans as she ate. I watched her from time to time to gauge her reactions to Merry, but whatever had passed between them in the church, they seemed nothing more than polite acquaintances at the table. Beatrice, I suspected, could engage in a little social duplicity, but Merry was as disingenuous as a baby rabbit. If he harboured any unsuitable feelings for her, he would never be able to conceal them, and he most definitely would not be able to devote himself so single-mindedly to his chicken. Still, I was determined to discover what their tête-à-tête had been about, and resolved then to run Merry to ground and force the truth from him by whatever means necessary.

The conversation turned general as we made our way through the roast and game courses—saddle of beef and then the MacIver grouse—before Tiberius took charge of the discussion once more. J. J. continued to serve discreetly, but her eyes were attentive, and I was certain she was making mental notes of everything.

"I am glad you introduced the topic of Lorenzo's fossil, James," Tiberius began smoothly. He had not touched his plate but instead held his wineglass up to the light, scrutinising the colour as it shaded to paleness at the meniscus. "It is, in fact, because of Lorenzo that I asked all of you here."

We had just started on the sweet course—a jellied and creamed apricot concoction of Julien's that would have merited a knighthood had he served it at Windsor Castle—when Tiberius rose to his feet and cleared his throat. Collins quietly poured out champagne at the sideboard and placed a coupe in front of each of us. Delicate bubbles raced upwards through the pale straw-coloured wine, and I could smell the crystal-sharp fragrance as each burst on the surface.

Our attention turned to Tiberius, and silence, taut and expectant, settled over the table. He raised his coupe. "I should like to propose a toast to absent friends, specifically Lorenzo d'Ambrogio."

No one spoke as he went on. "There are a few of you—Veronica, Beatrice—who never met Lorenzo, so this may possibly bore you. And four of you—Stoker and Merryweather, Timothy and Elspeth—who can only remember him vaguely. But, James, Pietro"—he raised his glass to each in turn as he named them—"we knew him. He was a brother to us. And we knew Kaspar and Alexandre and Benedict as well. Our dear friends, taken from us too soon. We must toast their memory," he added, pausing for us all to respond and drink with him.

"Dreadful business," James said quietly, looking thoroughly uncomfortable as most British men do when confronted by actual emotion.

"Gone too soon to the arms of their Maker," Timothy added sententiously.

The count crossed himself and said something in Italian—or perhaps Latin. He was not near enough for me to hear him clearly, but the intention was apparent. He was blessing their memories.

"Indeed gone too soon and, yes, an entirely dreadful business," Tiberius agreed. He paused again for dramatic effect. "But then murder usually is."

CHAPTER

22

The response to Tiberius' announcement was shocked silence. Merry gaped and Stoker's brows drew together in a forbidding line whilst the countess stared in wide-eyed astonishment. Augusta's sangfroid did not desert her. It was a point of honour for some ladies to appear unruffled at any provocation, and she did not fail to rise to the challenge. She merely looked serenely at Tiberius and waited for him to continue, while Pietro flushed angrily. The Greshams exchanged puzzled glances. Only Sir James made a noise—a grunt of annoyance.

"I told you last night this was in bad taste," he began.

Augusta turned to her husband. "Last night?"

Sir James waved her off. "Nothing to trouble you with, my dear. Tiberius has a bee in his bonnet is all." He turned to Tiberius with a meaningful look. "I told you, this is rubbish, and far beneath your dignity as a gentleman."

Beatrice cut in sharply. "I don't understand, Tiberius. What are you talking about?"

Tiberius did not look directly at her as he spoke but slowly swept his gaze around the table. "Twenty years ago, we enjoyed a house party very like this one. Some of the faces were different," he said with a glance at me. "But most of you were here. Most of you knew Lorenzo d'Ambrogio and you remember his tragic end."

He paused and Elspeth shook her head. "But you said *murder.* What did you mean by that?"

Timothy made a quelling gesture to quieten her, but Tiberius replied.

"I meant, Elspeth, that someone does not believe Lorenzo's death was an accident," he said pleasantly. "That someone is clearly in pursuit of vengeance, and has begun murdering the ones they hold responsible." He paused and looked around the table. "Us."

"But, my friend, your own father was the—what is the word for the English official?" Pietro turned questioning eyes to the rest of the table.

"Magistrate?" I suggested.

"Sì. The magistrate," he said, labouring to pronounce the syllables distinctly. "It was the late Lord Templeton-Vane who decided it was an accident, and of course it must be so."

"Pietro, my father, like all aristocrats, had a habit of bending justice to his will. The verdict returned was the one he insisted upon. He was involved in covering up the true cause of Lorenzo's death."

"Murder." On Elspeth Gresham's lips the word became a thrilled whisper.

"Murder," Tiberius said, inclining his head.

"For god's sake," Stoker muttered. I understood his annoyance. Tiberius' intention was clear: to set the cat amongst the pigeons by introducing the notion that Lorenzo had been murdered to the entire party, but it was a thoroughly foolish stratagem. Almost as foolish as inviting a houseful of prospective murderers to stay, I reflected. But I had encouraged the idea, and I ought to have remembered that Tiberius was very much his own man and would always do precisely as he pleased.

Augusta was pale but composed, the trembling of her earrings the only sign that she was upset. Beatrice's complexion had gone spectrally white, and the men seemed to be struggling with various states of outrage, anger, disbelief, and horror.

Tiberius went on. "I showed these to the gentlemen last night, but I think we do an injustice to the ladies not to include them in our discussion. You see, it isn't just Lorenzo's possible murder that concerns us. It is the recent deaths of Kaspar von Hochstaden and Alexandre du Plessis."

Augusta turned in obvious puzzlement. "Kaspar? Alexandre? You mean the others who were here that summer?"

"Indeed," Tiberius confirmed. "Both of them dead within the last few months, and—I have reason to believe—by the hand of Lorenzo's avenger."

Shocked silence reigned for a moment until Tiberius produced the infamous cuttings from his breast pocket. He opened them and handed each to Sir James with a motion that he should pass them around the table. Sir James flung them aside, lips working furiously in silence as Tiberius continued to speak. "Benedict Tyrell's death, occurring as it did, many years ago and under tragic circumstances, does not concern us. His end was unfortunate, but incontrovertibly the result of his missionary activities. We need consider him no more. However, these are obituaries for Alexandre and Kaspar. Please observe the annotations in the margin. It is apparent that although Alexandre and Kaspar appeared to have died from natural causes, they were both, in fact, murdered. And the assassin wishes me to be the next."

The cuttings made their way around the table. Having studied them at length in Bavaria, Stoker and I merely handed them on. Merry looked thoroughly distressed and could scarcely bring himself to touch them, while Timothy Gresham seemed to take a bit too much interest in handling the pages. His colour rose and his rabbity little nose twitched in anticipation of some new drama. Elspeth seemed more composed, although she hurried through the reading, while Augusta studied the cuttings with care, murmuring a low imprecation. Beatrice's expression was one of horror, although I caught a flash of what may have been something sharper—interest? Excitement even? It was not pleasant to think that anyone could view the situation as intriguing, but it was easy to imagine Beatrice holding court at a dinner party in some grand Manhattan mansion, relating the entire affair to an enthralled audience. It would indeed make for scandalously good conversation, I realised, so long as one did not know the victims.

But her husband showed more delicacy. Pietro read the pages slowly, twice, before placing them carefully onto the table, his expression thoughtful.

Pietro spoke. "So you invited us here to warn us?"

"Something like that," Tiberius said with a grim smile. "After all, if I am next, then it follows that the rest of you are in peril as well. And forewarned is forearmed. You see, my friends, I did not invite you here to celebrate the memory of those we have lost. I invited you to discover once and for all who murdered Lorenzo d'Ambrogio."

Edwin Booth could not have managed a more dramatic delivery. Tiberius stood, elegant and exquisitely groomed, in the middle of that enormous beast, the rib cage forming gleaming red walls around us, the entire scene lit by the guttering glow of candles. If anyone had captured the image in a photograph, it would have looked like Lucifer himself had taken to entertaining.

And the expression on his face would have done justice to that fierce and princely fallen angel. He was angry, righteously so, and he did not scorn to show it.

Sir James guffawed in obvious disbelief as Augusta pursed her lips, clearly feeling the entire evening in poor taste. Beatrice said nothing, but her hand had gone to her mouth and she kept her eyes fixed upon her plate. Elspeth shook her head in silent denial.

The others were not so circumspect. Merry, clearly overcome by the pure drama of the moment, burst out laughing. Gresham began a lengthy oration on the evils of wicked talk, while the count began declaiming vehemently in Italian. Stoker and I exchanged glances. Clearly Tiberius believed his approach was the best, but it would have been helpful if he had at least given a warning that he meant to toss a bomb into the proceedings.

Tiberius held up his hands. "Be quiet. Timothy, it is not idle gossip but reasonable conjecture based upon the facts. Pietro, you would do well to remember that we have slander laws here in England. And, Merryweather, if you do not cease that *noise* this instant, I will have Stoker sew your lips together and I cannot think it will take much persuading."

Merry gaped. "But you cannot be serious with your assumptions, Tiberius."

"As the grave," his eldest brother assured him.

"But you are accusing your friends of *murder*," he said slowly.

"Not all of them," Tiberius replied with a smile of devastating malice. "Just James and Pietro."

At this, fresh histrionics broke out, this time with Augusta lending a coldly decisive opinion on the matter of People Who Are Clearly Unwell. "Perhaps you ought to examine his lordship, Timothy. I think he cannot be in his right mind at *all*," she finished with chilly hauteur.

"I appreciate your concern, Augusta," Tiberius responded politely. "But accusing your husband of murder does not fall within the realm of derangement. In fact, I rather like him for the crime. Pietro strikes me as a trifle too fastidious for so brutal a deed. If he meant to murder anyone, I think he would do it with the flourish of a Florentine—a stiletto between the ribs in a flutter of silk."

He tipped his head as his gaze rested upon Timothy Gresham, who was perspiring heavily. "Now, I suppose, in fairness, I ought to include you, Timothy. After all, you were here then, and you were very much a part of our little group." Gresham gave a strangled noise and Tiberius went on. "Although, I must admit, I cannot see that you have the stomach for it, to be frank. No, James has the grit and the—I do hope you will pardon any offence, for none is intended, I assure you— the *earthiness* for such a killing. After all, whoever murdered Lorenzo must have actually put his hands upon him, a fellow we all considered to be a friend. Can you imagine the nerve it would take? The cold physical brutality to touch someone you have befriended, knowing you are about to take their life? To hold that life in your hands and then with a single, hard push . . ." He trailed off as he mimed the activity.

The count burst into passionate Italian again, a distinctly unmusical rage clipping each syllable sharply as he gesticulated to underscore his meaning. Sir James' complexion was empurpled with anger as well. Timothy Gresham was pale with a faint green cast to his skin.

"Tiberius," Stoker said softly. Tiberius gave a short nod, acknowledging he had heard and agreed the thing had gone far enough.

"I have shocked you, my friends, and I cannot apologise, for that was my intention. I only hope that one day the innocent will forgive me as we do our best to bring a murderer to justice."

With that, he raised his wineglass and drank deeply. The others stared at him in varying degrees of horror. I lifted my glass and said in ringing tones, "To justice."

The other two Templeton-Vanes joined me, and even the count calmed himself enough to drink. Elspeth did not touch hers, but Augusta put her glass to her lips and took a token sip, clearly relieved to have something more conventional to do. Timothy Gresham compressed his lips and touched nothing, while Sir James quaffed his entire glass in one go.

He set it down hard upon the table and I heard a distinctive crack. "I'll not forget this, Tiberius. None of us will. It is a mortal insult."

"Only to the guilty," Tiberius returned in a silken voice.

It proved to be a provocation too much, and Sir James lunged for him. In the melee that followed, glassware was broken, candles upended, and a considerable amount of food and drink dashed to the floor along with several pieces of a particularly fine Sèvres dinner service. Augusta leapt to her feet, upsetting her chair as she shrank back against the ribs of the Megalosaurus. Seeing Sir James grappling with Tiberius, the count dove into the heart of the action, although whether it was to assist James in throttling their host or Tiberius in throwing him off, it was difficult to say. Gresham dove under the table, while Merryweather stared in disbelief and Elspeth quite competently dealt with the assorted candles, stamping out the rogue flames one by one.

I looked across the table at Stoker, dodging an arrangement of roses as an epergne went flying. "Are you going to do something?"

Stoker, who had been consuming his dish of abricot impérial throughout Tiberius' antics, continued to eat. "Why ought I?"

"Because Tiberius is possibly outnumbered. Two to one," I pointed out.

Stoker snorted. "It would take more than that to best him."

"Well, if you won't help him, *I* will," Merry said stoutly as he jumped to his feet. He tore off his dog collar—doubtless feeling it inappropriate for a clergyman to engage in violence whilst dressed in the symbolic raiment of his profession. He darted around the trio now thrashing upon the floor before giving a whoop and throwing himself into the fight.

"Now you will have to go," I advised Stoker. "Merry is going to get himself hurt."

"That mightn't be a bad thing," Stoker replied calmly as he scraped up the last of the cream. "He would learn to look before leaping."

Augusta reached down, the pearls upon her bosom trembling with emotion. "Go and put an end to this, Revelstoke," she ordered. "You are the only one strong enough to head James off now he has a head of steam."

Stoker did as he was bade—he was always considerate of the wishes of ladies. But he did so with an air of resignation, first licking the last of the cream from his spoon and then stripping off his coat. He did not warn them, merely waded into the fray as unconcerned as Moses striding into the parted Red Sea. He managed to put himself between Sir James and Tiberius just as a lucky blow from Pietro sent Merry flying. It is a point of generosity on my part to assume the blow was the purest good fortune. From the little I could see, Merry was fortunate not to have been knocked unconscious by the sauceboat the count had taken up to use as a weapon.

"Now, that is unsporting," I said to no one in particular. "Gentlemen should only use fists in a friendly brawl." By this point Pietro had turned his attention to Tiberius and was preparing to put his sauceboat to use once more. Stoker was occupied with Sir James and doing handsomely, I observed. But Tiberius had been addled by a considerable blow from a flying epergne and it seemed entirely unfair for Pietro to attack him under such circumstances.

Since the other gentlemen were all otherwise occupied, I rose to the occasion. Just as Pietro raised his hand, poised to strike, I hefted one of the candelabra, heavy and dripping with wax. It hit him in the hand, knocking the sauceboat over and singeing his sleeve before I blew out the flames.

He whirled around, spitting unprintable Italian phrases which I shall not repeat in these pages. (The gentle reader will never need to know how to tell a person their mother is the daughter of a whore's pig in the Venetian dialect, I am certain.) Seeing it was a lady who assaulted him, he dropped the sauceboat and turned back to Tiberius, preparing to thrash him barehanded.

He landed a particularly nice left cross, opening a small cut on Tiberius' browbone. Tiberius returned the favour, slamming one fist into Pietro's nose and causing it to erupt like Vesuvius, blood pouring down the spotless white linen of his evening shirt. He screamed in rage and I grabbed him by the coattails, holding him like a rearing horse. Matters had got entirely out of hand, I decided, and I was about to tell him so when a shriek rose, so loud and keening it nearly shattered the remaining glassware.

The scuffling ceased and we turned as one to the source of this new commotion. Beatrice was still in her chair, head thrown back, eyes glassy as she arched her spine in a violent spasm. Across from her, Augusta's mouth was still slack with horror as she raised a hand to point.

Beatrice was convulsing.

CHAPTER
23

In an instant, the brawling was forgot as Stoker—having hauled Sir James off his feet by his collar—dropped the baronet and went to Beatrice. Before anyone else could respond, Stoker swept her rigid body off the chair and into his arms.

"She must have air," he said, forcing his way past Pietro as the count attempted to wrestle Beatrice from Stoker's grip.

Pietro, streaming blood and swearing in both gutter Italian and English, followed, landing a number of blows to Stoker's shoulders as he ordered him to release his wife.

Timothy struggled out from under the table where he had taken refuge at the beginning of the fight, and together the rest of us hastened to the clearing outside the Megalosaurus. The flames of the cressets streamed like crimson banners against the night sky, and the Megalosaurus itself glowed malevolence from its glassy eyes.

Around the edge of the clearing, the entertainers and servants stood in openmouthed horror. It took the musicians a moment longer to grasp the gravity of the situation. They had just struck the first notes of "Danse Macabre" when Collins, white-faced with shock, gestured them abruptly to silence.

With superb presence of mind, Collins whipped a tablecloth from one of the serving tables and spread it on the grass, ducking back into the shadows before Stoker laid Beatrice gently upon it. The little countess was staring up with unseeing eyes, her brows raised and her mouth curved in a tight smile. Pietro dropped to his knees beside her, clasping her hand and babbling words of endearment as Timothy hastened to take charge. Stoker ceded his position to allow the physician to take her pulse, but just then she arched again, so that the whole of her body was balanced upon her heels and the back of her head. It was terrible to witness, and even J. J., who had looked upon all manner of sordid things, seemed shaken by the sight. She kept to the edge of the clearing, an unobtrusive witness to it all, and I made a note to seek her out for a private conversation as soon as possible.

Suddenly, Beatrice gave a deep shudder and collapsed back onto the ground. The fit that had come upon her was finished, but the expression on her face did not change—that strange, otherworldly smile and those wide eyes.

Timothy put his finger to her neck and then bent swiftly to her chest, placing his ear just above the neckline of her gown. He remained there for a moment that stretched into eternity, no sound except the rustle of the cresset flames and Pietro's muted, pleading whispers as he begged Beatrice to live.

Slowly, reluctantly it seemed, Timothy sat back on his haunches and looked at Pietro. "I am so sorry," he said.

For a long moment, the world hung in silence. Then a grievous wail, a great, horrible lamentation, split the air. Pietro collapsed, hands covering his face. To my astonishment, it was Merryweather who went to him, putting his arms around the poor man while Stoker retrieved his evening coat and laid it reverently over Beatrice's face.

Augusta succumbed to emotion, weeping silently in her husband's arms.

"How?" I heard her wail against his shoulder. He patted her, disarranging her hair a little. Timothy retreated to a garden bench, head heavy in his hands, while Elspeth went to sit next to him and offer some comfort. Tiberius, his face quite pale, motioned to Stoker and then to me. We joined him a little distance apart, just far enough so the others could not easily overhear.

His expression was grave. "I presume there was nothing you could do?"

A muscle twitched in Stoker's cheek. "You may presume that if there was anything at all to be done, I would have done it."

Tiberius looked almost apologetic. "I did not mean to cast aspersions on your willingness or your abilities. Only to clarify that there was no hope."

"None whatsoever."

Tiberius was silent a moment. "When Pietro has had time to accept what has happened, we will take her up to the house and lay her out with dignity. I will tell Collins to have Mrs. Brackendale prepare a suitable room for Pietro. He will not wish to sleep in the same room as—" He broke off and waved his hand to where Beatrice's shrouded form lay.

Stoker regarded him with frank astonishment. "You cannot be serious."

"I am perfectly serious," Tiberius assured him. "She must be treated with all due dignity until we are able to have the undertakers in."

"Undertakers?" Stoker hissed the word in a whisper. "You cannot have the undertakers. You must call the coroner."

"I *am* the coroner, or had you forgot?" I was not entirely surprised. In most areas of the country, the most prominent landowner held the office of coroner and was entrusted with seeing justice done. In the case of sudden death, it was the coroner's responsibility to hold an inquest and establish the means of death by presenting evidence to a jury of the public. Such affairs were usually grand entertainment for the locals, held in pubs and open to all.

Stoker folded his arms over the breadth of his chest. "Then you know the necessity of an inquest in the eventuality of sudden death—" He broke off as he realised the MacIvers were looking curiously at us, no doubt wondering what the two brothers could possibly find to argue about at such a time.

Tiberius cut his eyes at them and back again. "We must discuss this in private."

Stoker opened his mouth to remonstrate, and if Tiberius had given him a quelling look, he might have persisted. Instead, his elder brother stared at him with such an expression of beseeching that Stoker clamped his lips together. He gave a single, sharp nod and Tiberius turned to the other gentlemen.

"Let us bear her into the house with the dignity she deserves," he said quietly.

Merry, who I surmised had been speaking words of clerical consolation to Pietro, rose and came to his elder brother at once. Sir James detached himself from his lady, consigning her to Timothy with a hopeful look. Timothy took Augusta's arm firmly in his. Elspeth joined them, looping her arm about Augusta's waist. I was rather surprised that Augusta should seem so badly affected. She had seemed to me a lady of grit and self-possession, but, as I reflected, if Timothy Gresham, a trained physician, could be so deeply shaken by the sudden death, then it was not surprising that Augusta had been shocked nearly to the point of insensibility.

Behind them, I caught sight of J. J.'s cap disappearing into the shadows as Collins directed a pair of servers to bring a table forward as a makeshift catafalque. I knew I should have to speak firmly with her to keep Beatrice's death from becoming a lurid headline, but that was a problem for another time. Instead, I applied myself to Pietro, gently taking him into my charge as Stoker and Tiberius lifted Beatrice with infinite care onto the table. At this Pietro gave another final ululation of grief and collapsed into my arms.

I held him, murmuring words of very little consolation, I was sure. He sobbed openly on my shoulder as I held him fast. Sir James and Merry joined Tiberius and Stoker, lifting the table to carry it to the water's edge and onto the trireme. The rest of us assembled in the other boats and we rowed back the way we had come, conveying Beatrice up to the house with slow and sober dignity. It was a grave and terrible procession, wending through the gardens, past the shocked faces of the rest of the staff who had heard the news of Beatrice's collapse. Once inside Cherboys, the men shifted her onto a sheet and conveyed her up to her room, where she was laid gently upon the bed. Pietro fell to the floor, clutching her hands, and Augusta went to him. She turned to the rest of us.

"I will stay with him," she said firmly. She seemed to have recovered herself, her manner decisive although her colour was still bad and her hands shook as she reached out to clasp Pietro's.

Tiberius turned to Sir James. "A drink. Go to the drawing room. Merry will make certain you have whatever you require," he added with a meaningful look at his youngest brother.

Merry, as he had done since Beatrice's collapse, rose to the occasion. "Of course."

"I will go with them," Elspeth Gresham said quietly.

The sad little trio left us, Merry suddenly seeming taller and more certain of himself with a task at hand. Tiberius looked to me and gathered Stoker in with a glance. "My study. Now."

He turned on his heel and strode from the room. He said nothing until we were closed in his study, locked away from prying ears. He poured a quick whisky and downed it in a single go. He poured another and then flung the glass, shattering it against the marble mantelpiece.

"Tibe," Stoker said, using the childhood nickname I had heard only a handful of times previously.

Tiberius turned to him with naked emotion in his eyes and then to me. "I did not intend for this. Whatever you think of me, you must believe that."

"Tiberius, that was never in doubt," I assured him. "This was a dreadful misfortune. Beatrice's heart was weak, to be sure, but you could not have imagined that it would give out so suddenly or in such a dramatic fashion." I stopped as I noticed the brothers were staring at one another, Stoker's expression meaningful as Tiberius shook his head. I ought to have seen it before, but I can only claim that the rapidity of the evening's unexpected events had been so marked that I had not had time to reflect upon the implication.

"Oh," I said, sitting heavily upon a convenient hassock. "She was murdered."

I looked to Stoker for confirmation and he nodded gravely, but Tiberius made a gesture of impatience.

"Her heart was bad," he said in a tone that brooked no argument. "She clearly died from her heart troubles."

Stoker made an effort to speak gently. "Yes, she did have a heart condition. And yes, her death was due to her heart failing her. But this was not due to natural causes. She was poisoned, if I had to guess."

"You do not have to guess," Tiberius told him firmly. "In fact, I require nothing whatsoever of you."

Stoker ran a hand over his hair, ruffling the ebony locks. "I know you are distressed, but you must face facts."

Tiberius gave him an imperious look. "Facts? The musings of a former naval surgeon?"

Stoker managed to hold his temper in check, but a cold fury seemed to have settled on him as he spoke. "You may dismiss my experience as you like. However, these are not mere musings. I have seen this sort of poisoning before. Did you note that terrible smile upon Beatrice's face as she died?"

Tiberius' nod was grudging.

"The risus sardonicus, the rictus grin, is a contraction of the facial muscles not found in a simple cardiac attack. It is indicative most frequently of tetanus—a disease from which we know Beatrice did not suffer—and poison, specifically strychnine. Furthermore, strychnine poisoning is associated with the sort of convulsions Beatrice demonstrated in her death throes. Strychnine in its most toxic form is derived from the strychnine tree, sometimes known quaintly as the dog button. Its scientific name is Strychnos nux-vomica, not to be confused with Strychnos ignatii, St. Ignatius' bean, which also contains lethal amounts of strychnine, as do many of the plants and trees of the family Loganiaceae. While small amounts of strychnine are believed by some physicians to have a stimulating effect and are prescribed in health tonics—"

"Enough!" Tiberius roared. "Very well. You have proven that you know a very great deal about poisons. It changes nothing."

"Tiberius, you must call an inquest," Stoker insisted. "I will give evidence. I know what I saw."

Tiberius said nothing but merely stared at Stoker coolly. Having once deserted him, the Templeton-Vane sangfroid was firmly in place and Tiberius would not succumb to emotion again.

I rose from the hassock and turned to Stoker. "Tiberius is right," I said slowly, finally understanding. "There can be no inquest."

"But there must—" Stoker began.

"No, there mustn't," Tiberius countered swiftly. "So long as the deceased has been seen by a doctor recently and has a condition to which the death may easily be attributed, the matter may be resolved by the coroner's own judgment. That is the law."

"Tiberius"—Stoker's voice was a growl—"she was murdered."

"And she will have justice," Tiberius promised. "But not through the law."

"How can you say that?" Stoker demanded. "You *are* the law here."

"And as soon as a jury is convened, the matter would be out of my hands," Tiberius said.

"Furthermore, who do you think they will blame?" I asked Stoker gently. "If she were poisoned, it must have been at someone's hand. And whose hands prepared the last food she ever ate?"

He gawped at me. "You cannot mean to suggest you think Julien poisoned Beatrice," Stoker demanded, his colour rising angrily.

"Certainly not! But this is not about the truth—it is about what people will believe," I reminded him. "Julien is a dark-skinned French-speaking immigrant to our shores. You must realise people will assume him guilty on the strength of those qualities alone, no matter how unjust."

"The moment it is put into record that Julien's food was the last thing Beatrice ingested, it is finished for him," Tiberius said, pressing the point home. "His employment at the Sudbury Hotel, his reputation—all of it, wrenched from him for no better reason than he was in the wrong place at the wrong time."

Stoker sighed. "Of course we must protect him," he began. Tiberius had been watching him closely, but something eased a little when he realised Stoker meant to let him have his way.

"Excellent," he said smoothly. "So, we are in agreement. You will say nothing and allow me to conduct my business as coroner as I see fit."

Stoker clamped his lips shut and gave a short nod. He was clearly seething, and I had reason to know his moods could last for some time. I turned my attention to Tiberius instead.

"It is strange," I began, "that Beatrice should be the victim of this latest attack. It is far likelier that her death was a mistake."

"A mistake?"

"She means that someone meant to poison Sir James or Pietro instead," Stoker put in. "Or perhaps they meant to poison you."

Tiberius bared his teeth in a smile. "How kind of you to care."

Their tempers were clearly rising and I hurried on before a proper quarrel could break out. I had no desire to spend the rest of the evening either stitching one of them up or setting bones. "It was cramped in the Megalosaurus. The servers were constantly jostling one another and us. It would have been an easy matter for any of them to have slipped something into the food."

"What do we know of the servers?" Stoker asked.

I held my tongue, wondering exactly how to broach the subject of J. J. I could not bring myself to believe she was in any way involved in Beatrice's poisoning; the very notion was laughable. I might distrust her motives occasionally, but though her ethics might be pliable, she was no more capable of violent crime than I.

I was further inclined to protect her because she might prove useful. It was possible that her reporter's eye had observed some small detail which might shed light on the evening's horrors. And if that were not enough, I was acutely aware of Tiberius' distaste for the members of her occupation. He had little use for the press and none whatsoever for the journalists who wrote on sensational topics. If he learnt that I had known of her presence in the house and not informed him, he would be less than pleased, and placating an angry viscount was a complication I did not need.

I turned to Tiberius, who responded to Stoker's question with a shrug. "Some are regular staff. Collins will vouch for them, I have no doubt. You know how it is—everyone in service here has family who has worked at Cherboys since God wore sailor suits. Julien brought some down from London—kitchen help and servers. I will ask him in the morning, but I believe they are all well-known to him from the Sudbury. None would have had motive to poison anyone at the table."

"Money?" Stoker guessed.

"I suppose it is possible that one might have been bribed," Tiberius agreed grudgingly.

"I think not," I said firmly. "First, do not complicate matters. We already have a murderer amongst us that we know of in Lorenzo's killer. We need not look further afield."

The brothers Templeton-Vane turned as one to look at me, their expressions eerily identical. They were skeptical, and I went on, attempting to give voice to my conviction. "But beyond that, this is a personal crime—even if Beatrice were an unintentional victim. Someone is targeting the remaining Seven Sinners. They are calling the tune, as a conductor will command an orchestra. There is a good deal of power in that. The cuttings," I reminded them. "They were designed to stir fear, to inflict terror in the next victim. This murderer has amused himself by contemplating the horror he has created. Would he wish to accomplish his aim at a remove? Or would he want to be there, directly on hand to witness the final crescendo?"

"How dreadfully theatrical," Tiberius mused. "But you do make an excellent point, my dear. Whoever is responsible for these crimes does strike me as the sort of monster who would enjoy watching the death throes of an enemy rather than pay someone to do the deed for him."

Tiberius rose, straightening his waistcoat. "I am going to ask Timothy to give Pietro some sort of sedative and encourage the poor man to rest. There will be much to do tomorrow, but nothing more at present."

Outside the room, we found the Greshams, sitting on a velvet bench in almost identical attitudes of shock. Tiberius had to call Timothy's name twice before the fellow roused himself.

"What's that? A sedative, my lord? I am afraid I haven't anything suitable with me," Timothy said feebly.

If Tiberius was surprised by Timothy's reluctance to attend to Pietro, he did not have a chance to address the matter directly. Elspeth spoke up.

"Mrs. Brackendale will. You gave her a small bottle of laudanum when she had the toothache several months back, remember?"

"Then it will doubtless be used up," Timothy said.

Elspeth's tone was one of exaggerated patience. "No, she didn't care for the effects. Preferred oil of clove." She turned to Tiberius. "You know what a frugal soul she is, my lord. I'm quite sure she would have kept it by should it come in handy."

Beatrice's death seemed to have affected our previous bonhomie. Gone were the forenames and comfortable familiarity. No more "Tiberius" but "my lord" instead. With the spirit of the house party dampened, the Greshams appeared to have remembered they—like everyone else in Dearsley—were dependent upon Tiberius' goodwill.

"Excellent thinking, Elspeth," Tiberius assured her. He gave Collins, hovering discreetly in the background, the necessary orders and turned back to bid the Greshams good night.

"A pity it has ended in tragedy," he remarked.

"Such a lovely young lady," Elspeth said wistfully. "It seems a crime when a thing of beauty dies."

"Indeed," Tiberius said. "I will send word when Pietro decides what arrangements he wishes to make. I presume he will want to take her back to New York, but perhaps he will have her buried in Italy with his family. I cannot image he will wish to remain in America without her, but of course, he is far too upset to make any decisions at present. Good night."

We all made the proper noises of farewell and the Greshams were given their wraps as one of Tiberius' carriages came around to the forecourt to collect them. Elspeth stepped out the door with alacrity, as though she could not take her leave quickly enough.

But at the last moment, Timothy Gresham paused and turned back, looking up at Cherboys with an inscrutable expression. Then, with a shudder and a shake of the head, he followed his sister into the night.

CHAPTER
24

Upon the departure of the Greshams, I went directly to my room to change. I removed my evening gown and dressed in my simple day dress of dark blue cloth, both for its sober colour and the fact that the fabric would not rustle. I pinned a ribbon of black silk to my sleeve, the best I could do in a nod to mourning without a proper black dress. I kept my evening slippers. They were fitted with thin soles that would be silent upon the floor. Noise is unwelcome both in a house of mourning and in detectival pursuits.

My preparations completed, I sat in a little armchair, reading Ovid as I listened to the various comings and goings in the next room. I heard Tiberius' low rumble, followed by Pietro's impassioned protestations. Eventually, his gulping sobs gave way to the sound of movement. Through a crack in the door, I saw Pietro leave, supported by Tiberius.

"I have had Collins prepare a room for you just down the way. I know you would not like to be far from her, but you must rest," Tiberius was telling him.

I waited until I heard a door along the corridor open and shut before slipping out of my own room and moving on noiseless feet to the door of Beatrice and Pietro's suite. The corridor was deserted.

I eased open the door. Inside, a candelabra had been left burning. Beatrice had been laid out with care, her garments smoothed and a thin sheet of fine linen draped over her.

Next to the bed, Augusta knelt in silent prayer. I paused as she finished, rising from her knees and giving a little start as she noticed me. She reached for my hand.

"I did not mean to disturb you," I began.

She shook her head and squeezed my hand tightly before dropping it. "I do not think anything could disturb me more than this," Augusta said with a vague gesture towards Beatrice's recumbent form. "I wanted to sit with Pietro as long as he remained. I didn't like to leave him alone."

She said nothing more, but I understood her implication. His grief had been extreme, violent even, and there was simply no way to know what he might do.

"Tiberius will remain with him," I assured her. "He has secured a bit of laudanum to help him sleep."

"That is a mercy at least. That poor man." She turned again to the figure on the bed.

"She looks peaceful," I murmured. "And so terribly young."

Anger veiled Augusta's features for a moment, but when she spoke her voice was limned only with sadness. "Folk will think it is not such a tragedy as she was already ill. But someone has played God here. A dangerous practice," she added, primming her mouth.

She smoothed her skirts briskly. "Mrs. Brackendale said the maids will come and wash her and lay her out properly. Beyond that, I imagine Pietro will have to decide."

"I would like to sit with her a few moments," I ventured.

Augusta's smile was mournful. "Of course, my dear. You are nearer in age to her than I. This must be particularly difficult for you. A reminder of the fate that awaits us all." To my surprise, she dropped a swift kiss to my cheek in passing.

The door shut softly behind her and I conjugated twenty verbs in the Corsican dialect before I moved. I wanted to make quite certain I would not be disturbed. I had searched the MacIvers' suite earlier, but not that of the Salviatis, and I regretted the omission deeply. Whether Beatrice's death was a dreadful accident or a pointed attack directed at Pietro—for the loss of his bride was clearly a far more terrible eventuality than his own murder—a search of their possessions might prove informative.

I twisted the key in the lock, hoping to purchase a little more time for myself should anyone else appear to pay their respects to the fallen contessa.

I had just moved to the bedside table when I heard a noise in the dressing room. An intruder! In my haste to change, I had forgot to slip a set of minuten into my cuffs. My evening corset did not permit the addition of a blade, and I had neglected to strap a knife to my calf. I did not even have my trusty cheese wire tucked in my pocket since Stoker still had possession of it.

I should have to find a weapon closer to hand. I hefted the nearest candelabra, mercifully unlit, and stood behind the door, arm upraised. I do not know how long I might have maintained the posture—the candelabra was solid silver and excessively weighty—but almost immediately a shadowy figure slid out from the doorway of the dressing room. I brought the candelabra down, but before it could connect, the figure spun. A steely grip banded my wrists and I dropped the candelabra to the thick carpet as I was shoved against the wall, pinioned from shoulder to shoe by a body that was as unyielding as iron and as familiar as my own.

"Stoker," I hissed. "What in the name of seven devils are you doing here?"

"Waiting to examine the body. I thought the rest of them would never leave—"

He stopped suddenly, as if only just then realising how entangled we were, limbs and breaths commingled in a posture that resembled our more passionate embraces. My thigh was trapped between his, my wrists bound by his palms and pinned to the wall. I was as helpless as one of my own specimens, and to my astonishment, I felt a rush of sudden—

"Veronica. Your expression has gone glassy again. What the devil are you thinking about?" he demanded as he released me. He seemed singularly unaffected by our proximity, but I noted his own respiration was laboured and a pulse beat wildly in his throat. I resisted the urge to nip at it lightly with my teeth and forced myself to reply in a casual tone.

"I was simply wondering how you managed ingress to this suite without detection."

He pointed behind him to the window of the dressing room. "The creeper on the wall. It goes right up to the floor above. An easy way to get around provided one has a good head for heights." Which of course he did. As a surgeon's mate in the navy, he ought to have had little cause for swinging nimbly amidst the sails and masts, but I knew he had done so out of a natural affinity for climbing. I had witnessed his skill with such feats myself, and on one memorable occasion his abilities had saved our lives.*

Stoker turned to the figure on the bed, his expression grim. "Far too young for such an end. I cannot perform a proper postmortem, but I can examine her and possibly gain some insight into how the poison was administered." He paused. "It is not entirely decent, to handle the dead."

It was perhaps the first time since our reunion in Bavaria that he had spoken to me without restraint, and I responded with instinctive reassurance. I touched his hand. "Decency will be in finding who did this."

I turned away as he bent to his work. He would, I had no doubt, be as swift and decorous as possible under the circumstances, but I knew he would prefer not to have an audience for this part. A full postmor-

---

* *A Murderous Relation*

tem examination would require scalpels and scales and all manner of equipment. It would also be impossible to conceal, necessitating a complete cutting open of the deceased in order to survey the internal organs. But a deft and careful investigation of her corpse might reveal some hitherto unknown clue.

While Stoker busied himself with Beatrice's body, I set to examining Pietro's things, a new and terrible hypothesis occurring to me. What if Pietro himself were the murderer? It seemed unthinkable that so devoted a husband might have harmed his own beloved wife—and his grief had appeared entirely genuine. But it was quite possible he had struck and missed his target, killing Beatrice instead. And then mightn't his elaborate show of mourning have comprised as much guilt as grief?

I made a thorough search of the wardrobe and drawers that held the count's clothes. Nothing of interest to be found in any of them, not even his pockets, which I turned out carefully. His clothes and accessories were of excellent quality, the country tweeds and evening suits all tailored in Manhattan and Savile Row. His shoes were made in Florence, his toilet water in Paris. His reading material was a stack of biographies of great composers with a selection of poetry and a traveller's guide to the great spas of Europe. I riffled the pages, but nothing came out, and his travelling desk proved just as fruitless. It was filled with memoranda and letters from various friends scattered around the world. I settled onto a hassock and read for some time, skimming the letters from friends and relations, noting the brisk social chatter and exchanges of gossip. I hunted for some clue of dastardly deeds, yet I was destined for disappointment. Pietro was as he appeared, a well-travelled gentleman of means and excellent good taste. But there was not a single hint that he was our murderer.

Frustrated, I moved on to Beatrice's things. It felt ghoulish to explore the belongings of a woman whose corpse still lay cooling on the bed, but I steeled myself and set to work. Like her husband, Beatrice wore exquisite and expensive garments, everything bearing Paris labels from the most exclusive ateliers. Her toilet set was mother-of-pearl and her shoes had a pretty little trunk of their own, each pair shrouded in a bag of soft linen. Her reading material, I was not surprised to find, tended towards the light French romances that Stoker loved so dearly. Apart from one. At the bottom of the stack of books lay the worn little book she had been reading in the garden, its soiled blue cover a marked contrast to the smartly bound French volumes. As I handled the blue book, a frisson shivered my spine. It was not that I had deduced it logically. It was that I *knew*, even before I opened the cover.

Scrawled there was an inscription which I read three times before I found my voice and called softly to Stoker.

He looked up in some annoyance. "Veronica, I am trying to—"

"I know what you are trying to do," I said impatiently. "But you must see this."

I moved to his side and held up the book, pointing to the frontispiece.

He read the inscription and his eyes widened in astonishment as he worked out the Italian. "But that says—"

"'Property of Beatrice d'Ambrogio.'" This was written in a childish scrawl, the letters fat and uneven. Below it, in a handsome, formal copperplate hand, it said, *For my Stella, on the occasion of her seventh birthday. From her beloved brother, Lorenzo.*

CHAPTER

25

S toker sat heavily in one of the armchairs by the fire as my mind raced ahead. "Lorenzo d'Ambrogio's sister. Tiberius mentioned one, but he said her name was Stella," he said.

I shrugged. "A pet name, no doubt. We have been told Lorenzo was devoted to her and that she was much younger. An indulgent elder brother might well call his sister his 'Star.' Tiberius mentioned Lorenzo's parents were shattered by his death and followed him to the grave the next year. He said he heard the whole family were dead, yet clearly little Stella survived."

"Beatrice was raised in America," he pointed out.

"But her Italian was fluent, idiomatic even. And she was raised by her aunt and uncle in New York. It makes perfect sense that once her parents died, Stella would have been shipped off to relations in America. Her mother's sister was wealthy and the child would have been grieving a tremendous loss. Even if there were family still in Italy to care for her, sending her to America to begin anew under fresh circumstances would have been a kindness."

"It is possible," he allowed.

"A thing easily confirmed by Pietro," I said briskly, moving to the door.

Stoker surged out of his chair and slid his body to block mine. "Where do you think you are going?"

"To speak with Pietro, of course," I told him. I attempted to edge around, but he stood with his back to the door, arms folded over his chest.

"Not a chance in seven hells," he said flatly. "For all we know they were working together and he is just as responsible for Kaspar and Alexandre's deaths as she was. Damnation, he may have undertaken a scheme of revenge upon her behalf without even informing her of the matter."

I paused, canting my head and giving the possibility all the consideration it deserved. "You astonish me," I said, smiling.

He relaxed a little, dropping his hands to his sides as I went on.

"You astonish me that after all this time and the variety of experiences you have endured, you still do not understand the first thing about women." I prodded his chest, but he would not be moved.

"It is possible," he said through gritted teeth.

"It is *not*," I countered. "Beatrice and Pietro were devoted partners, but it was entirely obvious that she was the dominant figure. She had a pretty face and gentle ways, so you cannot see it, but I can assure you, Beatrice was very much the one who wore the trousers. Here," I said, turning to retrieve the count's portfolio. I riffled through the papers. "Look here. Letters from various friends and relations addressed to him on his travels. In this one, his sister specifically mentions that she is upset Beatrice chose the spa in Germany instead of the one she recommended in Switzerland for Beatrice's health." I thrust the letter into his hands, leaving him to puzzle out the Italian on his own as I flicked hastily through the pages of the guidebook I had found amongst Pietro's things on a sudden hunch. I pounced with a soft cry of triumph. "And in case you wonder which spa it was, *here*," I said, producing a page with an entry that had been neatly underlined in pencil. "They stayed in Baden-Baden, the very spa town where Kaspar was killed."

"Then why didn't Pietro admit to being in the same town when we discussed Kaspar's death?" he shot back triumphantly. "There was no cause to conceal it if his purpose was innocent."

I puzzled over that a moment as he continued to loom over me, radiating victory. I snapped my fingers. *"Because he did not know.* Wait a moment," I said, searching through the various papers in the portfolio until I came to a pair of train tickets. "I did not realise the significance at the time, but see this. Pietro and Beatrice were at the train station, departing Baden the day of Kaspar's death. She had already set in motion the events that would kill him, but they left before the news became public knowledge, ensuring that Pietro never realised Kaspar had been there or what she had done."

"The tickets are for Paris," he said grudgingly.

I surveyed an envelope addressed to Pietro at his hotel in Paris and pointed to the date. "This puts them in the city at the same time as Alexandre's death. And they would have had no need to leave Paris immediately because there would be no reason to suspect them, nothing to connect them to Alexandre's sudden demise." I pressed home my point. "Beatrice has organised this entire affair," I said with conviction. "Think too of Pietro's obvious distress when Tiberius was speaking tonight. Pietro must have known she would be anguished at the mention of Lorenzo, but what if it was something more?"

"Such as?"

"Pietro and Beatrice quarrelled last night. I heard nothing of use, only raised voices and a single word—'morto.'"

"Veronica, have you no better use for your time than listening to the petty arguments of married couples through walls?"

It was on the tip of my tongue to explain that it was J. J. who first discovered the Salviatis arguing, but I had made up my mind to conceal her presence until I had learnt all I could from her.

I smiled thinly. "Regardless of your opinions on how I spend my time, they *were* arguing."

"About death," he finished thoughtfully.

"About death. This was shortly after Pietro learnt about the cuttings from Tiberius. He may have recognised her handwriting in the margin, realised he and Beatrice were at hand when Kaspar and Alexandre were killed. And then confronted her with her murderous scheme for vengeance."

"Painfully melodramatic, but possible," he said grudgingly.

"Not just possible. Likely. I hinted obliquely to overhearing the quarrel and Beatrice fobbed me off with a story about Pietro scolding her for overtaxing herself, but I think it was far more than that. I think he realised, for the first time, that he had married a woman capable of murder."

"Then why is she there," he said, pointing to the shroud on the bed, "and not reveling in the success of her homicidal schemes?"

I opened my mouth to explain, then snapped it shut. "I don't know."

"Perhaps he realised at last what she had done and decided to stop her in the only way he knew how?" Stoker suggested.

"What an appalling suggestion. He was devoted to her and his grief is real," I said firmly.

"Married people have been known to be murderous upon occasion," he reminded me. His fingertip went to his scar, almost absently, and I knew he was thinking of his former wife and the nefarious way she had treated him.

"Yes," I acknowledged finally, "but can you honestly say that you *see* it here?"

"No," he said at last. "I cannot." He was silent a long moment, lost in rumination. "It would have been natural to mention she was Lorenzo's sister, the little Stella he adored. The rest of them had actually met her as a child. She knew Sir James, Tiberius. The purpose of this house party was reminiscence. *Why* not reveal she was Lorenzo's sister?"

"Quite obviously, she could not have done so," I said. "It would have made her the logical suspect."

"And since Pietro concealed this, he must be at least her accomplice if not her partner in the murders," Stoker concluded smoothly. I caught then the gleam of pleasure in his eye as the trap snapped closed.

"Botheration," I muttered.

"Admit it," he urged. "Admit that I am right."

"I shall do no such thing," I countered. "His grief when Beatrice was found dead was profound, nearly unhinged. You cannot persuade me that he falsified such a display."

"I do not need to persuade you," Stoker said. "I am content to be right whether you acknowledge it or not."

"You are most certainly *not*—" I broke off, holding up a hand in a gesture of truce. "It is bad form to argue in front of the corpse. Let us agree that we are divided on the question of Pietro's guilt. We will interrogate him gently in the morning."

Naturally, even so simple a suggestion was met with intransigence if not outright rage on Stoker's part. "You cannot seriously believe we can permit him to roam freely when he may well be a murderer."

"Feathers! The man is prostrate with grief. He is in no fit state to lurk about the house, killing people. Besides which, he has been dosed with laudanum. If you are nervous, put a chair under your door and sleep with your candle lit."

"I am not nervous for me," he said through gritted teeth. "But you will remember we are here on Tiberius' behalf."

"I knew you cared about him!" I grinned. "He will be delighted to hear it."

"Veronica, you are, under absolutely no circumstances whatsoever, to relate to Tiberius any concerns I may have for his well-being."

"You love him," I crowed. "Admit it. He is your brother and you love him."

"I will admit no such thing. I will say that upon occasion, I do not entirely detest him."

"Progress indeed," I said. "But I am firm in my conviction that Pietro is no danger to anyone in his present condition. Now, what did you discover from your examination of Beatrice's body?"

He launched into a highly technical and deeply dull explanation that went on for some time before he concluded with the confirmation that she had indeed been poisoned by strychnine with little indication of how the thing had been done or the size of the dose. "Although," he finished, "with her heart troubles, she was unusually vulnerable. A normal young woman of rude good health, such as yourself, might be made violently ill from some toxic matter but weather the storm. The same amount could well kill a person with Beatrice's infirmity."

"The question is, who would view Beatrice as a threat?" I mused aloud. I went on. "Imagine you have committed the most grievous of acts, that of murder. You have taken a young man's life. Perhaps it was a crime of the moment, perhaps it was done with deliberation and intent. You had motive to kill Lorenzo d'Ambrogio and you did it. And you got away with it! Now twenty years have passed. You have prospered, perhaps you have married—all but Timothy Gresham have taken wives, after all. You have made a life for yourself. But always in the back of your mind, the knowledge lurks, squatting like a toad. You bear the mark of Cain. Suddenly, you are thrown back into the company of the men you knew at the time. Only now two of them are dead, quite close together. And then Tiberius shares the cuttings he received. Kaspar and Alexandre have been murdered out of vengeance for an act you have committed. And it is very apparent that sometime, perhaps very soon, you must pay for what you have done."

"My god, Veronica," he broke in. "Spare me the rest. I think I understand. You believe Lorenzo's killer has a guilty conscience. And that conscience has prompted him to believe he is at risk for retribution."

"Precisely. And somehow, he has discovered Beatrice's true identity, penetrating the secret she has worked so hard to keep. Naturally, he assumes she is picking off her brother's possible assassins one by one."

"And knowing the delicacy of her heart, he strikes before she can accomplish her revenge," he finished. He gave a slow nod. "It does seem logical enough, I grant you."

A lesser woman might have preened at the praise, but I spared no time for such pleasures, choosing instead to press my point home.

"And that means Beatrice was conclusively murdered," I said flatly. "The only other possibility is that she happened to fall victim to some accident in the kitchens. Perhaps poisonous mushrooms in the consommé?"

"No," he assured me. "We ate from the same tureen of consommé. If the mushrooms had been toxic, we all would have suffered. The same is true of any unwholesome food. Julien is thoroughly cleared, although I wonder if that was the murderer's intention . . ." His voice trailed off, but I leapt upon his meaning instantly.

"How clever and how utterly diabolical! To administer the poison somehow so that Beatrice would collapse at the dinner. We would obviously think her heart had given out, but even if anyone suspected poison, the next logical conclusion would be that she perished from something she ate."

"Leaving Julien the deliberately chosen scapegoat," he finished grimly. "When we discover who did this, I swear I will take him apart bone by bone."

We. The word did not escape my attention, and I felt a delicious rush of warmth clear to my toes from the sound of it. I smiled. "That puts Julien completely in the clear, as you say, but only if we run the murderer to ground and bring him to justice ourselves."

"I was rather afraid of that."

CHAPTER

26

We spent the next quarter of an hour pleasantly debating the most suitable course of action—if "pleasantly debating" can encompass a dispute comprising hissing whispers over the body of a dead woman. In the end, Stoker gave way. I chose to believe he was persuaded by my arguments, but it is also entirely possible he surrendered simply as a means to ensure I stopped talking. In any event, I emerged from Beatrice's room victorious. We repaired to our respective rooms and I fell at once into a deep and restorative slumber, waking only when Lily arrived with my breakfast tray. She puttered about, polishing a grate that already shone as brightly as any mirror, as well as inspecting my clothes to see if any buttons needed tightening or boots shining.

After several minutes of her dawdling, I sighed and drained the last of my cup, pushing it towards her.

"Lily, if you want to talk about the countess, do pour yourself a cup of tea and sit down. Your restlessness is most disconcerting."

She tried to refuse, but her eagerness to please a guest in her master's house and her desperation to indulge in a little idle talk about the most dramatic thing to happen in her young life were too much to resist. I nudged her along by pouring the tea myself and dropping in a considerable amount of sugar. I never take it in my tea, but I could see from the way her eyes lingered on the snowy lumps that she was a devotee.

"Now," I said, handing over the cup and patting the bed. "Come and sit. If Mrs. Brackendale wants to know what has kept you, you may tell her that I needed the hem of my evening gown whipped."

"Yes, miss," she said, sipping nervously at the tea. She was timid as a rabbit to begin with, but half a cup of India's finest brew and she was talking animatedly.

"Nanny is most distressed. Mr. Collins used one of the best sheets for covering the poor lady and Nanny said it's proper Irish linen, embroidered by nuns, and part of Lady Templeton-Vane's trousseau, irreplaceable, which Mr. Collins ought to have known, and she said it's the rankest disrespect to come into a house and simply take as you please, and then Mr. Collins said the poor lady was dead and he would be"—her voice dropped to a thrilled whisper—"*damned* if he begrudged a woman a shroud. And they both looked to Mrs. Brackendale to settle the matter, but she was having none of it, and now neither of them is speaking to each other or to her, so everything is at sixes and sevens belowstairs. And one of the scullery maids has gone back home. She refuses to sleep in a house where there is death," she intoned darkly. "She says the spirits of the dead do not rest so long as they are aboveground and it isn't as if the poor lady were going to be buried soon, so goodness only knows how long she will lie there. And worst of all," she added, her eyes widening in horror, "poor Polly was away yesterday evening—her mother was poorly and she went to tend her. Well, she come back today and went directly to do the countess's room, only she hadn't heard yet about the lady being departed, and Poll got the absolute shock of her life when she went into the room to see her just lying there under the shroud."

"The good Irish linen shroud, embroidered by nuns," I put in.

"Exactly. So Poll runs down to the kitchens and fairly shrieks the house down and goes into hysterics so badly that Mrs. Brackendale has to slap her to bring her to her senses, and it was the right thing to do, I say, even if she is my cousin. Heaven knows she ought to have a slap or two even on a good day just to get her to mind her work, but Polly took it amiss that she should be struck when she was simply suffering from shock. And Mrs. Brackendale said she would do far worse to a miserable slattern like Poll who couldn't even be bothered to put on a fresh cap and apron, and Poll did not like that one bit as the laundry maid never brought her a fresh set and she had to put on what she wore yesterday that was soiled. Then Mrs. Brackendale said it was a low trick to try to throw blame on the poor laundry maid when everyone knows the girl has never been quite right in the wits. Poll said the little fool should never have got the post because she can't remember from one day to the next where the linen room is and only got the job because she is Mrs. Brackendale's niece. And Mrs. Brackendale slapped her again and that was it. Poll gave her notice right then and there and said she'd marry the undergardener after all in spite of turning him down three times since she's had her eye on the new blacksmith. So I've all this wing to do as well as lend a hand in the kitchen," she finished breathlessly. She looked mightily put out and I felt a little dazed after that comprehensive recital of the domestic dramas that had been unfolding belowstairs.

"The coal miners have unions to make their working conditions acceptable. Perhaps chambermaids ought to do the same. Now, you have certainly earned a moment of rest," I told her. "More tea?"

"Lord love you, miss, that's kind, but I've the rest of the rooms to see to yet, and Mrs. Brackendale will have my guts for garters if she finds me lounging like a lady of leisure."

"I understand. Where is Lord Templeton-Vane this morning?"

She rose and picked up the tray. "With the doctor, miss. They've gone to have a look at the poor lady."

"Lady MacIver?" I asked with a start. "Is she unwell?"

"No, miss. The one what's dead."

I uttered a word that made Lily's eyes pop nearly from her head and thrust the bedclothes aside. "The investigation is afoot and I am still abed!" My favourite fictitious detective, Arcadia Brown, would *never* be so dilatory in sleuthing out the truth.

Lily beat a hasty retreat whilst I washed and dressed with a speed that would have done any man proud. I was just fitting a few minuten carefully into my cuffs as I dashed from the room. I nearly collided with Tiberius and Timothy Gresham as they emerged from Beatrice's room.

"Ah, Miss Speedwell," said Timothy, blinking nearsightedly through his spectacles. "You are a lovely sight upon such a sad morn." In another man I might have called it a leer, but he was so good-natured about his admiration, waggling his winsome little rabbit nose, I could not take offence.

"Yes, we are all quite distressed over Beatrice's sudden death. I suppose you were, with your professional acumen, immediately able to determine the cause?"

It was unsubtle enough of an enquiry to make Tiberius cough gently into his sleeve. "If you will excuse me, Timothy, I am afraid I have estate business. Veronica." He inclined his head, giving me a warning look as he went.

We watched him go, following behind at a sedate pace. The good doctor seemed distressed. He shook his head and made a clucking noise, rather like a frightened chicken. "Poor lady! We had a frank conversation about the state of her health the other evening and it was most distressing. I recognised the signs, you see. A rare and difficult heart condition. She said weak hearts were the curse of her family and that they seldom made old bones. She had visited several spa towns on the Continent for her health, but I cannot think it would have made much of a difference. No, she needed perfect quiet and serenity, and I advised her as much. Rich food, exhilarating company, exciting surroundings—these things are far too stimulating for one of her delicacy. Alas," he finished, pursing his lips.

I smiled gently. "Surely you are not suggesting the dinner party was in itself fatal?"

Timothy Gresham fluttered his hands a little. "Not at all, my dear. But you must admit, the sheer *strangeness* of the setting would be enough to afflict someone with a delicate constitution."

"The setting was unique," I admitted.

"And the topic of discussion was most unsuitable for ladies," he said. He leant near and I smelt carbolic soap and the smoky aroma of fried ham. His breakfast no doubt. "There are folk in the village who say it was less than respectable," he said in a whisper. "I do not mind telling you, I am not pleased to find my name attached to an event that is being spoken of as *disreputable*."

I wondered if Nanny MacQueen had perchance been discussing the evening's activities with the villagers. Being even tangentially a part of such an exotic and dramatic affair must surely have proven too tempting a subject for discretion. I put a hand to his sleeve, and his colour, impossibly, seemed to deepen further. His breath came quite quickly and I began to fear for his health if I kept him much longer. "Do not distress yourself, Dr. Gresham. We know the dinner party was unconventional, but even Her Majesty the Queen would have found nothing amiss. At least until the accusations of murder were hurled about." He fanned himself with a damp handkerchief and I went on. "So, after further reflection, you are still quite certain as to the cause of the contessa's death?"

"Oh yes, yes," he said, waving the handkerchief in my direction. "There is no doubt in my mind whatsoever. And since I had so very recently treated her for the same, it may all be handled quietly, with dignity and decency, for which I am very glad for her husband's sake. Pietro is thoroughly distraught, poor fellow."

I thought suddenly of the bones upon his mantelpiece at Wren Cottage. The bones of a megalosaur. He had grown up on this coastline, hearing stories of tremendous, history-making finds. Had he coveted Lorenzo's dinosaur? A creature of such distinction would bring respect and wealth to the person who discovered it. Granted, Timothy seemed a little lacking in ambition, but that he enjoyed his comforts was apparent in how neatly Elspeth kept their home, making certain everything was just as he liked it. What if he wanted the dinosaur for himself? Might he have ventured out that fateful and stormy night to excavate some of the bones? Could Lorenzo have discovered him in the act? It might not even have been intentional. It was easy to imagine, a quick tussle on the crumbling cliff top, a slip of the foot, and Lorenzo d'Ambrogio, the beautiful and beloved, lost forever.

And I thought too of the fact that Timothy Gresham had treated Beatrice for her heart condition. Did he supply her with a remedy? Perhaps her discussion of her rare heart condition had alerted him to the fact that she was Lorenzo's sister. Timothy did not have the strongest nerves. Even now he twitched and flinched, clearly overwrought at the circumstances. Perhaps he had found the temptation too great to resist. He was a physician with access to strychnine. He had only to give her a bottle of medicine and recommend she dose herself to strengthen her heart. Even if the mixture were bitter, as strychnine was known to be, she would doubtless swallow it down obediently. And then her death would be a fait accompli, even if he were completely absent from the scene.

I roused myself to find Timothy Gresham staring at me oddly.

"Yes, they were a most devoted couple," I said, returning to the conversation. We had reached the bottom of the stairs and he put out his hand. "Good day, Miss Speedwell."

I took his hand reluctantly. It was trembling and a little damp. He left then, scattering the contents of his bag before he went.

"I think you have made a conquest there," rumbled a familiar voice. Stoker stepped out from behind a statue of some round-hipped nymph with a basket of ripe fruit.

"I mean to marry him and settle down to being a country doctor's wife," I said, wiping my moistened hand upon my skirts.

"How touching. May I give the bride away?"

"She would have to belong to you first," I replied tartly.

But he was smiling, a smile I had not seen in a very long time. It was the sort of smile which said we were once more upon the course of a murderer, sleuthing out a villain in a chase which would engage our instincts and test our wits.

"What did our village physician have to say?" he enquired.

"He maintains that Beatrice died from natural causes and as he had treated her for her heart troubles within the last fortnight, he was perfectly willing to accede to Tiberius' wishes that it should be officially so."

I half expected him to indulge in a little profanity at the confirmation that Beatrice's death was to be formally attributed to natural causes, but he surprised me. He merely gave a grave nod.

"Perhaps it is for the best," he remarked, passing a hand over the shadow of whiskers at his chin.

"You astonish me. You were so insistent upon the need for a proper inquest last night."

He shrugged. "What difference will it make now? The most important thing is that Julien is not made to suffer by any inference that he was involved since she collapsed at the dinner party. Besides, if Beatrice, as Lorenzo's sister, is responsible for killing the others, then justice has been served. And if Pietro is involved, then he suffers as well. I have never seen a man so devastated by loss."

"You saw him this morning?"

"Before breakfast. I thought he might need a little nourishment, but he would take nothing. Augusta tried, bless her. He is utterly shattered by Beatrice's death. Still in shock, I think. I wouldn't be surprised if he simply wasted away after this."

His demeanour was subdued, quite unlike his usual vigour. Through all of our collective perils, he had stood his ground, fighting through them with the ferocity of one of the more predatory jungle cats. Even when Fate had shown herself at her most malicious, he had found some reserves to battle on. But he seemed a shorn Samson now, divested of his strength and oddly vulnerable.

I put a hand to his cheek. "Stoker—"

He covered my hand with his own and drew it gently away, pressing a kiss to the palm before dropping it suddenly. "Now is not the time, Veronica. This business seemed troublesome enough when it was only a flight of fancy we were discussing in Bavaria. But now it has come home to roost, literally," he said with a touch of asperity. "And if we do not discover who has done this—"

"You really are worried about Tiberius," I said in some amazement. I had thought Stoker's prickliness since our reunion in Germany was due to our ongoing disharmony, but I realised he had taken the threat to Tiberius very much to heart.

His smile was rueful. "I cannot say I am enjoying the experience."

"It is entirely permissible to form attachments to one's kin," I informed him. "In fact, most people do."

"You haven't," he pointed out.

"Yes, well, my family are either megalomaniacal villains or royal wastrels who will not acknowledge my existence. Tiberius is worth twenty of any one of them."

"I suppose he is," Stoker said slowly. "But make certain he never hears that. I shan't hear the end of it."

"Too late," said a cool voice.

CHAPTER

27

Tiberius' footsteps had been soundless on the carpet runner. He beckoned. "In my office, if you please." We made to follow him, but he paused and turned, fixing Stoker with a smug smile. "And do not think I shall let your feelings pass unremarked, little brother." He swung round on his heel and led us to his office.

Stoker's lip curled as he mouthed a series of imprecations towards Tiberius' back. I resisted the urge to smile. We were once more upon the chase, quarry scented and hunt engaged, and I vowed as I settled myself across from Tiberius' wide desk that we would prevail.

I was a little surprised at the office itself. His study was a grand affair, vast and hung with bottle green velvet and ornamented with sculptures and globes and enormous folios laid open for examination. The office, in contrast, was a workman's room. The desk bore the scars of penknife and ink, and the blotter was full of random jottings, quick memoranda and aides-mémoire. Shelves filled the walls from floor to ceiling and each was stuffed with ledgers and boxes of files. An enormous marrow rested on the edge of his desk and the room smelt agreeably of leather and damp wool. A door led to the east terrace and next to it were a series of pegs upon which hung oilskin coats, a hat of great antiquity, and dog leads in various states of wear.

"Tiberius, if I did not know better, I would think you actually turned your hand to work," I observed.

"I do," he said dryly. "In fact, I am rather good at it, much to my dismay." He gestured towards a large piece of slate hung by the door. It was covered in chalked numbers and a series of abbreviations that were as impenetrable as hieroglyphics to me. "I have calculated that with careful investment in new equipment and putting two more fields to the harrow, we might see an improvement next year of some seventeen percent."

"I am thoroughly impressed," I told him truthfully.

He grinned. "Now ask me about my stud activities."

I laughed, but Stoker gave a growl low in his throat and Tiberius rolled his eyes heavenwards. "Shall I have them send in a raw steak for your dinner? You sound positively feral. Besides, Veronica knows I mean her no insult."

I smoothed my skirts over my knees. "Tiberius, we did, as it happens, engage in a bit of detectival work last night."

"I expected you would," he said with a sigh. "I might as well have flapped a red flag in front of a Pamplona bull. Go on, then. What did you discover?"

Swiftly I related our discovery of Beatrice's identity, as well as the fact that she had been the one responsible for making certain the Salviatis were within striking distance of Kaspar and Alexandre at the times of their deaths.

He listened attentively, toying with a paper knife as he did.

"Of course, we cannot say for certain if Pietro knew what Beatrice was doing or if he was a full partner in her scheme of revenge," I concluded. "In fact, Stoker and I are rather divided in our opinions upon the matter. I believe he is entirely innocent of her machinations, but Stoker insists otherwise."

"It hardly matters now that Beatrice is dead," Tiberius began.

"It bloody well does!" Stoker erupted from his chair. "Tiberius, if Pietro aided her in these murders, then he is still a danger. To you, to James, to Timothy Gresham, possibly."

I did not object to this last point, but I rather liked Timothy for the murderer. I always think one cannot entirely trust physicians. Far too many of them liken themselves to gods with their ability to play at life and death.

Tiberius appeared to consider Stoker's words before shaking his head. "I cannot sanction further sleuthing games on my behalf."

"Games!" The word erupted from Stoker. "Might I remind you we undertook this matter at your behest."

"Yes, and now I tire of the whole thing." Tiberius always affected a world-weary mien, but I saw real emotion underpinning his attitude. This was not ennui; something darker and more implacable worried at him.

"You feel guilty," I said simply.

"Of course I bloody well do!" he roared in a creditable imitation of his younger brother's wrath. "Beatrice was a young and vital person. Yes, I know she may have been responsible for Kaspar and Alexandre's deaths, but I can understand that. God knows I would have torn apart a dozen men with my bare hands if it had kept Rosamund safe."[*] Tiberius seldom spoke of his late beloved, but I knew the wound ran deep, to the bone, a scar that would never entirely heal. I was not surprised that he would sympathise with Beatrice, connected as they were by shared loss.

He went on. "You must remember, I knew her. So many weeks we spent at the d'Ambrogio villa, little Stella always tagging along after us, just to be with her cherished Lorenzo. And how he adored her! I used to wonder what it must be like to be the object of that kind of

---

[*] *A Dangerous Collaboration*

devotion. God knows I never felt that sort of affection in this place."
Stoker's brows raised and Tiberius hurried on. "With Lorenzo's death,
everything was taken from her. Everything—not just her brother but
her parents, her home. Whoever was responsible for Lorenzo's death
murdered a part of that girl as well, and if she elected to take her revenge, then I will do nothing but applaud her for it."

He stopped suddenly, his colour high.

"But, Tiberius," Stoker began gently.

Tiberius made a slashing gesture with his hand. "She has paid for
her crimes, whatever they were. Enough. Let her rest in peace. Let
them all. I am finished with it."

He turned back to his paperwork and I realised we had been dismissed. I would have expected Stoker, under more ordinary circumstances, to have stayed and argued with Tiberius. Instead, he rose and
walked from the room without a backwards glance.

I followed hard upon his heels and he did not stop until he reached
the staircase hall, whirling to fix me with a bewildered stare. "What in
the name of seven hells was *that*?"

"I know," I said by way of consolation. "Tiberius is quite wrong, of
course. Whoever murdered Beatrice must be brought to justice—"

"Not that! His . . . his feelings. I didn't know Tiberius had them."

"Of course he does."

"He never shows them," Stoker retorted. "To anyone. He hides everything behind that cool façade of urbanity. But that"—he raised a
hand and pointed back towards Tiberius' office—"that was something
I have never before seen. He was . . ."

He trailed off, clearly at a loss.

"Vulnerable?" I suggested.

"Exactly so. Vulnerable. I cannot say that I much enjoyed it."

"Of course you didn't. Not a single one of you Templeton-Vanes
can speak of such things with equanimity. If you were made uncom-

fortable by the knowledge that Tiberius might have liked a closer relationship with his brothers, how much more uncomfortable must he be?"

Stoker thought it over for a long moment. "It was never encouraged," Stoker said finally. "Father always pitted us against one another. Partially for his own amusement. He enjoyed our battles. But he also believed it would make men of us, make us stronger if we never needed to rely upon anyone else. He wanted us self-sufficient. Like islands."

"Continents, more like," I muttered.

"You are a fine one to talk. I do not seem to recall that allowing yourself to depend upon others is one of your accomplishments," he said stiffly.

Ah, the difficulty between us had reared its head again at last. But as Stoker had reminded me before our interview with Tiberius, this was most definitely not the time.

"I think," I said calmly, "that we ought to speak with Pietro. Whatever Tiberius says, we must learn the truth about whether he collaborated with Beatrice in her murderous endeavours. And we *will* learn the truth, by whatever means necessary."

"Certainly," Stoker said, following me up the stairs. "Shall I get my thumbscrews and meet you in his room?"

I did not bother to reply. In the end, it required nothing more than the mention of Beatrice's name to open the floodgates of Pietro's emotion.

The room Tiberius ordered prepared for him was in the nursery wing, on the side of the house opposite the wing where Beatrice now lay. I rapped softly at the door and it was opened by Augusta. She looked deeply weary, dressed in sober black, and I cursed myself again for not travelling with a plain mourning costume in order to be prepared for any eventuality.

"Good morning," she said in a low voice. "He has just dropped off to sleep again, the effects of the laudanum. I am afraid I was dozing myself." I glanced past her to where Pietro lay atop the coverlet, fully dressed in his evening clothes from the night before.

Augusta covered a yawn with her hand and immediately apologised. "I did not sleep well myself."

"Never mind," Stoker said kindly. "You have been very good to him, but you must not neglect your own rest. Have you eaten?"

"A bit of toast was the most I could manage," she said with a wan look.

Stoker's voice took on a tone of command. "You must keep up your own strength, Augusta. Go to your room and ring for food and hot, sweet tea. Lots of it. Eat everything they bring you and then sleep."

Augusta, like all women of strength, appreciated a firm hand. She fairly blushed as Stoker ordered her about. "If you insist," she murmured.

Stoker watched her go with frank appreciation.

"A most remarkable woman," he said. "Thoroughly nurturing."

I snorted. "Men. You are the same the world over," I grumbled as we entered Pietro's room, closing the door behind us.

"How so?"

"Forever wanting to return to the nursery to be coddled by some woman and her comforting bosom."

He made a choking noise in response, but I ignored him, turning my attention to the count instead.

"Pietro," I said softly, kneeling beside the bed. His eyelids looked bruised, pale purple with the shock of what he had endured, I supposed. They fluttered briefly before coming open. His pupils were wide and black.

"Veronica?"

"Yes, Pietro. I am here. Do you remember what has happened?"

He gave a groan and covered his face with his hands. I was prepared to slap him should he succumb to hysterics, but he gathered himself manfully and when he dropped his hands, his cheeks were only faintly damp.

"My Beatrice," he murmured. "My beautiful Beatrice."

"I am so very sorry for your loss," I told him. He grasped my hand.

"Thank you, cara," he replied.

"We know who she was, Pietro," Stoker said softly. I gave him a sharp look and he subsided into the chair Augusta had recently vacated. I had a notion that Pietro would respond much better to a woman's gentle touch than Stoker blundering about like the proverbial bovine in the china shop. Besides which, Stoker's remarks about Augusta's talents for nurturing stung a little. She was not the only woman who could be consoling.

Pietro's eyes flared wide, but he did not attempt to deny it. "Oh."

"Lorenzo d'Ambrogio's younger sister," I said in an encouraging voice. I thought he might tell us more if we approached him obliquely. "How did you meet her?"

A smile, brilliant as the summer sun, broke over his face. "At a ball in New York. Given by one of those new millionaires—her aunt's husband, as it turned out. Beatrice went to live with them a year after Lorenzo died. Their parents, you see, never could they cope with the loss of their beautiful son, their only boy, their precious treasure. Heart troubles abounded in the d'Ambrogio family, and their father died from the shock of losing Lorenzo. After that, the mother wasted away from a fever in a matter of months. And they left my angel, my Beatrice. There were other relatives in Italy who might have cared for her, but it was felt that her mother's sister was the best choice. She wanted her desperately—she and her husband had no children of their own. And a change of scene could only be good for the child. So she went to live amongst strangers. She took her uncle's name and she became theirs. But never did she forget that she was a d'Ambrogio, never did she forget her mother tongue."

"It must have been a delight to her to meet someone from her home," I ventured.

"The moment she heard my name, she insisted upon sitting out the next dances to speak with me. We created a scandal," he said with a wistful smile. "She was a graceful and successful debutante, and the sons of industry were dangled before her as prospective husbands. But the minute we began to talk, everything else fell away. She remembered me, you see. I had often visited the d'Ambrogio villa and she knew me as a very young man. I ought to have known instantly—she had something of Lorenzo about her," he added, his face contorting with grief. I laid a hand upon his and he squeezed it compulsively. He did not relinquish it as he went on.

"I hardly dared to believe she would return my love, but for both of us, it was as if Lorenzo had come alive once more. All I treasured in his spirit—the sweetness, the sense of honour—she possessed even more. And in me, she found the link to the brother she had adored." It all sounded faintly distasteful to me, as if Lorenzo had been a member of their marriage, a dead man inserting himself into their union. But if it had brought them both comfort, then who was I to judge them?

"She told me about her heart troubles. We knew we would not have long together, a handful of years, but it would be enough for us. So we married. And I brought her to Italy with me. She wanted to see her country again before . . . before she became too ill to travel. She insisted on seeing the villa where she had been born. One of the old family servants was still there. She had kept a few boxes, things belonging to the d'Ambrogios. She very kindly offered them to Beatrice once she realised who Beatrice was. Very kindly," he added, twisting his lips into a mockery of a smile. "It would have been better for us if she had burnt the lot. They were Lorenzo's things. After Lorenzo died, old Lord Templeton-Vane had his belongings packed up and shipped to the d'Ambrogios in Italy. But his parents, they had never been able to bring themselves to open these boxes. Beatrice wept for three days straight before she could bear it. Inside were his clothes, his shaving things. And his journal."

His hand made an ineffectual gesture towards the coat draped at the foot of the bed. I retrieved it and he indicated the pocket. Inside I found a slender notebook. The cover was stamped with the same small gilded bee as on the cover of the book Beatrice had been reading in the garden.

Pietro explained. "There were dozens of these notebooks amongst his things, but this was the last. He used them every day for notes to himself, little sketches and memoranda. Sometimes he wrote them up as journals. He preferred very small notebooks so they took up little room in his pockets. He was careful of his tailoring," he said with a ghost of a smile. "Always a dandy."

I riffled the pages, smelling the mustiness of the years locked within.

Pietro went on. "When Beatrice read the notebook, she was changed. She explained to me that it contained evidence Lorenzo had been murdered but not by whom. She was enraged, tormented by grief. I consoled her," he said, his eyes filming with tears. "I explained to her that we must let the dead bury the dead. We had no guarantees, you understand, of how much time we should have together. Her health, it was so precarious. I could not bear for her to spend a single day in unhappiness. I thought she agreed."

"But she did not," I pressed.

He covered his eyes once more. For a long moment there was no sound in the room except the ticking of the mantel clock and the count's mournful breathing. At last he composed himself and resumed his tale. "She did not. I had no idea. I swear this upon my honour, upon my soul." He grasped my hands in his and rose up in the bed, his eyes glittering feverishly. "You must believe me. I will swear upon everything I hold holy. I did not know."

"When did you learn the truth?" I asked gently.

"After dinner, the first night. Tiberius showed us the cuttings about the deaths of Kaspar and Alexandre. The threats written in the margins—I knew her hand immediately. I concealed my horror until we were alone and then I confronted her. We quarrelled, but I understood her. She was avenging Lorenzo. It was a blood debt, you understand. And blood debts must be paid."

He lapsed back onto the pillows, a ragged sob escaping his throat.

"And now it is finished. The gods have taken her, my precious Beatrice." He rolled towards the wall and covered his face with his hands.

CHAPTER

28

We left Pietro in a somber mood. It was difficult to view a man's grief when displayed so nakedly. Such exhibitions of emotion are more common to the Latinate temperament, and I was not certain whether to admire his connection to his heartfelt sensibilities or deplore them with stout Saxon resolve. In any event, Stoker and I were silent as we left him. It seemed obvious we should have a council of war, and without being overheard. As so often happens betwixt two souls with such strength of attachment, we intuited each other's thoughts and made our way outside. There is nothing so revivifying as fresh air, and too much time inside has a deleterious effect upon Stoker's mood. We passed through the door to the terrace and our footsteps led us to the rose garden, and where I would have paused at the little bower, Stoker continued on in the direction of the Megalosaurus.

"Surely you have spent enough time with the creature," I began, but he turned with a vaguely triumphant air.

"I had a word with Collins last night and told him to leave all as it was. I intend to investigate the scene of the crime."

I smothered the urge to stamp my foot. I ought to have considered such a step, and it was thoroughly galling to realise he had had the presence of mind during the tumult of the previous evening's events to secure the place.

"I presume you are satisfied with Pietro's reactions," I began as he rowed us across to the island. "At least enough to absolve him of being Beatrice's partner in vengeance. He knew nothing of her activities until the night before her death."

"Which he may have engineered himself in order to stop her murdering again."

"You are determined to think the worst of him! But how?" I asked. "By what method would he have introduced the poison?"

"Direct consumption," he assured me. "There was no mark of a hypodermic syringe upon her person. And preparing an inhalation of the stuff is extremely dangerous as well as difficult. It would require scientific knowledge and equipment, neither of which Pietro possesses. Far easier to feed it to her."

I pondered this, ignoring his remarks about Pietro. "You say you are certain it was not in the dishes we shared last night, but perhaps a dose was slipped into a portion served only to her?"

He shook his head. "Strychnine is bitter, notoriously so. There is no dish that might mask it except a very strong coffee and we had none before she collapsed."

"Then perhaps some refreshment sent to her room earlier in the day?" I suggested.

"That is the trouble. I have been thinking, and her collapse was so swift, so sudden. Part of that may be attributed to her heart condition, but it also speaks to a large dose taken quite near the time of her death."

"How near?"

He shrugged. "Given that she wouldn't have required as large a dose as a healthy woman to kill her, I should think an hour? Perhaps more? It is an imprecise thing under the best of circumstances and I have no means of investigating properly."

I smiled in triumph. "And during the whole of the dinner, Pietro was seated nowhere near Beatrice. He could not have poisoned her." I broke off, frowning. "In fact, no one could. If, as you say, strychnine is bitter—"

"One of the bitterest substances on earth," he assured me.

"And it was not fed to her at the table, then when and how?"

"That is what we must determine," he said as the little boat bumped against the island's shore. He tied it off and strode away, leaving me to catch him up. Just as we approached the monster, I stopped, pulling Stoker to a halt. He opened his mouth to remonstrate, but I clapped a hand over it, tugging him behind a handy rosebush.

"Veronica, would you care to explain exactly for what purpose you have waylaid me?" he demanded in a furious whisper.

"There is someone inside the Megalosaurus," I whispered back. "No doubt the murdering fiend has returned to the scene of his crime to retrieve a clue that would implicate him in Beatrice's death."

"Of all the cotton-headed, wool-witted— How can you possibly know that?"

"I heard a snuffling noise just as we came near to it. There! I heard it again."

"I have thorns in my sit-upon parts," he said aggrievedly.

"I have no doubt you will recover in due course," I told him firmly. "But whilst you sit and nurse your injuries, I will be unmasking a villain."

There is no substitute for the element of surprise in such situations, and I had no intention of wasting the advantage that Fate had so kindly presented to me. With that, I launched myself from the concealment of the shrubbery and into the belly of the beast. It is my custom, at these kinds of critical moments, to employ the tactics of the Viking berserker or the Maori and issue a battle cry in order to strike terror into the heart of my foes. In this instance, I chose a particularly chilling one, delivered in the original Gaelic.

"Sons of the hounds, come here and get meat!"

With the Celtic invocation still rolling in my throat, I burst into the Megalosaurus, ready to do battle with whatever dastardly malcontent had taken Beatrice's life. I landed in a half-crouch, hands curled into fists and knees flexed, teeth bared in a snarl. Instantly, I was assailed— a heavy blow landed squarely in my solar plexus, driving the wind from my lungs and causing me to drop to my knees. At the same time, a foul-smelling liquid drenched me from head to hem, leaving behind an oleaginous green slime. Hampered by the pond-like condition of my hair hanging in my face, I could see little except shapes in the gloom of the dinosaur. I leapt up with a roar, flinging myself in the direction of the shapes. I made contact with one and hurled it to the ground, deeply gratified to hear its shriek of pain.

"Surrender, villain!" I cried.

"For god's sake, Veronica!" I heard Stoker behind me, exclaiming in astonishment.

"Stand down, Stoker, I have the matter in hand and the other miscreant may be armed," I ordered. I drove my knee into my prisoner's softer parts—the stomach, I guessed, and was rewarded with another shriek. "Explain yourself!"

"She might if you left off suffocating her," Stoker said sternly. He shoved me aside and I pushed my hair out of my face in time to see him hauling J. J. Butterworth to her feet. She whooped in air as she looked at me reproachfully.

"Good gad, Veronica," she said hoarsely as she put a hand to her side. "I think you have cracked a rib."

"Well, it is as much as you deserve for attacking me," I pointed out. I saw from the silver vase lying on the floor that she had hurled one of the epergnes at me. The foul-smelling liquid was the flower water in which the blooms of last night's arrangements had been quietly, warmly rotting. Decaying petals festooned my hair and dress and I shook the fetid matter from my soaked skirts.

"Attacking you! You are the one who burst in here as if all the loosed demons of Hell were after you," she retorted. "What was that you shouted?"

"The battle cry of Clan Cameron," I told her. "It is said to strike terror into the heart of the clan's foes. And I thought you were a murderer," I pointed out, mildly annoyed that Stoker had taken out one of his vast red bandanna handkerchiefs and was using it to wipe a few stray droplets of stinking water from his sleeve whilst I stood quietly dripping from every possible part of my anatomy.

"Veronica," Stoker said, his voice dangerously quiet, "you do not seem at all surprised to see J. J."

Before I could reply, a low moan sounded from the depths of the beast. A second person was still concealed in the shadows, and I peered into the gloom to see Julien huddled on the floor, a bottle of excellent cognac cradled in his arms. He snuffled softly and I crept near, careful to keep my damp person from despoiling his clothes. I needn't have bothered. Julien, usually so fastidious that not a mark could be found upon the pristine white of his chef's coat, was thoroughly disheveled. His velvet cap had been discarded and his coat was streaked with various substances, none of which I cared to identify.

"Julien," I said gently. "Are you quite all right?"

"Of course he is not," J. J. snapped. "He is distraught about what happened last night."

Julien let out another low moan, this one punctuated with long phrases in sobbed French. I recognised one word—"ruination"—and put my hand to his arm.

"Of course you are not ruined," I said stoutly. "You are in no way responsible for what happened to Contessa Salviati."

He lifted mournful eyes to mine, his swollen and swimming in tears. He smelt strongly of cognac and sugar. He continued to bewail his fate, and I listened for some time before my patience began to ebb.

"My dear fellow, I am quite fluent in French, but I am afraid my skills are not equal to your Caribbean patois, particularly when you are sobbing half the words. Now, dry your eyes, there's a good man, and tell me what troubles you."

He did as I bade him, wiping his eyes upon his already untidy sleeve. He gave a great gulping snuffle and then took a bracing sip of cognac. "The mushrooms. I gather them myself for the consommé. From the forest. What if I made a mistake? What if I have killed her?"

He finished on a low moan, dropping his head into his folded arms.

Stoker put a consoling hand to his shoulder. "It was not the mushrooms, Julien. It was strychnine."

Julien lifted his head, eyeing Stoker suspiciously, as if not daring to hope. "You are certain, my friend?"

"I am," Stoker returned stoutly.

"You have done the tests of the chemicals?" Julien demanded.

"Well, no," Stoker admitted. "There is to be no inquest, and without a proper postmortem—"

Julien gave another moan and took a long pull at the bottle of cognac. "All of my fine cooking, the dishes I have created, the triumphs in my kitchens. It will not matter. There will be talk. The story will go abroad. I cooked in a house where a lady met her death. They will whisper that it was my fault and I will be finished."

"Who on earth would carry a story like that—" I broke off, flicking an unwilling look at J. J.

It took only a moment for her to interpret the implication. When she did, she turned an unattractive shade of puce, then very white, the colour draining from her face and leaving her freckles to stand out, livid, against the parchment paleness of her skin.

"How dare you," she said softly. "After all I have done? All the secrets I have kept? All the promises I have honoured? Even now you doubt me? Julien is my *friend*."

Before I could speak, she fled, pushing past Stoker as if he were made of papier-mâché.

I sighed. I should have to make amends for that, but reconciling with J. J. was a problem for another hour. Together we hefted Julien to his feet and Stoker put an arm around his waist, pulling Julien's arm over his shoulders.

"There you are, my friend," Stoker coaxed. "Come along with me to the kitchens. We will have some food and some black coffee, good strong stuff."

Julien gave a deep sniff. "I brought my own supply of beans from Martinique. I will not drink the gutter water you English call coffee."

"Yes, I will grind the beans fresh," Stoker promised. He urged Julien forwards, pausing to brush his lips to my ear as they passed me. "Do not think for a moment we are finished with this," he warned.

They left me to the wreckage of the dinner party, feeling a little deflated. I deplored such scenes and I was not accustomed to the dart of regret I felt at my treatment of J. J. She was correct; her behaviour merited more kindliness, and I owed her at the very least an apology and at the most, a story.

I resolved to rectify matters in due course, but I had an investigation to pursue. Wet through and stinking of fetid flower water, I got to my knees and worked my way methodically through the debris of the dinner party. There were masses of shattered crystal and broken porcelain, to say nothing of the scraps of food, puddled wines, and cracked candles. I turned everything over carefully, but I found nothing.

Thwarted, I wiped my hands on a discarded piece of napery and left the Megalosaurus to make a brief toilette. I dressed in my hunting costume for no other reason than the rush of confidence it always provided. And as I picked up the dress I had discarded and felt the book I had tucked instinctively into its pocket, I realised I held a clue no one else did.

I had Lorenzo d'Ambrogio's notebook.

Clean and tidy once more, I descended the stairs to find a bit of quiet in the library, but to my dismay I was not the only one to choose its hushed comforts. Ensconced in one of the large leather armchairs was Augusta. A recent fashion paper was lying open upon her lap, but she was gazing pensively into the cold hearth.

"I always find an unkindled fire to be a melancholy thing," she said as I came near, rousing herself to greet me with a faint smile.

"There is a fire in the morning room if you are chilled," I told her.

She shook her head. "Collins has already offered to light this one. I am fine. Only saddened, as must we all be."

She motioned for me to take the chair opposite, but I hesitated. "I did not mean to intrude upon your solitude."

"My solitude! My dear, you do me a service, I promise. My own thoughts are necessarily unhappy ones. I only knew her for two days, and yet I admit I am shaken."

"As was Timothy Gresham," I observed. "For a physician he seemed quite distressed to preside over a death."

"A kindly man," she said. "A pity he never married. He would have made an indulgent but affectionate father, I think."

"At least he has Elspeth for companionship," I offered.

Augusta was too well-bred to sink to cynicism, but a curious little light glowed in her eyes. "Do you think so?"

"Do you not?"

She considered a moment, canting her head as she thought. "I have never been able to plumb her depths. She is a curious soul, our Elspeth."

"I thought that you knew her well, from that first visit to Cherboys."

"Knew her? Yes. Well? No. I do not believe anyone knows her well, perhaps not even Timothy. She is a solitary person, not easily given to forming friendships."

"She seems fond of you," I ventured.

Again that gleam in her eyes. "Elspeth is easily impressed with social position. She values knowing 'Lady MacIver' rather more than she values knowing 'Augusta.'"

"What was she like then, when you first met her?"

Augusta tipped her head back, resting it on the chair as she looked at the ceiling. It had been painted with a scene of Mars preparing for war, a singularly unsuitable theme for a library, I should have thought. But the brushwork was excellent and the colours sublime. It was also subversive. I noticed that Venus was distracting the god of war whilst her tiny winged son, Cupid, made away with his enchanted armour.

"Do you see that little cloud in the corner?" she asked, pointing upwards with a graceful hand.

"The one with the cherub peeking out?"

"That was Elspeth. Always watching, never *doing*. The rest of us used to get up to silly games—Blindman's Bluff, charades, that sort of thing. It was just boisterous fun, but she always gave the impression she disapproved of our little romps. She was forever wandering off, book in hand, usually to read on St. Frideswide's chair. It was her great escape since Timothy has no head for heights and could never abide going there to find her. And when she did join us, she always gave the impression she had better things to do with her time. We began to make a point of eluding her. Not very kind, in retrospect, but perhaps we may be excused on the grounds of youth and thoughtlessness," she said with a wistful look.

"I think none of us are as kind as we could be," I told her frankly.

"You are too gracious by half." She paused and glanced about the library. "It is curious. I always associate her with this room. Lord Templeton-Vane was very generous with his books. He gave us the run of the house and told us we were welcome to read anything we liked. Elspeth was forever turning up and borrowing books—natural history. I thought she was a dreadful bluestocking. My mother would never have permitted me to be found reading such serious books! But with no mother to guide her and only Timothy to act as guardian, she was perhaps not chaperoned as she might have been."

"Your own mother was here at the time?" I asked. I knew the answer, but feigning ignorance is, in my experience, the simplest way to introduce a topic of conversation.

"Oh heavens, yes." Her smile turned rueful. "We used to make a game of eluding her when we were at our most high-spirited. We were forever wandering off through the gardens or into the little copses where Mamma would never think to look. But I would never have been permitted to visit James here if she had not come. My virtue had been auctioned to the highest bidder, and it was to be protected until my wedding night."

"But I thought—" I broke off. There was no polite way to phrase my enquiry, but Augusta merely laughed, and it was a kindly laugh.

"I do not mean it literally, my dear. James had not a bean, bless him. It was my father who had the wealth. James was heir to a title and an estate he would never be able to afford to keep without my money. So, our fathers struck a bargain. James' blue blood in exchange for my gold. Their grandsons would be the benefactors of both. Does it surprise you to know such things happen?"

"No," I told her truthfully. "Only that you speak forthrightly. Most people make a huge pretence about it."

"I am a pragmatic woman, Veronica. And I pay you the compliment of recognising that you are as well. There are far worse foundations for a marriage than security. James' family had been marrying their cousins for two centuries. They needed fresh, vigourous blood and an infusion of cash. My family wanted the sort of respectability that comes from thousands of acres and a title. Everyone was made happy."

"A sound enough basis for a marriage, provided affection comes in the wake of such an arrangement."

"Respect and consideration are the most one may expect at the outset," she told me. "One is indeed lucky when affection follows."

Her frankness upon the subject led me to an indelicate enquiry. "And has it for you?"

She smiled. "How could one not feel affection for James? He is a good man. And he is an excellent father. He denies me nothing, and whenever he is made aware of my preferences, he is amiable enough to acquiesce to them."

"Made aware? He does not intuit them?"

She laughed, a rich, mellow laugh. "My dear, have you ever met the man who could intuit a woman's wishes? No, do not answer. If you have, I should be extremely envious and I should not care to be jealous of a new friend. Let it be sufficient to say that I have contentment in my marriage, and that is more than most women in my position."

"Did you never wish for more?"

"What more? You mean a grand passion?" She paused and looked heavenwards again, pointing to the god of war and his purloined armour. "That is what happens when grand passions are involved. Mars is seduced and his very purpose is thwarted. He lost sight of what is most important to him and love robbed him blind."

"A valuable lesson for us all, I suppose," I said.

"Indeed. I suppose you think me very mercenary," she said, smiling again.

"Not at all. I admire your willingness to view the truth through an unclouded glass."

"Illusions are the playthings of children. And we are women grown," she reminded me. She rose and shook out her skirts. "I have been too much with my own thoughts today and I am growing morbid. I think I will pay a call upon Nanny MacQueen. I met her when I was here last, and she might like some little delicacy from the kitchens."

"It is kind of you to think of her," I replied. I regarded Nanny Mac-Queen's cottage with the same degree of pleasure I might contemplate the gates of Hell.

Augusta smiled wearily. "If there is one thing I have learnt in my years of Good Works, it is that thinking of others can be a blessed respite from thinking of oneself."

She left in a rustle of skirts. For all her forty thousand acres, her sons, and her title, I did not envy Augusta MacIver. She had made a common bargain—exchanging her youth, money, and beauty for the security of an ancient title and the position it purchased within society. She had leveraged it to become one of the most celebrated hostesses in London, the sort of woman whose table accommodated ministers and ambassadors, philosophers and aristocrats. And yet there was a vein of some emotion I could not precisely identify that ran within her. Not regret, for she seemed contented with her lot. Nostalgia perhaps, for the girl she had been and the other choices she might have made?

Whatever my musings on Augusta MacIver, they had no bearing on the matter at hand. Alone at last, I settled myself in one of the window embrasures, tucking my feet up under my skirts. The heavy velvet draperies were drawn back but loosely, so that the deep folds concealed me from the casual visitor to the library. I had no wish to be interrupted as I perused Lorenzo's notebook, and the light was excellent. I took an apple from my pocket and munched contentedly as I studied the slender volume. It still smelt of leather, but faintly, and the little gilded bee upon the cover was nearly undetectable. There were marks on the cover, seawater, perhaps? And the entries were made with whatever Lorenzo had had to hand—a stub of pencil, a stray pen, the nib unmended and spluttering ink in blots. A corner of the book had been nibbled away—rats, I thought, with some distaste, and other pages bore the stains of a life well travelled: food, wine, candle grease.

It was easy to see where he had sketched on the fly, rendering his impressions in a few bold strokes. In other places, he wrote more carefully, dating his pages and heading them with his location. He matched his language to the setting, switching from lyrical Italian during what was apparently the last few days the party were in Florence to somewhat stilted English for their stay at Cherboys. There were misspellings, some corrected with a single, elegant stroke of the pen as he struggled to find the proper word. He spoke kindly of Lord Templeton-Vane—it always surprised me when someone had a good opinion of the bête noire of Stoker's childhood—and he waxed poetic about the cliffs themselves. The entry written the day he discovered the fossil was rhapsodic, evidenced by his lapsing once or twice into his native tongue. The following pages were full of sketches of the various bones in as much detail as he could manage without the skeleton being fully excavated. There were little jottings in the margins, aides-mémoire regarding mundane matters such as a coat sent to a tailor or a donation given in aid of a countryman who had fallen upon hard times. There was a note to remind him to reply to his sister's letter, and I felt a dart of pity for Beatrice, knowing how she must have lamented seeing a reference to herself in her beloved brother's journal.

There was much talk of the fossil and his plans for it. He was adamant that the creature should end in a museum for the twin purposes of scientific study and public edification. One entry was apparently written in a passion, the pen scraping deeply into the page as he re-

corded his outrage that a portion of the cliff had crumbled away, taking several small bones with it. He lamented the fact that the fossil
would be incomplete, although the bones themselves, sketched in detail, were obviously of modest significance, making up the very tip of
the beast's tail. He had carried his complaint to Lord Templeton-Vane,
wanting security to be set over the exposed bones, but instead his
lordship had forbidden anyone access to the site, explaining that a
portion of the cliff had become dangerously unstable.

The last several pages were blank. It was apparent this was the final notebook he kept, proven by the date on the last entry and the
thaumatrope tucked into the back. I remembered Merry's recollection
of the little toy and the fact that Lorenzo had intended it for his sister.
It was, as Merry had said, a bit of card with a bird on one side and a
cage on the other, two strings extending from the sides. I twirled it,
causing the little bird to fly in and out of the cage, a simple optical il-
lusion and yet magic to a small child.

I replaced it in the back of the notebook and reviewed the final entry
with care. Previous notes were devoted to the fossil and Lorenzo's regret
that Lord Templeton-Vane had forbidden its excavation on the grounds
that the cliffs had become too treacherous. Lorenzo seemed to accept this
even as he deplored the necessity for it, but the last entry was different.
With its bold handwriting and little errors of syntax or spelling, it conveyed a feel for the young man, offering a peek into his personality.

*The local villagers seem certain the coming storms will be harsh
ones, full of heavy rain and most powerful winds. I do not like to
abuse the ~~hospitlty~~ ~~hosipitaly~~ hospitality of my host, but it is a thing
that must be done. Of course, the [word obliterated by rats] wishes
to help me and I am grateful for the extra pair of hands. I have had
a note of conciliazion, assuring me that all will be well. Perhaps we
can at last settle the matter between us once and for all. We will slip*

away after the others are abed as this work must be secret, but I am
uneasy tonight. Has someone been exvacating the bones of my fossil?

I gave a soft cry of triumph. Lorenzo had believed his fossil at risk
and was determined to protect it, both from the depredations of late
summer storms and from possible thievery.

I turned the page, but this was definitely the last, and dated the night
Lorenzo fell to his death. It was proof he intended to go to the fossil and
it was proof he did not mean to go alone. It was this passage that persuaded Beatrice someone was responsible for her brother's death, and I
could not fault her reasoning. Lorenzo was meeting someone else,
against Lord Templeton-Vane's contraventions, secretly and in the
storm-tossed darkness, for the purposes of saving his fossil. There was
the cryptic hint at some quarrel hitherto unmended, and Lorenzo's
mention of his unease. What bone-deep disquiet had he entertained
about the night's work? And more importantly, why had he not heeded
it? Was it merely the danger of removing the bones of the dinosaur from
a crumbling cliffside that unnerved him? Was it the violation of the
rules of hospitality by thwarting Lord Templeton-Vane's wishes? Or was
it the primeval fear of being alone in the dark with a foe?

Of course, all might have been revealed had it not been for the word
destroyed by rapacious rats, I thought darkly. I held the book to the light,
attempting to make some sense of it with better illumination. It began
with "strang," and by an heroic effort, I managed to detect the beginnings of an "e" as well as the final letter: "r." "The stranger!" I read aloud.
"How very peculiar." Peculiar indeed because no one staying at Cherboys
ought to have been a stranger at that point. The Seven Sinners had been
travelling together for some months. The Templeton-Vanes and their staff
and neighbours and other guests were not strangers to Lorenzo.

I flicked through the pages again, looking for another mention of
the word, and found only two. "The stranger is quarrelsome with me

today," ran one entry, but the rest of the page was devoted to a sketch of the Pineapple Pavilion done in a puckish style. The other mention was even less instructive. "I must make a decision about the stranger soon. This situation cannot endure." Cryptic and entirely unhelpful, I decided. I pocketed the book and continued to think. The word "stranger" was a curious choice. It conveyed a sense of alienness, a person apart. Had he meant it playfully? Was it a pet name given because this was an individual with whom he shared little?

But there are other connotations for the word in Italian, I remembered. It may also mean "foreigner," and perhaps *this* was the meaning Lorenzo intended to record. Of course! I realised with a thrill of certainty. He was travelling with six other men, five of whom were not his countrymen. Only Pietro, another Italian, could be excluded from this list; only Pietro could, with certainty, not have been the person with him when he died. And this accounted for why Beatrice had never suspected her own husband. Pietro had not suffered her vengeance because she understood that he alone of the Sinners could not have been responsible for Lorenzo's death. Only the others, not Italians, were potential murderers.

The "stranger" was clearly Lorenzo's pet name for one of his friends, a friend who had engaged in some conflict with him, possibly over the fossil. Instantly my mind went to Kaspar von Hochstaden. He too had been a keen fossilist. Had he resented Lorenzo's find? Jealousy was rife even amongst amateur natural historians. He might have deplored the fact that Lorenzo had succeeded in unearthing this glorious monster, which promised to be the find of a lifetime. Had he quarrelled with Lorenzo over its fate? Over how the excavation should proceed? Lorenzo hinted at such disagreements with the "stranger," whoever he might be.

From my conversation with Sir James, I recalled that Lorenzo had a keen sense of honour. Would that honour cause him to include a fellow fossilist in his find even if the glory belonged solely to himself? I had a fair grasp of Lorenzo's personality, I believed. It seemed entirely in keeping with what I knew of him that he might have, out of generosity, consulted Kaspar. Perhaps in his moment of triumph, he had reached out to the German to include him and later had cause to regret it. It was all supposition, of course, but it was possible. Whoever the "stranger" was, he had clearly accompanied Lorenzo to the cliff that fateful night.

And whether Lorenzo's death was accidental or due to some more malicious intent, his companion at the time had never come forward, never offered an explanation which might have given comfort to those left behind. This naturally led to the conclusion that the other party bore some responsibility. It may have been as small as failing to offer sufficient aid or it may have been as calculated as outright murder. In any event, there was a failure of heart, of courage, in permitting Lorenzo's death to go unexplained.

Little wonder this document had sent Beatrice upon her errand of revenge. With only these few scant lines, she had constructed a plausible hypothesis—that someone had been with Lorenzo when he died and they had failed to save him. Was this worthy of her vengeance? Certainly not, but to a mind already twisted by the devastating losses she had suffered, the injustice of knowing Lorenzo had been robbed of his life whilst his companion had apparently gone on with theirs, it must have made a sort of grim logic. The fact that by killing each of the Sinners she must necessarily have killed a number of thoroughly innocent people seemed not to have troubled her at all. That spoke of a ruthlessness I had not detected in her, and a flaw I must deplore. Justice, for all that the law makes a stranger of it at times, must be carried out with the greatest care.

No justice that imperiled the innocent could ever be true, and Beatrice's recklessness spoke volumes as to her rage. I did not much care for the common habit of ascribing certain views or habits to a natural character, but Beatrice was a Florentine, and that city had certainly had its share of bloody quarrels. Feuds and disputes between families were the stuff of legend, and only by settling scores could one satisfy the family honour. I ran a finger over the little bee cipher on the cover. How obliged she must have felt, the last of the d'Ambrogios, to avenge the lost members of her family—not just Lorenzo, but the parents whose deaths were hastened by his tragic loss. And how much more must she have felt the burden of this, knowing that her own days were to be short in number.

I felt a sliver of pity for her, but no more. I could understand her methods and her motivation; I could even sympathise, but I could not condone. She had ensured the deaths of Kaspar von Hochstaden and Alexandre du Plessis, and she had received her just deserts. Now, it was entirely possible that she had, in murdering them, achieved her vengeance, but I doubted it. Someone at Cherboys had deduced that she was the author of their deaths and taken pains to ensure she could not kill again. Was it to exact justice for Kaspar and Alexandre? Or was it to make certain she could not come for them? It was entirely possible that Lorenzo's companion that dreadful night was still at large, killing Beatrice to protect himself, eliminating her before she could eliminate him.

Or her, I realised with a start. I turned feverishly through the pages again until I came to the sketches of the missing bones from Lorenzo's fossil. And I knew precisely where I had seen them before.

CHAPTER

30

The excitement of the chase sped my steps as I hurried along the footpath towards the village. Not even the sight of a particularly handsome Purple Emperor flapping at the edge of the duck pond could slow my pace, although I regretted the lost opportunity to perhaps find a chrysalis to carry back to London and nurture to fruition in my vivarium. But this was too important a mission to permit any deviation from my path. I had recognised the elegant little drawings in Lorenzo's book. It had taken me a moment to place them, but my mind whipped back to the morning in Wren Cottage. Whilst Augusta and Elspeth made polite conversation, I had spied the assorted trinkets arranged upon the mantelpiece—china shepherdesses and porcelain ducks. And tucked in amongst them, a handful of tiny bones of so distinctive an appearance there was no mistaking them. They were the very bones sitting on Elspeth Gresham's mantelpiece. I had assumed they were Timothy's bones, but how blinkered I had been! How could I have overlooked the possibility that the natural historian in the family was not the brother—with his weak head for heights—but the sister? The lonely, awkward sister who preferred books to beaux and fossils to fancy dress.

I arrived at Wren Cottage in a fever of anticipation. I stood upon the step, composing myself as I reached for the brass knocker. I rapped once, twice, thrice, sharply—as sharply as the judge would rap the gavel to pronounce sentence upon the murderous Elspeth Gresham. I had not thought to bring a weapon beyond the usual minuten tucked into my cuffs and my customary corset blade, but I did not believe she would prove difficult to subdue. I had the advantage of surprise, youth, experience, and a comprehensive grounding in one of the more obscure of the martial arts. If nothing else, a stout scream in her face should shock her sufficiently to render her hors de combat.

It occurred to me only belatedly that it was rather unsporting of me not to reveal my deductions to Stoker, but with the wager on the line and his current mood, I far preferred to present him with a fait accompli in the form of a confessed murderess. I waited upon the step, anticipation rising as I listened to the click of footsteps upon the flags of the hall. Someone was coming near, ever near, and at last the door was flung back. Elspeth stood, enveloped in a starched pinafore, her colour rosier than I had yet seen it, looking almost attractive. A wisp of hair was loosened from her chignon, softening her face, and to my astonishment, she smiled.

"Veronica! You must excuse my appearance. I have been at the canning. The raspberries will not wait, you know. Come through and join us in the parlour. It is the morning for visitors, it seems," she called over her shoulder as she led the way into the small parlour.

There, lounging insouciantly in her best armchair, teacup cradled in his hand, plate of cake on his knee, was Stoker. He smiled lazily at me as Elspeth surveyed her tea table. The cat was back and with it a spaniel of great antiquity. It lifted its head to peer at me through age-misted eyes, broke wind audibly, then settled back to sleep.

"Oh dear, we've run out of sugar." Elspeth clucked her tongue. "I'll fetch more." She bustled out of the room, leaving me alone with Stoker and the flatulent spaniel.

"Hallo, Veronica," he said, sapphirine eyes agleam. "I see we both had the same thought."

"I hardly think so," I said with a tight smile at Stoker. "I have come for a *very specific* purpose," I told him. I turned deliberately towards the mantel, but the bones were missing.

"Looking for these?" he enquired. He held out his free hand, and there, nestled in his palm, were the bones.

"Indeed," I said, clipping the word sharply.

"I suppose you think they are of significance," he went on.

"I know they are. There are sketches of them in Lorenzo d'Ambrogio's notebo—"

Too late, I bit off the word. Stoker arched an imperious brow, every bit as much an aristocrat as Tiberius in that moment. "Now, Veronica, surely you did not resort to such a low and underhanded stratagem as stealing the private property of a gentleman?"

Any general worth his salt knows that the high ground is always preferable, but when one finds oneself in a morass, the best tactic is to ride straight ahead at the enemy in the hopes one may break his courage.

"I did what was necessary in order to solve this case," I told him loftily. "There are sketches of *those* bones," I said, pointing for emphasis, "in Lorenzo's notebook. He was upset they had been stolen from the fossil. Those same bones have been resting upon *that* mantelpiece," I said, pointing again, "for twenty years. They might have been taken by Timothy Gresham, but it was not he who held forth on the subject of Mary Anning at dinner the first night. It was Elspeth. She stole the bones and she murdered Lorenzo d'Ambrogio over a fossil."

A gentle cough came from the doorway. "I did not, in point of fact, kill Lorenzo," Elspeth said as she entered with a bowl of sugar. She seated herself behind the tea table and poured out a cup for me. "You needn't fear it is poisoned, dear. Stoker and I have been drinking from that pot." She paused, and her expression, usually so sedately sour, looked almost amused. Her eyes even *twinkled* as she handed me the cup. "But do not sweeten it if you fear the sugar. I did just bring it in from another room."

Stoker reached out and, with great deliberation, added two large lumps to his cup. She did the same, and they both stirred and sipped. I drank a little of my tea to be polite, and she gave a satisfied nod. "Well then. If you were truly persuaded I was a murderess, you would not have taken refreshment from my table. I must say, I know I ought to be thoroughly offended, but it is rather exciting to be suspected of such a thing! I have been so dull for so long, it is gratifying to know someone thinks I am capable of more than just putting up the jam and calling upon the poor and needy."

"I am certain the poor and needy appreciate your efforts," Stoker said kindly.

She waved a hand. "No doubt. But one can only dispense so much beef tea and knit so many socks before half a lifetime is gone and there is nothing to show for it." Her mouth lapsed into its usual sullen lines for a moment. "I thought it would all be quite different, you know. *I* was different. At twenty, I wanted nothing more than to study fossils, to excavate, to make a name for myself like Mary Anning. I used to roam the cliffs for hours on end, digging, always digging. I ruined my complexion and my hands, according to my mother, and no gentleman would ever want such a freckled, windblown creature for a wife. But I did not care. I knew what I wanted, more than anything in the world. I would find the greatest fossil ever discovered. It would be named for me, and when I had dug it out of the earth, I would sell it to the highest bidder, some grand museum or person of royalty who would pay a prince's ransom to own it. And I would go to London to see it delivered and men of science would shake my hand. I would give lectures about how I had found it, me, Miss Elspeth Gresham of Dearsley." Her eyes had taken on a faraway look as she spoke, but she gathered herself with a shake. "Well, young people can be very stupid, and I was very young. Such a silly dream, but it was mine. Until Lorenzo d'Ambrogio came." Her mouth twisted and she took a deep draught of her tea.

"And he discovered your fossil," Stoker said gently.

"The first half hour he looked!" Her tone was frankly exasperated. "I had been digging for years, *years,* and he managed it in an afternoon. I burned with it, but oh, how I loved that fossil! I had found the first hint of it, you see. The month before, some of the cliff had come away and brought a bit of bone. It was not much, hardly more than a splinter, but I knew something great was locked in those cliffs. I thought of it as my fossil, even though Lorenzo found the rest of it. I found it first, *first,* mind you."

She paused and gave a sharp nod as if to stake her claim. "But that wasn't good enough for Lord Templeton-Vane. I asked him for men to help dig it out, I was that convinced it lay just out of reach. One good effort would have exposed it for all to see. But the cliffs were precarious and he was worried he might lose a good farmhand or two if we pressed on. So he roped off the cliffs and forbade anyone from going near. I had hopes of persuading him, but he was immovable, the old devil." She paused and looked at Stoker. "Begging your pardon, I know he was your father."

Stoker shrugged. "I assure you, I have called him worse and often to his face."

She picked up the thread of her tale. "Some weeks later, Tiberius and his friends arrived. They did as they were told so long as the old lord was about, but one day he had to go out on the farms, and Tiberius thought it would be a great lark to do a spot of digging and see what they could turn up. And that Lorenzo finds my beautiful beast! They were carrying him around on their shoulders like a conquering hero—for finding *my* fossil."

"And presumably Lord Templeton-Vane heard of it when he returned home and refused them access to the cliffs again?" I ventured.

She nodded. "He roared and fussed and stormed about at being disobeyed. Lorenzo was most apologetic, the perfect gentleman," she added sourly. "It never occurred to him to apologise to *me*. He'd never have found the beast if it had not been for my excavations. Lord

Templeton-Vane wanted to make amends for keeping him away until the cliffs could be shored up, so he hosted a dance. We were invited, you know. Timothy and I. And I had to sit there whilst they toasted him, Lorenzo d'Ambrogio, finder of lost wonders."

She paused, her lips working furiously. "It was the greatest thing I ever found, and it wasn't even mine. Timothy knew I'd been the first to discover a bit of it, but he wouldn't say boo to a goose, not if that goose were surnamed Templeton-Vane! 'Mustn't be churlish,' that's all he said to me. And the rest of them, pouring out rivers of champagne. I fairly burned to tell them what I thought of it all. But I looked around that ballroom, at the gathering of men, so sure of themselves, so privileged. And what could I possibly say against that? For all my airs, I was a country doctor's daughter. I knew not to speak crossways to my 'betters.' So I swallowed my pride with my champagne and I went home and vowed never to speak of it again. And I gave up fossil hunting forever."

She had flared with indignation during her little speech, but the fight seemed suddenly to go out of her. She picked the cat up onto her lap and stroked it, putting her face against its fur. It purred, low and softly, as if to give consolation to its mistress. When she had collected herself, she resumed her tale.

"The very next night the storms came. Everyone stayed inside, shutters battened. We knew it was going to be a bad one, we did. And I wet my pillow with tears, thinking of my beautiful fossil. I knew the cliffs wouldn't hold under that kind of weather. I'd been clambering around them the whole of my life. I knew them like the back of my own hands." She held up her hands, surveying the lines and spots of age. "I never did have a lady's hands. My mother used to bathe them in milk and send me to bed wearing gloves, but I was happiest with the good Devon soil beneath my nails. I was limber as a limpet in those days. I could outclimb any man. But I would never have dared those cliffs in that storm. It was a fool's errand. I knew my fossil would be lost, and I grieved for that. But I will admit I laughed myself silly thinking that Lorenzo d'Ambrogio would get his comeuppance when *his* great find was washed into the sea."

Catching my look of interest, she smiled. "I don't mean his death, Veronica. I mean the sheer fit of pique he would suffer at claiming such a discovery and having Nature herself snatch it back. She was always on my side, Mother Nature. I woke up the next morning, and it was as if the breath of God had blown across the land. Apple trees in the orchard uprooted, tiles from the roofs half a league away. Even the cows were wandering about looking as if they'd just been to Paris and back. And then the news came that Lorenzo d'Ambrogio was missing. We set out, all of us—yes, even me—to find him. I knew at once where he'd gone because I'd wanted to go so badly myself. No one who loved that fossil could have rested easily that night. But where I valued my own life more than the bones, Lorenzo hadn't any such qualms. I was the one who found him, lying at the base of the cliff where it had crumbled away into the sea. He had landed upon stones, great boulders, and you would have thought he'd have been ugly, but he wasn't. He looked like Icarus, dashed from the heavens."

She paused and rubbed her face into the cat's fur again. When she looked up, her eyes were bright with unshed tears. "You wouldn't think it would upset me all this time later, but to see such beauty taken in its prime. Oh yes, he was beautiful. I don't imagine you would have realised it at the time, Stoker," she said with an arch smile, "but he was. Even as I hated him, I could see he was the loveliest man I'd ever meet. The sort of otherworldly beauty you read about in fairy tales, the beauty of enchanted princes, the beauty that is cursed for it never brings happiness. Ganymede, cupbearer to the gods." Into the solemn silence that followed, the spaniel broke wind again.

"Did you know that Beatrice Salviati was his sister?" I asked.

She opened her mouth, then closed it again, shaking her head. "No. She seemed familiar somehow, but not in any way I could place. I can see it now. She had his grace, a way of holding herself. Poise, I suppose you'd call it. Perhaps something about the nose. Poor lady."

I flicked a glance to Stoker and he stirred himself, putting his cup aside and sitting forward to address Elspeth. "Beatrice believed that Lorenzo's death was not accidental."

Elspeth shifted, startling the cat, who leapt from her lap and straight onto the top of a bookshelf. Elspeth had gone quite pale and she took a hasty sip of her tea. The cup clattered a little in the saucer as she put it down.

"That is a dreadful thing to contemplate," she said at last.

"But possible," Stoker pressed gently.

She thought a moment, then nodded, her expression grave. "Yes. It would take someone very brave or very foolish, but yes. He might have been . . . pushed."

Stoker and I said nothing, and she went on. "I realise that puts me squarely under suspicion. I had motive, I suppose, if I were a thoroughly irrational creature acting solely out of jealousy over the fossil. And I was good with heights and a skilled climber, all of which I have just admitted to you—very foolish if I did in fact kill him. I've also made no secret of my antipathy towards him, which is again rather shortsighted if I shoved him over the cliff. Wouldn't a clever murderess have pretended to like him, claimed to be terrible with heights, feigned a complete disinterest in fossils? Wouldn't a clever murderess have at least hid the bones from sight?" she demanded, pointing to the little group of bones.

"Indeed," said Stoker amiably. "Of course a *very* clever murderess would have done exactly the opposite and pointed it all out to us as you have just done. A double bluff."

She smiled in spite of herself. "I am not that clever, Stoker. I am petty. I bear grudges and I nurture resentments. But I am no murderess. I did not push Lorenzo over that cliff. I did not kill Beatrice. You must look further afield for your villain."

CHAPTER

31

We took our leave shortly thereafter. As we paused upon the threshold, I turned back to Elspeth. "Did you really give up fossil hunting after discovering your Megalosaurus?"

There was a melancholic sweetness to her face, the sort of expression a woman might wear as she bids farewell to a lover going off to war, knowing she will not meet him again.

"I did. I hadn't the heart for it after that. But lately, I have begun to realise how much I miss it. I was never so alive as when I dug among the dead."

With that, she closed the door upon us and we left Wren Cottage. Stoker drew in a great lungful of the sweet late summer air. It was scented with roses and phlox, the last gasp before the gentle decay of autumn settled in. The spaniel trotted on its antique legs after Stoker, lifting its head for a pat. He obediently bent down and ruffled the threadbare ears.

"I sincerely hope Elspeth is indeed not a murderess. We have entirely too many dogs already and if you bring that walking sofa cushion home with you, I shall not be responsible for my actions."

He continued to fondle the creature's ears, a barely suppressed smile twitching the corners of his mouth.

"You needn't look so pleased with yourself," I told him waspishly. "You were just as incorrect as I."

"But I relied solely upon my powers of deduction," he replied in lofty tones. "You, my deceitful minx, resorted to larceny in order to arrive at the same conclusion as I. Yours, therefore, was the greater misstep. You had far more resources, and yet you fared no better—worse, in fact. For I arrived earlier than you. Remind me again, Veronica. How well do you enjoy losing a wager?"

"I have not lost yet," I answered through gritted teeth.

He sent the spaniel trotting back to its mistress and we took the shorter footpath to Cherboys, pausing where a bit of it branched off to Nanny MacQueen's cottage.

"I am sorry about J. J.," I ventured. "I ought to have told you she was here."

"I ought to have guessed," he said with a shrug.

"You astonish me. I thought you meant to hold a proper grudge about that."

"I have plenty of other things to hold a grudge over," he assured me.

I held up a hand. "Perhaps ere you begin to catechise my faults, you will be good enough to give me the benefit of your medical knowledge."

He folded his arms over the breadth of his chest. "About?"

"The strychnine. We have established it could not have been introduced in the food at dinner. But the strychnine might have been introduced into Beatrice's tonic."

He considered it a moment, then shook his head. "No. She must have consumed the poison after leaving the house."

"How can you possibly know that?" I demanded.

"Because she did not have the bottle on her person. I handled her body when I performed that extremely rudimentary postmortem. I took the liberty of looking over her clothing. She had no bottle with her, and she did not have it with her the previous night. Perhaps it was not her custom to carry it with her in the evening, particularly when it would have been a simple thing to go upstairs or to send a servant for it. The extreme nature of her attack suggests the poison was a large dose, administered on the island."

"Botheration," I muttered. "Then we are no nearer to clearing Julien as a suspect. I hope he is better after his little outburst this morning?"

"Sleeping off the better part of a whole bottle of Napoléon cognac."

"I thought brandy was the only spirit known by that designation."

"No, I mean cognac that actually belonged to Napoléon. Julien was given a case by a grateful client and always travels with a bottle for emergencies."

"Well, I suppose being suspected of murder might well count as such," I allowed.

"Would you care to come with me to visit Nanny?" Stoker enquired, a gleam in his eyes.

"I would rather be tortured by one of the lesser demons in Hell, thank you," I replied cordially.

He was still laughing when I left him.

I wandered slowly back towards Cherboys, thoroughly vexed with Elspeth Gresham. A lady had no business going around not murdering people when she had excellent motive, plausible means, and the correct temperament. Elspeth was decisive, physically strong, and by her own admission capable of coaxing along a seedling of a grudge until it flowered.

"How dare she be innocent," I muttered. "It is *most* inconsiderate."

So irritated was I that I took the long way round, circling the Pineapple Pavilion. As I passed the back, I heard voices within. My senses prickled. I could not have said why, precisely, but there was something of a hushed, furtive quality about them, and I realised it was high time to engage in a little harmless eavesdropping.

I eased into the shadows of the pineapple, moving on silent feet towards the French windows. They had been thrown open to admit the luscious air, no doubt, and this permitted me to hear everything so long as I crouched.

"I do hope it shan't cause trouble if I am discovered here. It is the *family* part of the estate, after all." The first of the two voices was female, purring as distinctly as Elspeth's cat.

A male voice, earnest and kindly. "Oh no, no. It is quite all right, I assure you. You are my guest, as such. I mean, your request for confession demands privacy. Now, I cannot say that I have much experience with confession. My father was very High Church, but my own ambitions have always been much more modest." He broke off for a moment, and I could well imagine the gentle blush on Merryweather's cheek. "Of course, if I can give comfort, then it is my bounden duty to hear whatever you have to tell me."

"It is not so much what I can tell you as what you can tell me," the female voice replied. It was still catlike, but the sort of cat that waits mercilessly outside the hole of a trembling mouse, anticipating its next meal.

"J. J.," I mouthed furiously.

"You see," she went on in that oleaginous tone, "I am not really a maidservant. I have come in disguise, as it were."

"Oh, I say! How extraordinary," Merry replied.

"Indeed. I am, in fact, a connection of your brother Stoker's. And Miss Speedwell's. I have upon several occasions been with them in the course of their investigative adventures."

"Investigative what?"

"Adventures. Do you mean you don't know? Your brother and Veronica Speedwell are responsible for unmasking several murderous villains. They have imperiled themselves in the course of justice more times than I can enumerate!" She paused and pitched her voice lower, conspiratorial, coaxing him into her confidence. "If you were to see your brother's bared torso, you would note the fresh scars upon his person, the marks of bullet and knife inflicted upon his flesh by desperate fiends."

"When have *you* seen my brother's bared torso?" was Merry's shocked reply.

"I nursed him," J. J. returned, doing an excellent impression of insulted modesty. "I have assisted and indeed even led them, upon occasion. We are close as the proverbial peas in the pod. I came down with Julien d'Orlande because I feared this very thing would happen— *murder.*" She breathed the last word out in a thrilled whisper.

Merry made a noise of protest, a sort of whimper, and I could well imagine him thrusting his hands through his hair. "I cannot credit it. My brother and Veronica, involved in murder."

"In the solving of it," she corrected hastily. "They are servants of justice, Father. As well may you be."

"Me? How so?"

"I believe you may have information about the murder that has taken place within the walls of Cherboys."

"Murder!" His exclamation resounded through the tiny pineapple and I could well imagine J. J. wincing as she shushed him.

"Not so loud, I beg you! We must be clever. There is a murderer on the loose, I am certain of it. Stoker and Veronica are as well. And I am assisting them," she said.

"But then won't you be in peril as well?" Merry sounded troubled.

"Ah, but not as much as they," she said. "For I have a secret weapon, a stalwart companion and helper in this endeavour." She must have given him a nod or a wink, for he made a choking sound.

"Me? You want me to help you find a killer?"

"You need not fear, Father, no harm will come to you, I promise. But you may well know something that could assist me in unmasking the miscreant who took Beatrice Salviati's life. You could be the key to solving this mystery."

"But how?"

"You may have seen something. You were sitting next to her at the fateful dinner. How was her mood?"

With that, they were off. They spent the next several minutes discussing Beatrice's disposition that evening as well as the movements of the staff serving the food and drink. I might have put a stop to the interrogation, and I was even poised to charge in to rescue Merryweather, when I realised I might use whatever J. J. gleaned from him to my advantage. I did not much care for the fact that she discussed our detectival exploits with him, but family feeling would prevent him from spreading tales abroad. Stoker and I both preferred for various reasons to keep our involvement in such investigations secret. It was enough to know that justice was satisfied by our efforts. Justice—but not always the law. We had little faith in the established systems that governed our island. We had, both of us, fallen afoul of what was strictly legal, and we were thoroughly convinced that justice was the superior aim. And listening to Merry's discourse might well provide a piece to the puzzle.

But crouching is devilishly hard upon the ankles, no matter how supple they may be, and I was forced to change position to stretch them. In doing so, I missed one of J. J.'s questions and heard only Merry's response. "No," he said slowly. "I think she was well, except perhaps a bit overexcited. She had to take a little of her tonic."

"Did she?" J. J.'s voice sharpened with interest. "I never saw her drink it at dinner."

"Oh, not at dinner. On the boat on the way over. She took a deep drink of it and made a sort of face. It must be terribly bitter, but medicines often are, aren't they?"

I caught my breath. This then was how the poison had been introduced. Stoker, I reflected with an emotion very like glee, had been entirely incorrect.

I waited until Merry's footsteps receded. I was still crouched in the shadow of the pineapple when J. J.'s voice came, clear as a bell, through the open windows.

"Did you hear anything of use, Veronica?"

She peered around the window, smiling broadly.

"From that angle, you resemble nothing so much as that fiendish cat of Lewis Carroll's," I told her. "Nothing but a smug smile and an air of self-satisfaction that is deeply unattractive."

"Now, now. You needn't be nasty just because I managed to coax some information from the young parson."

"Coax! You told him you wanted to make Confession," I protested.

"I did. I confessed to being here under false pretences."

"You did not tell him you are a reporter," I retorted. "You are a journalist, J. J. One of that most reprehensible and parasitical fraternity."

"I am a teller of truth. I am an upholder of justice. I am—"

"Do spare me the moral righteousness. It was very wrong of you to use young Merryweather in that fashion."

Her small hands curled into fists and her bottom lip was slightly outthrust.

She was clearly sulking and I took a deep breath. "You are still angry about what happened earlier. And I am sorry. I ought not to have implied you would sell a story about Julien to further your career."

"Bloody right I wouldn't." She sighed. "Veronica, do you know how exhausting it is? Trying to make something of myself? This world belongs to men and yet I am just as clever and just as canny and just as good as any man on any newspaper in the country."

"Better," I told her. "And I do know. I know you have looked out for your friends, and I ought to give you more credit for your loyalty. Again, I am sorry."

She seemed taken aback by the frankness of my apology. Finally, she gave a grudging nod. "Accepted. And I wouldn't have had to investigate on my own if you hadn't changed your mind about working to-

gether. You seemed to be having second thoughts last night even. Why
did you come over all cold at the dinner? It couldn't just have been
about making certain Stoker didn't find out I was here. He is annoyed,
but his temper is nothing to be afraid of."

She was quite correct in that regard. Stoker's eruptions were vol-
canic, sudden and full of loud fury, but seldom significant. I enjoyed
them as a prelude to other activities, largely because I knew, in my
marrow, that Stoker was incapable of harming a woman.

"I was annoyed that you took it upon yourself to search the Salviatis' suite after I specifically told you not to," I admitted.

She furrowed her brow. "When?"

"Yesterday. Just before the dressing bell. I saw you leaving their
room."

"You did not," she said roundly.

"I saw the back of a maid, and she had a black dress. All of the staff
maids wear blue."

"It was not I," she insisted. "I did as you asked and stayed well clear
of the guest rooms." She paused, folding her arms over her chest. "You
really do think the worst of me, don't you? I was not in the Salviatis'
suite, but what if I had been? Did it never occur to you I might have
had a good reason for it? No, you presumed to know best and expect
me to fall in line. I have my own life to lead, you know. Not everything
in the whole of the universe revolves around you. You are not the *Earth*,
Veronica."

"If by 'universe' you mean 'solar system,' then I feel I ought to point
out that ours is heliocentric."

She let out a little shriek of rage and stamped her foot as she left
me, demonstrating a considerable fluency in profanity as she went.

"Botheration," I said again, to no one in particular.

CHAPTER

32

I left the folly in a state of agitation. I was not pleased to have quit things in such a state with J. J. I had, if I am honest, as I have sworn to be within these pages, few women upon whom I would bestow the appellation "friend," and fewer still to whom I would entrust my most confidential thoughts. J. J. had been admitted to the former, and it was a signal failure upon my part that she had not yet been admitted to the latter. She had proven herself, time and again, a faithful friend. She had upon occasion behaved with understandable deceit; my own hands were not clean upon that score. I had misled, lied, manipulated, and from time to time committed modest crimes in the pursuit of justice. How could I blame her for doing much the same in the cause of earning her bread? For, let us be clear, that was her aim. She invoked the principles of truth and justice, but as much for practicality as for ideals. She had to buy her crust, the same as the rest of us, and it was to her credit that she chose to do so in as difficult a manner as she had. She aimed high, she aimed true.

And although I had often been the author of her thwarted hopes, she had never done me harm because of it. In fact, she had within her grasp the means to do me tremendous evil for a considerable profit, but never had she swerved from her vow of secrecy where my true parentage was concerned. What a story she might have made of it! Her name would have graced the front of every newspaper from London to Lucknow. She would have been feted and feasted, immortalised as the woman who broke one of the greatest scandals ever to involve the British monarchy. She might have rocked the throne itself, toppled it even, such was the potential power of that secret, and yet never had she wavered. She was a stalwart heart, was J. J. Butterworth, and I had not appreciated her friendship as I ought to have done. Loyalty was a quality I claimed to prize, but I had not lived the proof of my proclamations.

Such were my musings as I wandered the grounds at Cherboys. The hour of luncheon had passed, but I had no appetite. I was restless and moody, and I had learnt through painful experience it was best not to inflict such humours upon others. Better to indulge my ill-temper on my own than have to make apologies later, I decided. I avoided anyone else, seeking out the most remote parts of the estate until I roused myself from my torpor and realised I had, without intent, taken the footpath that led to the cliffs.

Perhaps the sea air would blow the cobwebs away, I hoped as I climbed the narrow path. Here and there a gull shrieked, their high voices ominous against the broad blue sky. Clouds were gathering on the water, casting long grey shadows over the waves that whipped up, the foamy manes of the white horses riding across the endless rippling plain of the sea. As I walked, my mind went again to the quarrel with J. J. Something tugged at my consciousness, and I puzzled it over as I walked. J. J. claimed not to have been the maid, but I knew the woman I had seen could not have been one of the regular staff at Cherboys, who would have been wearing blue. Therefore it must have been someone else, dressed in black, wearing apron and cap in an effort to conceal her features. Someone who needed a moment of access to Beatrice's room to introduce the poison to the tonic bottle. Someone who would have had the opportunity to retrieve the tonic bottle later.

As I reached the top of the climb, I realised I was not alone, and I understood that Fate had been directing my footsteps all along.

Perched on the boulder above the crumbling cliff top was Augusta. She was very still, staring out to sea as the wind tore at her hair, blowing it free from pins and net. It rippled behind her, a banner of burnished red-gold. From a distance, the silver strands were invisible, and I could imagine her as she must have been, twenty years ago, ravishing auburn locks tumbling free as she romped and cavorted with the young men around her.

"It was you," I said. I had not intended to speak. The words came of their own accord, and for a long moment, I thought the wind had borne them away, unheard.

But at last she turned her head and I saw that she had been weeping, tears still coursing down her cheeks.

She did not move as I came near. She simply sat, Niobe in her tears.

"Would you like to tell me about it?" I urged. "I am an excellent listener."

She turned back to the sea, then began to speak, her voice tight with emotion. "Do you know what it is to love? To really love someone?"

"I think so."

"You mean Stoker," she said.

"Yes."

She nodded. "He is a good man. He is worthy of your love. Lorenzo d'Ambrogio was not worthy of mine."

She fell silent again and we watched the gulls wheel and dive, darting into the sea for a catch and climbing again, shaking the seawater from their wings.

"You met him here, when you were first betrothed to James, is that right?"

"I had met James precisely twice before our fathers made the arrangements. My mother was so pleased, she fairly glowed. 'A title in the family. Little Gussie will be a lady.'" Augusta cut her eyes at me. "Have you ever heard anything so revolting? They called me 'Gussie' as if I were a cow in the field, munching on clover. And that's all I was in the end. Mamma wanted nothing so much as respectability to go with the new money. She hired all the best tutors—dance, elocution, etiquette. I was taught everything. Everything except what to do with my heart."

She paused and heaved a sigh that seemed to come from her very bones. "But I was reconciled to it. I knew I would never be permitted to choose for myself, and James was nice enough. I could manage him. I could make a good life for myself. And it would have all been perfectly fine if I had just stayed in London and waited for him. It was Mamma's fault, you know. She's the one who insisted we come. She knew I was reconciled but not enthusiastic. It was never enough for her that I did as I was told. I had to *want* to be perfect for her. I had to enjoy the things I was made to do, the endless lessons, the dances, the posing in tableaux like a dressmaker's mannequin. I went to all the fittings for my trousseau. I let her choose everything, just as she liked it. I never complained, not *once*. But neither did I exclaim and prance about with shining eyes, wittering on about my fiancé like other girls did. And one day she shook me by the shoulders, saying I was unnatural and cold. She inveigled an invitation out of Lord Templeton-Vane for us to come and join the house party. I think she believed if I saw James, spent more time with him, I would fall desperately in love and she could pretend it was all a love match instead of a grubby little business arrangement."

She broke off, turning once more to the sea. "So we came and James was here, but I hardly noticed him. Who could notice a James MacIver when there was a Lorenzo d'Ambrogio in the world?"

"I heard it said he was beautiful," I ventured. "Like Ganymede." Elspeth Gresham's comparison seemed apt.

"Cursed cupbearer to the gods. Yes, that is perfect. The worst part was that it didn't matter to him. He never used it, not the way most men might have done. He treated everyone precisely the same. I think I might have been able to resist my feelings if he seemed to try. But he never did. He was exquisitely courteous with everyone and he had no idea what effect he had on people. It was, quite simply, devastating. At least to me."

"You fell in love with him."

"Love!" Her expression was bitter. "The anguish of it was like nothing I have ever known before or since. It settled into my bones like a cancer. It ate at me, day and night. I was feverish with it. I could not eat, could not sleep. I never dared to imagine he might feel the same. But then Lord Templeton-Vane decided to throw a ball. A whim of his, he thought the entertainment would make up for forbidding Lorenzo and Kaspar the right to excavate until the cliffs could be made secure. Lorenzo danced with me. It was the first time he had touched me, and I thought I would kindle into flames right there in the ballroom. And there was champagne. So much champagne," she said with a rueful smile. "It went to my head. I had eaten nothing, which pleased Mamma greatly. She always thought it was elegant to be thin, and I was wasting away for love of Lorenzo. Mamma drank too deeply that night too. She slept in the room adjoining mine, but I could hear her, snoring away from the effects of the wine. So I crept out and went to Lorenzo's room. I did not intend to go to him. I felt like a sleepwalker, moving as if underwater."

Her expression was dreamy as she reminisced, and I wondered if she remembered it thus in order to remove all responsibility from herself for what followed. Sleepwalkers were innocent of agency, I reflected. They passed, ghostlike, and could bear no blame.

"His door was unlocked. I went in and simply climbed into his bed. He was dizzy with wine and wanting, I think. He did desire me," she said with sudden fierceness. "He had resisted it because of his friendship with James, but when he had me there, in his arms, there was no refusal. There was only *us*. At least until morning. I crept back to my room before Mamma awoke. I pretended to be asleep, pretended that everything was the same, but I was changed, you understand. I had been loved, for myself. Not for Papa's money or Mamma's little sophistications. I had been loved as a woman."

She turned to me with a smile. "I suddenly understood the story in the Bible, when Eve eats from the fruit of the tree of knowledge and all is revealed to her. I was enraptured. I could not wait to be married to James then."

"James?" I started in amazement. "Not Lorenzo?"

"No," she said, her lip curling in scorn. "I wanted to lie with Lorenzo as a means of exorcising the demon from my soul. I believed if I did that with him, I would be past it, free of my torment and able to marry James without regret."

"But you were in love with Lorenzo," I reminded her.

"Love is a notion for poets and children. I knew what mattered in the end was security, Veronica. A security I could never have with Lorenzo. If I pursued a life with him, what would that have been like? Living always with that sickness in my blood, forever at the mercy of that feverish need. No, it was not to be borne. I knew him carnally and that was the end of it. I was ready to marry James and be a proper wife to him."

"What happened?" I coaxed.

The lip curled again. "Lorenzo happened. He insisted we meet privately, which I tried very hard to avoid. But he cornered me in the library after tea and said that we would have to be married. I was terrified, you understand. He was so insistent that his honour was involved. I had thought of it as an act of pleasure, entered into by willing participants. He thought of it as some sort of contract, a promise! There was no time to dissuade him. I begged him to wait a day or so until I could break the news to Mamma, and he agreed to keep it secret. I had so little time to plan, but he left me no choice. I don't think I intended to do what I did, not then. I simply wrote him a little note, telling him that I knew the fossil would be in danger and that I would help him to excavate it before it could be lost. He would tell no one else. That was how deep his sense of honour went. He knew he was violating the wishes of his host, so he would do this secretly. He went along to the cliffs, biddable as a lamb. I teased him when he got there about carrying love notes in his pocket. He handed over the note I sent him and swore he had told no one of his intention to go out. And then he asked me once more to marry him."

"You refused him," I said.

"I was not given the chance," she replied. "Lorenzo told me that there was simply no other option. That as much as he wished me to marry James, he could not permit it. *Could not permit it.* As if it were up to him! He had decided his honour must be satisfied, and that could only happen if he confessed everything to James and married me himself. Lorenzo spoke of the sacrifice he was willing to make, the sacrifice." She fairly spat the word. "As if I were some nobody he had plucked from the gutter. I was good enough to marry a baronet with forty thousand acres but not good enough for the d'Ambrogios. He told me how his mother would weep at the marriage, how it would affect his little sister's chances of a suitable match when her elder brother had married an untitled Englishwoman, but it must be endured. We were going to live with them, his family in Italy, and suddenly I understood what the rest of my life would be like, in a country where I did not speak the language, on sufferance, the little English whore Lorenzo had defiled and married because it was the proper thing to do."

Angry tears sprang to her eyes. "I did not mean to do it, not even then. I swear it. But when he kept repeating how awful it would be but that it must be done to satisfy his honour as a gentleman, I could not bear it. I knew there was no way to persuade him to keep silent and let me marry James. He thought it disloyal. He was shocked I even suggested it, and I saw then something I had never thought to see in his eyes—contempt. He hated me a little for being willing to deceive James so easily, and yet he still swore he would marry me. Because he *must*."

The words fell like stones from her lips. "And before I knew what I was doing, I put my hands in front of me, like this," she said, holding out her arms, "and I pushed him. I did not even push him very hard. He simply was not expecting it. He flew backwards, into the darkness of the storm. He gave a short little cry, and then I heard the sound of his body hitting the rocks below. I hear it still. It is a terrible sound, the breaking of a body. I did not intend for it to happen, but it was the only way."

She lapsed into silence then and we watched the sea rising and listened to the cries of the gulls, so like a keening human voice.

"Did you know someone was bent upon avenging Lorenzo's death?" I asked after a little while.

She nodded, the wind teasing her hair. "James received a set of cuttings, just as Tiberius did. The message was slightly different. He wasn't told he was next, only that vengeance for Lorenzo was coming."

"Did he share them with you?"

Her expression was mocking. "Share them? My dear Veronica, James would never burden a genteel female mind with something so distasteful. No, he hid them, like a naughty child. I needed the address of the headmaster of our boys' school and James was out. So I looked in his blotter and there the cuttings were. I was horrified that someone might have guessed what I had done until I saw the envelope. They were addressed to James, not to me. My secret was still safe. At least I thought so—until Tiberius invited us here."

"Why come? It was a terrible risk," I pointed out.

"Staying away would have been a greater one. I had to know who was sending the wretched things. Clearly it was someone who didn't realise what I had done, but there was the terrible possibility they might discover it somehow. That is the worst of it, you know. Being responsible for such an act means you are always looking over your shoulder, wondering if there was something you missed, something you forgot. Something that might come back to haunt you."

"When did you realise Beatrice was Lorenzo's sister?" I asked.

"Almost as soon as I met her. There was something unsettling about her I could not put my finger on. We shared a train compartment with them coming down, and I engaged her in conversation, trying to discover if we had met before. But it was not until we were at Cherboys that I saw it. When I cut her silhouette. I had done Lorenzo's, you see. As my scissors moved around the curve of her image, something in the profile. And I knew, as suddenly and as surely as if she had told me herself. This was his little Star, his beloved Stella. And she had come to bring vengeance for him. I felt cold to my marrow because I understood if she had come for some innocent purpose, she would have made herself known to us. What would be more natural than to speak of him, to ask us to share the memories of the brother she had lost? The fact that she concealed her relationship to Lorenzo meant she was cunning. There was something too watchful about her. I saw her, scrutinising each of the men in turn—Tiberius, James, even Timothy Gresham. She wondered about each of them. But it never occurred to her to wonder about Elspeth. Or me."

"A frequent oversight when one is hunting murderers," I confirmed. "One often fails to consider the female can be deadlier than the male."

"Yes, we can," she said. "It was so terribly easy, you know. She dosed herself with that tonic for her heart, and it would be child's play to introduce something lethal. I presumed Timothy would have a suitable substance at the dispensary, and I was right."

"Strychnine," I supplied.

"Yes. Used in small doses as a stimulant but entirely fatal in large amounts. And compounded into salts. The easiest thing in the world to tip into her bottle of tonic. A quick shake and they dissolved. The best part was that I needn't be anywhere near when Beatrice poisoned herself. It would be entirely her own doing."

Hardly so, but I was not prepared to argue the point with Augusta. She rose and gathered her hair into her net, pinning it as neatly as she could with the wind whipping around us. She paused and took a last look around, from the deep blue water stretching as far as the eye could see to the lowering grey skies just beginning to drop gentle rain upon the waves.

"Come along," I said. "It is time to tell the others."

I held out my hand for hers, intending to support her in what must be the most difficult conversation of her life.

"My sons," she began, and for the first time, her voice broke. She clasped my hand tightly. "I cannot have them know what their mother is."

"There are ways," I began.

"There is one way," she said, and she stepped near the edge.

"Do not jump!" I cried. "Augusta, your death will change nothing."

A smile, sweet as a seraph's, illuminated her face. "Oh, I did not mean mine."

And with that, she jerked hard upon my arm as she pivoted, flinging me over the edge of the cliff towards oblivion.

CHAPTER

33

I did not, as the clever reader will deduce, die—in spite of Augusta
MacIver's best efforts. I fell some distance, too startled to scream,
before being jerked to an abrupt halt, my skirts snagged upon some
outcropping or other. It was my custom in the wild to wear trousers,
but I gave a fervent prayer of thanksgiving for the breadth of fabric and
the stoutness of my tweed skirts as I hung, dangling like a marionette
against the side of the cliff. I could not see what merciful projection
held me fast. I only knew that I was, for the moment, safe.

I was also, I realised, in the gravest of perils. Whatever held me aloft
could easily prove unequal to the task and give way, sending me hur-
tling down at gravity's mercy. Below, the sea churned angrily about the
cluster of boulders which had been Lorenzo d'Ambrogio's undoing. I
dared not move for fear of dislodging my precarious position, and I
dared not shout for help lest I alert the murderous Augusta to the fact
that her attempt upon my life had failed. The edge of the cliff provided a
bit of overhang, concealing me from view should anyone stand even at
the very brink of the precipice. Chance would not provide me a savior.
No one would *happen* upon me. I should have to wait until hue and cry
had been raised over my absence and a search party had been sent. But

even if they had recourse to dogs and villagers, they would not easily find me. And if Augusta were clever—which she had proven to be, having two undetected murders to her credit—she would arrange to help search the cliffs, where she could "discover" my body. When she failed to do so and realised I was still clinging to the rock like a limpet, she would doubtless take the opportunity to finish me off.

A worrisome state of affairs to be sure, particularly as whatever kindly outcropping I had snagged my skirts upon felt rather less secure than it had a mere moment before. I do not think it was my imagination that I was sinking, easing lower with each passing second. I was heavier as well, for the rain had begun to fall in great, gusting sheets, the water soaking into my garments. If the cliff face did not fall away, I might simply prove too weighty to remain where I was.

Such thoughts were not helpful. I considered how I might climb up—impossible. And how I might climb down—improbable. There was nothing to do but swing gently in the wind and hope for the best. As I did so, I thought naturally of butterflies. I am never happier than when contemplating lepidoptery or Stoker, but I could not bear to entertain any thoughts of him. What would I have thought of? The way his eyes crinkled with laughter when he was amused? The way they brightened with ardour whenever they saw me? The manner in which he expressed himself, eloquently and with such originality of thought that he never failed to surprise me? That he was a source of endless delight and infuriation? Certainly not. And I most definitely could not afford to think about the notion of never pressing my lips once again to his heated flesh, never twisting my fingers into those tumbled ebony locks as I arched—

"Veronica, what in the name of the oozing wounds of Christ are you doing down there?"

I did not dare to look up, as much for fear of falling as for revealing the state of considerable emotion to which I had been reduced.

"I am in a position of mortal danger," I informed him, shouting to be heard over the wind.

"I can see that. Do not move," he ordered. "I am coming."

There are, I maintain, no sweeter words in the English tongue. *I am coming.* And come he did, descending on a rope with the swift, masterful dexterity that recalled his long experience with both travelling shows and naval vessels. He came to rest gently beside me, looping one steely strong arm about my waist. I rather imagined he would mistake my tears for rainwater, but he knew better. As soon as I was safely within his grasp, he spoke as mildly to me as a newborn babe.

"There you are, safe as houses," he said, his lips against my temple. "I have you." He held me fast as we rose slowly into the air, twisting gently. I clutched at him as we were lifted. The cliff face passed in front of us, and I was glad we were not facing the sea itself, grown angry with the storm. It hissed and boiled below our dangling feet, and I focused my attention instead upon the sheer wall of earth in front of us.

"Stop!" I shrieked suddenly. I leant forward and Stoker's grip gave way. I felt myself falling once more unto oblivion, windmilling my feet as I succumbed to gravity. This was it, then, the very end for me, dropping into eternity with the inevitability of a stone. I brushed my fingertips against Stoker's sleeve as I fell, my last touch on this earth him. I opened my mouth in a soundless scream as his hand clamped around my wrist at the last second.

Simultaneously, the rope jerked to a halt and Stoker was caught between, the quick whiplash of the movement causing his shoulder to make a wrenching, snapping sound as he arrested our fall. He saved us, putting his own body between mine and certain death, and not for the first time. I came to rest against the face of the cliff, dangling below him and twisting gently.

"Veronica, kindly explain what you are playing at," Stoker demanded through gritted teeth.

"Look!" I ordered with a shaking finger. Before us was the projection that had halted my headlong fall, saving my life. A scrap of my skirt was still snagged upon it, and as I freed it, I realised it was a bone, shining white against the dark brown crumble of the cliff.

"That is the rib of a Megalosaurus. It is the fossil," Stoker breathed. "It was not lost when Lorenzo died. At least not all of it."

"And it has chosen now to be revealed again. We must excavate!" I reached to scrabble at the cliff, but Stoker took matters into his own hands. With a great, guttural moan, he flexed his arm and pulled me up and into his arms.

"Bring us up!" he called, and the rope jerked again. I had time only to free one small piece, a fragment of the great beast still locked within the cliff.

We were hauled rather gracelessly over the lip of the precipice and we lay for some minutes breathing heavily. Tiberius and Merry stood, bent and heaving, ropes clutched in their hands as they recovered from their efforts. On the ground, Augusta lay senseless, a bruise darkening her jaw.

"What happened to her?" I asked.

Stoker regarded her coolly. "I do not, as a rule, approve of striking women. But I think we might make an exception for her."

"You punched her?" I demanded.

"No, I did," said Merryweather. I stared at the youngest Templeton-Vane in astonishment. "Well, she tried to murder you, Stoker said, and if we let her go back to the house she might have got away, but you were about to die, and it all got rather confusing and I am afraid I lost my head."

I rose and went on tiptoe to press a kiss to his cheek. "You did very well, Merry. I think we will make a man of action of you yet."

CHAPTER
34

It was not until we had reached the house and after I had been closeted for some time with Tiberius, explaining what Augusta had revealed, that I was able to attend to my poor battered body. I sustained rather more in the way of injuries than I had realised at the time. My arms were terribly sore, my legs bruised, and I was thoroughly chilled. Lily filled the bathtub with steaming water and stripped off my ruined clothing before plunging me bodily into the bath. She scrubbed me free of mud until the water ran clean and helped me to towel myself dry and dress in a fresh gown. She had just pinned my hair into some semblance of order when Stoker appeared, arm neatly bound in a linen sling and looking a little the worse for wear.

Lily, sensing our wish for privacy, scuttled away before she could be asked.

"Are you quite all right?" I asked, nodding towards the sling.

His smile was faint. "Rather better than usual after one of our adventures. No scars from this one. Just a wrenched shoulder."

He sat heavily in the armchair by the window and I went to perch on the hassock, content to sit at his feet, at least for the moment. "How did you know about Augusta?"

He grinned. "Nanny, of course."

"Nanny?"

"She is remarkably insightful about her own sex, you know. When I went to visit her earlier she said she noticed something when Augusta was here twenty years ago, a sort of heightened awareness in her whenever Lorenzo was around. She did not much care for it, given that Augusta was engaged to be married to James. So she took to keeping a weather eye upon her. She saw Augusta coming back to the house the night Lorenzo died."

"She knew Augusta killed him and said nothing!" I was indignant that the peevish old woman hadn't cared to share her observations earlier.

"Nanny knew nothing of the sort," Stoker corrected. "She merely saw Augusta coming into the house. She might have been anywhere."

"Feathers. It was a filthy night, everyone said so. The storm of the century," I reminded him. "She knew perfectly well where Augusta had been."

"Be that as it may," Stoker said severely, "she had no cause to accuse anyone. Augusta was a guest, remember. And the house party broke up the next day. Why would Nanny have made trouble at that point when Augusta might have had a perfectly logical explanation? And Nanny did not believe she had been up to no good, at least not murder. She thought they'd been having an assignation."

"They had been." I related swiftly what Augusta had told me about her interlude with Lorenzo. "Where is she now?"

"Tiberius has had her locked in her room, with Merryweather and Collins standing guard." I had dispatched Merry on a quick errand to the village, but he had sent word through J. J. that my suspicions were correct. I looked forward to hearing him fit one last piece of the puzzle into place.

Stoker went on. "James is furious, of course, demanding she be released, claiming it must have been an accident that you fell. Tiberius wants him to hear your version of events."

I smoothed my skirts and patted my hair. "Unto the breach, then. Let us screw our courage to the sticking place."

Stoker escorted me to the library, where Tiberius sat in lordly state behind the great polished desk. Chairs had been arranged in a semi-circle in front of it and Pietro sat in one—or rather, slumped, for his usual urbane pose had abandoned him. He looked like a broken doll, flung aside and abandoned. His eyes were red-rimmed and swollen from weeping, but he was composed, his hands folded in his lap. He gave us a nod of acknowledgment as we entered. No sooner had we seated ourselves than Sir James arrived, blustering and puffing and furiously indignant.

"I will have the law on you for this," he spat at Tiberius. He refused a seat but paced, uneasy as a panther, behind the chairs. But he stopped the instant Augusta appeared, pale and dry-eyed, accompanied by Collins and Merryweather, who stood behind her chair as she sat. Behind them, J. J. slipped into the room as unobtrusively as a mouse. She had had only a few minutes to complete an errand I had set her, but a quick wink told me she had been successful. She took a chair against the wall and waited in demure silence.

"My dearest," James began, flying to Augusta's side. But she held up a hand and gestured towards the chair next to her. He looked confused a moment, then seated himself. He patted her hand awkwardly, murmuring words of reassurance mingled with bombastic asides to Tiberius threatening everything from litigation to bodily injury until at last Tiberius abandoned his pose of languor and roared a single word. "Enough!" He accompanied this with a slap of the hand on the desk, the thud reverberating through the room. It was so unlike Tiberius to have recourse to bad temper that James lapsed into silence.

Tiberius addressed him directly. "I know you are outraged at the insult done to your lady, but I assure you it was entirely necessary. And it is the least of what she deserves." James gaped in astonished umbrage, but Tiberius ignored him, turning instead to Pietro. "I am sorry, my friend. This will be painful in the extreme, I have no doubt. But it must be done."

Tiberius looked at last to Augusta. "Twenty years ago, you murdered Lorenzo d'Ambrogio. Yesterday, you murdered his sister, Beatrice. And today you attempted the murder of Veronica Speedwell. Have you anything to say for yourself?" He made a swift aside to James. "I can feel you working up to another outburst, and believe me when I say I am fully capable of having you forcibly gagged. You will sit and listen and your wife will speak for herself."

"Aye, that she will." James looked to his wife, his brows beetling angrily. "Tell them what madness this is, Augusta. And then we can be gone from this place and these people *forever.*" He fairly spat the last word, but even as he said it, his expression changed. Something in her looks, her stony acceptance of Tiberius' charges, must have alerted him. He shrank suddenly and the next words to slip from his lips were a feeble whisper. "Augusta? Augusta, *no.*"

"Yes, James. Everything Tiberius says is true. I might quibble about whether I murdered Lorenzo. It was not my intention, but I am the reason he was there on the cliffs that night, and although I did not plan to push him over, I did." Stoker and I exchanged quick glances. She might claim not to have deliberately orchestrated his death, but I thought of the setting. If she was determined to speak away from the house, where they might have been overheard, she could have lured him to the pineapple folly for their confrontation, or any one of a dozen discreet spots that would have been far more comfortable on such a filthy night. Instead, she had insisted upon meeting at the cliff, that most precarious of places.

Almost imperceptibly, Stoker moved his hand as if to write, and I understood what he meant. On that fateful night, Augusta had taken pains to retrieve the note, the one physical clue that would have tied her to his death. Surely that, if nothing else, spoke of premeditation.

James gave a faint cry at his wife's confession, but she seemed not to notice his anguish. She went on in a calm voice, resigned, or perhaps eager even, to acknowledge her deeds. Confession, they say, is good for the soul, and I wondered if she longed for absolution, for someone at last to understand her.

She went on. "I realised who Beatrice was the first night, and I knew then she was my enemy."

"But why?" Timothy Gresham ventured. "Why did she not say, poor lady, who she really was?"

Tiberius looked to Pietro, who stirred wearily in his chair. "She had a scheme of revenge, a plot to avenge her brother."

He paused and Tiberius prompted him gently. "A plot she had already undertaken by causing the deaths of Kaspar von Hochstaden and Alexandre du Plessis."

Pietro nodded. "I knew nothing of it. I did not understand what she meant to do, I swear it upon everything I hold sacred. If I had . . . never would I have brought her here." At this, he gave himself up to weeping, deep, violent sobs wrenched from his very soul. The sound was terrible, a despairing howl into the wilderness, and Merry went to him, putting an arm about him to offer consolation. At last Pietro subsided, wiping his eyes with Merry's handkerchief. All the while, Augusta stared directly ahead, as if his enormous, consuming grief had nothing to do with her.

When his sobs had subsided to quiet snuffling, Tiberius went on. "I had deduced that someone was targeting the Seven Sinners, but I did not know who or what their purpose might be. But gathering the remaining Sinners here seemed the best way to bring matters to a head. And so it did, because Augusta recognised Beatrice as Lorenzo's sister."

"But how could you have known Beatrice was behind the deaths of Kaspar and Alexandre?" Timothy asked of Augusta. She pressed her lips together and did not reply. Instead, I ventured an answer on her behalf.

"Augusta was suspicious of this house party from the beginning, pricked by a guilty conscience and by the fact that you, Sir James, received a set of cuttings of your own—just like the ones that Tiberius received."

The assembled menfolk looked decidedly astonished and I relished the moment before explaining. "Sir James was the recipient of an identical set of cuttings—cuttings which indicated he too would fall victim to the wrath of Lorenzo's avenger. If," I pointed out icily, "he had bothered to share that information when you disclosed yours, Tiberius, it would have immediately become obvious that Pietro was the only remaining Sinner who had not received a set. We would have suspected him at once of being the avenger—or Beatrice."

Sir James' moustaches twitched guiltily, but I went on. "Sir James concealed the cuttings from Augusta because he did not wish to alarm her. And because he was innocent of the crime of killing Lorenzo, he believed the whole thing a distasteful joke. But when Augusta found the cuttings quite by accident, she understood the danger. It was necessary then to come to Cherboys and confront the killer of Kaspar and Alexandre herself."

I paused and drew breath for the next part of the tale. "Augusta detected the resemblance between Lorenzo and Beatrice the first night they were here. She had cut Lorenzo's silhouette and noticed their matching profiles when she cut Beatrice's. If any doubt about Beatrice's identity remained, it was settled once and for all the following morning when Augusta and I both saw Beatrice in the rose bower, reading a book—a book marked with the d'Ambrogio crest of a golden bee. Augusta even made a point of handling the book after Beatrice left it behind. She would have recognised the cipher." I turned to Augusta for confirmation and she nodded.

"Lorenzo lent me a book once," Sir James put in slowly. "Bound in blue leather and marked with a bee."

"As I imagine all of the d'Ambrogio library was marked," I told him.

I turned to Pietro for confirmation. He nodded. "There were not many things left when her family died, but a few of the books were still in Lorenzo's belongings sent from England. All of them were marked with the family colours and crest."

That point settled, I resumed my narrative. "After seeing the resemblance and the book, Augusta realised that Beatrice must be Stella, the lost d'Ambrogio. After all, who better to seek vengeance for Lorenzo than his beloved little sister? She must have survived the fever which killed her mother—and we know Beatrice grew up in America. Yet she was not reared by her parents. She mentioned her aunt and her uncle, but never a mother or father."

Pietro spoke up, his voice quiet. "She was sent to New York when she was orphaned. Her aunt and uncle had the raising of her. They were kind and had much money, but still my Beatrice never forgot where she came from and all that she had lost."

"Indeed," I said. "And Augusta determined that Beatrice would have to be eliminated before she discovered the truth of what happened the night Lorenzo died. The only question was how. When Augusta realised the extent of Beatrice's heart troubles, she understood she had the perfect means by which to eliminate her. A little tampering with the heart tonic, something lethal added to the medicine, and Beatrice would no longer be a threat. Adulterating the tonic had the added advantage of meaning that Augusta need not be at hand to administer the poison herself."

Sir James gave me a triumphant look. "There you are mistaken, my girl. My wife is no Borgia! She is not in the habit of travelling with deadly poisons."

"But she needn't be," Stoker said evenly. "At dinner the first night, she spoke with Timothy Gresham, comparing notes on treatments at rest homes. I heard them discussing the uses of stimulants. Strychnine is frequently used as such, and it would have been reasonable for her to assume she would find a supply in the dispensary. And if that failed, surely something in the dispensary would serve her purpose."

I picked up the thread of the narrative. "She needed only a moment's access to the dispensary and she was lucky. She did find strychnine salts. Easily dissolved, quick, and invariably fatal, if gruesome." Sir James made a moan of protest, but I forged on, addressing Merryweather. "You have paid a visit to the dispensary this morning, have you not, Merry?"

He blinked, as if surprised to find himself a speaking player in the drama unfolding before him. "Yes, I did."

"And?" I prompted.

"Timothy Gresham was about to leave on a call—yesterday's confinement has complications—but he supplied the information you requested. A new bottle of strychnine salts which ought to be full is nearly empty."

"The dispensary cupboard ought to be locked," Stoker put in with a frown.

"I did ask him about that," Merry said. "Apparently he is forever forgetting to take the key out of the lock when he leaves the dispensary, especially if he goes in a hurry."

"Slapdash," Tiberius remarked. I had a feeling Timothy Gresham would be spoken to sternly about his habits in future.

I resumed my tale. "So Augusta has secured the necessary poison. There was only one moment of real risk for her—a narrow escape from detection. When she emerged from the dispensary, she saw me coming down the lane, a potential disaster if it could later be proven that Beatrice had died from strychnine secured at Timothy's dispensary. She could not be seen *coming* from the dispensary. But she could be seen to be *going*."

Sir James blinked. "I do not understand."

Stoker understood at once. "Augusta simply slipped out of the dispensary and instead of walking down the front path, she turned and knocked on the door so it would appear she had just arrived."

I nodded. "It was a clever stratagem, and it speaks to Augusta's audacity and quick thinking, as well as her ruthlessness. Now that she had the poison in hand, she had only to introduce it to Beatrice's tonic. It was simple enough to do so. A quick visit to the Salviatis' suite when no one was about, and she took the precaution of disguising herself as a maid. Unfortunately for her, I happened to glimpse the back of her as she left the Salviatis' room during the time the tonic must have been poisoned. She was wearing the apron and white cap of an upstairs maid, but a black dress."

"And none of the upstairs maids at Cherboys wears black," Tiberius finished.

"Precisely. The chambermaids here all wear blue, and Augusta had not brought a blue dress with her. Even if she had, it certainly wouldn't have been plain enough to pass for a maid's frock. But, like many ladies, Augusta always travels with a simple black dress should she be unexpectedly required to put on mourning. A quick visit to the laundry to purloin a spare apron and cap, and her disguise was complete if imperfect. After all, who scrutinises the attire of a maid? Anyone passing her quickly would take her for one of the staff.

"She administered the poison, Beatrice obligingly died, and all that remained was to remove the tonic bottle from Beatrice's pocket—easily done when she sat with Beatrice's body. Someone might notice later that the tonic bottle was missing, but it might easily be presumed to have been mislaid in the commotion. She could not risk the bottle being tested should there be a proper inquest. That task accomplished, Augusta thought she was free. Until she realised she had overlooked one crucial piece of evidence. We saw Beatrice reading a poetry book belonging to Lorenzo. But it was a book he had carried with him during the visit to Cherboys. The only way Beatrice could have got her hands on it was if it had been shipped to Italy after his death with the rest of his things as Pietro has confirmed. And that meant that Beatrice had his notebook."

"His notebook?" Sir James looked startled.

"His notebook," I confirmed. "Augusta had written Lorenzo a note, summoning him to a rendezvous on the cliff the night he died, and she was clever enough to retrieve that note before pushing him over. But she could not know whether or not he had written about the meeting in his notebook. She ought to have taken it from his room the night he died, but I suppose she was too upset to think of it," I finished.

"And the next day, Father ordered all of Lorenzo's things packed up and sent to his family in Italy. She had no chance to retrieve it then," Tiberius put in.

"Correct. But she needn't have worried. The notebook does not mention her by name. Only his conversations with the 'stranger.'" A ghost of a smile touched Augusta's lips, but she said nothing.

"Lorenzo, he loved his nicknames," Pietro said faintly. "Beatrice, his little star. And he called Augusta the stranger because she was the newest to our group. He said it with affection, I think."

I wondered. His feelings towards Augusta seemed complicated in the extreme. If he, with his burdensome sense of honour, found himself attracted by his friend's fiancée, perhaps referring to her only by a nickname was a means of holding her at arm's length. But that was a secret Lorenzo had taken to his grave.

Sir James puffed out his cheeks, his moustaches trembling with emotion. "This is a fine story, if you like melodrama and the destruction of an innocent lady's reputation. But you'll find no proof of it because it never happened. And without proof, my solicitors will bring suit against every last one of you. I will hound you until you've nothing left but the clothes on your backs and you will have to sell those just to afford air to breathe, d'you hear me?" He looked at each of us in turn, fixing us with an accusatory stare.

I turned to J. J. "That, I think, is your cue."

Sir James blustered again as she rose and came to stand beside my chair. "Must we be bothered by the tittle-tattle of maids now?"

"This young lady is not a maid," I told him. "J. J. Butterworth is an investigative reporter frequently published in the *Daily Harbinger.* She is a journalist of note, and I believe she has a piece of evidence pertinent to this case."

I gestured and J. J. reached into her pocket. Wrapped in a handkerchief was a small glass bottle shaped like a scallop shell. I turned to Pietro. "Count, do you recognise this bottle?"

"Yes, it is the bottle my Beatrice used to carry her tonic. It is engraved with her monogram."

J. J. turned the bottle so that Sir James and Tiberius could see the silver cap, incised with B D'A S.

"Undeniably Beatrice's tonic bottle, the one used to poison her with strychnine—the one Augusta took from her dead body as she lay upstairs," I said.

Pietro gave a low, mournful moan.

"Where did you find it?" Tiberius enquired.

J. J. nodded towards Augusta. "In Lady MacIver's dressing room. Not even hid properly, just stuffed into her toilet case." It had occurred to me that the missing piece of the entire puzzle was Beatrice's tonic bottle. If Augusta had—as I believed—retrieved it after poisoning Beatrice, she would have had no opportunity to dispose of it. I had instructed J. J. to begin her search as soon as Augusta was released from her room. The fact that she had arrived in the drawing room a scant few minutes after Augusta meant she had made quick work of the task—and knowing J. J. she had hared down to the drawing room so as not to miss a second of the proceedings.

Tiberius nodded gravely. "Incontrovertible evidence, I think, James."

"You dared search our things! You sneaking, conniving, little—" He surged out of his chair, but before he could lay a finger on J. J., I plucked a minuten from my cuff and drove it into his wrist.

He howled in outrage and fell back, plucking the pin free and sucking at the bright red bead of blood that welled up.

"I'll have you up for assault for that," he assured me.

"Do feel quite free to bring charges," I said with a tight smile. "And I will be certain to make sure that J. J.'s newspaper publishes every detail of what has happened here."

He puffed again, like an adder will before it strikes, but Stoker raised a lazy finger.

"Sir James, I literally have one hand tied, but I will still thrash you into the next century if you threaten either of these ladies with violence again."

Something in his face gave Sir James pause, for the baronet changed tack. He subsided into his chair, muttering, his complexion quite puce, as I looked at J. J. She flicked me a glance of annoyance. We had had the situation well in hand, but some men will only ever respect the strength of other men. It was frankly exhausting.

J. J. slipped the bottle back into her pocket and returned to her chair.

After a long moment, Sir James turned to Augusta. "But why? Why would you want Lorenzo to die? You barely knew him."

Augusta roused herself at last, turning to her husband with a look of contempt. "Barely knew him? I lay with him, James. I knew him, carnally. You made rather a bad bargain in our marriage, I am afraid. You got no virgin bride on your wedding night."

Angry colour suffused his cheeks. "Augusta, it is not your fault that bastard forced you—"

Augusta's laugh was sharp and cruel. "Forced me? I *seduced* him, James. I wanted him. And I had him."

"I do not believe it," he said stubbornly. "I cannot believe it. You are unwell, these are sick fancies."

"Fancies! James, my god, can you not face the truth like a man? Shall I tell you what it was like? Perhaps then you will believe it. Very well. I went to his room. I took off my clothes and I got into his bed. I touched him and I kissed him and we did whatever we liked with one another. It was the only time in the whole of my life I have understood what it meant to be satisfied."

The lash of her words must have stung him deeply, for James shook his head, dumbly, as a donkey will do when it cannot decide in which direction to go.

Her anger subsided as soon as it had flared, and when Augusta spoke again, it was milder, a note of pity threading her words. "But I did not want to marry him. I wanted to marry you and he would have prevented it. He said he would tell you everything because of his precious honour. You would have broken our engagement and I could not have that."

It took a moment for the full implication of her statement to penetrate his shock. "Do you mean to say you killed him solely to marry me?"

"Yes, James. I wanted our life together. Our homes. Our boys. And I did what must be done in order to make that happen."

She raised her chin, daring him to sit in judgment on her, and I realised then she was not sorry. She justified what she had done, and moreover, she would do it again if faced with the same choice.

Something of this must have finally communicated itself to James, because he looked at her in horror. "You do not regret it, do you?" he asked in a hoarse whisper.

"No," she said, folding her hands calmly in her lap. "I regret nothing."

"You're mad," he said, shrinking back in his chair. "I do not know you."

"I did what must be done," she repeated.

"You killed a man!" James said, shrinking further still. "You killed a man."

"A man who would have destroyed any chance at the life we have made for ourselves," she told him.

"But Beatrice—" he began.

"Beatrice would have happily killed me for the sake of vengeance," she said shortly. "You cannot blame me for that."

"It was cleverly done," I told her. "Murders committed with audacity and a complete lack of fear. The only loose end was Lorenzo's notebook."

"It haunted me," she said. "I did not even know if the thing still existed or if it had been with the rest of his things. And even if Beatrice had it in her possession, had Lorenzo written anything damning in its pages? I had to try to find it."

"That, with the tonic bottle, was why you volunteered to sit with her body when she was first carried up to her room," Stoker said.

She nodded. "Yes. But there was no time. As soon as Pietro left her, I had only a moment to retrieve the bottle before you came in and sent me off to bed. I had to sit up half the night, waiting for James to fall asleep so I could slip back downstairs and search again. I spent ages, looked through everything, but still I could not find it. I began to hope that Beatrice had never had it."

"It was with me," Pietro said wearily. "When we quarrelled the previous night, she showed me the notebook as proof that Lorenzo had been murdered. I confiscated it, told her I would keep it with me until we had the chance to discuss things properly. I held it as a bond for good behaviour, told her if she harmed anyone else, I would burn it, this treasured possession of her brother's. I kept it in my pocket. It was still in my evening coat when she died."

"And then we come to the matter of attempting to take Veronica's life," Tiberius said wearily. "There is no possible justification, Augusta."

"I pushed her," she said with astonishing frankness. But she seemed almost relieved, as if she had lived too long behind a mask and was content for everyone to know her as she actually was. "I pushed her quite deliberately. I intended for her to die, and that is premeditation." She smiled at Tiberius, a ghost of her usual winsome expression. "Is it to be the hangman's noose for me?"

James, who had been silent through the recitation of her crimes, leapt suddenly at her, hands at her throat, screaming abuse as he throttled her. Stoker and Tiberius dragged him off, pinioning his arms at his sides. Still he flung invective, spittle flecking his moustaches as he trembled in rage. Augusta had scarcely attempted to defend herself, putting her hands up only for the worst of the blows. Her hair had come undone and she smoothed it, her fingers shaking a little as she did so.

Stoker eased James back into his seat. "Stay in that chair or I will lash you to it," he warned. James' colour was not good, mottled red and white, perspiration dampening his brow. "You are not my wife," he said to Augusta as he subsided into his chair. "I renounce you."

"But she *is* your wife," Tiberius pointed out. "And you are responsible for her."

"I am not responsible for that monster," James began. He broke off, dropping his head in his hands. "Oh, my poor boys! What's to become of us? The scandal of it all will ruin them."

The room fell to silence, broken only by his ragged breathing and the ticking of the mantel clock. At length, I ventured a suggestion.

"It does not have to be their ruination," I said. James lifted his head. Augusta did not even turn to look, so spent was she by the confrontation.

"What do you mean?" James demanded. "This means the law and prison and a trial, all of it written up in the most lurid newspapers for all and sundry to see. She will be hanged, damn you. And the MacIver name, dragged through the mud and tainted forever."

"What if it were not?" I asked. "What if there were a way to keep her name out of the newspapers? What if she were not hanged, and no one ever knew about any of this?"

They turned to me as one and I laid out my idea, elaborating and building as I went. When I finished, silence reigned once more until Tiberius spoke. "It must be left to Pietro to decide. It is his justice which must be satisfied."

James turned anguished eyes to Pietro. "Please, man." His voice broke as he pleaded. "I do not ask it for her. But for my boys. It is the only way they may have a hope of escaping this. And she will pay. I promise you that."

Pietro drew in a deep breath, letting it out slowly. The weight he had been manfully shouldering seemed to drop away. "Beatrice believed vengeance was the only way. But I am a modern man. And I believe justice which harms the innocent is no justice at all. I will agree, James. For the sake of your sons." James gave a broken exclamation of gratitude as Pietro held up a hand to stop him. "But I will have a confession from her hand, and witnessed by those in this room. I will keep it as my insurance that she will never be permitted to go free."

"Done," James said, putting out his hand. Pietro took it after a moment, and it was finished, a gentleman's agreement that disposed of a murderess without so much as a look in her direction.

CHAPTER
35

Augusta was once more locked in her room, but she made no attempt to escape. The next morning, when the closed coach arrived, she emerged, dressed soberly, in a plain black gown, no jewels or fine lace. The coach from Milverton House had brought the director of the asylum and two muscular attendants, who escorted her into the carriage as we watched from the hall. She did not turn back, although the doctor tarried on the step.

"I assure you, we will take excellent care of her ladyship," the director said to James. "I am only sorry to hear that she has proven insensible to the remedy of fresh air and change of scene that you have provided her here," he added, looking around. "And I hope that we may, in due course, nurse her back to her full capacity."

James smiled coldly. "Her ladyship's reason has entirely broken down. She cannot ever return home, no matter what progress she makes in your facility. Do we understand one another?"

The director, who had been genial, now adopted a graver mien. "We do indeed, sir. Say no more. I will see to it that she is comfortable and well attended, but we shall not anticipate her leaving Milverton House."

"Correct," James said. "And we will not require correspondence from her. It would only upset my sons."

"Naturally," the director replied, nodding. "These are sad cases, but you must put it behind you now. She is in good hands, and no longer your concern."

He bowed, lifting his hat as he made his good-byes. Just before he reached the carriage, J. J. emerged from the house, clutching a small carpetbag, Tiberius holding her firmly by the arm.

"Do not forget your other patient," he called. The director turned back.

"Ah yes. The young woman you telegraphed about. Melancholia, you said?" He peered at J. J., who looked downcast, her eyes fixed upon the stones at her feet. "Yes, I see it. We will be happy to take her into our care. I will write within the week to let you know how we get on. She looks young and healthy enough. I am certain she will respond well to treatment."

Stoker started forward, clearly about to protest, but J. J. flashed him a warning look as I put a hand to restrain him.

We stood upon the step as the director leapt into the carriage, slamming the door behind him. The driver sprang the horses and they were away. Tiberius guided James back into the house and Stoker turned to me. "Would you care to explain?"

"I owed J. J. a story. She pointed out to me that I have been significantly less of a friend to her than she to me, and I wanted to rectify the situation. So I arranged with Tiberius that she would be committed to Milverton House for a period not to exceed a fortnight."

Comprehension dawned on his face. "Nellie Bly," he said, invoking the name of the intrepid American journalist who had recently spent ten days in an asylum, emerging to write an exposé on the treatment of the insane to clamorous acclaim. And not only acclaim; it was hoped that the brutality of the situation of those locked up for their mental woes might be mitigated with proper reform. Already, some institutions were exchanging small, dark rooms and inhumane treatment for sunshine, fresh air, and a little human kindness, and J. J. was determined to accomplish the same in England. Thus far no female journalist had possessed the courage of Miss Bly, but J. J., for all her sins, was never one to shrink from a challenge.

"Precisely," I affirmed to Stoker. "It required only enlisting Tiberius to help." Committing a woman to an asylum was, under the present laws, a matter of terrifying ease. It wanted only a man of standing to swear to a woman's mental state to have her held against her will. And if the man chose, he could have her liberated with equal simplicity. Tiberius had promised to ensure J. J.'s timely release from the asylum.

"I am surprised you got him to agree," Stoker told me.

I smiled. "J. J. and I appealed to his better nature."

"I wasn't aware he had one."

"He feels responsible for the way matters ended—and for the fact that I was very nearly killed. This is an opportunity for him to help do some real good for once. Perhaps he might make a practice of philanthropy."

The entire system was one calculated to accommodate abuses of the worst kind, and I was happy to see J. J. championing the cause of the unfortunates who had been locked away from the world. I had little doubt she would effect great things.

"Who knows?" I said to Stoker. "Perhaps she will create such a sensation that our laws will be changed to help those who are most powerless."

"The very laws that helped us to lock up a murderer," he countered.

"Her husband did that. We just suggested it," I reminded him. "And would it really have been a better thing for her to have been arrested?

Tried by a jury? Hanged in a public execution for all to see? What would that have done but feed sensationalism? It would not bring back her victims and it would only have created new ones in her children as they suffered through the trauma of having a mother made so notorious."

"They will suffer for not having her love, her presence," Stoker said wistfully, looking up at the façade of Cherboys. He had been only twelve years of age when his own mother died, and I wondered if he felt her presence here.

"Is that why you never come back here?"

He nodded slowly. "Sometimes, when I turn a corner too quickly, I imagine I can smell her perfume or hear the rustling of her skirts. A fantasy, perhaps."

I tucked my arm through his. "Come. Let us walk to Dearsley churchyard. We can cut late roses for her grave. It is time you put your ghosts to rest."

O ver the next few days, the remaining guests departed. James mapped out a plan to visit his sons' schools in turn to explain as much as he could to them, whilst Pietro arranged for Beatrice's body to be taken to Italy to be buried. Tiberius was able to have Lorenzo's casket disinterred, and so Lorenzo d'Ambrogio would at last lie in the land of his fathers, his sister at his side. Perhaps this would bring peace to them both. And to everyone's astonishment, Merryweather accompanied him. He had shown a flair for pastoral work, providing gentle comfort to Pietro in his hour of grief, as well as a surprising capacity for practical detail. There was still one last thread remaining unwoven to this sorry business, but I did not trouble Merryweather to explain why Beatrice had gone to see him the day she died. It was simple enough to imagine what had transpired. There was no erstwhile dalliance with Merryweather, only a grieving sister who had gone incognita to pay her respects to the grave of her brother. Whether Merry had discovered her wandering in the churchyard or found her in prayer inside St. Frideswide's, it did not matter. She had concealed her true purpose with that particular brand of charm I should always associate with Beatrice d'Ambrogio Salviati. Besides, I was rather abashed at having suspected Merryweather of such indelicacy as an inappropriate flirtation with a married woman. I had grown fond of him, and it occurred to me as we discussed his imminent departure that I should miss him as he embarked upon his travels.

"It will do the boy good," Tiberius said with a shrug. "He has never been abroad and he might learn a thing or two. Besides, the vicarage is still under repair and I have given permission for him to engage a curate. The new fellow can preach Sunday sermons for a while." So Merry set off with Pietro for Italy to lay Lorenzo and Beatrice to rest and perhaps to experience some Continental consolations in time.

After they had gone, a melancholy quiet settled over Cherboys. Stoker and I packed up our things, prepared to take our leave the following day. I was less than pleased that the Megalosaurus was to accompany us, but there were worse things lurking in the garden at Bishop's Folly already, I reflected. Patricia the Galápagos tortoise, for one. And Stoker was delighted to take possession of his childhood playhouse once and for all. He spent the whole of that day cleaning it meticulously and overseeing the packing of the beast. He returned to the house late, taking dinner on a tray in his room, and I wondered if he were perhaps avoiding me.

If he were, I could not blame him. It had been brought home to me during the course of this investigation that for all my skills as a lepidopterist, I was rather lacking in one or two other areas. I had built myself a fortress, stone by stone, each hewn from my upbringing and experiences in the world. Meeting Stoker had caused my defences to crack—to crumble entirely, I had thought. But the return of Harry

Spenlove in our previous adventure had shaken me badly. Stoker had accused me of not trusting him, but how could I when my confidence had been so grievously tested? My judgment had been wrong, catastrophically so, with regard to Harry. How then could I rely upon it ever again? How would I ever be able to fully trust any man when I had been so incredibly mistaken about that one?

Because Revelstoke Vortigern Templeton-Vane was no ordinary man, I reminded myself. From the moment of our acquaintance, he had proven that he was there, always, eternal and unchanging as the Earth itself. His own heart had been so badly flayed that only scraps remained, and yet he risked them with me. He was unique in every possible way, my equal in courage and curiosity, and I understood that the love of such a man was as rare as a jewel.

But how to show him I was, once and forever, his? He had made me many demonstrations of his affections, and yet where was *my* grand gesture? We had neither of us the inclination for marriage, but there had to be some action that might show him precisely what I would risk for him.

I brooded over the question for some time before my gaze fell upon the volume of Ovid that always accompanies me upon my travels. I took it up, and the *Ars Amatoria* fell open to a much-loved page. I had even pencilled lightly below my favourite passage. And then I knew exactly what to do.

I might have changed once more into the garments I had purchased in Paris, those designed to ensorcell and enchant, but I did not. Stoker had loved me first as a woman of action, a scientist who dared all and feared nothing. I donned instead my working costume, the apparel of an explorer, dauntless in the face of certain peril. From my flat boots to my trousers to my neatly buttoned shirtwaist, I was the very picture of competence and daring.

When I was ready, I went onto my small balcony and straddled the balustrade, edging onto the stone coping that ran just below. It was narrow, that coping, scarcely four inches wide, and I had to go slowly as I made my way towards the corner. I had one or two close calls with gravity and one particularly nasty moment involving a gargoyle, but above me, light glowed from Stoker's window, beckoning me ever onwards. I eyed the stout creeper that grew around it, the lacy tendrils surrounding the embrasure, the leaves gilded by the illumination from his room.

Unfortunately, the stone coping ended there, just a few feet short of my destination. I perched upon my little ledge, assessing my options, until my toes began to cramp and I had to make a decisive move.

"Fortune favours the bold," I reminded myself sternly as I launched my body into the ether. At the last moment, I grasped the creeper, arresting my fall. I hit the wall with an audible thud, and after a moment, I heard the window above me open. A dark and beloved head appeared, the face scowling into the night.

I hissed and he looked down, his mouth falling open in astonishment.

"Veronica, what in the name of Christ and his assorted saints are you doing down there?"

"I have come to woo you!" I called back.

Catching my tongue between my teeth, I began to climb. It was not an easy endeavour. Hampered by the slickness of the creepers, twining and vining their way across the stones—it had rained earlier that day—I slid back several times before coming near enough that Stoker was able to reach down and offer a hand. His other arm was still bound in its sling, and he winced a little as he hauled me over the parapet and into the room. I pushed off with my toes to help lighten the burden for him, but I rather miscalculated and we landed with an audible thump on the floor, Stoker upon his back with my body draped fully over his recumbent form.

He lifted his head, gasping a little, although whether from pain or passion, I could not be entirely certain. "Veronica," he managed, but I laid a finger over his lips.

"No. It is my turn," I told him firmly. "You were right to be angry with me for not coming to you at once when I discovered Harry and I were not married. I was, quite simply, afraid."

"Afraid?" He blinked furiously. "Of what?"

"Afraid of an unguarded heart, of giving myself fully to anyone again after making such a wreck of things the first time. I have shielded myself from true friendships, from you. Always I have held something back so that I could never again be so hurt from my own mistakes."

I paused and drew a deep breath. "But no more. Stoker, I loved you when the world was new. I love you now. And I will love you until the Earth is burnt away and the stars themselves turn to dust. For we are two souls with but a single thought, two hearts that beat as one."

He smiled, a slowly ripening smile that promised everything. "You learnt Keats for me."

"Learnt Keats? My beloved, I would burn the Earth to cinders and blow the ashes to the four winds just to be near you. Now, take me to bed and let me show you."

We did not, in fact, make use of that particular piece of furniture for some hours. There was the floor—made comfortable by an especially plush carpet—a hassock which proved a singularly useful prop, and an armchair just commodious enough for us to accomplish a position which I am reliably informed by certain obscure volumes of Roman poetry is called the Leaping Dolphin.

By the time we at last tumbled into the bed, it was more in the interest of repose than recreation, and we slept intertwined until dawn streaked the chamber with the first rosy shimmers of the new day. I gathered my garments and crept hurriedly down the back stairs to my room just before Lily appeared with my morning tea tray.

"How are things this bright and beneficent morn, Lily?" I asked as I poured a gently steaming cup of Assam.

She shook her head. "Sixes and sevens, miss. Polly came back—she decided she would rather work under Mrs. Brackendale than marry the undergardener after all—but she has given notice yet again."

"Whatever for?" I asked. The comings and goings of the maids were not of particular interest, but I liked Lily and I was feeling extremely cordial to everyone that morning. (Physical congress, I have often observed, is as revivifying to the spirit as to the body, and the congress I had just enjoyed invigorated me enough to make me feel quite benevolent indeed.)

Lily went on as she tidied the room. "She says her room is haunted, she does. Claims she were up the whole of the night, hearing such moanings and groanings as would make your hair stand on end."

I paused in my sipping. "Where is her room, exactly?"

"The upper floor, this side of the house, miss. Above Mr. Revelstoke's room," she said as she built up the fire. I drank more tea as she went on. "It were just the house settling, I told her, but she said no house ever made such sounds as that. Bangings and rattlings and thumpings until all hours. Not a wink of sleep she got."

"Oh dear," I murmured. She finished with the fire and turned.

"Why, miss, you've gone quite pink. Is the fire too hot, then?"

I sipped my tea. "Everything is just fine, Lily. Just fine indeed."

CHAPTER

36

Stoker and I took our leave of Cherboys shortly after breakfast. I thought it best to depart before we drove any more of Tiberius' staff away in fright, and Stoker was eager to get his Megalosaurus back to London.

"Will you come with us?" I urged Tiberius. "*The Secret* is shortly to open at the Adelphi. Perhaps you would care to be there for opening night?"

"Tempting, but no," he said. "I think I might do a bit more 'lording' here. I mean to apply myself to my obligations for once and take a personal interest. Pity me, pet. I may have to learn about *drains*," he said, pulling a face.

"A little honest work will do you good," I told him. "Well, if you will not come, perhaps I can persuade Elspeth to visit. I promised to take her along to the Hippolyta Club to listen to a lecture or two."

"She might be in a fair way of *giving* a lecture," he said, nodding to where the lady herself was flying up the drive, skirts belling like sails in the wind. Her skin was browner, the freckles standing out on her cheekbones, and her hair was gilded by the sun. Gone were the pernickety lace collars and instead she wore a stout striped pinafore over a loose skirt and trousers similar to my own design—a pair of Timo-thy's cut down, I imagined. She held a bone aloft and cried out in tri-umph as she reached us.

"I found it!" she exclaimed, holding it out for us to see. "This is the first sign of a new Megalosaurus. And one quite unlike any ever dis-covered before."

"You have been digging!" Stoker said happily. He is never more de-lighted than when another natural scientist shares their finds. Joy shone from her face.

"I have indeed. When Veronica described the bone her skirts were caught on, I knew it must be from a Megalosaurus and I was right." She brandished the bone in front of Tiberius. "It is still there. Or rather, *they* are still there. The one I discovered twenty years ago was a juve-nile compared to this. This is perhaps a parent or elder sibling. It is the find of the century," she crowed.

"Are you certain?" I enquired, peering closely at the bone. To my untrained eye, it looked insignificant, much too small to bear the weight of such august expectations.

But Elspeth replied with a fluent lecture on the finer points of the specimen, going on at length about the thing in such minute detail that I was left in no doubt about its consequence. She looked like a bride, radiant and confident in her conquest.

"Of course, it will take a good deal of time to dig it out—Timothy will have to see to the jam making," she added, her eyes glinting in satisfaction. I was not entirely convinced Timothy would resent the jam making, and there was every possibility he would prove more tal-ented at it than his begrudging sister.

An anxious frown touched her brow. "That is if I still have permis-sion to dig? That bit of cliff does belong to Cherboys."

"The fossil is entirely yours," Tiberius assured her.

She turned glowing eyes to Stoker and to me. "I told him of my suspicions and his lordship gave me permission to dig. And men to help excavate. *And* he has had the cliff shored up to make it as safe as possible."

"If you require introductions to the appropriate societies, you have only to ask," Stoker told her kindly.

She fairly danced as she gave him her thanks and then dashed away, back to her fossil. "So much left to dig!"

Stoker looked at his brother. "Well done," he said quietly.

Tiberius waved a hand. "It has come to my attention that there are one or two things I might have managed a little better," he said.

"You mean I was right to tell you not to meddle by holding this house party," Stoker put in.

Tiberius smoothed his cuffs. "I was entirely correct to do so. Beatrice wanted me dead, and I have no doubt she would have accomplished it had I not forced her hand by inviting everyone here. But I am grateful for your assistance. And to show my appreciation, I brought you a present back from Bavaria."

He signaled to Collins, who came forward with a small crate. Even before the thing was opened, I knew what horrors lurked within.

"A wolpertinger!" Stoker exclaimed. Between that and the Megalosaurus, he should be busy indeed.

Julien appeared then to say farewell. "Are you not returning with us?" I asked in considerable disappointment. Sometimes Julien's pastries were the only means of coaxing a good mood out of Stoker when he had overworked himself, and I will admit to a certain fondness for his *pets de nonnes* myself, although why anyone should choose such a ludicrous name for such a delectable pastry eluded me. Nuns' farts indeed!

"No, I remain here for a few more days, until his lordship and I have settled the details."

"Details?" I looked to Tiberius while Stoker amused himself by plucking shreds of excelsior from his new wolpertinger.

"Julien and I are going to be men of business together," Tiberius said, smiling at Julien. "We are opening a restaurant, a very exclusive establishment catering to extremely discriminating tastes."

"We shall call it d'Orlande's," Julien said.

"We bloody well shall not," Tiberius countered.

"We will argue and then I will cook my ortolans à la d'Orlande for you and you will agree with me," Julien said, with the perfect assurance of a man who knows his worth.

"We will see," Tiberius replied.

He turned to kiss me farewell, and I held out my hand. "Are you not forgetting something? Five guineas, your lordship."

He patted his pockets with an air of regret. "And me without my notecase! How distressing. I suppose I shall have to owe you."

"Tiberius, you are the most—" I would have argued with him, but just then I caught sight of Nanny MacQueen barrelling down the steps of Cherboys. "Never mind," I said hastily. "I will see you in London." I returned his kiss and offered another to Julien, who handed me into the carriage. I moved to the far side and sat very still, as a mongoose will when confronted with a cobra.

Nanny kissed Stoker soundly on both cheeks, her good-bye punctuated with reminders about the importance of clean teeth and regular bowels. Stoker, with a hint of desperation in his voice, promised to attend to both. As he bent to kiss her, she grabbed him by the ears and pulled him further down, whispering something just loud enough for him to hear. He smiled in reply. "Yes, Nanny."

He vaulted in to sit beside me, carrying the wolpertinger with exquisite tenderness. The coachman snapped the reins to start the team on our brief journey to Dearsley station. Lily waved a handkerchief in farewell while Nanny stood on the steps, giving me a baleful look.

I fairly itched to know what he had promised Nanny in parting, but it was beneath my dignity to ask. But I had a dreadful suspicion it had something to do with me.

As we bowled along, leaving Cherboys behind, Stoker continued to fuss over his wolpertinger with a care bordering on adoration.

"You cannot seriously intend to hold that appalling creature all the way back to London," I protested as he settled it onto his knee.

It was frankly hideous, its lips drawn back into a snarl to reveal long, yellow fangs. The hare's ears were long and cunning while the tiny antlers affixed to its head were nothing short of ludicrous. The wings, liberated from some unidentifiable bird of prey, had been stiffened with wire to stand proud of the body, spread with the malevolence of a bat in flight.

To Stoker, however, it was a thing of perfect beauty. He regarded it with all the fond infatuation of a father to his newborn babe. He fairly crooned to it as we travelled back to London, and I realised I should have to make my peace with the little beast if we were to enjoy any sort of domestic harmony. It assumed pride of place on Stoker's desk, and when the Megalosaurus arrived for installation on the grounds of Bishop's Folly, his happiness was complete. Of course, Lord Rosemorran's children instantly adopted the Megalosaurus as a sort of playhouse as Stoker had once done, and he was forever chasing them out of the monster.

One afternoon in late September, he was driven to evict Lady Rose, the youngest of Lord Rosemorran's impetuous offspring and by far the most troublesome, with the promise of violet creams and a lesson in one of the less lethal varieties of physical combat. They were still negotiating terms—Lady Rose had the advantage of him in that she was perched atop the Megalosaurus, and as any general knows, she who commands the highest position enjoys the advantage—when a small packing crate arrived bearing my name in an unfamiliar hand.

I used a prybar to access the contents and was delighted to find a small potted goat willow tree. Hanging from the branches were a collection of *Apatura iris* chrysalides, the unfinished form of the magnificent Purple Emperor butterfly, one of our most tremendous native beauties and indigenous to Devon. A short note accompanied the offering.

My dear Veronica, it read, *I hope you will accept this gift from one natural scientist to another. In friendship, Elspeth Gresham.*

I marvelled at the little pouches, spun from the finest filaments to nurture the larvae as they completed the transition from immaturity to imago. With infinite delicacy, I carried the arrangement to my vivarium and placed it tenderly in a quiet corner. In the warmth and serenity of the vivarium, they would finish their journey, affording me the opportunity to study them at length. It was a thoughtful and generous gift, and I felt abashed that I had suspected Elspeth of various villainies instead of recognising a woman who suffered acutely from dashed hopes. I wondered how my own life might have been stunted had I never discovered my passion for lepidoptery or seized the chance to make it my life's work. And I felt a rush of gratitude for the benevolence of a universe that had looked kindly upon my talents and given me scope for the exercising of them.

As I sat musing, a gentle movement caught my eye. One of the chrysalides, a little darker and a bit larger than the rest, swung on its branch. I came closer, witness to the moment when the creature within would stir forth for the first time. It is not a quick thing, the birth of a butterfly, but it never fails to enchant the curious mind. This tiny creature had crawled upon its branch with its caterpillar's Herculean resolve and settled in to sleep the long sleep of the ages. And when its time had come, it had courageously pushed itself free and into the bright new world. I watched as the chrysalis fell away and the imago emerged, struggling a little with wings heavy and damp. It drooped on the branch, resting from its ordeal before shuddering its wings, testing them. I held my breath as it stretched out, reaching for the air.

And then it fell, dropping away from the branch and all the safety it had known, plunging towards certain destruction. But before it came to disaster, its wings took hold of the ether, bearing it upwards in a drifting, mazy spiral. It circled my head in a flutter of those jewel-like violet wings, and I laughed aloud for the sheer joy of it. There was no magic so elemental nor so moving as that of metamorphosis. I went to the door of the vivarium and threw it open. My new friend hesitated between the warmth of the interior, safe and quiet, and the fresh, bright, beckoning world beyond.

"Go now. You have everything you need," I told it.

It circled my head again, then drifted away into the garden. It flew towards a shrub, then looped back, pausing for just a moment to perch upon the leathery head of Patricia, the Galápagos tortoise, like a frivolous piece of millinery. This time when it flew off, it lifted itself above the shrubbery and up into the slanting sunlight. I heard Stoker's laugh as he retrieved Lady Rose and the barking of the dogs, circling in excitement. The air was heavy with the fragrance of the latest of the summer flowers, brave and bonny, and high above my head was the butterfly, circling ever upwards.

It flapped once more and then lifted itself away and into the blue beyond. Stoker turned to me, Lady Rose perched on his shoulders, and he smiled, a smile that would cause my heart to swell within my chest even if I saw it a thousand times.

"Be brave. You have everything you need," I murmured to no one in particular. "Everything indeed." Excelsior!

AUTHOR'S NOTE

The Megalosaurus as described here is accurate according to the beliefs of Veronica's contemporaries but varies greatly from the current ideas of what it may have looked like. The suggestion that the earth was formed at 8 p.m. on the evening of October 23, 4004 BC, was published in 1650 by James Ussher, Archbishop of Armagh. This hypothesis was supported by research into the chronology of the Bible and was defended into the nineteenth century. For more on the excavations of fossils and the impact on natural history and theology, Shelley Emling's *The Fossil Hunter* about the life of Mary Anning is highly recommended. In recognition of her extraordinary contributions to natural history, Lyme Regis erected a statue to Mary Anning in 2022.

On December 31, 1853, a dinner was held inside the model of an iguanodon, an event so curious, it made the pages of the *Illustrated London News*. The menu was not nearly as enticing as the one served by Julien d'Orlande. The iguanodon was modeled by Benjamin Waterhouse Hawkins for the Crystal Palace Exhibition and stretched to thirty feet in length.

ACKNOWLEDGMENTS

I am eternally grateful to the Berkley/Penguin team, who constantly amaze me with their talent and dedication. Particular thanks to Claire Zion, Loren Jaggers, Tara O'Connor, Candice Coote, Craig Burke, Ivan Held, Jeanne-Marie Hudson, Christine Ball, Jessica Mangicaro, Jennifer Snyder, Angèle Masters, Amber Beard, and the behind-the-scenes folks in Sub Rights, Audio, Sales, and Marketing. A special tip of the chapeau to the Art folks, who are determined to outdo themselves with every Veronica cover, and much appreciation to Jomie Wilding and the Writerspace team.

Tremendous thanks to Pam Hopkins, Ellen Edwards, and Danielle Perez, because of whom Veronica has found such a happy home with such stalwart champions. And to Michelle Vega as we begin the next stage together. I can't wait for what lies ahead!

Enormous gratitude to the librarians, booksellers, readers, reviewers, bookstagrammers, bloggers, and interviewers who have shown this series so much love.

To my family, my author pals, my friends, my Twitter crew, my Blanket Fort—thank you. The words are small, but the gratitude is huge.